The Wrong Sort of Wife?

Elise Chidley

First published in Great Britain in 2008 by Orion Books,
an imprint of The Orion Publishing Group Ltd
Orion House, 5 Upper Saint Martin's Lane
London WC2H 9EA

An Hachette Livre UK Company

1 3 5 7 9 10 8 6 4 2

A CIP catalogue record for this book is
available from the British Library.

ISBN (Hardback) 978 0 7528 8898 9
ISBN (Trade Paperback) 978 0 7528 8897 2

Typeset by Deltatype Ltd,
Birkenhead, Merseyside

Printed in Great Britain by
Clays Ltd, St Ives plc

The Orion Publishing Group's policy is to use papers that
are natural, renewable and recyclable products and made
from wood grown in sustainable forests. The logging and
manufacturing processes are expected to conform to the
environmental regulations of the country of origin.

www.orionbooks.co.uk

For Patrick

Acknowledgements

I'd like to thank Peter Robinson for his good judgement and guidance. I'm also deeply grateful to Susan Lamb, Kate Mills, and Genevieve Pegg of Orion. And of course I'd like to thank those who read the book early on and said encouraging things: Creina Beattie, Debbie Lynn, Odette Watson, Julie Camarillo and Clodagh McCoole. Laura Hatto deserves mention for helping with some key research. And most of all, my thanks go to Patrick for his unwavering support.

Chapter One

The kitchen cabinets at Back Lane Cottage were at an awkward height. The average man would find them a stretch. The average woman, standing on tip-toe, might just be able to reach the underside of the cupboard doors, if she had very long fingernails. Lizzie Buckley's fingernails, bitten to the quick for the first time since she was twelve, were nowhere near long enough.

All in all, the cottage was the most inconveniently laid-out place Lizzie had ever seen. What prankster of an architect would put the only bathroom downstairs? And why had it seemed a good idea to put the stairwell in the dining room? Then there was the hallway, with its odd shape and multiple doorways. James would call it a criminal waste of space. There wasn't much you could do with the room except hang a chandelier – and maybe let the children loose on their tricycles.

The contrast with the home she'd just left couldn't have been greater. Mill House in Gloucestershire, so ancient it was probably listed in the Domesday Book, had been renovated to within an inch of its life. To look at its weathered limestone exterior, you'd never guess that every possible convenience – cappuccino-maker, ice-dispenser, twenty-jet power-shower – had been tucked away amid the lovingly-preserved period features. Back Lane Cottage was old, too, but not old enough to be interesting. Just old enough to be awkward.

The trouble was, by the time Lizzie had noticed all these flaws, she'd already decided that Back Lane Cottage was the house for her.

The garden won her over before she even stepped out of her

estate agent's car. Not that it was a beautiful garden. Far from it. It was little more than a field – rough, lumpy, nettle-infested and riddled with rabbit holes. Compared to the Sissinghurst-inspired garden at Mill House, it was laughable. But it was huge and hemmed in by big trees. Best of all, it was very well fenced. Just the place for her three-year-old twins – once she'd cleaned it up, of course.

Inside the house, the bedrooms were ideal. There was a tiny one, perfect for an office, and a big stately one complete with its own fireplace – a bit grand for a newly-single mother, but never mind. The third bedroom made the house irresistible. It was long and bright, lit by two large windows with deep sills, which would be perfect for the sunflower seedlings, piggy banks, birds' eggs, pebbles, pine cones, shells, you name it, that sprang up around the twins wherever they went. These untidy and sometimes smelly collections had always been an eyesore among the gleaming antiques at Mill House. But in this ramshackle place, they'd fit right in.

As Lizzie stood in the doorway of this room, picturing twin beds beneath the windows, she felt a little warm glow of excitement building somewhere in her chest. She put her hand to the place in surprise. It was days since she'd felt anything but a cold lump of misery there.

She could work with a house like this. She could turn it into a home.

But if Lizzie was sold on the house, her estate agent wasn't, which seemed odd. Then again, her experience of estate agents was limited. She hadn't needed one since her student days when she and her friend Tessa had been in hot pursuit of any sort of two-bedroom flat they could actually afford. Of course, when she'd married James he'd already been in possession of Mill House, and they'd moved in at once without ever considering that perhaps they didn't *have* to live in it.

Even though she was a novice in the world of estate agency, Lizzie could have sworn that she understood the basic motivation of the profession: to unload houses onto clients as quickly as possible. So she was surprised by this woman's determination to drag her away to see another house, one with a '*very* well-maintained garden, *loads* of updates, and a more conventional lay-out'.

'Is the rent the same?' Lizzie asked, opening the tiny fridge a second time and peering into it. Back Lane Cottage was already more expensive than she'd imagined.

'Actually, it's a bit more,' the agent admitted, 'but then it *is* furnished, and you said you wanted furniture.'

Looking out of the kitchen window to the rolling fields beyond, Lizzie sketched a careless gesture. 'Furniture's not a big issue,' she said, inaccurately. 'We can always sleep on blow-up mattresses at first.' She wasn't doing much sleeping at the moment, so beds, or lack of them, made very little difference to *her*. The twins, of course, ought to have something between themselves and the carpet.

'But this place is so isolated. Fantastic for a big family, yes, but for someone in your situation? Wouldn't you want to be closer to town? And do you really think you'd manage with no dishwasher?' The agent watched Lizzie warily as she spoke, perhaps wondering if she was going to burst into tears, as she had several times the day before.

'But look at the view,' Lizzie riposted, determined to remain dry-eyed and rational.

The agent cleared her throat and shuffled through some papers. 'Just a *little* look at the next property?' she pleaded. 'I'm not really comfortable with the idea of you and the kiddies all alone in this place. To be honest, I'm only showing it to you as a yard-stick. We have a mantra at our office: "Show the worst first." Not to *scare* anyone into anything, you know, just to give the client a realistic idea of what's out there.'

Then Lizzie understood. She was supposed to have fled from this place with quaking heart, only to snap up the next house in pure gratitude for its dishwasher and upstairs bathroom.

Well, it wasn't going to happen. After yesterday's dreary tour of one miserable little semi after another – all that was available in the price range she'd originally suggested – Lizzie was tired of looking at houses. Besides, she couldn't keep making the exhausting round trip to Kent from Gloucestershire, couldn't keep asking her friend,

Maria, to baby-sit the children. More importantly, she couldn't expect James to stump up just *a bit more* so that she could have loads of mod cons.

'I don't want to see any more houses,' she said, surprised by the firmness of her own voice. 'I've made up my mind. This is the one I want.'

And if the rent on this place stretched the joint bank account a bit further than was comfortable, too bad. Maybe it would make James come to his senses.

It was all so simple, in the end. A week later, they were in.

Lizzie didn't take a stick of furniture out of Mill House. She wouldn't have had the nerve. The furniture was as integral to that house as her nose was to her own face. She'd chosen none of it herself; many of the pieces had originally come from the manor house, so it was possible they belonged to James's parents. Besides, she hadn't wanted to suggest anything as irrevocable as a division of the marital spoils. On moving day, she simply walked out of the house with her luggage and turned the key, leaving it fully furnished – and ready to receive them all back again at a moment's notice.

At the back of her mind she was still hoping – quite fervently – that James would suddenly see how ridiculous this whole situation was, how massively he'd over-reacted, how impossible it was that the two of them could live apart.

That was partly why she'd left. If he could no longer glance casually out of the library window at the manor and see the building that housed his family, maybe he'd finally see the light and realise what he'd done – both the enormity and downright misery of it all. It wasn't that she wanted him to come crawling back to her – a sheepish shuffle would probably do the trick – but if he didn't make some kind of move towards reconciliation some time soon, she didn't know how she was going to keep getting out of bed every morning.

So she left Mill House tidy but not at all vacant, secretly telling herself that she'd be home again before the roses were in bloom. When she pulled up at Back Lane Cottage later that same afternoon and dragged four suitcases, three inflatable mattresses, a folding table, an old computer, sundry bits of hand luggage and two bags of groceries over the threshold, she realized she was treating this whole 'move' like a camping trip.

When she finally released the children from their car seats, they spilled out into the desolate garden and chilly house with shrieks of glee, excited to the point of hysteria by the novelty of the unfurnished rooms, which they were seeing for the first time. They weren't demanding tenants; even the dark and dusty garden shed delighted them.

But Lizzie was shaken by the emptiness.

The newly-painted magnolia walls seemed to echo. In every room, a bare lightbulb hung dejectedly from the ceiling. In amazement, Lizzie noted that there were no towel racks in the bathroom, no bathroom shelves or cabinets of any kind, not even a humble toilet-roll holder. How come she hadn't noticed all this the day she'd viewed the place?

Standing in the cold, bare bathroom, Lizzie felt suddenly helpless and deeply afraid. How on earth would she cope with this stripped-down life? She must have been mad to think she could make a home of this place, temporary or otherwise. It had all the comforts of an abandoned barn. OK, so she'd often poked fun at the splendidly tasteful Mill House interiors, mostly because they'd made her feel inferior, but at least she'd always been comfortable. In fact, she'd been more than comfortable. She'd been living in the lap of luxury, travelling first class — and now she was in the cattle truck.

Shaking the excess water off her hands, Lizzie abruptly realized that she hadn't heard a squeak out of the twins for a good twenty minutes or more. Silence was never golden when it came to pre-schoolers.

She stuck her head out of the door. 'Alex! Ellie! Where are you?'

Nothing.

'Alex! Ellie! Come quick, I have a surprise for you!' That usually worked and luckily she had some emergency Smarties in her handbag.

Still nothing.

With an exaggerated sigh, she began a quick tour of the downstairs rooms. Nothing.

Irritation began tipping into alarm as she went out into the bleak, unkempt garden and carried out a hurried reconnoitre of the few bushes and trees. All she found was Alex's toy fire engine, abandoned in the rough grass. She stuck her head round the corner of the house and surveyed the nettle-infested side garden. Not surprisingly, the twins weren't there, either. Alex would be bringing the house down by now if he'd wandered into the nettles. For a big bruiser of a boy, his pain tolerance was pitifully low.

Now her heart was definitely beating too fast. Giving up all pretence of calm, she sprinted into the house and up the stairs. Without a stick of furniture, there was nowhere for them to hide; not even a built-in closet. But as she flung bedroom doors open one by one, she was greeted only by the smell of new paint and a silence that seemed to hum.

Calling their names, she broke into a run down the crooked passageway. As she rounded a corner, she managed to trip over her own feet, catching her arm on the textured white wall as she fell. Then she was up and running again, down the steep stairs, across the bare boards in the dining room, and out into the garden. Perhaps she'd left the gate open; perhaps even now the twins were capering merrily across some field, unhindered by an ounce of common sense between them to keep them out of bramble patches, away from angry bulls, and safe from poisonous mushrooms or paedophiles walking their dogs.

But the gate was closed.

Could they have climbed it? It was too high for Ellie, that was certain, but perhaps Alex could have boosted her up?

Oh God, how could she have lost the twins within hours of bringing them to their new, single-parented home? She might have known she couldn't do this on her own, not after days of panic and insomnia. She wasn't competent. She could barely look after herself, let alone the children. She'd better call the police.

Then she remembered the shed. 'Never come in here alone,'

she'd told them earlier when they poked their heads in to look at its sad jumble of discarded garden implements. Encouragement enough.

And, of course, that was exactly where they were, closeted in the lovely, mysterious, giant Wendy-house, with the door firmly closed to keep out meddling mothers. She heard them chatting away as she paused beside the door, trying to slow her breathing and get a grip on her overblown emotions.

'Alex, this box is a table,' Ellie was chanting insistently.

'We got to keep dah monsters out,' was Alex's equally insistent reply.

Lizzie threw open the door with a resounding smash.

'Dah monster!' Alex cried, and both children began to screech in only half-feigned terror.

The cortisol was obviously sloshing about in Lizzie's veins. Her anxiety immediately morphed into fury.

But she'd learnt a trick that had saved her sanity and the children's hides in just this sort of situation many times before: count to forty-seven before you open your mouth. She did so, as slowly as she possibly could, and, by the time she reached twenty, she was no longer itching to smack bottoms. By twenty-five, the children had stopped screeching and were studying her with a mixture of apprehension and curiosity. By thirty-five, she'd noticed Ellie's box table, complete with newspaper tablecloth, a leaf plate, some gravel for food, and a solitary diner in the form of Panda the panda. By forty, she'd taken in the stout stick in Alex's grubby hand, dangling at his side now but no doubt ready for action should a bona fide monster suddenly burst onto the scene. By forty-seven, she was able to speak, not yell at a volume that would have assaulted the ears of their only neighbour, as yet unknown to them.

'Children,' she said evenly, 'I told you not to come in here. Didn't I?'

They nodded. In the past few days, Lizzie had seen this watchful look on their faces many times, most recently when they'd squeezed all the toothpaste into the tooth mug. Mummy was no longer the tolerant woman she'd once been, laughing off minor incidents like raw eggs smashed all over the tiles and sudden haircuts with the kitchen scissors. No, Mummy had become a wild force, given to crashing around like an electrical storm on a summer's day.

'Do you know *why* I told you not to come in here?'

They looked at her in silence for a while.

'Iss dirty,' Ellie finally said.

'Iss dange-riss,' Alex answered at almost the same instant.

'Right,' Lizzie said, and pursed her lips. Both children were still studying her intently. By their expressions, she could tell they were braced for anything – shouting, arm-waving, door-slamming, foot-stamping, even a Mummy in tears. Since James had left them, she'd been losing her temper at the smallest provocation, despite renewing her vow every night to remain patient, calm and rational with the children.

She took another cleansing breath.

'This shed is not only dirty, but also dark and nasty. It's full of broken glass. You could cut yourselves.' She gestured at the litter of shards beneath a smashed window.

'Yes, Mummy,' came the chorus.

'It's full of old paint cans and bottles of turpentine and who knows what else.' Really, she had a good mind to complain to the landlord about all the odds and ends the previous tenants had abandoned. It was no stretch of the imagination at all to picture the twins settling down with paper cups and an assortment of bottles – engine oil, anti-freeze, rose pesticide – for an impromptu garden-chemical tasting.

'Yes, Mummy.'

She decided not to mention the pitch-fork and garden shears. Best not to draw Alex's attention to such bounty.

'So you must never come here alone.'

'We won't, Mummy.'

'Never, ever. Promise?'

'Pwomise, Mummy.'

'Right. It'll be dark soon. Let's go and clean up now.'

Obediently, the children trailed behind her back to the house. Using paper plates, she rustled up a meal of bread (no butter), miniature cheeses in red wax, tiny pots of fromage frais, wrapped cereal bars, and juice in foil pouches with straws. The children, sitting cross-legged on the carpet in the lounge, fell upon this uninspiring fare with shrieks of joy. Anything in bright packaging was in their eyes superior by far to home cooking, be it ever so gourmet. Which it seldom was. But still.

With her mouth full of purple fromage frais, Ellie announced, 'Daddy will fix the shed an' make it nice an' not nasty.'

Alex, who was working on rolling his red wax into a malleable ball, looked up with bright eyes. 'Yesh, Daddy woll fix it!'

Lizzie massaged her eyebrows with all ten fingers. 'Daddy will not fix it,' she said at last, her voice rising. 'Daddy will not be staying in this house with us. Daddy is living with Gran and Granddad at the moment. You'll be seeing him a lot, but not here, not in this house.' How many times would she have to tell them before it sank in?

'Daddy will fix it,' Ellie screamed suddenly, and threw her plate across the room.

A hush filled the house as the three-year-old contemplated her crime. The cheese seemed to roll for ever, while the fromage frais pot went head-over-heels, spattering purple blobs on the beige carpet.

Then Lizzie found herself doing it again: crying in front of the children. Sort of crying, at any rate. No noise came from her throat, but the tears were slipping freely down her cheeks, as if she had some kind of incontinence of the ducts. Wordlessly, she got up and began retrieving the paper plate and bits of food. Wordlessly, she dumped everything down in front of Ellie again and retreated to the kitchen.

She was standing at the sink, dabbing at her face with a tissue, and looking out over nettles towards the great open space of the field beyond the garden, when she heard them pattering hesitantly over the linoleum.

'Mummy?'

'Mmm?'

'Iss OK, Mummy. Everything woll be all right if you have a nice little nap. You jus' tired, Mummy,' Alex said earnestly.

For good measure, Ellie added, 'You look 'stremely pretty today, Mummy.'

And it was all her fault, all of this.

Of course, she could clean up the shed for them. Throw out all the dangerous chemicals. Sweep away the broken glass. Hang the sharp tools up high so that Alex couldn't get his hands on them. Get a chain and padlock.

But that wouldn't solve a thing, not a solitary thing.

Still, she needed to stop crying, for the children's sake. Taking a deep breath, she told herself that this was just a temporary jaunt anyway, a stop-gap adventure, a detour. She and James would look back on it in a few weeks' time and howl with laughter.

The irrational, miserable side of her brain wasn't convinced. Never mind, as soon as she'd managed to get the children to sleep, she'd take out the large slab of milk chocolate she'd hidden in one of the high cupboards, and then she'd be able to make it through the night.

Chapter Two

'Gosh, it looks different with your things in it,' said Ingrid Hatter, drinking a brew made with a one-cup teabag in a Tesco mug, and shamelessly assessing her surroundings. 'The other people had so much stuff the place was bulging. The rooms look much bigger like this.'

After a week as tenant of Back Lane Cottage, Lizzie was wondering if she'd allowed loneliness to get the better of good judgement when she'd invited her neighbour in. The Hatters lived a stone's throw away in a picturesque renovated barn with a conical oast that looked like a fairytale tower. For a well-heeled, middle-aged woman with an expensive accent, Ingrid had a surprisingly inquisitive gleam in her eye.

Lizzie followed that gleaming eye around the room. There wasn't a picture on the wall as yet, but Lizzie had bought an oak bookshelf from a second-hand shop in town, and a comfortable wheat-coloured sofa from Ikea – the cheapest furnishings she could find. It seemed you couldn't function without some squishy piece of furniture to flop down on at the end of the day.

The memory of the trip to Ikea, on her second day in the house, made Lizzie shudder. Traipsing around the enormous warehouse with the twins in tow had been exhausting enough, but then she'd found she couldn't stuff the boxes of sofa parts into her vehicle. Close to tears, she'd had to wheel the teetering trolley back inside and line up all over again to arrange for delivery.

The sofa had arrived only yesterday and she'd spent a good part of the night putting it together, alternately sobbing and cursing because James could have done the job in fifteen minutes – but

11

then, if James had been there in the first place they wouldn't have had to assemble a sofa at all.

When the thing was finally set up, the sight of it in her living room made her feel suddenly hospitable. So when she'd spotted Ingrid over the garden fence, out walking her tiny dog, she'd rashly invited her in. And now here Lizzie was – without a scrap of make-up on her face, in a crumpled T-shirt she'd worn for three straight days, her unwashed hair scraped back in a pony-tail, her voice hoarse from lack of use – entertaining!

If Lizzie was a wreck, at least the living room didn't look too bad. In addition to the sensible sofa, she'd splurged on some ruinously expensive but rather gorgeous scatter cushions in scarlet, gold and peacock-blue. Now, every time she looked at the cushions, she felt a jab of remorse. She was in no position to be impulse-spending, especially not on frills and furbelows like cushions.

At the windows fluttered beaded Indian muslin drapes, the palest shade of old gold, found in the bargain bin of an Indian shop in Tunbridge Wells. She didn't feel at all guilty about those. The four framed photographs she'd packed carefully at the bottom of her suitcase were the only other ornamentation in the room. They stood on the bookshelf, commanding attention.

Ingrid stood up, went over to the cabinet, and took a good, long look at those four portraits. One was of Lizzie and her old friend, Tessa Martin, at a beach in Greece when they were about twenty, looking tousled and tanned and happy. Two were studio shots of the twins at various stages of babyhood. Ingrid Hatter lifted up the largest photograph, a family portrait, and turned it to the light. 'This is your husband?' she asked. 'Very photogenic, isn't he?'

Lizzie winced. James was good-looking enough on paper, but photography couldn't hope to convey his full magnetism. He was far more impressive in the flesh, when he could do that quirky thing with his eyebrows and flash his dimple at you.

In real life, James was the sort of person who lit up a room when he walked in. Rooms had definitely been darker for Lizzie since he left.

Despite the dimple and unwitting charm, James wasn't a lady's man at heart. For years, his over-riding passion had been rugby; he'd been some sort of star player at university. He wasn't even a flirt, not on purpose. But he had a way of locking eyes with people, even in casual conversation, that was very gratifying. This unconscious mannerism left women, and even men, believing they'd made a huge impression on a man whose good opinion was worth having.

Even after she married him, Lizzie was aware that when they entered a restaurant or pub together, all the single women (and many of the attached ones) nudged their friends and hissed, 'Oy, look what just walked in!', as if Lizzie and her wedding ring were invisible.

Not one of these women would be able to get her mind around the fact that this man's marriage had faltered in quite the way it had.

'Yes, that's James,' Lizzie said. 'He, um, he's not actually here with us. We're, sort of, having a bit of a trial separation right now.'

Lizzie's palms were sweating and her face felt tight, as if horribly sunburned. How embarrassing if she should burst into tears. Apart from the estate agent, she hadn't yet told anyone outside Laingtree village that she and James had split up – not her best friend, not her sister, not even her mother. At first, she'd put off telling them in the hope that there'd be no need, that James would turn up one evening with his suitcase and perhaps a bunch of tulips. As the crisis deepened, she found that she just couldn't face telling anyone; apart from anything else, the details of the whole thing were so ... so *toe-curling*. And then there was the awful feeling that if she put the sorry situation into words, it would become set in stone, irreversible, a fact of life.

Of course, everybody in the village knew about the separation without having to be told by Lizzie. Her mother-in-law had seen to that.

According to Lady Evelyn Buckley, Lizzie had never adapted to village life. Hankering after the bright lights of London, she'd wilfully scuppered her own marriage, depriving her children of their father so that she could reclaim her fast-paced sex-and-the-city lifestyle.

Lizzie was a little flattered, really. Lady Evelyn clearly had no idea how many Saturday nights Lizzie had whiled away, in her single days, eating cereal on her sofa in front of the TV.

But even if she'd ever had a racy lifestyle, she couldn't see how she was supposed to be reclaiming it with three-year-old twins in tow.

Lizzie knew about her mother-in-law's version of events because her closest friend in Laingtree, Maria Dennison, had filled her in. Naturally, Maria hadn't heard the gossip first-hand. But Maria's boyfriend, Laurence, had heard various editions of the rumour in the pub. As a friend of James's, Laurence was given all the dirt on treacherous Lizzie.

And, of course, there was also the conversation Lizzie had over-heard in the Wisteria Rooms when she'd popped in to buy some sticky buns for the children. She and the shopkeeper had stared at each other, frozen with embarrassment, as Lady Evelyn's distinc-tive, carrying voice boomed out from the table tucked around the corner from the till.

'Yes, he's back at the manor for the moment,' Lady Evelyn was saying. 'No, we're not that surprised ... That's right, not out of the top drawer ... one of those lower-rung public schools ... it's the children one feels sorry for ... Oh no, the Christmas party business was pretty much par for the course ... Often felt I should just drop a word about her clothes ... Poor chaps around here, never knew where to look ... One used to call that sort of girl a tart ... Yes, something very *loose* about her. You only have to watch her eat ...'

Lizzie and the shopkeeper both glanced at Lizzie's ample bust, which, even in a baggy sweatshirt, managed to look indecent. Blinking quickly, Lizzie had taken her change and bolted, leaving the sticky buns behind in her haste.

With an effort of will, Lizzie forced her mind away from the Wisteria Rooms. Much better to concentrate on her new neigh-bour.

She loved the picture Ingrid was scrutinizing so frankly. It was the only decent shot of all of them together, and she was darned if she was going to put it face down in a drawer, let alone tear it up, as she believed was *de rigueur* in this sort of situation.

It wasn't the usual sort of family portrait. It had been taken by a photographer who worked only in black and white, with an old-fashioned manual camera. The woman had come to Mill House in Laingtree late in the afternoon one Midsummer's Day, more than half a year ago now. 'Let's see what the light's like outside,' she'd suggested.

The light had been like honey, or well-steeped tea held up to sunshine. The photographer asked them to group themselves as they might after a picnic. James lounged on his elbow, elegant and obliging. The children, bandy-legged toddlers then, immediately began to jump and climb all over him. Lizzie sat behind James with her legs folded to one side, looking busty and slightly awkward because of the effort of holding her back straight and sucking her stomach in.

About thirty photos had been snapped machine-gun style, but Lizzie and James had chosen this one, which had caught him smiling up at her through his floppy fringe in a moment that looked like the sharing of a secret joke, while the children used his long body as a hobby horse and climbing frame, their baby faces full of wicked delight at having Daddy at their mercy.

James was the centre of that picture. Every eye was on him, every family member touched him, every twinkle and sparkle was aimed at him. James. How on earth was she living and breathing here in this strange house without him? The ache of missing him was constant, underlying all the rest: the anger, the confusion, the out-and-out fear.

'When I was your age, people had more respect for marriage,' Ingrid said, setting the photograph back in its place. 'Single women didn't feel they had the right to go after family men the way they seem to nowadays.'

Lizzie had to smile at her visitor's convoluted way of asking whether James had run off with another woman.

'Oh no, it was nothing like that,' she said. Would everybody assume she was the scorned wife? 'It was … well, it was me. I was the one who ended it.'

This wasn't strictly true, if you were going to split hairs. James had been the one to pack his bags and go. All the same, Lizzie had definitely caused him to leave.

The whole débâcle had started with a blunder. One tiny, irreversible blunder, like a misplaced chip with an ice pick that sends out a spider-web of cracks and makes the whole glacier come crashing down.

If Lizzie hadn't been so useless with computers, she'd probably be in her kitchen at Mill House at this very moment, doing something happy and domestic, like sanding away the scratches Alex had made on the kitchen table.

If she hadn't woken up that day with a sore head and a sense of grievance because the four hours of sleep she'd snatched between Alex's nightmare and Ellie's bed-wetting incident had been marred by James stealing the duvet and then not-quite-snoring every few seconds …

If she hadn't looked out the window to see yet another iron-grey sky brooding over trees bent double by the wind …

If she hadn't felt a pimple forming like a unicorn's horn between her eyebrows …

If Ellie hadn't insisted on wearing her sparkly cowboy boots to nursery school …

If Alex hadn't found a rusty compass somewhere and started gouging out train tracks on the table for his Thomas the Tank engine …

The ifs were endless. The long and the short of it was, everything had conspired that morning to propel Lizzie into a seething great huff.

But the straw that broke the camel's back was probably the sight of her mother-in-law, dressed in some sort of oilskin overcoat, traipsing through Lizzie's garden with an enormous pair of shears, pruning things right, left and centre without so much as a by-your-leave.

Glancing feverishly out of her window at the overcoat ducking about in the shrubbery, Lizzie fired up the computer and found herself writing things that normally she didn't put into words, not even to herself.

From: lizbuckley@hotmail. com
Sent: 12 April

Janie, do you ever feel you need a mini-break from being married – or is it just me?

Lately, I've been fantasizing an awful lot about switching lives with a single woman (But don't tell Mum, whatever you do.). I mean, things are just so much simpler when James is away on business. I can have a boiled egg for dinner with the kids, watch room makeovers and plastic surgery on TV, turn in early – oh, and not feel guilty that the main thing (the only thing) I want to do in bed these days is sleep.

Another great thing about those business trips: if I have to get up in the night to deal with a twin while James is away, at least I'm spared the seething resentment I normally feel when I finally stagger back to bed to find that he hasn't even surfaced out of his REM cycle.

To be honest, I'm a bit worried, Janie. All the romance is gone. I've picked up too many pairs of soggy underpants off the bathroom floor, I think. (There's obviously a gene in men that stops them from seeing clothes on the bathroom floor. Or any other floor, for that matter.) Those evenings when James starts lighting candles and putting on mood music and giving me that come-hither look, I just have this awful, dull feeling that I really can't be bothered with all that. Give me a cup of tea and a good mini-series any day. Oh, and a box of chocolate digestives.

Maybe his mum is right. Maybe he shouldn't have married me in the first place. Maybe I am too common-or-garden for the lofty Buckleys. I'm sure the right sort of girl would've breezed through pregnancy, childbirth and the never-ending fall-out without turning a hair. The right sort of girl wouldn't have let herself go, either. She wouldn't now be overweight and overwrought. The right sort of girl, no doubt, would be a lady at the table, a cordon bleu chef in the kitchen, and a whore in the bedroom. Frankly, I'm more the TV dinner, flannel pyjamas, bore in the bedroom sort.

Sorry to be such an old misery, but I just had to get it off my chest. Next time I'll confine myself to pearls of sisterly wisdom about pregnancy, I promise. Good grief, look at the time, got to crack on with things before school pick-up. By the way, is the ginger working for your morning sickness?

Lots of love

Lizzie

She read it through once, corrected a couple of typos, and then pressed 'Send'.

It was only when her computer displayed a snappy, efficient note that 'Blue Monday' had successfully been sent to james.buckley@ hotmail.com that Lizzie began to realize she'd made a considerable mistake.

With the quickness of hindsight she knew immediately what had happened. She had typed 'ja' for her sister Janie in the 'To' box, and the helpful e-mail program had prompted James's address. It always did this, and she always kept typing until Janie's address popped up. But this time, perhaps because she was tired and miserable, she'd simply hit the enter key.

Why wasn't there a big 'Unsend' button on the toolbar? Surely she wasn't the first person to send a hugely embarrassing note to the wrong address?

Lizzie, who took pride in knowing very little about computers, then spent a fruitless half hour on the internet researching how to recall sent mail. She learned that she should save any message with sensitive content as a draft for a couple of hours to give herself time to mull it over. If she was in the habit of sending notes in haste, she should be using BigString.com – whatever that was – so that she could yank her mail back, or better still, get it to self-destruct. This advice might perhaps come in handy for future gaffes, but what about her current predicament? The consensus seemed to be that, if you were using a web-based programme, you could kiss your e-mail goodbye once it left your mailbox.

At first, and this seemed amazing to Lizzie later, she wasn't all that perturbed. She'd felt sheepish, yes, and she could remember suppressing the urge to bang her head against the wall. But she certainly hadn't panicked. As the day wore on, though, and she waited in vain for James to call in for his daily chat – a ritual he'd never skipped in the six years of their marriage – she began to feel distinctly uneasy.

Every now and then, she'd nod decisively and go over to the phone. Once or twice, she even dialled the number of his office in Chipping Norton. But they had a tradition that she never called him at work in case she interrupted a meeting with clients or caught him at some crucial creative moment. She only phoned him in emergencies – when she was in labour, if a child knocked out a tooth on the playground, that sort of thing.

She didn't want him to think this was an emergency.

If only he'd just ring, she'd be able to say carelessly, 'Did you get the e-mail? Isn't it a riot? I bet I scared the pants off you just for a moment.'

As the afternoon dragged itself towards the children's tea-time and no call came, Lizzie's mind began to race. The situation was beginning to look less promising with every tick of the clock. How on earth was she going to get herself out of the dog box this time?

By 6 p.m., she had a plan.

She put the children to bed a good half-hour earlier than usual, warning them that if they dared come downstairs on any pretext whatsoever, they would never watch Noddy again. Then she launched into action.

She'd decided that the only way to give the lie to the awful e-mail was to prove to both her husband and herself that she still fancied him rotten.

This should be easy enough to do, she reckoned. Yes, she was a bit out of practice, but she was sure she could still do the Dance of the Seven Veils or similar. Better set the scene with the old wine-soaked candlelit dinner.

If she'd had her wits about her, she'd have organized a babysitter and booked a table at a restaurant. Instead, she found herself rooting through chicken nuggets, fish fingers and French-cut green beans in the freezer. At last she came upon a box of rock-solid green Thai chicken, bought from the local let-us-cook-for-you-we-do-it-much-better shop. Perfect. She managed to excavate it from its box, then dropped it with a clunk into an authentic-looking clay casserole dish before sliding it into the oven – so much more romantic than microwaving it seven minutes before they were due to eat. She didn't have time to be messing with rice; they'd have to make do with defrosted naan bread. Then she jammed two bottles of white wine into the freezer before dashing upstairs to have a bath, shave her legs, pluck her eyebrows, cover up the unicorn pimple, apply perfume to her pulse points, smear body glitter all over – and wind herself up in clingfilm.

She'd read once in a glossy magazine, in the sort of article that gives advice on how to seduce your man and spice up your love life, that no red-blooded male can resist the sight of a woman wrapped in a skin-tight strapless dress, especially one that is totally transparent. Such a dress, the magazine advised, was easily constructed from items you already had on your kitchen shelves: namely, clingfilm.

Apparently, if you looked both dressed to the nines (strappy heels, lots of make-up) and naked at one and the same time, you were guaranteed to drive your man into a frenzy, the likes of which you'd never witnessed in all the years of your marriage.

Creating a dress from a roll of clingfilm was surprisingly difficult, single-handed, and the results were ... interesting rather than seductive, as she'd been led to expect. To her own critical eyes, she looked like a good-sized portion of de-boned, skinless chicken breast wrapped up for a long stay in the refrigerator. Still, it was the thought that counted, wasn't it? And she was sure she'd look better by candlelight.

Hastily, she flung a red satin robe over the clingfilm and headed back to the kitchen. The wine wasn't quite chilled but it was at least below room temperature. She poured herself a largish glass and then began working on the special effects: candles, perfume, gas fire, acoustic guitar music. Then she made a quick search of the bookshelves for something that would help put her in the mood. By some stroke of luck she found an ancient copy of Jilly Cooper's *Riders*, probably left over from the days when Mill House was a holiday rental – a definite improvement on her current book, which was about serial murders, especially as some thoughtful person had dog-eared all the sex scenes. She broke out a small bar of chocolate, too, because she'd read somewhere that it was an aphrodisiac.

The only trouble was it was difficult to concentrate because she kept thinking she could heard his car coming up the driveway, but it never was.

Around 9.30 p.m., James let himself in quietly and went straight upstairs. After all that ear-straining, she hadn't heard his car at all, and was only alerted to his presence by the sound of his feet on the stairs. For a while she sat in the living room, waiting for him to come back down. When nothing happened after ten minutes, she had no choice but to follow him upstairs.

'James, what are you doing up here?' she called softly from the dark passageway. Maybe he was looking in on the children. Such little angels, when they were asleep. But she would kill him with her bare hands if he woke them up.

'James?'

Was he going to punish her with the silent treatment?

But then, in a perfectly normal voice, he called quietly, 'In the bedroom.'

And there he was, in the room where the children had been conceived, packing a suitcase very neatly and methodically. Even then she didn't panic; after all, he was always going off on business.

But when he looked up, the expression on his face stopped her cold.

At that precise moment, she began to appreciate that the damage was far worse than she could ever have imagined.

'Do you have an early start in the morning? Is it Scotland again?' she asked in a scratchy little voice.

'No, I'm leaving tonight.'

'But ... do you have to be on site at dawn or something?'

He shook his head. 'No, I mean I'm leaving home. Leaving *you*,' he added for the sake of clarity, smoothing down an armload of silk ties.

'*Leaving?* You mean, like … like walking out on me? What … because of that stupid e-mail?' She could barely talk at all now, her throat felt so tight. Why had she ever stopped noticing how beautiful he was, how smooth his skin, how excellent his teeth, how glossy his hair?

For a moment his hands stopped fussing with clothing, and he took a piece of paper out of the breast pocket of his jacket. He hadn't even removed his jacket, she registered with some remote part of her mind; he really meant business.

He'd printed the damned thing out. He must have been reading it over and over again. Already, it had a grubby, much-fingered look.

'Give that here,' Lizzie gasped, and snatched it out of his hands. Then, with amazing ferocity, she tore it into a million pieces – or at least ten. 'It was a mistake, that's all, just a stupid mistake.'

'Yes, of course it was, and you can explain everything, right?'

'Yes, and don't make me sound so bloody predictable,' she hissed, remembering, but only just, to keep her voice down. 'Look, I really messed up; I should never have written any of that down. You see, it means less than nothing! *Less* than less than nothing. It was just a rant. I was just letting off some *steam*, for God's sake. Girls say stupid things like that to each other all the time, but we always know it's nothing *serious*. And now you're blowing it out of all proportion.'

'Lizzie, don't try to make this my fault,' James said quietly. He was so calm, which was the worst thing of all. 'It's all there, in black and white. I'm not sticking around where I'm not wanted. What's the point?'

'Rubbish, James, it was the hormones talking. Nothing's wrong with our marriage except I got all introspective and weepy at the wrong time of the month.'

James sighed and began moving steadily again between the cupboard and his suitcase. 'No excuses, Lizzie. I'm just beyond all that, now. The note was pretty plain. You've gone off me in a big way. You fantasize about being single. For God's sake, you fancy chocolate *digestives* more than you fancy me.'

She realized then that, beneath the veneer of calm, he was probably as angry as she'd ever seen him. But anger was good. It was closely related to passion, after all. Perhaps this was the moment for her big move.

She made a dive at his hand, trying to grasp it in hers, but it was impossible to wrestle him away from his socks and boxers. He fended her off gently and resumed his packing.

'Will you stop that flaming fussing about for a moment and *listen* to me?' she hissed through her teeth. He did indeed slow down for a moment, but held onto a bag of First Class airline toiletries, to show that he wasn't to be distracted for long.

'Remember how it used to be in the beginning?' she asked, as huskily as she could. 'Remember when we were at it like rabbits, night and day, barely stopping for meals or even trips to the loo?'

James said nothing, his face still set against her.

'Well, look, I want it to be that way again. I really do.' In one fluid movement, she threw aside her robe and stood revealed in the clingfilm dress.

He gaped. Literally. Stood and gaped. Made no move to embrace her or rip the plastic from her body. Just stood. And gaped.

'Well, what do you think?' she asked nervously. 'Personally, I thought I looked a bit like leftover chicken breast, but then you're a guy. Do *you* think it's sexy?'

His face broke into a reluctant, lop-sided grin. 'I'm afraid I'm forcibly reminded of raw sausage rather than chicken breast.'

'Sausage. We could work with that. Sausage could be ... kinky.' Lizzie wriggled her encased body in what she hoped was a suggestive way.

For a glorious moment a light leapt in his eyes and he gave a quick, hastily suppressed guffaw. OK, so he was supposed to be reeling with lust not merriment, but laughter was definitely better than excessive gravity accompanied by non-stop, automaton-style packing.

But the sudden laugh, ironically enough, upset all Lizzie's best-made plans. From down the passageway came a familiar loud wail. Alex. Both of them knew there'd be no shutting him up without a parental visit. If they didn't react quickly enough, he'd be on his scooter wobbling his way to their room.

'I'll go,' said James.

When he returned about fifteen minutes later, Lizzie was under the duvet, the plastic wrap crumpled in the bin. She stared at her husband with beseeching eyes.

'Coming to bed?' she asked as lightly as she could, hoping they could turn it into a storm in a teacup even now.

But he shook his head, and she saw that he'd brought his shaving things and toothbrush from the bathroom.

'It's no use, Lizzie,' he said. 'It's over. The light's gone out for you. Let's just be honest and do what we need to do.'

Lizzie felt as if an enormous stone had been tied to her foot and someone was about to shove her gently off into the river.

'But ... think of the children. You couldn't possibly leave the children?'

'I've done nothing but think of the children all day,' James said. 'I think the best thing I can do for them is to leave immediately. Make a clean break. I mean, they're still so little now, they'll hardly notice.'

Now, in addition to tying a heavy stone to her foot, someone had painlessly tapped some enormous artery, and all the blood was draining out of her body.

'Let's face it, they don't see an awful lot of me,' James said quietly. He sat down on the bed beside Lizzie but didn't touch her. 'This way, they may even end up seeing more of me than they did before, if I take them on weekend outings and things.'

Weekend outings. His mind was ranging far ahead. He had made the mental leap hours ago, she realized.

She saw then that he'd been crying at some point, perhaps in the dark room as he rocked Alex to sleep.

'James,' she whispered, 'it doesn't have to be like this. I don't want you to go. I love you, you know I do. Please stay. *Please!*'

He shook his head. 'I can't do it, Lizzie. I can't end up like Dad.'

'What do you mean?'

He kept on shaking his head. 'Don't pretend you can't see it. Mum just about tolerates him but that's all. It's a joyless marriage, a farce. They should've had the guts to end it years ago. Anyway, just ... just tell the children I've gone away on a business trip, for now. I'll be in touch. We'll sort things out.'

Then he stowed his toiletries, snapped shut his suitcase and left, pausing only to retrieve his golf clubs from the closet.

She heard the front door close softly, then the car start up and creep away along the driveway.

She lay for a moment like a seal who'd been clubbed on the head. He couldn't be gone. How could he be gone? He'd come back. He'd be back before sunrise. Of course he would.

Shivering, she dragged herself downstairs to lock the door, snuff the candles, and throw away the blackened mess that was still in the oven. The bottles of wine in the freezer she forgot about entirely, and by morning they had exploded.

He didn't come back that night, and every time she spoke to him on the phone he remained firm in his resolve: they had to make a clean break. He wasn't coming home.

But there'd been a moment when she'd had a chance of getting him back. If only Alex hadn't chosen that precise fraction of a second to wake up and bellow, she could've explained things to him; could've made him understand that even though everything she'd written in that note was sometimes true, it was also *always* true that she loved him with a deep and unswerving passion that neither time, nor resentment of his underpants on the floor, nor the ebb and flow of her body's demands could ever diminish.

In her starkly minimalist living room in Back Lane Cottage, Lizzie became aware of her guest, Ingrid, looking at her rather hard. How long had she been moping in her chair with the family photo pressed to her left breast? Really, if she was going to make a success of this new life, she had to get a grip.

She stood up. 'To hell with tea,' she said. 'Do you fancy some Chardonnay?'

Ingrid's eyes nearly shot out of their sockets. They were getting a real work-out today. 'Wine?' she asked, snatching a quick look at her watch. 'Well, it's a bit early in the day perhaps, but why not? Just this once.'

So Elizabeth Buckley, née Indigo, and her neighbour, whom she'd met only hours ago, sat down with a bottle of wine between them at eleven o'clock in the morning. And because Lizzie lived alone, except for two uncritical three-year-olds, who happened to be taking a nap at the same time, and because Ingrid's daughter was at school and her husband was flying a passenger jet to Canada, no one was ever the wiser.

By noon, when the bottle was empty and an almighty wail had suddenly erupted from upstairs, Lizzie and Ingrid had decided that raising children was exactly like running an egg and spoon race in waist-deep water, that the government was made up of a bunch of self-seeking exhibitionists, that Jane Austen was the cosiest novelist in the world, and that reality TV was a cop-out designed to save the BBC money and dumb down the population. Best of all, Lizzie hadn't burst into tears even once.

By the time Ingrid had helped Lizzie make peanut butter sandwiches for the children's lunch, an unlikely friendship had been cemented.

That afternoon, Lizzie stood in her garden with her hands in the pockets of her raincoat, staring in fresh wonder at this place she'd so impulsively rented.

What on earth had she taken on? It wasn't so much a garden she was assessing as a field, complete with rabbit holes and enormous patches of nettles. Also a fair amount of litter. The dying-away remains of daffodils were the only indication that anybody had ever done anything to the land.

For a moment, Lizzie simply stood in the steady drizzle, feeling a bit woozy from the wine and very bleak, as she watched Alex and Ellie, in their all-enveloping yellow rain gear, run about on the so-called lawn. Who was she trying to kid? The garden was a mess, she was a mess, the house was a mess. And she, Lizzie, feeling about as energized as a hibernating snake, was supposed to push up her sleeves and sort it all out? In the knowledge that she might only be here for a short time anyway? Back to bed with a box of chocolates sounded like a better idea.

Then she gave herself a good shake. She couldn't, *couldn't* let the children assume it was normal to live like this, however briefly.

Right, she told herself, I'll start on the nettles; they're definitely the ugliest and most hostile things in the garden. The rabbit holes we'll leave for another day.

Wasting no more time, she stamped off to the tool shed where she slipped on her brand new gardening gloves and gathered up her brand-new fork and trowel. Nobody would suspect for a moment that she'd never gardened in her life. An excellent landscaping service, supervised and supplemented by her mother-in-law, had more than adequately taken care of that side of things at Mill House. Lizzie's vague idea of starting a vegetable garden had been unceremoniously nipped in the bud by Lady Evelyn.

Before Mill House, she'd shared a tiny, gardenless flat with her friend Tessa in Ealing Broadway. Before the flat, she'd been in student digs, and before that she'd lived at home, taking her mother's gorgeous garden in Surrey entirely for granted.

She was amazed, now, at how quickly she was able to make real inroads on the thickets of nettles choking the flower beds. There was something strangely satisfying about pulling whole clumps of the tall green weeds out by their roots, and liberating a sparse sprinkling of seedlings that just might turn out to be plants and not weeds. Soon she'd built up an impressive pile of the prickly stuff, and went to fetch the rickety wheelbarrow from the shed.

'Don't touch, don't touch!' she called as the twins trotted up, determined to help her fill the barrow. 'This is the nasty plant that stung you yesterday, Ellie, see? Mummy's wearing gloves; only Mummy can touch.'

As she waggled her yellow gloves at the children, a black and white collie suddenly bounded up out of nowhere and began jumping at her hands.

'Madge, get *down*. Heel, *heel*,' a furious voice called from the direction of the tumbledown garden gate.

Lizzie held her hands above her head, but this seemed to excite the dog more than ever.

The twins were reacting predictably: Ellie yelling at the top of her lungs, presumably in terror, while Alex jumped about excitedly, shouting, 'Dog, dog, *dog*!'

Out of the corner of her eye, Lizzie saw a burly figure vault over the gate.

'Down, Madge, down,' the stranger yelled for the umpteenth time. 'Get over here *now*!'

With her master now in striking distance, the dog jumped one last time at the gloves, half-knocking Lizzie over. A firm hand landed under her elbow and steadied her. Lizzie righted herself quickly and swooped down to pick up Ellie, who was still shrieking. With the bony but strangely powerful little girl clamped to her in a limpet-like grip, Lizzie turned to the stranger.

Her mind registered that he was fairly young, rather heavily built without being overweight, and deeply tanned. He was dressed in a damp T-shirt and jeans, and steam seemed to rise from his curly dark hair. Not an unattractive man, she couldn't help noticing. With her free hand, she found herself surreptitiously tucking away some strands of hair that had escaped from her pony-tail. Not a good idea with dirty gloves on. She stopped at once.

Now that his dog had given up assaulting Lizzie, the stranger seemed to have lost all sense of urgency. By rights, he should have had the animal by the scruff and be dragging it towards the gate. Instead, he was standing with his arms folded, muscles bulging, smilingly watching the culprit.

'Excuse me, would you kindly get your dog out of my garden?' Lizzie said, not quite as severely as she would have liked. 'Can't you see he's scaring my children?'

She gestured at the offending animal, who was now sitting in front of Alex, offering to shake paws.

The stranger had the gall to smile. 'Of course,' he said quickly. 'I'm awfully sorry. Madge used to play with the kid who lived in this place before you. On the way over here, I did explain to her that the family had moved to Hong Kong, but she couldn't have been paying attention.'

Lizzie started to laugh but quickly turned it into a cough. She composed her face into a frown and shrugged ungraciously. 'Just try to make sure she doesn't jump over our fence again. Ellie here has a sort of phobia about dogs.'

Just at that moment, Ellie wriggled out of her mother's grasp like a piece of wet spaghetti and sidled up to her brother.

'He likes tickles here,' said Alex, demonstrating a scratch behind the dog's soft ears. Tentatively, Ellie put up a hand to touch the fur.

'Yup, and Madge is a ferocious specimen of the breed,' the dog's owner laughed. Actually, it was rather an appealing laugh, as if he were inviting her to share the joke. Her lips quivered slightly, but by now the man had turned to the twins and was hunkering down beside them.

'It's a she, not a he,' he told Alex. 'Her name's Madge and she's five years old, which is about thirty-five in dog years.'

Alex attempted a knowing whistle. 'Mummy iss firty-two,' he said impressively. 'Madge is vewy old.'

'Gosh,' said Madge's owner, squinting up at Lizzie through the drizzle, 'thirty-two. I would never have guessed. She doesn't look a day over twenty-five – that's three-and-a-bit in dog years.'

Lizzie held the man's eyes for a moment too long. She felt a tiny glow of pleasure, but shook it off immediately. Honestly, who did he think he was, this complete stranger, to come leaping into her garden and start ... well, *flirting* with her in front of her children? For all she knew, he could be an escaped lunatic or a confidence trickster.

'Look, could you just get your dog and go?' she asked. 'I don't know who you are or what makes you think our garden is a public footpath, but I've got quite a lot of weeding to get on with. The actual public footpath, if you're interested, is thataway.' She pointed with her tiny garden fork.

The man stood up and shrugged. 'OK but I'm not a crazy dog-walker. I'm a landscape gardener. I do the Hatters' garden every couple of weeks, once a week in the summer.'

Lizzie's eyebrows rose. She had taken Ingrid Hatter for one of those master gardener types, because the grounds around the barn were so fabulous. At the moment her lawn was awash with blue-bells, like the floor of some ancient woodland. 'I thought Ingrid did her own garden.'

The man laughed and casually threw a stick for Madge, who dashed after it, panting. 'You should have seen the barn a year ago,' he said. 'The garden was pretty dismal – even worse than yours, as I remember. The bluebells were all but choked out by weeds.'

The twins began to scream with joy as Madge brought the stick back and laid it down at her master's feet. He gave it a kick, and the dog went bounding off again.

Lizzie watched the animal scrambling over her molehills and rab-bit holes. Pointless to be offended by his aspersions. He was only stating the obvious, after all. 'It is pretty dismal, isn't it? But I have big plans for it. Look, I've already made a start, pulling up all those nettles.' She gestured proudly at the sodden pile, which was about as tall as Ellie.

'I see,' he said, and wandered over to kick at the weeds with his boot. 'Thing is, you'll be pulling these up all summer because the runners are still under the ground. Look, I'll show you.' He bent down and poked around in the dirt until he found what he was look-ing for, then gave a great tug and yanked out a long, tough strand of root, ripping up a line of soil and lawn as he did so. 'Come and see, there are hundreds more of them.'

Lizzie crouched down beside him and looked at the network of runners he had uncovered just beneath the surface of the flowerbed that ran around the house. Her heart sank into her wellies. Why did things always have to be so much more complicated than they looked? Why couldn't it be enough just to pull the nettles out and cart them off in a wheelbarrow? She'd felt so competent only minutes ago, amassing her enormous pile of weeds at record speed.

The stranger laughed. 'Don't look so down in the dumps about it. It's not a train smash. You just need to spray with a weed killer that will get down to the runners. Oh, and by the way, you have ground elder.' He cupped a pretty-looking leaf in his hands.

'And that's ... good?'

He shook his head. 'Sorry. That's definitely bad. It will swarm all over your borders and smother whatever you have in there. You need to get rid of it, too. Pulling it up will do no good at all. It'll just keep coming back. The best solution is to dig this stuff up with a fork, roots and all.'

He turned aside to throw the stick for the dog again.

Lizzie sighed and threw down her garden tools. 'On that cheerful note, I'm going to pack it in for the day – possibly for ever. Do you realize you've just turned my molehill of a garden into a complete and utter bloody mountain?'

'Yup, making mountains out of molehills is part of my sales patter,' he grinned. 'If you like, I'll come and help you with it some afternoon. We could get it done in a few hours between the two of us.'

Lizzie gave her best attempt at a sneer. 'And how much do you charge? Twenty quid an hour?'

He hooted with laughter. 'Where on earth have you been living, woman? Around here, we gentleman gardeners don't leave the house for at least forty-five. But I wasn't trying to sell my services. I was genuinely offering to help you out, just to get you started.'

Lizzie gaped. 'Why on earth would you do that?'

He shrugged. 'Dunno. Easier than asking you on a date, I suppose.'

'But ... but ...' Lizzie gestured helplessly towards her children, currently dabbling in the mud created by the visitor's excavations among the nettle runners. Madge had taken this as a sign to get digging, too. 'Why would you think I'd go on a date? Have you not noticed? I'm a married woman. I have two children, for crying out loud.'

The man folded his arms again and frowned. 'That's not what the grapevine says,' he complained. 'You were advertised as newly single, you know. Has someone been spreading misinformation?'

All of a sudden, Lizzie felt chilled to the bone and slightly sick.

She should never have confided in Ingrid Hatter. Clearly, the woman was already gossiping about her, and it was only hours since they'd spoken.

'Children!' she yelled, too agitated to be amused that her visitor nearly jumped out of his skin at the sudden bellow. 'I'm giving you *three* to get back inside.' Lowering her voice, she added, 'Look, I'm not interested in dating you or anybody else. If I want a gardener, I'll look in the local paper.' Then, at the top of her decibel range, she called, 'Right, Ellie, right, Alex, that's *one*, that's *two* ...'

With the usual shrieks of delicious terror, the twins threw down their muddy sticks and scuttled towards the open door. Lizzie flicked the wet hair out of her eyes and stomped, in squelching wellies, after them.

'By the way,' a voice called just before she was able to slam the door, 'my name is Bruno.'

Chapter Three

When Lizzie finally reached the head of the queue at Boots, the pharmacist was looking down, making a note on a yellow post-it. Lizzie cleared her throat. 'Tessa,' she said very softly, and the woman's head shot up.

For a moment neither of them spoke. Then the pharmacist threw down her pen and clapped her hand to her mouth.

'My God! Lizzie,' she hissed, and a huge grin banished every trace of her professional mien. 'What on earth are you doing here?'

Lizzie was grinning from ear to ear, too. She handed over a tube of toothpaste and some Calpol. 'How *are* you?'

With a bemused look, Tessa Martin began ringing up Lizzie's meagre purchases.

'Bloody hell,' she muttered, glancing at the line of customers behind Lizzie. 'Why on earth didn't you pick up the phone and let me know you were coming? By the way, you do know you can't give this syrup if you're dosing with any other form of paracetamol, right?'

'Course I know. My best friend's a pharmacist; I helped her swot for her ruddy exams. Remember?'

'Just doing my job.'

'Look, can you maybe take an early lunch and come for a chat? I only have until twelve, then I have to get the twins.'

Tessa glanced at her watch. 'You want me to take lunch at ten-thirty in the morning? Hang on, let me see what I can do.'

She handed Lizzie her receipt and change, then disappeared behind the the dispensary. The people in the queue began to clear their throats and shuffle their feet. Luckily, Tessa soon reappeared, shrugging on a coat, handbag over her arm, followed by a resigned-looking male colleague sporting a white coat and a thin blond pony-tail.

Lizzie hurried after Tessa as she jay-walked across the High Street into a prosperous-looking coffee shop that was packed to the rafters with women. Animated groups of trendy thirty-somethings, presumably stay-at-home mums, chatted loudly over lattes. The smaller tables were occupied by harried-looking lone mums watching over babies and/or toddlers. One table was heaving with disgruntled pre-schoolers scrapping over a box of crayons.

'Too crowded,' Lizzie said at once.

'You should see it on a Saturday morning,' said Tessa. 'It's the only decent place in town. And look, there's someone leaving now – the sofa at the back. Quick, let's nab it.'

She darted off, fighting her way efficiently around tables towards the comfortable-looking sofa, which had barely been vacated before Tessa slid neatly across the seat. Lizzie followed with a grudging smile. Tessa had always been the trail-blazer at pubs and clubs, she remembered, clearing a path through wall-to-wall bodies with a mixture of charm and sheer physical force.

The moment Lizzie arrived, slightly pink from the heat and bustle, Tessa stood up. 'Sit with your legs across the cushions,' she ordered. 'I'll get the coffee.'

Lizzie studied her friend from afar while she stood in line.

Tessa Martin, dark-haired, athletic and good-looking, had been Lizzie's best friend since their school days at a small, nurturing but rather shabby girl's boarding school in Surrey. The two had flat-shared as students and during their early working years.

They'd owned one used Vera Wang dress and one Prada handbag between them, which meant they could never attend the same black tie event simultaneously. There were times when Tessa had first dabs on the dress even if it wasn't strictly her turn, because Lizzie wasn't always able to squeeze into it. Unfortunately (or perhaps fortunately) they couldn't share shoes because Tessa's feet were too wide and flat, a fact that had always given Lizzie a secret kick.

Tessa had been bridesmaid at Lizzie's wedding (not wearing the

Vera Wang), and pregnant Lizzie had been matron of honour for Tessa three years later. In all the years they'd known each other, they'd had only one serious falling-out. The tiff had been over a dark and brooding Scot named Angus. His pressing phone calls to Lizzie had been mysteriously intercepted by Tessa, who, through a combination of low cunning, shameless flirting and a campaign of ruthless misinformation about Lizzie, had managed to deflect his attention from Lizzie towards herself.

Tessa's only defence afterwards was that she'd been of unsound mind due to a massive rip-tide of hormones unlike anything she'd ever dealt with before. Apparently she'd never been so attracted to a man in her life. Luckily for the friendship, Angus had turned out to be a bit of a wind-bag and bore. Tessa had been thoroughly ashamed of her wanton behaviour after the fact, and since then had considered herself under a moral obligation to be on Lizzie's side no matter what.

Lizzie, who'd never been that interested in Angus anyway, had been secretly amused to see Tessa making a bit of a fool of herself. After all, Tessa was always the sensible, practical one, the woman who dispensed advice from her unassailable position of strength as someone who had it all together and absolutely never messed up.

Lizzie had no idea where Tessa got her confidence from. OK, so she was good at lots of things, tennis and running, chemistry and biology, making small talk with strangers, choosing clothes, walking into a room and somehow causing everyone to notice her, and decorating tiny flats with bits of flea-market junk so that they looked like something out of the pages of a home décor magazine. But if Lizzie had been Tessa, she'd probably have worried that her calves were too muscular and that her ears lacked the usual quotient of lobe.

Lizzie could make a list of her own virtues: good at synchronised swimming, dancing, writing silly verse for children, understanding what people really meant when they were saying something entirely different, changing nappies, and making up jokes (but not telling them). She was also improving at cooking and better than most English people at French. But no matter how many items she added to the list, she knew she'd never be able to walk around with one-tenth of Tessa's bullet-proof self-confidence. As it happened, Tessa's pushiness had stood Lizzie in good stead on many occasions, and she didn't begrudge her it at all. In fact, most of the time she wished she could borrow it.

The sound of Tessa setting coffee mugs down on the table brought Lizzie out of her reverie. Just coffee, no cakes, she noted with disappointment. Never mind, she'd buy herself a big, sticky bun afterwards. She'd enjoy it more anyway if Tessa wasn't watching her eat it.

Tessa plonked herself down beside Lizzie and took an experimental sip of her latte. 'Mmm, lovely. Not too hot. Now Lizzie, out with it. Why on earth have you turned up out of the blue in Sevenoaks? It's not like you to expect me just to drop everything at a moment's notice. What's going on?'

Lizzie felt her stomach tighten and her mouth go dry. Time to go public.

'Tessa, I've been in Sevenoaks about ten days already. You see, I . . . I live here now.'

Tessa choked and coffee flew inelegantly out of her nose. Lizzie silently handed her a paper napkin. While Tessa was mopping up, Lizzie stumbled on with her story, glad not to have her friend's frank eyes on her.

'I've taken a house in Back Lane, it's called Back Lane Cottage, and I've managed to enrol the twins at a nursery school in Chipstead. Today's their first day, so I'm a bit stressed out. Ellie was bawling when I left, but I phoned and they said she'd settled down. I must say, it's going to be bliss having the two of them away in the mornings again. I'll be able to get something done for a change. I'm determined to finish my children's book and—'

Tessa held up a hand. 'Stop, Liz, stop, for God's sake. You're babbling. You've got to start at the beginning because I'm just not understanding anything you're telling me. What do you mean, you've moved here? Why didn't you let me know you were coming? And why do you keep saying "I" all the time, not "we"? Where's James, for God's sake?'

'So ... so James hasn't been in touch with you guys at all?'
Lizzie was stalling for time. Even though James was an old friend of
Tessa's husband, it was quite clear that Tessa hadn't heard a word
about the state of affairs *chez* Buckley. Tessa shook her head. 'OK.'
Lizzie licked her lips. 'James is, well, I think he's at the manor, but
he may be away on a business trip. He's not living in our house.
Nobody is right now. We're talking about putting it back on the
holiday rental market.'

Tessa simply gaped at her.

'The thing is,' Lizzie said haltingly, 'the thing is, Tessa, James
and I have ... kind of, split up.'

'You've split up? Oh God. Oh shit. Oh, Liz, I'm so sorry. Was
it another woman?'

Lizzie felt a flash of irritation. 'No, it was *not* another woman,
thank you very much. As a matter of fact, James didn't end it. I did.
Well, sort of, anyway.'

Tessa was shaking her dark head so hard she was in danger of dis-
lodging her hair grip. '*You* ended it? *You*? But ... but why? Why on
earth would you do such a thing? The last I knew, you worshipped
the ground he walked on.'

Tears filled Lizzie's eyes and she felt her mouth going into the
upside-down horseshoe shape she'd come to dread in her children.

Immediately, Tessa put down her coffee and began to pat her on
the back. 'Oh Liz, I'm sorry. I'm so sorry. You must've had your
reasons. I'm sure they were damn good ones. Look, here's a tissue.
Just take a deep breath. You'll be OK.'

After a moment or two, Lizzie had her voice back under control.
Sniffing only a little, she offered her sorry explanation.

'The thing is, Tessa, the main problem, you see, is ... well, I've,
sort of, gone off James a bit. Well, not so much James – more
just the bedroom bit with James. And, well, the whole marriage
thing just started to pall. I think it all started when I was pregnant, and it just got worse after the twins were born. I started to
have these fantasies about being single.' Lizzie's face was bright
red with the embarrassment of confessing this stuff, but she really
needed to make Tessa understand. Tessa had always been so good

37

at sorting things out, and she needed her help now more than ever before.

Tessa's eyes were wide with amazement, and she was probably biting her tongue to stop herself from bursting out with, 'You've gone off the bedroom bit with James *Buckley*? Are you insane?' but she managed to hold her peace. Not expecting such self-control, Lizzie paused for comment, but Tessa simply wiggled one hand to indicate she should go on with the story.

Lizzie took a deep breath. 'Believe me, it's not as if I didn't make an effort. I'd try to psyche myself up to get into the mood, but somehow I never really could. So then I just concentrated on … on putting on a good show for James, so that he wouldn't suspect anything. It was a bit exhausting, to be honest, but I thought if I could just keep it up long enough, then things would eventually get back to normal.

'The problem was, things never got back to normal because, well, because I kept feeling this huge, I don't know, resentment, I suppose – this big, black, angry feeling – and it was all aimed at James. You see, I had to change my life *completely* once the babies were born – no more career, no more sleep, no more free time – but James didn't have to change his in the slightest. And he still couldn't pick his own bloody clothes up off the floor!

'Then … then I sort of sent an e-mail to James about … everything. Well, the e-mail was really supposed to go to Janie, but I sent it to James by mistake. And it was all about how much easier life was when he went away on business, and … and how I'd rather have a good cup of tea than go to bed with him. That sort of thing.'

Tessa made a choking noise. Her eyes were so wide they would have popped out if she'd been a Pekinese. When the power of speech returned to her, she said in tones of wonder, 'You sent him an e-mail like that? By *mistake*?'

'Yes, yes. Don't gawk at me like that. I was sending an e-mail to Janie, just to get some stuff off my chest, but somehow I managed to zap it off to James instead. It's easily done, you know, just the click of a mouse.'

Tessa was shaking her head. 'My God, Lizzie. I can't believe it.

What a bloody nightmare. You poor, poor thing. You must be kicking yourself into next week.'

Lizzie's eyes began to mist up and her chin to wobble again. She hastily took a sip of coffee to give her mouth something to do other than turn into an upside-down horseshoe, but her lips wouldn't cooperate and next thing she knew she had coffee dribbling down the front of her jumper.

Tessa reached for Lizzie's hand, which was frantically rubbing at her jumper with a paper napkin.

'Don't worry about that now,' she said firmly, 'I've got a book about how to clean practically anything. Just get back to your story. So you sent him this e-mail, and then what?'

'Well, then he came home and packed his suitcase and left.'

'*Left*? What, just like that? No discussion? Didn't you try to stop him?'

'What do you think? Of course I tried to *stop* him. I wrapped myself up in clingfilm and cooked a romantic dinner and tried to lure him into bed, but it didn't work. He just seemed too ... sad for that sort of thing. Since then we've talked on the phone quite a lot, and he still thinks we're better apart.'

Lizzie said this last bit quickly, not wanting to dwell on the awful, abject phone calls, with her begging him to give things one more chance, and him listening in deafening silence and then saying things like, 'I'm not going to flog a dead horse, Lizzie.' Or, 'I'm pretty sure that ship has sailed, Lizzie.' Or, 'What's the point of trying to paper over the cracks?' She'd never realized he had such a rich storehouse of clichés at his disposal.

Tessa was looking at Lizzie in horror. '*Clingfilm*? OK, let's not even go into that. I just can't get my head around all this. I mean, surely it takes more to bust up a marriage? One stupid misdirected e-mail? I can't *believe* he thinks you're better apart. What about the children? What about Mill House?'

Lizzie was dabbing at her jumper again, as if her life depended on getting the brown stains out. 'We agreed that he should have the twins every second weekend or so. As for the house, we've both just left it. James is staying with his parents, when he's not travelling all over the country for work, that is. So now he's got this model of a bad marriage in front of him the whole time, just to keep him focused. You know how his parents more or less ignore each other? Separate suites? Separate safaris in Kenya? He thinks *we'll* end up like that if we stay together. Anyway, he's mentioned finding a place of his own, a bachelor pad.'

Her voice broke on the word 'bachelor' and then she really was crying, using the coffee-stained napkin to mop up her tears. Women at other tables were staring at them now, some shaking their heads, presumably in sympathy, although very possibly in disapproval at the unseemly public disturbance.

'You were right, Lizzie,' Tessa said. 'This place is too crowded. I just want to know one thing: why didn't you stay at Mill House? Surely he didn't turf you out? I mean, how will you pay the rent here? Will you go back to work? Wouldn't it have been better to carry on there, until something definite happened?'

Such as divorce, Lizzie knew she meant.

The effort to answer this 'one' question helped Lizzie bring her tears under control. 'No, of course he didn't turf me out. I decided to go of my own accord, but he thought it was a good idea. To be honest, I was gambling on him begging me to stay. Shot myself in the foot, really. Anyway, he's told me to keep using the joint account. I was glad to be out of there, in the end. It was horrible in the village, with everybody pitying me, and all the old biddies whispering about me in the shop before my back was even decently turned. But the worst thing was bumping into his folks all over the place.'

Tessa gave a sympathetic shiver at the thought. 'How did *they* take it, then?'

Lizzie pulled a face. 'His mum is saying ghastly things about me to all her ghastly chums. She crosses over to the other side of the street if she sees me coming. His dad is being so kind in that funny, sarcastic way of his, it makes me want to cry. When he heard I was going to move, he came round to the house and told me not to do anything silly. He said, "He'll be back, don't worry. Boys will be boys, but he'll come to his senses." He thinks James is having an affair, of course.'

'What about James? Did you keep bumping into him, too?'

'No. I didn't see him except when he came to take the kids out. It was horrible, knowing he was so close by, holed up in the manor. He might as well have been on the moon. As I said, after about a week of pure hell it dawned on me that one of us had better make a first move, and it might as well be me.'

'But why here? I mean, I know you've always said it's a nice sort of town, and you like the Kentish oasts and whatnot, but isn't it a bit far away from Laingtree?'

'Where else would I go? I can't go home to my parents – that would be too pathetic – and Janie's in Australia. So that left you.'

Tessa's face softened. 'You came all this way to cry on my shoulder?'

'That's right.' Lizzie gave a watery smile. 'Also, I don't want to make things too easy for James. I want him to have to get in his car and drive for bloody hours to see the children. He can just sit in traffic on the M25 and have a good, long think about what he's throwing away.'

Tessa squeezed Lizzie's hand. 'Yes, I can see what you mean,' she said. 'The M25 on a Saturday morning would make anybody sit up and think. Oh, Lizzie, why on earth didn't you come to me straight away?'

'Need you ask? How could I tell you over the phone? It's just too . . . well, it's unspeakable, really. Especially if you're not face to face with the person. That's why I haven't told my parents yet. Or Janie, for that matter.'

Tessa gaped. 'You haven't told your family that you've split up with James or that you've moved? Which?'

'Either, as a matter of fact. I'm just working out the best way to do it. I'm thinking I should load the kids up and drive to Guildford for lunch some Sunday. That way I could explain things properly. Phone calls just seem so . . . brutal. And then Mum could pass the news on to Janie. She calls from Sydney once a week.'

Tessa was shaking her head. 'Lizzie, you can't go on like this. Come on, you need to gird up your loins and make a clean breast of it *now*, not *some Sunday*.' She stopped and gave a short bark of laughter. 'Blimey, loins and breasts all in one breath. I must be ovulating. My advice to you, girl, is to go home, get on the blower and get it over and done with. Your parents are great. They'll understand. They'll give you some moral support. And so will Janie.'

On that rousing note, Tessa slid back her sleeve and looked at her watch. 'Oh my God, we need to get going. I should be back at Boots already. Look, Greg and I are supposed to be off to France for the weekend, but I'm thinking maybe I should cancel. I'm not sure you should be alone right now.'

Lizzie stood up and smiled, a big, genuine smile that lit up her swollen, red-eyed, woebegone face so that she looked almost like her old self for a moment. 'No, you go off to France. Have fun. I'll be fine. Honestly. I feel better already.'

Chapter Four

When you were married, you didn't drive over to your parents' house *alone* for Sunday lunch – well, alone except for your squabbling three-year-old children. You drove over with your husband. Obviously.

As a matter of fact, since she and James had been married, Lizzie couldn't remember a single weekend when she'd gone to visit her parents without him. He liked her parents. They liked him. Sunday lunch had always been a family affair.

Lizzie, therefore, was counting on her parents to notice that something was wrong the minute she stepped out of the car in Guildford. Her father would spot her, James-less, from the kitchen window. He'd hurry out with the baster still in his hands, and she'd dissolve into tears in his arms. Or her mother would be in the front garden, weeding, and she'd straighten up quickly, hand flying to her mouth in shock. 'Lizzie,' she'd cry. 'For God's sake, what's happened?'

Instead, as Lizzie pulled up outside the familiar two-storey mock Tudor house, she found herself altogether unheralded. Nobody was watching for her. Nobody had sensed that this was her hour of need. The lace curtains in the kitchen window didn't even twitch.

Was it possible they'd forgotten she was coming?

'I'm hungry,' Ellie grumbled as Lizzie unbuckled the car seats.

'Me, too,' groaned Alex. 'I'm hungwy like I'm eatin' somethin' right *now*!'

They ran ahead of Lizzie and fell against the back door, wrestling each other for the privilege of opening it. Lizzie followed them through the deserted kitchen, which at least smelled of roasting

43

meat, into the lounge where she found her mum and dad placidly watching TV.

Lizzie's father tore his eyes away from the screen with difficulty. 'Oh, good, you're on time. That's a nice change. Mind you, we'll still have to wait for the food because we calculated you'd be forty-five minutes late, at least.'

Lizzie's mum was bouncing both children on her knee and inhaling the scent of their hair in great gulps, apparently in complete bliss. 'Hello, love,' she called to Lizzie over her shoulder. 'Alex, you little monkey, what do you have in your pockets? They're digging into me.'

'Oh, jus' fings,' said Alex. 'Stones an' stuff. I'll show you.'

'I'm just going to finish watching this bit about global warming,' Lizzie's dad said cheerfully. 'Would you get James a Guinness? I put a couple in the fridge for him.'

'Yes, and put the kettle on, dear,' added her mother, admiring the contents of her grandson's pockets. 'I'm sure you'd like some tea after the drive.'

Lizzie took a slow breath and forced out the words, 'James. Isn't. Here.'

Now, surely, they'd notice something. Her mother's famous sixth sense would kick into action. They'd jump up and crowd around, offering Rescue Remedy or medicinal brandy.

'Oh. Working, is he? Still that house in Scotland?' Surely her father didn't usually sound this nonchalant?

'No. Not working. Listen, Dad, will you come into the kitchen?'

'In a minute, love. I'm just watching this programme.'

'Dad. Please.'

Her mother began to stand up, children screaming with laughter and clinging to her disappearing lap.

'No, Mum. Stay with the kids. I just ... I need to talk to Dad.'

Her father looked at her with narrowed eyes. Without a word, he put down the remote control and shot after her into the kitchen. With the air of a conspirator, he closed the door behind them.

'What is it, love? You in trouble? Smashed the car or something?'

'Smashed the——? Why would you think that?'

He shrugged. 'Don't know. Sort of thing that happens to women. Your mum did it once with the Renault. Remember that? She tried to have it fixed on the quiet, but I cottoned on.'

Lizzie shook her head impatiently. 'No, Dad, it's nothing like that. I wish it was. It's – oh, God.' She squeezed her eyes shut, then opened them again. 'He's left me.'

Her dad stood and looked at her for quite a long time. 'I beg yours?' he said at last.

'James. He's left me. Gone. Packed his bags. Moved out. Dad, will you *stop* staring at me?' And she burst into tears.

That was when the medicinal brandy came out. And the Rescue Remedy. And suddenly Lizzie's mother was in the kitchen, too, and Lizzie found herself stooping over to cry on that warm, familiar shoulder. Her mother still smelt of Yardley English Lavender. Was that a maternal obligation, never to change your soap or your perfume, so your children would always know the smell of you? Just recently, Lizzie suspected, her own smell had been a powerful cocktail of sweat and tears, with undertones of lime and gin.

Between sobs she muttered, 'The children. Got to pull myself together.'

But her mother said, 'You cry as much as you like. I've let them loose on a Milk Tray in the garden.'

Lizzie gave a snort through her tears. 'So much for lunch,' she said. 'I'm s ... sorry.'

Her father paced the kitchen restlessly, clutching a corkscrew in a white-knuckled grip. 'Never mind lunch. Where's the bastard now? Shacking up with his floozy, I suppose. I'd like to ... I'd like to ...' He made a disembowelling motion at crotch level with the corkscrew.

Lizzie gave a watery, shocked giggle. 'Dad. Don't. It's not like that. There isn't another woman.'

Her mother shot her a shrewd look. 'Another man, then?'

Lizzie gasped, appalled. 'No! For God's *sake*! No.'

'I meant *you*, not him, sweetpea. These things happen, after all.

A little flirtation with some friend of his, some chap you both know. Harmless stuff, but men over-react to these things. I mean, look at what's-her-name on *EastEnders*.'

'There's no other person *involved*.' Lizzie sank down into a kitchen chair and held her face in her hands. 'It's just us.'

All of a sudden, it seemed to Lizzie, that bald fact made everything so much worse.

'I'm so sorry, sweetie.' Her mother crouched down and patted her on the back. 'What on earth is it all about?'

Lizzie felt herself colouring to the roots of her hair and the soles of her feet. 'I . . . I really can't say, Mum. It's kind of personal.'

Lizzie's parents locked eyes. Then, simultaneously, her mother gave a tiny shake of the head and her father made a discreet throat-cutting gesture with his corkscrew. Knowing she wasn't supposed to be noticing this silent communication, Lizzie dropped her eyes quickly. Into the pregnant silence, her father said bracingly, 'Well, on the bright side, love, all of England will soon be a tropical island.'

Lizzie's head snapped up. 'What?'

'Global warming.' He threw out his hand in an airy gesture. 'We'll be the new Mediterranean.'

In spite of herself, Lizzie had to smile. 'That's nice,' she said. 'Maybe there'll be palm trees in Kent.'

'Cornwall's already got them,' said her dad. 'Here, have a glass of this Syrah. It's a beauty, isn't it?'

'Why Kent?' asked her mother keenly, like a bloodhound on a trail. You couldn't put much past Lizzie's mother once you had her attention.

Lizzie took a sip of the wine. 'Got a bit of a gamey taste, wouldn't you say, Dad?'

'Why Kent?' her mother asked again.

Lizzie put down her glass. 'Sorry,' she said. 'I should have told you before. Ages ago. The thing is, I've . . . moved there.'

From: janehawthorn@yahoo.com
Sent: 1 May
To: lizbuckley@hotmail.com

Lizzie, EXPLAIN! What does 'kind of personal' mean? Has he gone impotent or something?
   J

From: lizbuckley@hotmail.com
Sent: 1 May
To: janehawthorn@yahoo.com

  Not him, Janie. Me.
  L
  PS See attached note, Blue Monday. The first time round, attached bloody note went to James instead of you.

On Monday evening, Tessa arrived with a purple wig for Ellie, a water pistol for Alex, and a pile of Internet-generated research on post natal depression for Lizzie. 'Consider it a house-warming present,' she said.

'Couldn't you just bring a pot plant or a bottle of wine, like a normal person?' Lizzie complained, dumping the pile down on a kitchen counter. 'I'm not depressed. I'm just ... *depressed*.'

Tessa shrugged. 'It won't kill you just to look at the stuff,' she said. 'I mean, considering I stayed up half the night printing it out.'

'Really, I would've much preferred some French cheese, you know. How was France, anyway?'

Tessa spread her hands over her belly. 'I don't know,' she said with an enigmatic smile. 'We'll have to see. Come on, let's have the guided tour of the house, then.'

'Ah.' Lizzie nodded. Tessa and Greg's three-year quest to become parents was well-known territory. 'It was that sort of trip, was it?'

Tessa grinned. 'You know, I feel really hopeful this month,' she said. 'I think the timing was right, that's if you can trust the basal thermometer. But let's not jinx it with too much talk. Show me the house.'

'OK.' Lizzie gestured grandly at the space around them. '*La cuisine*,' she announced.

'It's very . . . white,' said Tessa.

'You ain't seen nothing yet.' With a certain grim pride, Lizzie showed her the rest of the place.

Tessa stood in the doorway of Lizzie's room, surveying the inflatable mattress under its jumble of linen, the piles of clothes against the wall, the fireplace full of ash, and the white sheets fluttering gently at the windows. She whistled softly between her teeth, momentarily speechless.

Lizzie waited for comment. When none was forthcoming, she said defensively, 'I like it. For now, anyway. It's airy and light and – and minimalist. I've had a bellyful of antiques and brocades and acanthus bloody moulding.'

Tessa tilted her head to one side and then the other. 'So when will you get furniture?' she asked.

'I have a bed. What more do I need? It's a bit like a cell in a monastery, don't you think? Spartan. Simple. Functional.'

'I think monks are tidier,' Tessa said. Then she surprised Lizzie by turning to her with eyes full of tears, and folding her in a tight hug.

On Tuesday afternoon, Lizzie took Tessa's research on depression into the garden so she could riffle through it while keeping half an eye on the children. She'd never really considered that she might be suffering from depression in an official sort of way, but she owed it to Tessa to take a look.

She took a secretive bite of her Mars bar, managing to conceal it from the twins, and began reading.

Most of the stuff was very heavy-going, but at last she came across a quiz similar to the ones she sometimes filled out in magazines on subjects ranging from 'Doormat or Doberman: What's *your* confrontational style?' to 'Flirt, Femme Fatale or Frump: What do your wardrobe choices say about *you*?' The nice thing about these quizzes was you could cheat as much as you liked.

Lizzie started answering the depression quiz. 'Do you find it difficult to fall asleep at night?' *No.* 'Do you feel as if you lack the energy to accomplish simple tasks?' *No.* 'Have you lost your appetite?' *Definitely not.* 'Do you find yourself eating a lot more than usual?' *Hang on, that's a bit personal.* 'Have you put on or lost a significant amount of weight recently?' *Bloody cheek.* 'Have you lost interest in sex?'

Lizzie put down the quiz in disgust.

At that moment a disreputable-looking vehicle towing a trailer loaded with garden machinery pulled into her driveway.

Hurriedly, she stuffed the Mars bar into her pocket before bundling up the depression papers and stowing them face-down on the doorstep, with a brick on top to keep them from blowing away.

A man got out of the filthy van in leisurely fashion and strolled towards the house. Lizzie couldn't help noticing that his arms were very brown and muscular, his hair very curly, and his eyes a bright and twinkling brown. In short, she couldn't help noticing that he was the cheeky bugger who called himself Bruno.

'I was in the neighbourhood,' he hailed her over the fence. 'Would you mind if I mowed your lawn?'

The children ran to the gate. 'Where's dat dog?' cried Alex. As if in answer, they heard a bark from inside Bruno's car.

Lizzie looked at the man with disbelief. 'You want to *mow* my *lawn*? Be my guest. Just don't expect me to pay you.'

'Don't worry,' he said. 'I won't charge a penny. I won't even expect payment in kind.' He gave a lewd wink. 'I just can't stand to see a garden look this way. Hey, don't pull that kind of face! I told you I did some tidying up for the people who lived here before, completely gratis and of my own free will. Ask Ingrid Hatter. They were hopeless with the garden, too. I cut back the hedge on the other side of the kitchen one weekend out of the goodness of my heart, not a single ulterior motive in sight. Of course, they did give me dinner and lots of white wine.'

Lizzie shrugged. The man was obviously slightly touched. Who went around working on other people's gardens just for the heck of it? 'Well, don't expect *me* to ply you with cups of tea, let alone white wine.'

'Wouldn't dream of it. I'll just drink out of the water bowl I brought for Madge.'

'You do that.'

She stamped back into the house, calling for her children over her shoulder. They didn't come, of course, so she had to go out and carry them inside, one under each arm.

Later, the man had the nerve to knock on her door. He was holding the bundle of papers on depression.

'It's just beginning to rain,' he said.

She took the papers awkwardly from his hands. One loose leaf flew off and floated gently to the ground. 'LOSS OF LIBIDO: CAUSATIVE OR SYMPTOMATIC IN POST-NATAL DEPRESSION?' the heading screamed. Lizzie swooped down to pick it up. 'You have a noisy lawn-mower,' she said, and closed the door in his face.

Storming back to the kitchen, Lizzie dumped the pile of depression research directly in the bin. Bloody Tessa! Not for the first time, she felt like wringing her friend's neck.

Another neck she'd have liked to wring was Ingrid Hatter's. Lizzie had gone off Ingrid completely the moment she realized that she – Ingrid – had been gossiping about her – Lizzie – with the landscape gardener – Bruno. So, when the two met the next morning, dropping off their black rubbish bags at the end of Back Lane, Lizzie was as frosty and stand-offish as she knew how. In Lizzie's case, this meant not offering to help Ingrid pull her countless rubbish bags off the roof-rack of her 4x4.

'I was saying to Clive last night what a treat it is to have someone really friendly in the cottage,' Ingrid bellowed as she lugged a bag off the roof and dumped it on the kerb in one fluid movement, completely oblivious to the fact that she'd ripped a good-sized hole in the black plastic. The odour that wafted through the hole was indescribably foul. Lizzie could do nothing but cover her nose and stand her ground. She maintained a stoic silence to mark her new hostility.

'By the way, I was just mentioning you the other day to this chappie I know who does our garden: Bruno Ardis. He's a bit of a dish, if you know what I mean, and single.'

Lizzie narrowed her eyes above the hand that was clutching her nose in a glare that she hoped spoke volumes.

'Don't worry, he's not just any old gardener, you know. He used to be something in the City – mergers and acquisitions, I think he said – but he got tired of the hustle and bustle, so he chucked it all in. I gather he could well have afforded to retire, but he decided to start up a little landscaping business to keep himself busy. Anyway, I happened to bump into him the *very* same day you had me over for tea. So I just told him that you'd moved into the cottage and might need some cheering up, you know. I filled him in about James and everything.'

Lizzie had a mental image of her Chardonnay-soaked neighbour accosting Bruno Ardis as he weeded her borders. Her eyes widened in horror. Thank goodness she'd been sparing with the details of the breakdown of her marriage when she'd had her heart-to-heart with Ingrid.

'So don't be surprised if he comes knocking on your door one day. Nice-looking chappie, as I said. Not a patch on your James, of course, but what a sense of humour. A bit of a flirt, too. If anyone can jolly you out of the doldrums, he can. There, that's the last of those bags for the week.' She kicked casually at an empty can of smoked oysters that had somehow made its way onto the muddy lane. 'By the way, if you ever need a baby-sitter, just give me a ring. My daughter, Sarah, has a way with the little ones, if I say so myself. And she's saving up for a ski trip to France next year. Toodle-oo.'

How did you bear a grudge against a woman like that?

Later that same day, Sarah herself arrived at the cottage to present her baby-sitting credentials. An awkward-looking teenager with a mouth full of braces, she blushed when Lizzie thanked her for coming over.

'I brought this,' she said, holding out a rainbow-coloured teddy bear. 'For the kids.'

Lizzie took it, touched. She called for the twins, and Ellie appeared obediently in the empty hallway. 'Look, darling,' Lizzie cried, aware that she was gushing, 'this is Sarah. From the barn next door. She brought you and Alex a teddy bear. Isn't it lovely? What do you say?'

Alex stampeded into the room at that moment. He snatched the new toy out of Lizzie's hand and hugged it to his middle. 'Ish mine,' he growled.

Ellie's own hand shot out and closed over the teddy's head. 'Snot yours,' she quavered. 'Iss for sharing. Mummy *said*.'

A vicious tug-of-war ensued. Lizzie smiled brightly at her guest. 'Twins,' she said. 'They're a teeny bit ... competitive. Thanks so much for coming over. I'm not sure I'll need a baby-sitter. I don't go out very much. But if I ever do, I'll be sure to give you a ring.'

She was about to close the door on the ugly scene when Sarah suddenly ducked into the hallway and knelt down beside the children.

'Help!' she cried in a gruff little voice. 'You're stretching my tummy! You're squishing my head! You're pulling my legs off!'

The twins stopped tugging at once and stared, round-eyed, at the stranger.

'Phew! That's better!' the gruff voice declared. 'I won't stay with you lot if you hurt me again. I'll go back to the barn.'

Alex was staring at the bear, now in Sarah's hand, with a deeply buckled brow. 'Sowwy,' he muttered. 'Dint mean to hurt you.'

'I'm sorry, too,' Ellie added. 'We got to take turns, right?'

'Right,' said the rainbow-coloured bear. 'So who's the eldest?'

'Me!' yelled Alex, slapping his chest.

'OK, you get to take me first,' said the bear, and shuffled along the carpet in the boy's direction.

'An' I take you next,' said Ellie happily. She smiled up at Sarah. 'Come see our room,' she invited.

Sarah glanced at Lizzie. 'Go ahead,' Lizzie said with a shrug. As they walked off, she heard Ellie asking, 'Why you got that shiny stuff in your mouf?'

For someone who didn't have a social life, Lizzie had a very busy doorbell. Moments after she'd come in from dropping the children off at nursery school the next morning, someone rang it long and loud.

In spite of herself, Lizzie's spirits lifted. She padded to the door – in socks, torn old jeans and an oversized grey sweatshirt – to see who it was.

These days she didn't bother about niceties like mascara and lipstick. It was quite enough effort just to drag a brush through her hair after she'd cleaned her teeth. Today she was looking particularly dishevelled because she'd literally grabbed her clothes from the puddle of unsorted laundry that lay on her bedroom floor. She was probably smelly, too, since she hadn't bothered to take a shower for a day or so.

'Oh. It's you.'

Twinkling up at her from the bottom of her doorstep stood Bruno Ardis, Madge at his side. Under his left arm he carried a bristling assortment of garden tools, and he'd taken the liberty of laying out several trays of seedlings on the steps.

'You up for some gardening this morning?' he asked.

It was hard to stonewall a man who'd mowed your lawn for free. Perhaps that was his strategy – though why he bothered, Lizzie couldn't imagine.

'What if I say no?'

'I'll just go and plant these next door. I'm sure Ingrid would enjoy a spot of colour in her front border.'

'I have to tell you, I hate people turning up to see me out of the blue.'

'Then you'll have to give me your phone number.'

To change the subject, Lizzie took a step outside and bent to examine the plants he'd brought. 'What are they?'

'Violas. Aren't they sweet? If we put them in now and look after them properly, you should get blooms all through the summer. They're pretty low maintenance, really. Just keep the soil moist and make sure the weeds don't choke them. Think you can manage that?'

'It's a wonder nobody has got round to choking *you*,' she snapped. 'Just because I didn't know about nettle runners and ground elder doesn't mean I'm brain-dead. It's just that I've never done gardening before.'

Bruno laughed and ran his fingers through his dark curls. 'A virgin gardener! And I get to show you the ins and outs. Lucky old me.'

Lizzie stuck her finger into the moist potting soil around one tiny, fragile plant. It had a single, perfect, purple bloom. 'OK,' she sighed. 'Let's plant the ruddy things, but please, no more of your wit. Let's just assume I'm scintillated and leave it at that.' After a sleepless night replaying her entire life in her head, and especially all scenes involving James, she was in no mood for sexual innuendo masquerading as humour.

'Ouch. What's the matter? Bad night's sleep?'

'Yup,' said Lizzie, taking a tray of plants and heading towards the front of the house. 'Nothing new there, though. I don't think I've had a decent night's sleep since my third trimester.'

He gazed at her with raised eyebrows. 'Since when?'

'Since the last months of my pregnancy, more than three flipping years ago,' she explained wearily. 'You can tell you've never been married. You just don't understand the language.'

'We can't plant these over there,' he said evenly, gesturing at the border she'd begun to attack with a trowel. 'No sun. I was thinking of the beds along the garden path, back here.'

He walked off to the shed – now cleared of toxins and crammed with outdoor toys – and came back with the rickety wheelbarrow. He loaded it with plants and tools, and trundled off to the bed near the gate. Then he picked up a long-handled fork and began turning the soil over. Grudgingly, Lizzie joined him, clutching a trowel. Madge kept dropping a dirty old tennis ball in front of Bruno, and he kept kicking it across the lawn. Lizzie didn't feel like talking, so she just stayed quiet and contemplated the dirt.

'As a matter of fact, I have been married,' Bruno said after a while. 'I'm a gay divorcée, just like you. That's sort of why I keep showing up on your doorstep. I know how it feels, those early days. Not a time to be alone in a new place. Ingrid's been a bit worried about you, too, to be honest. Said you were drinking wine at elevenses, that sort of thing. So between the two of us, we're keeping an eye. Anyway, my ex-wife and I didn't have kids, so I don't know the pregnancy terminology.'

For a moment, Lizzie was stumped. She simply sat back and looked at him, aware of a slight feeling of . . . yes, disappointment. OK, she'd always thought it a bit odd that Bruno seemed attracted to her, in her current state of disrepair. But it was still demoralizing to reflect that his flattering interest amounted to little more than a mercy mission.

He seemed a bit tense, talking about his divorce. Maybe he was still smarting. Maybe he suffered from insomnia, too, and, when he *did* manage to sleep, also woke with a horrible jolt, sweaty and panic-stricken because the other side of the bed was empty. Lizzie could feel her eyes filling with tears. She blinked, took up her trowel and began to dig furiously.

'I'm not divorced yet, and you're certainly not gay,' she said in a wobbly voice.

'Not such a deep hole,' he replied, gesturing at her feverish trowel. 'We want to plant it, not bury it.'

'OK, OK, I was just being thorough.' She was glad he didn't offer any sympathy. Sympathy always undid her.

'That's about right,' he said as she tipped earth back into the hole. 'Now, could you possibly fill this watering can?'

Lizzie trailed into the house with the large metal watering can, glad of the chance to blow her nose in private, but wondering why on earth there wasn't an outside tap. It was so awkward angling the can into the kitchen sink. Heading back out with the full can, slopping water on the sludge-coloured carpet as she went, she felt as if her right arm were being stretched several inches longer than her left.

'Why do men have muscles if they never do the grunt work?' she complained loudly. 'Why is it that with their massive biceps and triceps and . . . forceps, they're generally the ones sitting behind an office desk pushing a pen, while weedy women cart ten-ton toddlers and trolley-loads of groceries around?'

As she reached the doorstep, she saw that Bruno had company. Someone in sporty stretch pants and a trendy padded gilet was leaning casually against the garden gate, chatting to him. It took her a tenth of a second to realize it was Tessa.

Two unexpected visitors on the same morning. Really, it was too much.

'Tessa, what are you doing here? Why aren't you working?' She had to admit it, she was a little stung to see Bruno grinning so appreciatively at Tessa's legs.

'Yes, I'm delighted to see you, too,' Tessa quipped back. 'Can you spare me a minute, or should I come back later?'

Lizzie glanced at Bruno, who was busily planting violas. 'What do you reckon?' she asked.

'Oh, go ahead, have a cup of tea with your mate,' he said. 'I'm nearly finished here, anyway. Just hand over the watering can. You'll have to douse them some more later.'

'Can I at least bring you out a cup of tea?' Lizzie asked.

'Nah, thanks anyway, but I have to get on,' Bruno grinned. 'I'll take you up on it next time, OK? When you're alone.' And with a huge wink and nudging motion of his left elbow, he turned his back on them and set to work again.

'So that's Bruno, is it?' Tessa asked. Lizzie handed her a mug and a plate of chocolate digestives in the living room.

'So he tells me,' said Lizzie.

'Not bad,' Tessa pronounced, licking off the top of her biscuit. She only ever allowed herself one and she liked to make it last. 'Why didn't you say he was so yummy? The way you described him, I thought he was some pot-bellied, middle-aged loser with no mates.'

Lizzie shrugged. 'Is he yummy? I wouldn't know. I've pretty much lost interest in that sort of thing.'

Tessa snorted. 'Yes, he's yummy. You *must* have noticed.'

Lizzie sighed. 'OK, so he's not bad-looking. I didn't think that was so important. Why would you want to know? You're happily married. Aren't you?'

'Yes, I'm happily married. But I've still got eyes in my head.'

'All right, all right. So what's going on? Why'd you take the time off? It's not ...?' She didn't dare put the question into words. Had Tessa found out she was pregnant?

Tessa popped the last morsel of biscuit into her mouth and licked her fingers daintily. 'No, it's nothing like that,' she said. 'I won't know for a bit, will I? The thing is, Lizzie, I thought it was time we developed a campaign for you.'

'A campaign?'

'Yes. I mean, I just can't stand by and watch you give up without a fight. You *can't* let James go. You can't. The two of you are meant to be together. You've just got to snap out of this funk. I mean, you really have to get to grips with this whole no-sex-drive problem. If you can just get back to being your old self, I'm sure things will sort themselves out between you and James.'

Lizzie felt her colour rising. 'Tessa, really, I don't want to talk about it.'

'Lizzie, do you want him back or don't you?'

'God, Tessa, if only you knew how much.'

'Well, then. You've got to get off your backside and do something. I've already mentioned I think you might be depressed. I mean, clinically depressed, not just sad. I think you should consider getting some counselling.'

Lizzie shook her head. 'Tessa, talking to some stranger is never going to work. Not for me. It's sort of ... creepy and weird. And, you know, not very loyal to James.'

Tessa pursed her lips. 'OK. But did you read the research I brought you? Lack of libido is a common symptom of depression. And I think you're showing other symptoms, too.'

Lizzie raised her eyebrows and bit viciously into a biscuit. 'Such as?' she asked with her mouth full.

'Such as ... erm, well, you must admit you're not quite as much in control as you used to be. I mean, in control of yourself, your life. I mean, look at you. Look at your clothes, for heaven's sake. You must have grabbed those out of the laundry basket. And your hair. When did you last wash it?'

Lizzie felt her blood pressure beginning to rise. How dare Tessa go on about her clothes and her hair when her husband had just left

57

her? If this was her idea of being supportive, well, she could go and and suck eggs.

'For your information, I just read a magazine article that said you should leave your hair unwashed for about ten days every now and then in order to restore the natural oils.'

'So, this greasy look, it's actually a beauty treatment?'

'That's right.'

Tessa began a new attack. 'What about your weight, then? Is that a beauty treatment, too? It's feasible, I suppose. The French always say you have to choose between your face and your figure when you reach a certain age.'

'Excuse me?'

Tessa took a deep breath and said clearly, 'Your weight. You must have put on a couple of stone at least since Ealing Broadway days. I mean, you've never been the skinny type, but I bet you've had to buy a whole new wardrobe of, you know, *fat clothes*.'

Lizzie felt the blood rushing to her head, whether in humiliation or rage she hardly knew. What woman in her right *mind* said the 'f' word to her best friend? She couldn't have been more gob-smacked if Tessa had suddenly hit her in the face with a dead fish.

Obsessively combing out the tassels of one of the new cushions, and refusing to meet Lizzie's blazing eyes, Tessa staggered on. 'Look, Lizzie, this is my take on the whole thing: you had the twins, you got the baby blues, and somehow or other they never went away. Remember how exhausted you were when the little horrors were born, bless their hearts? You used to boast that you never got more than two hours of sleep in a row. And anybody could tell it wasn't *idle* boasting; you looked like death warmed up.'

Lizzie opened her mouth, but Tessa held up an imperative hand for silence and steamrolled on.

'I know you *chose* to stay home with the kids but I think you were bored as well as chronically sleep-deprived. Somewhere along the line you stopped watching your diet. I'm guessing you just didn't have the energy to continue the crusade. I mean, you always used to say you could put on five pounds overnight just by smelling a bag of fish and chips. And look at you now; you've just *devoured* five chocolate biscuits!'

Her tone of voice wouldn't have been inappropriate if she'd been accusing Lizzie of snorting five lines of cocaine.

'Well, for God's sake, woman, I've just lost my husband. Do you expect me to be *dieting*?'

Again, Tessa held up the hand. 'You're misery-eating, but I don't think you started when James swanned out.'

'He didn't *swan* out. It was more of a shuffle, what with that heavy suitcase and his golf clubs.'

But there was no stopping Tessa in full flow. 'My guess is you've been doing it since the twins were born. Misery-eating, I mean. I've been trying to screw up my courage to talk to you about your weight for ... hmm, at least three years. So, I'm thinking that the ... erm, well, the *weight gain* may also have affected things in the bedroom. Made you feel less, you know, interested.'

Lizzie simply stared at Tessa.

'Say something, Lizzie. You're making me feel weird, just gawping at me like that.'

'That's because you *are* weird. What kind of person makes up stories like that about their friends?'

'I'm not making up stories. Isn't it all true?'

'Well, for your information, I have *not* put on two stone. One and a half, that's all. Well, maybe one and three-quarters. And it's just my pregnancy weight, that's all. Everyone knows it's really hard to get rid of pregnancy weight. Plus, I had *twins*.'

'OK, so I got a few details wrong. But I'm right, on the whole ... aren't I?'

Lizzie knew her friend was spot on, but she couldn't help feeling betrayed.

'You've never had a baby, Tessa. You have absolutely no clue what you're talking about. So just shut up about it, OK?'

'No, I haven't had a baby, but that's not through want of trying, as you ruddy well know. I'll forgive you because I know you're just lashing out without thinking.'

'I'm lashing out? *I'm* lashing out?'

'Yes, you are, and no, I'm not. As I said, I've been thinking about this a lot, and I just think someone has to talk to you and, sort of, set you back on the right path.'

'And you're the one qualified to do that? You, the boyfriend snatcher of Ealing Broadway?'

'He wasn't your boyfriend and you didn't even want him. Don't throw *that* in my face.'

All of a sudden, Tessa was starting to look vulnerable, even tearful. Lizzie knew she'd been wrong to mention Tessa's fertility problems. It was a sensitive issue. But then, Tessa ought to have known that Lizzie's weight was a *super*-sensitive issue.

Still, she felt herself weakening.

'OK, so what if you're right? What if I am fat and depressed and that's why my marriage failed? What then?'

Tessa wiped her eyes with the back of her hands and then gave a deep sigh. 'Good girl,' she breathed, 'good girl. Now you're not in denial any more I can show you some stuff I've brought for you.'

Lizzie gave a snort. '*Denial?*'

'Oh, Christ, Liz, don't start all that again. All the righteous huffing and puffing and whatnot. Just hold on a moment; I have to run out and get something from the car.'

While Tessa was out, Lizzie took the opportunity to wolf down another couple of biscuits. She was brushing crumbs off the sides of her mouth surreptitiously when Tessa came back lugging a bulging black hold-all.

'That Bruno chap has gone,' Tessa remarked, setting the bag down on the floor beside the sofa.

Lizzie sat up in her chair, eyeing the bag. This was beginning to get interesting. She wondered if Tessa had brought in some control panties or corsets.

But no, Tessa began to unpack bottles and jars of what looked like vitamins or food supplements. Was it possible she had access to some experimental dieting drugs that would cause Lizzie's excess weight to melt away miraculously? Tessa spent some time lining up her bottles. Then she sat back and, assuming the earnest expression of a Tupperware party hostess, began what sounded like a rehearsed speech.

'Now Lizzie, I know you've never really had that much faith in alternative medicine, but I hope you'll have a little faith in my judgement, since drugs are my business. What I've got here is a line-up of all the alternative stuff that is supposed to have some effect on mood. So I've got SAM-e, that's for depression, St John's Wort, ditto, DHEA for vim and vigour, ginseng for energy, and a new one, Codonopsis, which is supposed to work just about as well as ginseng, and improve your memory, too.'

'What's the matter with my memory, for God's sake?'

'Nothing. Only, of course, you did forget my birthday last year. If your memory is beefed up that'll be a bonus, but we're really aiming to lift your mood and improve your energy levels. I've also included an iron supplement because you may be anaemic.'

Lizzie picked up a couple of the bottles and glanced at the labels. 'I have enough energy to do what I need to do,' she muttered.

'Right, but do you have enough energy to run around the block?'

Lizzie frowned. 'Of course I don't have enough energy to run around the block. Who does? Only complete nutters like you, that's who. The rest of us are quite pushed enough just getting on with our daily lives. And by the way, I read somewhere that too much aerobic exercise can have a negative effect on fertility.'

'You're probably thinking of what cycling can do to a man's sperm production,' Tessa riposted.

Lizzie frowned, trying to remember the magazine article she'd read recently while waiting to show Ellie's tonsils to the doctor. 'I'm sure they said something about jogging and a woman's ovaries. Anyway, you'd be well advised to do some research into *that*.'

'Good thing we don't have to worry about *your* ovaries.'

'*What?*'

Tessa grabbed her hands and squeezed them tight. 'Look, Lizzie,' she said urgently, 'everyone knows that exercise is one of the best treatments for depression. Gets all those endorphins pumping through the system. So ... so ... well, to cut to the chase – how about running the London Marathon with me?'

Chapter Five

Lizzie laughed loudly. Tessa had run the marathon years ago. But nobody mentioned marathons and Lizzie Buckley in the same breath.

'We both know I can't run the London Marathon, idiot,' she said fondly. 'Besides, it's over already, isn't it?'

'For *this* year. But I've decided to run next year. My thinking is that if I've got my heart set on running a marathon then I'm bound to fall pregnant.'

Lizzie nodded sagely. 'Ah, using reverse psychology on Fate.'

This was an old ploy of theirs. If you desperately wanted some man to ring you, you had to go out all day and not even *think* about the phone. If you wanted to meet a new man, you had to vow you were sick of men, and stay away from the places they congregated, like pubs, takeaways and television sets.

'Right,' said Tessa. 'Thank goodness somebody understands. Greg reckons you can't play mind games with Fate. I had to re-frame the whole thing and call it Murphy's Law before he'd go along with it. So I've given up on the baby thing and now it's all about the marathon. I'm going to start training this weekend – just some road work to get me back on track. Maybe a 5k race here or there. I'm really out of shape, and sex just isn't the workout they say it is. But it's OK because my training partner,' arch smile, 'is even more out of shape than I am.'

Lizzie stood up and began backing away into the kitchen. 'Steady on, Tessa. I've already said no.'

'Glad we're on the same page, Liz. Come on, I know you're up for it.'

'You're out of your tiny mind.' Lizzie was pleased with the assertive ring in her voice. But she was distinctly uneasy. Tessa was a *force majeure*.

Tessa held up a piece of paper from the hold-all. 'This is our first challenge,' she said. 'I thought we'd start off really slowly. So I've put us both down for a 5k fun-run in a couple of months. By then you should be able to handle the distance, no sweat.'

Lizzie kept shaking her head. 'I'm not doing it, Tessa. I'm not a runner, OK? I've never been a runner. I never will be a runner. Have you seen the size of my boobs?'

'Hard not to.' Tessa gave Lizzie's considerable chest a measuring look. 'But have you never heard of sports bras?'

'Sorry, Tessa, completely bloody out of the question.'

'Nonsense, I've bought you one already. Let me just say two words, Liz: Oprah Winfrey.'

Lizzie raised her eyebrows.

'That's right. Oprah Winfrey. Ran the US Marine Corps Marathon at the age of forty in four hours twenty-nine minutes. If she can do it, with her cup size, which I would hesitate even to guesstimate, then you've haven't got a leg to stand on, Miss 36D.'

'If I haven't got a leg to stand on, then I can't run, can I? Ha-ha.'

Tessa ploughed on as if she'd never even opened her mouth. 'So I'm giving you a few days to get used to the idea, and I'm leaving you some literature to pep you up.' She fished in the black hold-all, and emerged with a pile of magazines bearing scary titles like *Runner* and *Extreme Athlete*. 'Also the bra,' she said, flourishing a severe-looking article of corsetry. 'I think we should try to get out on Saturday afternoon for a gentle little run-walk.'

Saturday afternoon? Oh, thank goodness. 'Sorry, can't do it, Tessa,' Lizzie said joyously. 'What would I do with the twins?'

Tessa's hands stopped fussing for a moment as she turned her full attention on Lizzie. 'Liz,' she said slowly, 'the twins won't be here. Remember? You told me James was coming on Saturday morning to take them to Gloucestershire. You said how annoyed you were, because he got Sonja to phone and arrange it.'

63

Lizzie's heart did something funny. She couldn't believe she'd forgotten about the weekend visitation, even for a moment. Sonja had phoned several days ago, sounding apologetic and embarrassed, to say James had rung from Scotland and asked her to set things up.

Sonja was James's personal assistant. Lizzie had never had anything against her. She seemed a nice enough sort of girl, unobtrusive and good at her job. But when Sonja phoned to make arrangements for the weekend, Lizzie suddenly loathed her. How dared she be privy to the ins and outs of Lizzie's separation from James?

Since that phone call, Lizzie had been simultaneously longing for and dreading the moment when James would walk through the door of Back Lane Cottage to pick up Ellie and Alex.

On the one hand, she was anxious about letting the twins out of her sight for two whole days. Who would wipe their bottoms after potty time? Did James know that Ellie liked sugar sprinkled on top of her Readybrek and not mixed in? What if he left Alex unsupervised among Lady Evelyn's breakables? What if Alex bit somebody?

Then, on the other hand, what freedom to be alone in the house for a whole weekend. She'd finally be able to knuckle down to some writing.

Lizzie wondered what she'd do when James turned up on the doorstep. Throw herself down at his feet and beg him to take her back? Put on a brave front and wear some feisty new outfit in the hope of convincing him that she'd changed into a mysterious and desirable new person? Or just stand there like a lump in her grey sweats, not meeting his eye, fighting back tears as she kissed the children goodbye?

Another idea suddenly presented itself. What if she opened the door in trendy new running gear with slogans like, 'Just bloody get on with it!' written all over it, flashing a pair of those running shoes that lit up, and perhaps chatting animatedly on the phone to a friend about her training for the London Marathon? That would shake him up, and no mistake.

Tessa was still staring hard at Lizzie.

'Oh my God, you're right. He'll be here at nine on Saturday morning, according to Sonja. More like noon, I should think. Without me there to elbow him out of bed . . .'

An awkward little silence fell.

'You know what, Tessa?' Lizzie said after a while. 'I think I'll give this jogging thing a whirl. No promises, mind you. I'm not into self-flagellation. But I'll give it a go; see if I can at least manage that fun-run thingy.'

Tessa leapt up and gave Lizzie a resounding slap on the back. 'I knew you'd see sense,' she said happily. 'I'll drop by on Saturday at around four, then. Don't eat a big lunch, but don't skip any meals, either. I tell you, James won't be able to resist you when he sees the light back in your eyes and the bounce in your step again. Gotta get going now. Don't forget to start taking the alternative medicines. Especially the Codonopsis. Bye-ee!'

Twenty minutes later, Lizzie managed to find a parking spot somewhere in the vicinity of Chipstead village hall, where the twins went to nursery. Panting with exertion after a stiff walk, she strode with feigned confidence towards a group of women already gathered outside the doorway of the crumbling redbrick building.

'Hello there,' she called out to no one in particular. The women turned surprised faces to her. 'Don't you hate the parking here?'

The other mothers made non-committal noises, but nobody took up the issue. In fact, it seemed to Lizzie that they turned away as quickly as they could to resume conversations that didn't include her.

Lizzie told herself she didn't mind. After all, they'd all known each other since the start of the school year. They'd been meeting twice a day here, outside the village hall, for months, whereas she was a brash newcomer. It was bound to take them a while to warm up to her.

But still. It was discouraging. In this new town, these women represented her only real hope of a social life outside of her lifelong friendship with Tessa and her budding acquaintanceship with the Hatters in the barn.

Lizzie felt her bright smile fading as she ducked her head over her bag and dug around in it, pretending to be searching for something really important. She found a pencil and a scrap of paper and spent the next five minutes writing a to-do list, just so it wouldn't look obvious that no one was talking to her. 'Running shoes', she wrote. 'Light-up kind. Top-of-range lycra running gear. Sports bra.' The bra Tessa had given her was too small.

On Friday night, when most single women were out on the High Street, propping up bars or dining in girly groups at cheap restaurants, Lizzie was sitting in her upstairs office at her elderly computer, sipping a gin and tonic and checking e-mail messages, one ear open for noises from the children's room.

Ignoring a fresh spate of wails from down the passageway, Lizzie clicked on a note from James.

From: james.buckley@hotmail.com
Sent: 22 May
To: lizbuckley@hotmail.com

Dear Lizzie

Just to confirm I'm picking up twins first thing tomorrow. Expect me around nine.

James

Lizzie took a large gulp of gin and shuddered. Never in the long years they'd known each other had James communicated with her in such a cold and truncated fashion.

At least he'd written 'Dear'. Plain 'Lizzie' would have been too much to bear.

She took another sip of gin and rattled off a reply.

From: lizbuckley@hotmail.com
Sent: 22 May
To: james.buckley@hotmail.com

James

    I'll have them ready for you.

    Lizzie

James hadn't seen the children for more than three weeks. This wasn't because of Lizzie's move, but because he'd been away looking at a carriage house in Scotland. He'd now become such a big name in farm-building conversions that people were seeking him out across the length and breadth of the country. This meant he had to go on extended business trips, which he used to grumble about because he missed romping with the children at the end of the day.

Lizzie had looked forward to his trips as times when she could eat scrambled eggs or cereal for dinner. And go to bed at eight o'clock with a cosy novel, without being expected to exert herself between the sheets.

Now that she was free to do all of the above to her heart's content, she found she spent most nights scrabbling about on the inflatable mattress like an arthritic dog, trying to find a comfortable position. The small hours passed in a twilight zone of insomnia, panic attacks and bad dreams. She would have given anything – her left ear, both little fingers (what use were they anyway?), even her right arm – to have James's familiar bulk under the duvet beside her. Yes, even if his return meant marathon sex sessions every night.

Oh, to recapture those days when she'd enjoyed the marathon sex sessions.

In the misty past – before pregnancy turned her body into a stretch-marked pumpkin, before the twins came along and channelled so much of her love and energy into their tiny frames – she'd loved nothing better than to leap between the sheets with James Buckley.

At one point, long before they'd even met, leaping between the sheets with James Buckley had been her dream, the very sustenance of her imagination.

In those distant days, James frequented Lizzie and Tessa's grimy local, the Bird in Hand. Lizzie and Tessa used to call him Mr Rugby, because of the battered rugby jerseys he wore.

The moment he was spotted in the pub, the conversation between Lizzie and Tessa would go something like this: 'Psst, Lizzie! Red alert! Mr Rugby to starboard.' Tessa, of course, had done any amount of sailing.

Lizzie had done no sailing at all. 'Where is starboard?'

'That way, that way.' For discretion's sake, Tessa would point with a thumb. 'Whoa, Lizzie, don't look now. Crikey, you're so obvious. OK, *now* you can look. God, isn't he *gorgeous*?'

'Do you think he has a girlfriend?' Lizzie would ask.

'Several, I'd imagine,' Tessa would reply. 'Should I do the walk-by?'

Lizzie was always too wimpy to do the walk-by. She was saving it for an evening when she knew she looked spectacular, but sadly, that evening never seemed to come.

Tessa had no such qualms. She was always sure of her looks. She'd stand up, smooth her hands over her hips, and undulate past Mr Rugby and his crowd. But for one reason or another, he never seemed to look her way. He and a couple of cronies were always deep in some loud conversation about a rugby or football match, or the money someone had lost at the races. Sometimes there were girls in Mr Rugby's crowd. More vigilant than their male companions, they'd shoot Tessa poisonous looks and toss their highlighted manes like spooked thoroughbreds.

Never before had Tessa cast a man so many smouldering looks and received not a single smoulder in return. The whole situation began to rankle with her. Lizzie, on the other hand, didn't expect to make actual contact with the great Mr Rugby. She knew he was out of her league. Way, way out of her league. But a cat could look at a king.

Then she and Tessa went away one weekend in late summer to stay with Tessa's parents in Winchcombe, the Cotswold village where they'd retired. That Saturday morning, in a spirit of joviality ill-suited to the earliness of the hour, Tessa's father suggested they went berry-picking at Longborough fruit farm. Tessa wrinkled her nose and groaned, 'Oh, Daddy, I'm not five any more, you know.' But off they went, all the same, Tessa kitted out for the occasion in her oldest jeans and ratty T-shirt, found in a box of clothes in the garage, waiting to be donated to Oxfam, Lizzie electing to remain in her ancient, good-enough-for-the-country, floaty summer skirt.

Lizzie was never going to admit it to Tessa, but she was quite excited about the outing. There was nothing she liked better than strawberries, except maybe raspberries, and she planned to eat her fair share of both.

Tessa's father, whom Lizzie had been told years ago to call Harold, drove at speed down green, tunnel-like lanes lined with hedges and trees all leaning over the road to shake hands with their kith and kin on the other side. The Cotswolds fields were glorious, with rows of flourishing produce – wheat crops, barley, broad beans, even violently yellow fields of rapeseed. Tessa's father gesticulated at purple fields of lavender. 'Fill your lungs up with that,' he yelled above the noise of the engine.

'Oh, do close the window, Harold! My hair, my hair!' called Tessa's mother, whom Lizzie was supposed to call Babs.

But Harold was having too much fun. Possessing very little hair himself, he was hardly likely to understand why women shrieked so much on this sort of expedition – i.e. travelling at full throttle in a tiny car with all the windows open. The windows remained down and, released from the pressure to look well-groomed by a sense of being buried in the back of beyond, Tessa and Lizzie allowed themselves to get into the spirit of things. They threw back their heads and belted out cheesy songs along with the radio, careless that the wind was wreaking havoc with their hairstyles.

What with the heat and the wind and the singing, Lizzie – who was often described by her mother as peaky-looking and/or anaemic – was positively blooming, her cheeks and lips as rosy as a child's by the time they pulled up, in a scattering of gravel, at Longborough.

Having installed Babs at a table to imbibe tea and pat at her hair, the rest of the party left with cartons to pick strawberries. To Lizzie's eternal shame, she and Tessa and Tessa's dad were still singing snatches of 'We had joy, we had fun, we had seasons in the sun', when they walked into the first row of strawberry plants and collided with another strawberry-picker.

Lizzie was grinning back at Harold, who was trying a tricky tenor variation of the chorus, when she bumped into a solid wall of flesh. Harold and Tessa piled into her back. Head down, Lizzie observed a strangely attractive foot in a brown sandal. Feet were not normally attractive to Lizzie. They fell into two categories: functional at best; malformed and unsightly at worst. But these feet were uniformly tanned and graced with that rare thing, a set of elegant toes.

Lizzie just had time to take this in before strawberries began to rain down on her head.

She was blushing with embarrassment before she even looked up. 'Gosh, I'm so *sorry*!' she stammered as she raised her head, lifting her wild hair from her forehead with one flustered hand.

And then she stopped. Because, of course, she was staring into the surprised face and bright blue eyes of Mr Rugby.

'Here, we'll get them up for you,' Harold offered, not in the least perturbed. 'Clumsy girl, Lizzie! Come on, let's at least help the chap with his strawberries.'

Tessa, who'd been gaping as shamelessly as Lizzie, slowly began to bend down and gather fallen berries.

Lizzie was momentarily unable to move or speak, immobilised by a mixture of shame and shock. Who would have expected to see *anyone* at Longborough fruit farm, let alone the magnificent Mr Rugby? Until then, neither of them had even seen him in daylight, though Tessa once claimed to have glimpsed his back as he hopped onto a number 11 bus. He was, to the best of their knowledge, a creature of the night, an *habitué* of beery dens of iniquity such as the Bird in Hand. His handsomely battered face and piercing blue eyes, normally narrowed against cigarette smoke, did not belong among strawberries in the Cotswolds.

'Are you OK?' Mr Rugby asked. He had to ask several times before Lizzie finally nodded, and then quickly hung her head to hide her flaming face.

'Some of your berries are smooshed, I'm afraid,' Harold said, holding up a sample as evidence. 'They'd probably do for jam.'

Peering up through her hair, Lizzie saw Mr Rugby jiggle his eyebrows and grin. 'My mum will have my hide out drying on a fence by lunchtime if I take those back to her,' he said. 'She doesn't do jam. I'd better get some more.'

'We'll help,' said Tessa, who'd been fiddling with her frizzed hair and rearranging her ratty old T-shirt.

'Thanks. She turns away anything that's not quite ripe or isn't the right shape. They have to be a certain size, too. By the way, I'm James.' And he stuck out his large, tanned hand at Lizzie so she was forced to deliver her own into a firm handshake. 'Lizzie,' she breathed from behind her hair. Then he shook hands with Harold and Tessa. Lizzie's hand felt warm for hours. She contemplated never washing it again, but then she'd be left with the strawberry stains.

A funny thing happened that morning in the strawberry field. James decided he liked Lizzie Indigo more than any girl he'd ever met.

Weeks later, he explained himself to Lizzie. He'd liked her at once because she seemed so unpretentious, so *nice*. In retrospect, it was a godsend she'd been too self-conscious about her sweaty armpits and awful clothes even to look at him much. He'd found her diffidence intriguing, accustomed as he was to girls going after him like dogs after bacon sandwiches (not that he said this in so many words; just that it really didn't need to be said).

He'd liked her ringletty blonde hair, her pink face, her floaty flea-market skirt, her ample curves (that didn't need to be said, but he said it anyway, so he could see her blush), even the shape of her hands. Plus, he added, the *chemistry* was there. Lizzie thought she knew what he meant. There was certainly something chemical about the way her stomach turned to slush whenever he came near her. Also, her sudden loss of appetite that day indicated various chains of events that you could very possibly reproduce in a test tube, if only you had the right sort of chemistry set.

From the moment James joined them, the berry-picking became a bit of a party. That was one of the lovely things about him. Wherever he went, parties seemed to break out. Harold was wittier and more entertaining than he'd ever been before. Tessa was so animated she was swatting passing bees out of the air with her effusive hand gestures. And when they finally sat down with brimming cartons for a celebratory round of tea, Babs was suddenly as charming and queenly as Grace Kelly. Even Lizzie, still overpowered by a sense of being smelly and dishevelled, began to say a word or two as the morning wore on towards lunch-time.

James seemed delighted by them all. When they finally parted (James looked at his watch, groaned, and said he had to get the blasted berries back to his mother in time for lunch or he'd be court-martialled), he invited them round for cocktails on Sunday evening. His parents were having a bit of a do, he said. And no, of course his parents wouldn't mind if he went about inviting every Tom, Dick and Harry he bumped into out strawberry picking. They'd be tickled pink. More or less. At any rate, they'd encouraged him to invite his friends.

Even Harold seemed to expand with pride at being counted as one of James's friends.

It turned out James's parents lived not far from Winchcombe, in a village called Laingtree, which explained his presence in those parts. And he said that he, too, had to get back to London by Monday morning, so he'd be sure to get the girls to the station in time for the last train after the party.

The rest of Saturday was spent in a mad panic as Lizzie and Tessa scoured the length and breadth of Gloucestershire and neighbouring counties for something decent to wear. The high streets of Chipping Campden and Broadway were crammed with useless boutiques selling tweeds and wellies. Evesham at least had some normal clothes stores, but they couldn't find anything they liked even there. Nothing was sophisticated enough. Nothing was glamorous enough. Most importantly, nothing was sexy enough for cocktails with the man formerly known as Mr Rugby.

With barely an hour of shopping time left, they found a parking spot in tourist-thronged Stratford-upon-Avon and began yet another mad dash down the high street. This time they struck it lucky. Tessa, athletically built and of medium height, found a long, drapy black dress that made her look slim and leggy, especially on the left side where a slit went very nearly up to her waist.

Lizzie, tall and busty, decided to go for a safer look in case all the other women turned up in tweeds and wellies. She found some flattering black flared trousers and a well-cut, sleeveless chiffon blouse. Both of them splashed out on new sandals, and Tessa bought a family-sized bottle of sunless tanning lotion and a small bottle of Chanel Number 5 for good measure.

Preparations for the cocktail party began that very evening. On instructions from Tessa, Lizzie took a long shower and scraped away at her arms, shoulders and chest with a gritty apricot scrub. She then donned latex gloves and rubbed Tessa's fake tan lotion into every inch of skin that would be exposed by the grey chiffon blouse.

The one thing Lizzie didn't like about the sunless tanning lotion was its rather peculiar smell, but Tessa assured her it would have faded by the following evening.

Tessa herself rubbed several layers of fake tan into the bits of her that would be on display – most of her back (with Lizzie's help), her entire left leg, a sock-high portion of her right leg, her arms, most of her bust, and the tops of her feet.

By the next day, they had both developed glorious, nut-brown tans. It was true that Lizzie's neck had come out a little darker than she'd expected, but Tessa said they could easily fix that with an ivory foundation. Tessa's feet were, frankly coffee-coloured, but they reckoned nobody would pay too much attention to the bits of her below the hemline.

By six o'clock, the girls were showered, scented (rather heavily, to disguise the lingering smell of the tanning cream), and made-up. Harold had sprayed himself with Old Spice cologne and tweezered his nostril hairs. Babs, elegant in a spangly gold top bought for a holiday in Spain, shook her head at Harold's bright shirt and khaki trousers (also bought for Spain), but didn't go so far as to send him up to his room to change.

Tessa had her hand on the door knob when her father casually remarked, 'Oh, did I mention? James called earlier to ask us to bring our swimming gear. Apparently they have a heated pool.'

Lizzie and Tessa simply stared at each other, stiff with horror.

It was too late for more fake tan.

Then they both remembered at the same time. Thank God, thank God! They didn't *have* any swimming gear. That let them off the hook nicely.

'I've got mine!' Harold held up an orange Speedo.

'You're never going to prance around in *that*?' Babs asked. 'He had to buy it in France, you know. We were trying to swim in a public pool when these officials marched up and said he had to wear a Speedo or they'd chuck us out. They were selling the things at the desk.'

'Come on, Dad, you might as well *skinny*-dip as wear that thing!'

'I couldn't find anything else,' said Harold. 'Look, a heated pool is a heated pool. I'm not passing up on it.'

Babs and Tessa groaned.

Twenty minutes later, they were pulling into a stone gateway that opened onto a stately driveway leading to a sizeable pile of local limestone bristling with elaborately pinnacled towers and spires.

Babs's eyes were almost bulging out of their sockets. 'Good grief,' she said in wonder. 'Isn't it that posh conference centre and spa place? You know, the one where clients arrive by helicopter? There was an article about it in *Cotswold Life* just last month. The family converted a couple of wings of the manor into a sort of hotel, but they still live in the main wing. James could have warned us!'

Tessa and Lizzie's eyes were bulging, too. 'Christ,' said Tessa, 'they must be loaded.'

'And I'm wearing trousers from BHS,' whispered Lizzie, ready to turn tail and do a runner.

Tessa, who'd found her outfit in a boutique, was far from crushed. 'Nobody will know,' she said. 'They look great. And it's not as if you're going to be flashing the label.'

Babs rang the doorbell, and they all grinned nervously at each other as footsteps rang out sharply from within. The massive arched door swung open to reveal a thin, blonde woman of about sixty with James's piercing blue eyes but none of his friendly demeanour. 'Yes?' she asked in a far from hostessy voice.

'Um, you must be Mrs Buckley,' Harold stammered. He looked like a little kid, rolled-up towel tucked under his arm. 'Your son, um, James asked us over for the party. I hope he, um, let you know?'

'Oh, *that's* who you are.' The woman's nostrils fluttered and thinned. She was horribly glamorous in a pastel blue suit, possibly satin, that glittered like ice. 'Lady Evelyn,' she added cryptically.

'Oh no, I'm just Babs,' said Tessa's mother, preening slightly in her spangly top, obviously delighted that she'd been mistaken for somebody very uppercrust.

James's mother curled her lip slightly. 'No, I'm Lady Evelyn Buckley,' she said. 'You'd better come in. Nobody else is here yet, but I'll send James down to you in the conservatory.'

They filed into the flagstoned hallway, feeling distinctly sheepish, as if a) they were uninvited guests, b) their hostess didn't particularly like the cut of their jib, and c) they'd arrived unfashionably early, whereas in fact they were spot on time.

It was not a promising start, but from the moment James joined them, they were extremely glad they'd come. At first, he looked a bit intimidating in an open-necked white shirt and impeccably-cut dark jacket, not at all like the scruffy chap they'd met at the fruit farm. But he was so obviously pleased to see them that even Lizzie soon became convinced that he wasn't, after all, silently kicking himself for inviting them.

He set about mixing cocktails immediately. 'Get that down your necks,' he said, handing out glasses. 'You'll soon feel better. God, don't you hate the beginning of a party, when everybody's sober and squeaky clean, and people just stand around eyeballing each other?'

They took his advice and dispatched their drinks speedily. Soon, Lizzie began to feel a bit less like a badly-dressed gate-crasher and a bit more like the fascinating girl James seemed to think she was.

It turned out to be a wonderful party, even though Lizzie and Tessa were dressed for the wrong occasion in their sophisticated black. All the women were in garden-party pastels, and all the men were in sports jackets and very white shirts. Harold's Hawaiian look stood out, to say the least.

The sight of James in the magnificent setting of his ancestral home sent Tessa into overdrive. To think she'd hankered after him from the dim recesses of the Bird in Hand for so long, without any clue as to his real worth! Lizzie stood back with a little sigh to give her friend a clear field.

But Tessa was destined to toss her hair and flaunt her coppery left leg to no avail. James still thought Lizzie was the nicest girl he'd ever met.

After a couple of hours of fierce endeavour, Tessa conceded defeat. She'd lost the glittering prize, and she knew it. But she wasn't a girl to sulk, so she was soon flirting outrageously with a pleasant-looking old schoolfriend of James's.

Lizzie, meanwhile, felt that the bubble of happiness in her heart would lift her up and float her right out of the room if she wasn't careful. No matter how many horsey-looking girls in dusty pink or powder blue glided up and tried to steal him away, James remained at her side. And suddenly she was funnier than she'd ever been in her life. And more profound. And more incisive. She was Essence of Lizzie Indigo, at the height of her power and charm. Everything that was clever and quirky and likeable about Lizzie seemed distilled to perfection that evening. She glowed, she shone, she positively radiated wit, confidence and poise.

In this heady mood, she first met Roger Buckley, James's father. He strolled up to her as she stood briefly alone, while James was walking some departing friends to their car.

'Hello there. Elizabeth, I believe? Roger Buckley.' Nonchalantly, he lifted a monocle to one eye and gazed at her in frank appraisal.

To her own surprise, Lizzie burst out laughing. A *monocle*? Had he never heard of laser eye surgery? Or even contact lenses? Surely an ordinary pair of *glasses* would have done the trick?

As soon as the guffaw was out of her mouth, she clapped her hand to her lips. But Roger Buckley didn't seem offended. Rather, his eyes lit up with answering amusement.

'Please call me Lizzie,' she found herself stammering, all her wit, confidence and poise gone up in a puff of smoke.

'Lizzie. How delightful. I hope you're enjoying yourself, my dear?'

'I'm having a great time. Thank you. This is a fabulous place for a party, Lord, um, Buckley.'

Roger Buckley's mouth twitched. 'How kind of you to say so. We do our poor best.' And he jiggled his eyebrows at her, taking the sting of condescension out of his words. 'I'm not Lord anything, by the way. Just plain mister, but you can call me Roger if you prefer.'

Lizzie blushed very pink. She searched around desperately for something else to say. 'I believe the manor has been converted into a hotel, Mr Buckley?'

James's dad considered this remark for a moment, his head on one side. 'Not a hotel in the usual sense,' he said eventually. 'A venue for corporate entertainment. Conferences, conventions, re-treats, pow-wows, pat-on-the-back ceremonies – that sort of thing. Top-quality accommodation – four-poster beds, ball-and-claw bath tubs, eccentric plumbing, smoky chimneys, French chef, butler service and so on.'

'I see,' said Lizzie.

'We strive to reproduce the sensation of being a personal guest at a country house along the lines of Blandings Castle,' he explained airily. 'That's one side of the operation. The other side is much more mundane. We flog gym and spa memberships to the locals so they can use the indoor pool and treadmills, et cetera.'

'This pool?' Lizzie asked, gesturing through an archway of the conservatory to a long room in which she could just see a flash of blue water.

'Good God, no. We do our best to keep the punters out of our private quarters. There's another pool in the east wing. Olympic-sized. Stiff with chlorine because the old buggers who constitute most of our membership seem to be uniformly afflicted with urinary incontinence.'

She gave a shocked snort of laughter. 'And ... you're in charge of all that?' she asked when she'd recovered.

'Good grief, of course not. When would I play golf? I have an excellent manager who works himself to the bone because he gets a cut of the profits. I just keep an eye on the books, and come up with the occasional idea,' he said modestly. 'Well, must be trickling on now, my dear. I'm ... ah ... working the room, as they say in Los Angeles.'

She watched him walk away, a tall and elegant figure in a rakishly-cut sports jacket and what Lizzie believed was known as a cravat. He'd been so charming, yet Lizzie had a distinct sense that, in his own way, he was as formidable as his icy wife.

Then James returned bearing strawberries and champagne. He held up one luscious red berry between finger and thumb. 'The humble English strawberry,' he said musingly. 'A miracle in its own right. Can you face another one after yesterday?' She could, of course, and opened her mouth like a little bird so that he could place the berry between her lips. The tips of his fingers brushed against her mouth, and she shivered.

Yes, it was a wonderful party.

The only regrettable thing about the evening was the swimming.

Über-hostess Lady Evelyn had supplied spare swimsuits in a range of sizes. And by the time the invitation went out to take to the water, Lizzie and Tessa had forgotten why they'd ever had reservations about swimming in the first place.

The pool was in a flower-filled extension of the conservatory, with fat, naked cherubs peering down from massive oil paintings on all the walls. The cherubs were saved from vulgarity only by being very, very old.

In the late-summer evening, with soft sunshine streaming through the glass roof and walls, and diamonds of light bulging and undulating in the blue depths, Lizzie and Tessa couldn't imagine anything more delicious than diving into the silky water.

So they did, both of them. Entirely forgetting about Lizzie's farmer's tan (neck, chest and forearms only), and not giving a moment's thought to the sock-high tan on Tessa's right leg and her strangely brown feet.

At the time, they both wondered why a couple of people were

sniggering at them. And Lizzie did intercept a puzzled glance between James and his old schoolmate, who was still squiring Tessa.
But, with several martinis and a few glasses of champagne under her
belt and the bubble of bliss still floating in her chest, Lizzie wasn't
going to sweat the small stuff.

After the swim, she couldn't find her black trousers anywhere.
For a while she had to skulk around in a towel, a very low point
indeed. Then Lady Evelyn called for the attention of her guests and
asked in a carrying voice, 'I have a pair of black trousers here ...
let's see ... BHS, yes, from British Home Stores, so if you happen
to have lost them, would you please come and claim them now.'

Apparently they'd been found draped over a potted palm. Tessa
opined that one of the horsey girls in pastel had done the deed to
make Lizzie look 'a right charley' and scare off James.

James didn't seem to be scared off.

But later, as he drove them to Moreton-in-Marsh (it turned out
he was almost sober) to catch the train back to London, he said one
or two things that both of them would remember the next day in
toe-curling mortification.

'Interesting body art you girls were wearing tonight.'

'Huh?' Tessa grunted.

'The streaky coffee-coloured markings. Is that some kind of new
trend?'

'Washat?' It was Lizzie's turn to bear the burden of the conversation.

Both girls gazed at him with woozy incomprehension. Then the
penny dropped.

'Yesh, new trend, very cutting edshe,' Tessa slurred.

'Alla rashe in ... New York,' Lizzie added.

They drove along in silence for a while.

After a mile or so, James sniffed a couple of times. 'Odd smell in
here,' he said. 'Can you smell it? Perfumey at first, but then it sort
of gets you at the back of the throat. Come to think of it, I've been
noticing it all night.' Suddenly he clouted himself on the side of the
head. 'Oh God, it's not your perfume, is it, Lizzie? Now I've put
my foot in it. Is it one of those pheromone scents that are supposed

to be irresistible to the opposite sex? I have to say I don't think it really works. It's a bit off-putting, as a matter of fact. Not that I'm put off,' he added hastily. 'But then I have a strong stomach. Known for it.'

Of course, they grasped later that he was talking about the peculiar smell of the sunless tanning lotion, apparently still lingering under the Chanel No 5. Embarrassing, yes, but at least they now knew why James's mother nipped in her nostrils every time she came near them.

It was a miracle, really, that James called Lizzie at all after that. But he seemed prepared to overlook the funny smell, the streaky farmer's tan, the trousers from BHS, and the acquaintanceship with a middle-aged man who wore Hawaiian shirts and orange Speedos.

The fact of the matter was, James Buckley was smitten.

Needless, to say, Lizzie returned his interest, with knobs on. Because he was a lovely man; not just good-looking, but kind and self-deprecating and funny. Lizzie couldn't believe her luck, and nor could any of her girlfriends.

Much as everybody loved Lizzie, none of her friends could see that she had the sort of style to attract a man like James Buckley. She was pretty in an understated way, and sometimes, when she was very happy or very excited, she could even be beautiful. But she had the sort of face that wasn't very hardy. It was always teetering on the edge of some catastrophe – a pimple breakout, puffy eyes, a shiny forehead, or the blank, lifeless look that came over it when she was miserable. You didn't look at her and say, 'That girl has good bones.'

She had a nice enough figure, but, like her face, her body seemed poised on the brink of ruin. You knew, just looking at her, that a size ten was not her natural weight, that only by the strictest of vigilance was she keeping her abundant bosom, slightly rounded stomach and well covered thighs reined in. You sensed that her curvaceous body was just waiting to explode into outright plumpness, given half a chance.

Women saw this at a glance. But men were not quite as perceptive. In general, men didn't seem at all surprised that Lizzie had landed a big fish like Buckley. In fact, Lizzie had always had her fair share of male attention, a phenomenon Tessa had, perhaps too simplistically, put down to the size of her bosom.

Lizzie being Lizzie, most of her friends squelched down their jealousy and managed to be happy for her when it became clear that James Buckley's interest was going to outlast their first night in bed together.

After that first night, Lizzie knew beyond the shadow of a doubt that James was the one for her. She knew because she hadn't once thought about the cellulite at the back of her thighs. James made her feel so good, so special, so irresistible, that her excruciating self-consciousness about the cellulite simply fell away, along with her clothes.

At this point in her reveries, Lizzie abandoned the computer, ran downstairs, threw herself down on the sofa and began to howl like a dog. A mute dog, at any rate. She was well practised, by now, in silent howling, because she was darned if she was going to inflict her misery on her children. She'd let them down enough already.

Fits of grief came over Lizzie whenever she let her guard down, whenever she wasn't tending children, washing dishes, pulling up weeds or writing to her sister. Nights were the worst. She also broke down if she had to talk to anyone sympathetic on the phone, so, after a few days of fielding calls from her mother and concerned friends like Maria Dennison in Laingtree, she simply decided to unplug the thing.

Most nights, when Lizzie finally dragged herself to bed, she'd lie awake for hours, letting herself steep in the emptiness on the other side of the mattress.

Tonight, knowing that she was going to see James in the morning, Lizzie felt less likely to sleep than ever. When at last she crawled into bed, her brain began to work feverishly. She kept trying to turn the bally thing off so she could sleep, but on and on it went, relentlessly sifting through memories like a forensic scientist desperate for clues.

After a while, Lizzie jumped out of bed and unearthed a tape

Tessa had given her: *Ten Easy Steps to Self-Hypnosis.* Sinking back into bed with ear phones on, she closed her eyes and concentrated hard.

'You are lying on a beach,' a melodious voice informed her. God, have I got sunscreen on? Lizzie wondered. 'You hear the sound of the sea.' Waves crashed in the background of the soundtrack. 'You feel very peaceful and secure. You are ready to practise visualization. Close your eyes. Breathe in, breathe out. Now, picture one of the happiest days of your life ...'

Lizzie pictured herself standing in Mill House with a little white stick in her hands. The little white stick bore a faint but unmistakable pink line. Lizzie saw the kitchen door swing open. James burst into the room, eyes as bright as a summer sky. He was holding flowers. 'Are you sure? Are you sure?' he cried. She nodded and he pulled her hard against his woolly jumper and held her very close, squishing the bouquet of mixed spring blossom. They both stared in wonder at the thin pink line, and James laid his hand on the slight swell of her stomach – of course, Lizzie's stomach almost always swelled slightly, but this was different. The warmth of his hand seemed to go right through her ...

Lizzie ripped the earphones off her head and threw the portable cassette player aside. She should have known better than to try another of Tessa's fads.

She lay down again and put a pillow on her chest. She didn't want to hear her own heartbeat. It reminded her of the day at the doctor's office when they'd heard the second heartbeat, that awful moment when she'd thought: 'Oh my God, I'm carrying a defective foetus with two hearts.' And then her tears of relief when the doctor told them it was twins. James, bless him, had been like a little kid at Christmas. 'Two babies? We're having two at once? Lizzie, that's pure genius, my girl. Pure genius!'

Shifting to get comfortable on her gradually deflating mattress, Lizzie tried to count sheep. One one-thousand, two one-thousand, three ... Hang on, that was the way you counted the minutes between labour pains.

OK, so counting sheep wasn't going to work. Lizzie tried to

empty her mind and picture a river rolling down to the sea. Instead, she pictured herself in a puddle of broken waters on a black dustbin bag spread across the car seat. James was hunched over the steering wheel, driving with maddening care to Cheltenham hospital.

She'd never get to sleep, at this rate.

Visualization. Visualize something boring, like ... chess. Lizzie tried to picture a chess board. She had just moved the first white pawn forward when her mind threw up a snapshot of James, sitting in a chair beside her hospital bed, clutching her hand so hard she thought he might break some of the smaller bones, telling her she'd been superb, fantastic, unbelievable, his face even more elated and ecstatic than when England had won the Rugby World Cup.

Bloody hell, she might as well get up and have some hot chocolate and whatever was left of the ice-cream.

Chapter Six

Lizzie wasn't aware that she'd ever fallen asleep, but suddenly urgent voices were calling to her from far away, and hands were jostling at her shoulder, and she was trying to fight her way back to consciousness.

'Mummy, Mummy, somebody knockin' onna door!' Even in her sleep, she recognized Alex's insistent yell.

Then came a 'ding-dong' and a distant thudding.

Lizzie sat bolt upright in bed.

The thudding came again.

'Oh my God, what time is it?' She snatched up the alarm clock on the bedside table. Ten past nine. Unbelievable. She hadn't slept that late in years.

Ding-dong.

James. James was at the door, impatient to see the children. And she'd had such elaborate plans to impress him.

She'd made a special trip to the Royal Victoria Place, risking the terrifying indoor car park, to buy an extremely expensive black-and-white tracksuit and a pair of high-performance running shoes. She hadn't been able to find the type that lit up – those were only for kids, apparently – but the ones she had bought were pretty impressive.

She'd also splurged on some make-up that the woman behind the counter had sworn would give her a natural, radiant glow while fooling people into thinking she was wearing no make-up at all. And she'd planned to take a shower and blow-dry her hair to show off her new cut – only, of course, she'd forgotten to *have* the new cut – and splash herself with perfume. And she'd planned to have the house spotless, and the children all dressed and combed and fed, and the smell of percolating coffee wafting through the air. Then she'd planned to wave him in with the phone pressed to her ear, so that he could overhear her chatting nonchalantly about her training programme for the London Marathon.

Instead, she found herself stumbling to the door in her dreadful grey jogging bottoms, hair encrusted with dried-up tears, face smeared with yesterday's make-up, teeth unbrushed, hands shaking with nervous dread.

But it didn't matter really, because he didn't look at her. He just knelt down and held open his arms for Alex and Ellie.

For a moment, she studied this man who was still her husband, despite weeks of separation. He looked exactly the same. He just wasn't hers any more.

Dammit, he should look different. There should be some sort of mark on him to show that his world had crashed down on him, his children had been taken away, and he was back living with his parents at the age of thirty-seven.

He had no *right* to look unscathed.

She felt like punching him on the nose. No, she felt like leaning over and brushing the hair out of his eyes.

'I'll ... I'll just nip up and get their clothes,' she said in a crusty voice. Quickly, she cleared her throat.

He glanced at her, his face smooth and blank. 'Right. Are their bags packed?'

'More or less. Look, just go through to the living room and ... and make yourself at home. I won't be long.' *Make yourself at home.* God, why had she said that? He paid the rent, didn't he?

And now she really hated the house's layout, because she had to sneak into the bathroom to clean herself up, and the bathroom was more or less next door to the living room. James couldn't help but hear her sloshing around.

Still, some hosing down absolutely had to be done before she could face him again. Within about three minutes, Lizzie left the bathroom with a clean mouth, some very subtle coppery lipstick, and just a touch of blush across the cheekbones and brow, to try to bring her ashen face back to life. Nothing short of surgery could be done about the shadows under her eyes and the puffiness of her eyelids, unfortunately.

She took the stairs four at a time, burst into the children's room and began rummaging through their clothes, which lay exposed in baskets on an old bookshelf, for want of a built-in closet.

She stuffed a few outfits for each child into a hold-all, along with Ellie's panda and Alex's fire engine, then snatched up shorts, T-shirts and sandals. As an afterthought, she grabbed a couple of jumpers just in case the weather turned foul. Off she raced back to the bathroom to gather toothbrushes, a hairbrush and a few bath toys. Then she raced to the hallway and shoved tiny wellies and raincoats into the bulging bag. She checked her watch. About seven minutes. Not bad, all things considered.

In the living room, James sat reading a story to the children. He looked up when she came in, and all the animation in his face died.

'All set,' she panted. 'Here, would you get these on Alex while I do Ellie?' She threw him Alex's set of clothes. She was acting as if her life depended on getting them all out of the house as quickly as possible.

With great deftness, James began to take off Alex's pyjamas and coax him into his clothes. As he was feeding Alex's feet into his velcro-strapped sandals, he suddenly burst out, 'Look, I've contacted a lawyer. I thought it would be best to get things moving.'

Lizzie paused with her hands on Ellie's shoulders. 'A lawyer?' You'd think she'd never so much as heard of the profession.

'Yes. A divorce lawyer.'

'A *divorce* lawyer? Already? But ... oh, don't wriggle, Ellie ... but we haven't even talked things through properly.'

James raised his eyebrows, the famous eyebrows that could be so jaunty and playful. Not an ounce of skittishness between the pair of them today, unfortunately. 'I don't think there's anything more to say, Lizzie.'

'But ... surely we need a little time to ... you know, to get used to being apart? Before we rush into divorce?'

James heaved up a deep sigh. 'You're all set now, son,' he said, giving Alex's foot a little pat. The boy, looking anxiously from his father's face to his mother's, suddenly piped up, 'Wass dah-vorce, Daddy?'

For a moment, Lizzie's eyes met James's. She gave a tiny little shake of her head. He frowned back and widened his eyes meaningfully. 'Divorce?' she said smoothly, before James could get in with an answer. 'Divorce is something you don't need to know about right now, Alex. Mummy will explain it later. It's a ... a grown-up thing, not a kid thing.'

'Like din and tonic?' Ellie prompted.

'Yeah, like gin and tonic.' She wasn't going to meet James's eye any more. This really wasn't the right moment to announce to the children that their parents were planning to split the family apart by legal decree.

'Mummy's right, we don't have time to talk now, but we'll both explain it to you some time soon,' James said in a loaded voice. 'OK, are you ready? Come on, give Mummy a hug and kiss and tell her you'll see her tomorrow night.'

She knelt down and the children both threw themselves at her, half-suffocating her with their full body weight. And she was suddenly bathed in a panicky sweat. How could she possibly let the children out of her house and into James's car, and off down the lane towards the big, scary M25 without her? They were so little, only three; they needed their mother. What was she thinking? What was James thinking? She couldn't be expected to do this.

As if reading her mind, James suddenly said, 'Don't worry. They'll be fine. I haven't forgotten how to look after them.'

Lizzie had the grace to blush. 'Of course they'll be fine,' she said, straightening up, still holding onto the strong little hands. 'Just don't forget to brush their teeth. And don't let your mother give them too many biscuits before suppertime. Oh, and please remember that Ellie doesn't like rice and Alex won't eat mashed potatoes. It's easiest if you just give them pasta, really.'

James frowned. 'Mum doesn't really *do* pasta. Never mind, we'll manage. I'll have them back at around six or seven tomorrow evening.'

Lizzie stood in the doorway and watched while he strapped them into the car seats he'd had the forethought to buy and install in his car. Somehow, she resisted the urge to run out and give the seats a good tug to make sure they were properly fitted.

The engine sprang to life, and James rolled down the rear windows so that the children could wave and shout bye-bye at the tops of their voices. Then he did a quick reverse swoop and took off down the muddy driveway just a tad too fast for Lizzie's liking. She watched the car speed away between the tall green hedge and the rolling field of knee-high maize. Within seconds, it was gone.

Lizzie sank down in the doorway and stared at the empty driveway for way too long. Divorce, she was thinking. So. No going back to Mill House after all. But that couldn't be true. He was calling her bluff. Trying to scare her. Teaching her a lesson. Making a point. Anything, *anything*, except really and truly trying to divorce her.

'Morning, Lizzie. Are you waiting for something?'

Ingrid Hatter, walking her ridiculously small Jack Russell, had somehow crept up on her.

Yes, she *was* waiting for something. Only thirty-six hours and her children would be delivered back, right here, to her doorstep.

'Erm . . . no. Just . . . just looking at the garden. Planning my next move.'

'I see. So, this is your big child-free weekend, isn't it?'

'Yeah. They just left.'

Lizzie watched as the Jack Russell bustled up to her garden gate, cocked his leg, and let loose a perfunctory yellow squirt.

'He'll be limping by the time I get him back home,' remarked Ingrid. 'He has to christen every tree stump and fencepost along the way. Do you have any plans, then, for the weekend?'

'Plans? Yes, of course. Loads of plans. I'm going to be very, very busy.' Lizzie stood up briskly and pushed back her sleeves, as if about to get stuck into some monumental task without delay. She wasn't going to have Ingrid Hatter feeling sorry for her.

Ingrid looked at her doubtfully. 'Jolly good, then. But if you should happen to have a spare moment, pop over to the barn for a coffee. Or a glass of wine, if you like.'

Lizzie thought of the bottle of Chardonnay she'd forced on Ingrid before noon on the day they'd met. The woman probably thought she was an alcoholic.

'Thanks. But I should think I'll probably be too busy.'

'Right. But if there's ever a bit of a lull . . .'

'Quite. Well, must be getting on with things now. Have a good walk.' And she hopped backwards into the house and closed the door. Then she sank down to the floor in the hallway and resumed her dazed gazing. But somehow all the fun had gone out of staring into the middle distance, so, after a while, she got up and went into the kitchen, not quite sure what she was going to do there. Of course, there was a sinkful of washing-up from the night before, but she wasn't in the mood for standing around up to her elbows in suds. Besides, she hadn't even had breakfast. That was it, she'd have breakfast!

She went over to the freezer and took out the family-sized tub of vanilla ice-cream. Then she shuffled across the room, pulled open a drawer and took out a spoon. Just as she was swallowing the first cold and creamy mouthful, she had a sudden awful thought.

She'd let the twins leave the house without breakfast!

Before she even realized what she was doing, she'd snatched up the phone and dialled the number of James's mobile. His phone rang four times before he picked up and asked, just a trifle tersely, 'What is it, Lizzie?'

'Er . . . nothing major. Just . . . well, in all the rush the kids didn't get any breakfast this morning.'

'I know. They told me.'

'So, you'll get them something to eat?'

'No, they're getting too fat, they can stand to miss a meal.'

'Too *fat*?'

'I'm kidding, Lizzie,' James said wearily. 'As a matter of fact, we're just sitting down to a large breakfast in a pub. Fried eggs. And orange juice. And toast.'

'Oh.'

'And if they're still hungry we'll stop outside Oxford and get something else.'

'Right.'

'So that's it?'

'Yip. But ... ah ... I wonder if you could sort off ... not mention to your mother that they left the house without eating? She might get the wrong impression, think I'm not coping.'

'Lizzie, you know I never mention *anything* to Mum if I can possibly help it. Your secret's safe with me. But in return, I want to ask you a favour.'

A favour? That had a nice friendly ring to it. 'Sure, anything.'

'Don't keep phoning me every hour to ask about the kids.'

'That's the favour?'

'Yes, that's it. Don't keep phoning all the time. They're with me, they're fine. If there's any problem, you'll be the first to know. And I'll give you a call this evening so they can say goodnight. Right?'

'Right.'

Lizzie went back to her ice-cream, but it just wasn't doing the trick any more. She could hardly be bothered to let it melt in her mouth and trickle down her throat. So she stuffed it back into the freezer, went upstairs and climbed into bed.

She lay there for a while on the squidgy mattress under her white duvet, the spring sunshine streaming in through the sheets she'd rigged up as curtains, the sound of birdsong ringing discordantly in her ears. Why did birds have to be so bally *noisy*? Couldn't they just shut up and let a person sleep?

But it was no use. With or without a rowdy crowd of birds outside the window, her body knew it was ten-thirty in the morning.

So she got up and straightened the duvet. Then she went downstairs and had a shower, not bothering to wash her hair, but at least getting rid of any muskiness under the armpits. Feeling a little more positive, she threw her grey jogging bottoms aside and pulled on a semi-respectable pair of faded old jeans and a loose white shirt. What a pity the inside seams of the jeans were starting to go. They were so comfortable. It wasn't very uplifting to reflect that the wear and tear was being caused by her thighs rubbing together as she walked.

In the shower, she'd made some definite plans for her day. It was crucial to have plans, otherwise she'd find herself sitting on the doorstep and staring down the driveway again. First, she was going to do something practical and useful, namely, install the toilet-roll holder. She'd bought a nice pine-effect one and it was high time she got it up on the wall, if only to stop Alex from using the toilet-roll as an unravelling bowling ball. Then she was going to do something creative but also practical, namely, work on her children's verses. If she could only get them finished and maybe even find some sort of publisher, she would start to feel less panicky about the future.

There was no getting away from it: the future was beginning to look scary. If James wasn't using reverse psychology on her with this whole divorce thing, if he was for real, then there was no telling what would happen, nor how quickly. Certainly, James was fairly well off, but was he well enough off to support two households for years to come?

At the moment, she was simply using their joint bank account as if nothing had happened, and so far James hadn't second-guessed any of her expenditures. He hadn't even alluded to the fact that she'd opted for a three-bedroomed house when two bedrooms would have been enough. Nor that she'd chosen an expensive town.

But she knew that this state of play wouldn't last for ever. Either she'd go back home, or the unthinkable would happen. One day soon she might be faced with a fixed income in the form of maintenance payments, and wasn't maintenance always too little for the woman to manage on? She had no way of knowing whether she'd have enough money in the future to cover both the sizeable rent and the groceries, not to mention the massive winter utility bills and all the other mundane expenses of life that she hadn't had to worry about since marrying James.

It was clear she'd better start making some money of her own. Just in case.

A regular job was a last resort. Lizzie didn't have a lot of intractable opinions, but she'd always known she wanted to be around for her children, especially when they were little. Besides, she'd worked in PR before she got married and was fairly sure she wouldn't be able to find a well-paid similar job in her field in Sevenoaks. Commuting to London would be too risky, as a single parent. Even on a fast train, it would take her at least forty minutes to get back if there were an emergency with the twins. She didn't have the luxury of looking for a mediocre job in Sevenoaks. With the cost of childcare to consider, that simply wouldn't make sense.

No, her only option was to write a best-selling volume of nonsense verses for children. For some reason, this had always been her burning ambition ... well, ever since she'd given up the idea of being the Poet Laureate.

She had her late grandmother to thank for her writing aspirations. When Lizzie was eight or nine, she'd sent a humorous poem to Gran in lieu of a proper sixty-fifth birthday present. Gran had been deeply impressed with the genius of her fourth grandchild. She copied out the little rhyme and sent it off to her favourite radio station. For good measure, she also posted it to the 'children's corner' of her local paper.

In a massive stroke of good fortune, both the radio station and the newspaper liked the silly verse. It was read on air one Sunday morning, and published in the paper the following Wednesday. The paper later sent a cheque for £10; Lizzie had won their little creative writing competition.

As her grandmother proudly handed over the cheque at a family gathering, she'd pronounced, 'Mark my words, this child will go far. Keep every little thing she writes down. She'll be famous one day.'

As she grew up Lizzie had been convinced that, in the fullness of time, she would effortlessly pen the single most important body of verse of the early twenty-first century. But as time wore on, she found that whenever she actually picked up a pen and sat down to begin her life's work, nothing but nonsense rhymes ever came out of the nib. So she went through a period of readjustment, and instead set her sights on writing the greatest nonsense verse since *The Owl and the Pussycat* and *Green Eggs and Ham*.

You wouldn't think it would be difficult to buckle down and write enough nonsense verses to make up a book. But it was. It was terribly difficult. The most difficult part of all was ever finishing a verse she'd started. She'd started plenty. Possibly as many as sixty or seventy. But most of them – no, all of them – resisted closure in the most obdurate way imaginable.

But that had all been before she'd had a really important reason to finish the things. Now she had the most important reason of all: survival.

Well, maybe she was being overly dramatic. She would certainly survive if she didn't make a single penny out of her nonsense verses. She knew she'd always be able to count on James to pay his share, no matter how things turned out; he simply wasn't the 'dead-beat dad' type. She knew, too, that if push came to shove, she could move into a smaller place, maybe a semi or a terrace, in some less exalted satellite of London. In the worst case scenario, she could go somewhere really cheap, like Wales or the far reaches of Scotland. She could live in a croft, for example. That would be very economical, and the children would get used to shearing sheep and burning dung, or whatever it was crofters did.

But Lizzie hated moving. She hated it in general, and she would hate it in particular in this instance – because if she weren't so deeply miserable she'd be very happy here in Sevenoaks.

She liked the mad Hatters. She liked the plump, motherly woman in charge of the twins' nursery school. She liked having Tessa nearby. She liked the garden and the fields, the green lane and the hedgerows. She even liked the rabbits that kept playing havoc with the lawn. If she had to be out of Mill House for the summer, then she wanted to be here, in Back Lane Cottage, when the brambles on the fences eventually burst into masses of purple blackberries.

So. She wouldn't start looking for a job, not yet. For one thing, she was still hanging onto the hope that all this was just a blip in her married life. But just in case it wasn't, she'd have faith in herself and bury herself in her writing. Maybe nonsense verse would be the next big thing, maybe she'd strike it lucky and become, overnight, the second richest woman in England, pipped to the post only by J.K. Rowling.

She'd get busy just as soon as she'd put up the toilet-roll holder. It was a simple job. She just had to drill two holes and screw in two screws.

The only thing was, the drill bit didn't seem to want to go into the wall.

Most people would have given up after about the fourth or fifth assault on the plasterwork. But Lizzie was on a mission, and she wasn't easily deterred. She even tried drilling holes three-quarters of the way up the wall, where most people would be very surprised, if not downright dismayed, to see a toilet-roll holder. By the time she finally stood back, half-blinded by cement dust, she realized, with a little flip of her stomach, that the wall now had the pock-marked look of a room in which a fierce gun battle had taken place.

Lizzie knew she was beaten. She put down the hot drill and found a notepad. On a page headed 'Shopping List – House', she wrote, 'white wall-filler stuff' and 'industrial strength drill bit'.

It was difficult to move seamlessly from the scene of destruction in the bathroom to a session of inspired endeavour at her desk, but she was determined not to deviate from her plan.

Pausing only to make herself a cup of tea and grab a plate of short-bread biscuits, she was soon seated with pen in hand, scrawled-upon note book in front of her, and a perplexed frown on her face.

She was trying to decipher some doggerel she'd begun ages ago, about a little girl who would wear nothing but pink, however much her poor mother coaxed, begged and cajoled.

> *Millie, who was two, one day hopped out of bed and said,*
> *'I don't think I'll wear blue today, I don't think I'll wear red.*
> *I don't think I'll wear orange, I don't think I'll wear yellow.*
> *I don't think I'll wear anything' – her voice rose to a bellow –*
> *'I don't think I'll wear anything that isn't pink, pink, pink.*
> *'Cos that's just what I think, Mum, pink, pink, pink, pink, PINK.'*

That was fair enough, as far as it went, although the first line had a choppy rhythm. And there was more in the same vein. It seemed the little girl wouldn't eat or drink anything that wasn't pink, either.

> *At break of day Mum drove away to the shops at Dumbleton Bluff*
> *And into a shopping basket threw a strange hotch-potch of stuff:*

Strawberry chowder and pink sea bream,
Pink margaritas and pink sour cream,
Raspberry gumballs and pink caviar,
Strawberry tofu and pink cigars.

Margaritas? Cigars? Caviar? Bream? That couldn't be right. The only thing that struck the appropriate note was the raspberry gumballs. Even gum wasn't politically correct in some parenting circles, and cream was a prime cause of heart disease.

With a heavy sigh, she took up a pen and began to cross out the verse. Then she started racking her brain for replacement rhymes, but her brain was not cooperating. Her brain kept running on a track of its own: *I wonder if he decided to take them out for the day, or if they're running riot in the manor? I wonder if the weather's the same in the Cotswolds? Maybe the sun's shining there and they're playing hide and seek in the formal garden, annoying the paying guests.*

On a day like this, James might have decided to take them strawberry-picking at Longborough. But were the strawberries ripe in May?

It was no good. She threw down her pen and got up to put the kettle on. Come to think of it, she hadn't eaten much today. What she needed was a good lunch.

Fifteen minutes later, she was slumped in front of the TV with a pile of golden-brown toasted cheese sandwiches. She'd sort of forgotten the twins weren't there and made enough for three. She probably wouldn't eat quite all of them, although boarding school had conditioned her to clean her plate. Each well-buttered triangle gleamed with grease, and the cheese inside was melted to oozy orange perfection. She alternated mouthfuls of warm sandwich with sips of strong, sweet coffee. Bliss.

To finish, she ate the chocolate orange she'd been hoarding for well over a week. She couldn't believe she'd had the willpower to keep it that long. It just went to show she wasn't nearly as out of control as Tessa seemed to think she was.

Tessa.

Now, why did her stomach do an unpleasant clench, like a sea

95

anemone being prodded, at the thought of her friend?

Of course, she was still deeply annoyed with Tessa for that un-forgivable lecture about her supposed weight problem. But, as far as she could remember, the two of them had more or less patched up their differences once Lizzie had made her own unforgivable remarks about Tessa's infertility issues.

Yes, they'd patched things up and Lizzie had promised to ... Oh my God. It was Saturday. It was ten to four. And Lizzie had prom-ised to *go running* with Tessa at four o'clock this very afternoon.

In all the excitement of buying her new sports gear, Lizzie had somehow lost track of what the running shoes and tracksuit were actually *for*. Her mind simply hadn't ventured beyond the nine o'clock visit from James, at which time she'd been scheduled to knock his socks off with her hitherto unsuspected athleticism.

Currently, the splendid new running things were lying in a heap at the back of Lizzie's closet, price tags still attached, shoes still in box.

Obviously, there was no way she could go running this afternoon, granted that she could ever go running at all. The day had simply been too ghastly already. Besides, she felt slightly queasy after all that cheese and chocolate. And it was beginning to cloud over. It would probably rain. Even Tessa would have to see reason and let her off the hook.

Her stomach did the recoiling anemone thing again. Tessa had never been the type who saw reason – and the doorbell was ringing.

Tessa, dressed in lycra from top to toe, bounced on the garden path as if she had springs in her shoes.

'Hey, you're not ready,' she observed, without so much as a 'hello'. 'Am I early?'

'Well, yes, just a tad. Come in. How about a coffee?'

'No, no, I'll just look at a magazine or something while you change.'

'Oh. Erm ... I'm not actually planning to change.'

'What? You're never going running in those old jeans? Crikey, they don't look as if they could stand the strain.'

'Thank you very much. I'm not going to put them to the test.

The thing is ... well, I don't think today is a good day to start this running business.'

Before her very eyes, Tessa began to swell up like a bullfrog. She pulled her tummy in and inflated her chest and seemed to stand several inches taller than usual. 'You don't think *what*?'

'Look, at least come and sit down while I explain. You see, it's been an absolute shocker of a day. You won't believe how awful! First, I overslept and the kids had to wake me up with James already knocking down the door, and the house in a total shambles.'

'Really? But what happened? You were going to have everything ship-shape.'

'I know, I know, but I couldn't sleep last night. I finally conked out at around four in the morning. So, anyway, I had to answer the door in my grey jogging bottoms without a stitch of make-up.'

Tessa groaned. 'Aargh! Not the grey jogging bottoms?'

Miserably, Lizzie nodded. 'And then I had to run around packing and dressing children. Then just before James left, he ... he said something about a lawyer. A divorce lawyer.'

'Oh.'

'So you see. I couldn't possibly go running after all that. And to make matters worse, I've gone and mucked up the walls in the bathroom. Come and see.'

Moments later, Tessa stood and gaped at Lizzie's handiwork.

'What ... what were you doing?' she asked at last.

'Trying to put up this.' Lizzie held out the small, innocuous-looking toilet-roll holder. 'But the walls are steel reinforced or something. So now I've got to think about fixing this all up.'

Tessa simply nodded, eyes bulging.

'Then I decided to get down to some writing. But when I started working on one of the poems, I found I just couldn't do anything with it at all. It's absolute crap. They're *all* crap. The one thing I thought I could do, and it turns out I'm really rubbish at it.'

Tessa shook her head decisively. 'But Lizzie, that's just not true. I've read some of your stuff. It's not crap. It's funny. You know what I think? I think you're just really down on yourself today. You need cheering up.'

Thank goodness, Tessa *was* going to see reason, after all. Lizzie's spirits lifted. 'How about a gin and tonic, then? I've even got a lime, and we could put on a movie. *Bridget Jones*? Or if you're not in the mood for fantasy, maybe *Harry Potter*?'

Chapter Seven

'Remember to breathe,' Tessa shouted into the wind. 'Like this.' She began to run backwards, sucking air loudly into her nose, and panting it out through her open mouth.

'Stop ... showing ... off,' Lizzie panted back. 'I know ... how ... to breathe.'

'No, no, don't stop! Keep running! Remember, we *run* three hundred paces then *walk* a hundred. One-fifty-*two*, one-fifty-*three* ... *Keep running*!'

But Lizzie couldn't. She couldn't even keep walking. She stopped and bent over, cramming one hand into her side. 'You ... go ... on ...' she heaved. 'Got ... stitch.'

'A stitch *already*? You didn't drink or eat just before we came out, did you?'

Lizzie glanced up and pulled a face. 'Think I ate lunch ... bit late,' she puffed.

'Right. Next time don't eat for at least two hours before we go. What did you have, anyway?' Tessa was jogging on the spot in a thoroughly ostentatious fashion, like some kind of vindictive games mistress.

Lizzie dropped her head and crossed her fingers. 'Bread and cheese.'

'Doesn't sound like much, but remember dairy's not a good choice before you run. No salad? No fruit?'

'Oh ... and an orange.' OK, a chocolate orange, but Tessa didn't need to know every last little detail.

'Good. And I hope you've been drinking lots of water. Right, let's go. Best just to run through the pain.'

Lizzie straightened up gingerly. 'Ouch! But surely it's time to go back now? First time out. Mustn't overdo it.'

'Lizzie, we haven't even reached the bottom of the *lane*. The *house* is still in sight. Come on, let's at least get onto the main road. You'll thank me later.'

'Honestly, Tessa, I don't think I like this. I'm not cut out for it.'

'Shut *up*, Liz, and get running. Remember, you need the endorphins to jump you out of the depression. All part of the campaign! Save your breath for *breathing*.'

Tessa began to jog towards the end of the lane. With an enormous sigh, Lizzie gritted her teeth and shuffled after her.

'Run through the pain,' she whispered to herself. If she'd had any spare breath at all, she would have laughed out loud. Derisively, of course, not mirthfully. Right now, she was 'running through the pain' every minute of her life, just getting herself out of bed and living through each James-less day. Did she really need to be running through gratuitous pain as a *hobby*?

Still, at least relentless physical pain made a change from the relentless mental stuff.

Running and walking by turn, they inched their way through the most excruciating half-hour Lizzie had endured since the birth of the twins. They didn't cover an awful lot of physical ground – Back Lane was just around the corner when they crossed the main road and began working their way homewards – but by the time Lizzie reached the safe haven of her cottage again, she knew she had to knock this whole running scheme on the head before Tessa got completely carried away.

Lizzie sat on the steps, dry heaving, while Tessa did an exercise that involved wedging the ball of one foot on the edge of the step and then ramming the heel downwards. 'You really should be stretching, Liz,' Tessa remarked. 'You'll be sore tomorrow if you don't. Got to move that lactic acid around.'

'I'll be sore tomorrow, whatever I do. Are you finished? Can we *please* go in and get some water now?'

They stood in the kitchen drinking tap water from bright red plastic mugs.

'So that's it, then,' Lizzie said after her third cupful. She slammed the mug down on the counter. Tessa's eyebrow twitched. Lizzie never slammed things. 'My first and last run. That's my final word and I don't want to talk about it.'

That evening, over at the barn, Lizzie took a sip of bitter green tea and grimaced. 'Gosh, this stuff is revolting. And you say it's supposed to work wonders?'

Ingrid Hatter took a swig of her own brew and nodded sagely. 'Absolute wonders. Stops your stomach from absorbing the fat in food. Another piece?' She held up a heavy plate of fudge. Lizzie did a quick scan and selected the largest chunk. The sugar exploded on her tongue, and she sank back blissfully in Ingrid's battered kitchen chair.

'So, have you had a good day without the little people?'

Lizzie shrugged. 'So-so.' She didn't feel the need to go into detail.

'Did you manage to get through all the stuff you wanted to do?'

Again, Lizzie shrugged. 'Kind of.' Maybe it hadn't been such a good idea to come down to the barn after all.

'It must have been jolly awful to see your husband this morning,' Ingrid remarked out of the blue. 'I thought you looked quite shaken when I saw you sitting there on the doorstep.'

The fudge seemed to catch in Lizzie's throat. She began to cough. Ingrid stood up and patted her on the back. 'Have a sip of tea,' she advised.

Lizzie took a gulp and coughed a bit more.

'It ... it wasn't so bad,' she said at last. 'It was fine, really. It's not as if I haven't seen him at all since ... since we split up. He came to the house a few times in Laingtree to take the twins out. No, I'm quite used to seeing him. It really doesn't upset me.'

'No, of course not. Why would it? Here, have a tissue. Now, do you have any plans for tomorrow?' Ingrid was shamelessly nosy. Lizzie wondered why she couldn't help liking her, none the less.

'Shopping. And some gardening, I expect, if it doesn't rain. I want to spray weed-killer on the nettles.' Lizzie blew her nose.

'Any chance you'd come and help me with a car boot sale in Tonbridge? Normally Sarah gives me a hand, but she's staying over with a friend tonight.'

Sarah was the teenage girl with braces and a way with children. Ingrid's husband, Clive, was away flying a jet to Johannesburg. He seemed to be away more often than not.

'Gosh, I'd really like to, but I promised myself a lovely morning at the shopping centre. Retail therapy. Maybe even a manicure and a pedicure.' Lizzie blushed at the feebleness of her excuse, but really! She could think of nothing more dismal than a morning at a car boot sale in Tonbridge.

'Righto. Just as long as you have something to do. Don't like to think of you mooning around that house all by yourself.'

Lizzie suppressed a giggle at Ingrid's turn of phrase. 'Ingrid, don't worry. I'll be fine, I promise.' She gave an enormous yawn, partly as a way to ease herself out of Ingrid's kitchen, partly because she felt bone-weary. 'Anyway, I'd better get going now. I've got to … clean out the children's toy boxes while they're away. They never let me throw away all that plastic rubbish from the fast food places.'

'Golly, it's all go with you, isn't it? Another piece of fudge for the road?'

'Don't mind if I do,' said Lizzie, choosing a big one.

'Toodle-oo, then. And the offer still stands if you find yourself at a loose end in the morning.'

But Lizzie didn't find herself at a loose end in the morning. She went to bed early and woke up late, feeling stiff but strangely rested, and decided that she owed it to Ingrid to take herself off to Bluewater for some serious self-indulgence.

She didn't like shopping for herself any more; the lighting in changing rooms was just too brutal. But she could, at least, shop for the house. Back Lane Cottage – a blank canvas if ever there was one – opened whole new shopping vistas.

She'd never been able to buy much for their house in Gloucestershire. You didn't just go out and pick up a few priceless antiques and an original oil painting or two on your local high street.

When she'd walked into Mill House as a bride, the place had been fully decorated, a lovely *fait accompli*, not something to be mucked around with by an amateur like herself.

James had tackled the re-design of the original gamekeeper's lodge as one of his earliest projects, possibly before he'd even started shaving. The risk his parents had taken in giving him such leeway had been richly rewarded. He could so easily have destroyed the place's worth by tampering with its structure, but instead he'd added significant value. On its completion, Mill House had been rented out as a luxurious Cotswolds holiday cottage.

As a graduation present, James's parents had sold him Mill House for pennies on the pound. For years, the house had been a nice little earner for James, ensuring that even as a junior partner at his first job with a firm of architects, he'd been a man of independent means. With Mill House as security, he'd been able to wangle enough money from the bank to start his own architectural firm before he was thirty.

It was a charming house, but Lizzie had never quite shaken the feeling that she was a permanent house guest there. Even when she'd emptied the spare bedroom of its four-poster bed, painted it yellow and filled it with nursery furniture, she still hadn't felt as if the place really belonged to her.

But Back Lane Cottage – awkward, plain and colourless – was a place she could put her stamp on. To that end, she bought a tasselled table-runner in jewel tones, a toffee-coloured chenille throw, a lined wicker basket monogrammed 'Laundry', some paper-and-bead lampshades, and a bright, flower-shaped rug for the children's room. She also bought a vase and three bunches of tulips.

She hurried home with her purchases and began working on the house feverishly. She knew you could never undo a person's first impression, but she didn't want James to think she'd rented a complete dump.

She vacuumed the murky carpets, mopped the kitchen floor, opened all the windows, hung lampshades over naked lightbulbs, draped the throw over the sofa, arranged the tulips on the dining-room window sill, spread the runner on the fold-up table, and chucked all the laundry into the lovely new basket. Then she tidied away the children's clutter before arranging the new rug between their mattresses.

After an unusually virtuous lunch – an apple and scrambled eggs on toast – she went out into the grey but mild afternoon and began her pesticide campaign against the nettles.

Working in the garden suddenly put her in mind of Bruno. She wondered idly what he was doing with himself this dull Sunday afternoon, and had half a mind to call him up and ask him to help with the spraying, or possibly to get started on the exterior tap he'd promised to install. But somehow she couldn't do it, not today, when she was expecting James in the early evening. It wasn't that she felt guilty about her friendship with Bruno. It was just that it would be very awkward if he were there when James turned up.

When Lizzie had emptied three bottles of poison onto the weeds she stopped for a breather. By now the sun had broken through and the day had turned almost hot. On an impulse, she went inside and unearthed an old purple bikini from her pile of clothes. She must have brought it from Mill House by mistake. She hadn't worn it in years, but she was still able to fit most of her chest into its faded supportive cups. The effect was probably indecent, but it didn't matter because there was nobody around to see. Gathering a blanket, a pillow and a magazine, she went out and settled down in the sun. She'd give herself about twenty minutes just to relax, then go in and get cleaned up.

She'd decided that she'd offer James a cup of coffee to wake him up for the long drive home. Really, it was high time they started acting more naturally around each other. It would do the children good to see them sit down together and have, if not a cosy chat, at least a civilized conversation, one in which she hoped the word 'divorce' wouldn't figure.

The glare of the pages began to dazzle Lizzie. She closed her eyes and became deeply immersed in a relaxation exercise she remembered from years ago, when she used to go to an aerobics class. The best part of that whole class had been the bit at the end, when you were allowed to lie on a mat and listen to dreamy music while squeezing and releasing various bits of your anatomy.

She was squeezing and releasing her left buttock when a shadow fell over her.

She opened one eye. At first, blinded by the sun, she could see only a dark shape. As the silhouette came into focus, she realized it had curls.

'Bruno?' She sat bolt upright, hands flying protectively to her chest. 'For heaven's sake, what are you *doing* here?'

He held up a box of tools. 'It's the perfect day to put in that tap.'

Before Lizzie could remonstrate, her eye was caught by a flurry of activity in the bed where she planned to plant carrots and peas. Bruno's infernal collie, noticing the newly-turned soil, had taken it upon herself to excavate still further. The animal's front legs whirred in a blur of movement as she threw out a cloud of dirt behind her.

Bruno put his fingers to his lips and gave an ear-splitting whistle. The dog stopped digging immediately and came bounding over, snout covered in black earth, tail slapping foolishly from side to side.

'Stupid bloody dog,' Bruno muttered fondly. 'Sorry about that, Lizzie. Anyway, you just carry on with your sun worship, and I'll get started on the tap. We said the corner near the oil tank, didn't we?'

Lizzie, her hands still crossed over her chest as if she'd been caught naked, began shaking her head adamantly. 'Not a good idea, Bruno. Not a good idea at all. Look, it's very kind of you to come out on a Sunday and offer to do this, but I just can't have it. You've got to take Madge and go home, please.'

Bruno frowned and set down his tool box. 'Go home? Don't be silly, Lizzie. I'm here now; I might as well stay and do the work. I've gone out and bought all the bits, too. Let's just get it done so you can water your garden like a normal person instead of lugging around watering cans. I see you haven't watered the violas today, and no wonder.'

Lizzie stood up, draping the blanket around her shoulders like an enormous scarf. 'No, no, I can't have you here today. You see ... you see, my husband will be over later on. Bringing the kids back.'

She held his eye for a long moment. As comprehension dawned, his lip twitched slightly. 'Ah,' he said. 'I see. Awfully compromising if he arrived to find a strange man fitting a tap in your garden?'

Lizzie went pink. 'Well, you must admit, he'd probably think it a *bit* odd,' she said defensively. 'I couldn't pass you off as some sort of contractor, either, because everybody knows they don't work on Sundays.'

'What time is he coming?'

Lizzie shrugged. 'Six or seven. It's a long drive.'

'Look, it's not even four yet. This is a one-hour job. I'll be out of here long before he's off the motorway.'

Lizzie looked at him doubtfully. On the one hand, she'd give anything to shoo him away so that she could compose herself for her next encounter with James. On the other hand, it was going to be a long, dull afternoon unless she had some sort of distraction. Between the two of them, Bruno and Madge constituted a fairly sizeable distraction.

'OK,' she said at last. 'You can stay and put the tap in. But you've got to be out of here by five.'

'Piece of cake,' said Bruno.

'In that case, I'll go in and make some tea.' Lizzie didn't want tea nearly as much as she wanted a bra and sweatshirt.

'Right, I'll get busy.' Bruno hoisted up his tool box and strode off purposefully.

Still swathed in the blanket, Lizzie bolted for the house. She ran straight to the bathroom, where the brand-new, uninstallable mirror sat propped against the wall. Balancing the mirror on the hand basin, Lizzie threw aside the blanket and bent her knees until she got a view of her bust in its ancient bikini top. The effect was rather grotesque. She seemed to be sprouting breast tissue from under her armpits. What wasn't hanging out of the sides seemed to be bulging over the top. At least the important bits were hidden, though. She wasn't technically committing public indecency.

More alarming than the plenitude of flesh in the breast area was the plenitude around the midriff. It was clear that large tracts of her abdomen had not cottoned on to the fact that she'd stopped being pregnant more than three years ago. She glanced down at her legs. They didn't look too bad from the front, although they could have used a shave. But she was aware that the backs of her thighs were well-known harbourers of cellulite, not to mention the less-sensational but just as incriminating common-or-garden subcutaneous fat.

Looking at the big picture – even if only in sections, in a propped-up bathroom mirror – she was inclined to think her bikini days were over.

Bit depressing, she thought as she trudged into the kitchen to put the kettle on. It wasn't that the weather was frequently balmy enough to *warrant* a bikini, but it would have been nice to imagine you could get away with one if you felt like it.

She turned the tap to fill up the kettle, but it just coughed and spat out a single droplet. She sighed. Bruno must have turned the water off at the mains in order to get on with his outdoor plumbing. Tea would have to wait.

She was on her way upstairs to put on something decent when an urgent roar from the garden stopped her in her tracks. It wasn't the sort of roar you ignored. She ran outside, heart banging, hoping Bruno hadn't chopped off his finger, or been attacked by hornets.

He hadn't. He'd just gone and sawed open some pipe, which was now shooting water at him like a firehose.

'There must be two mains,' he yelled as she came into sight. He was trying, without much success, to stop the water with his palm. 'Any ideas where the second one might be?'

She hadn't a clue, naturally. A frantic search began, the two of them scampering around the garden, leaving no stone unturned, while Madge yapped maniacally and tried to savage the water jet.

The corner near the oil tank had all but turned into a swamp by the time Bruno located the second mains tap in the shack-like building that might once have served as a garage.

'Thank God for that,' said Lizzie as the sawn-off pipe finally dried up. 'I thought I was going to have to call the landlord. And he doesn't even know we're doing this.'

Bruno flicked the wet hair out his eyes. '*Now* I've got egg on my face,' he said with a rueful grimace. 'Here I was trying to impress you with the handyman bit, and I didn't even turn off the mains properly.'

Lizzie shrugged. 'Look, I wasn't going to be that impressed anyway ...' She trailed off and fell silent, because Bruno was taking off his shirt.

It was soaked, of course, so he had some excuse – it wasn't as if he was just doing a bald-faced striptease. But Lizzie wasn't prepared for the shock waves that ran through her as his taut stomach and muscular upper chest hove into view. Gosh. She hadn't realized she could still react that way. She'd thought that fizz was all gone.

She turned her eyes away chastely and was about to scuttle indoors when he said, 'Look, Lizzie, would you mind giving me a hand, just for a second? I need you to hold this in place while I screw this thing on.'

He held up a couple of pieces of hardware.

Lizzie opened her mouth to say that she'd be back in a jiffy, she just needed to change into something decent, but found herself muttering, 'OK, but don't you dare drip on me.'

He grinned. 'Why not? You're in a bikini. At least, I *think* that's a bikini.'

'Of course it's a bikini,' she said indignantly. 'What else would it be? Do you think I lie around outdoors in my underwear?'

He chuckled. 'Look, just come over here and hold tight a moment, and not so much chit-chat about underwear.'

Lizzie took a vexed breath, then found herself speechless. He was so close to her now that she could have leaned over and nuzzled her head against his gleaming bare chest. And his gleaming bare chest pretty much filled her view.

He took her hand and gently placed it on the pipe. 'Grip hard,' he said.

Averting her eyes from his skin, Lizzie did as she was told, but she couldn't resist stealing a couple of glances at his damp hair as he bent over his task. She was rather deep in contemplation of the way the sun bounced off the coppery highlights in his curls when a familiar voice suddenly called, 'Oh, so *this* is where you are.'

Lizzie froze in position like a guinea pig in peril.

She knew that voice. She knew it better than any other voice on earth. She knew every nuance of pitch and cadence in that voice, and right now that voice was icy with distaste.

'James,' she squeaked, losing her grip on the pipe.

Bruno's spanner immediately slipped, causing him to bash himself. 'Shit,' he cursed, dropping the spanner and squeezing his thumb tight in his right hand. All at once, Madge began barking at the top of her voice, the hair on her back standing on end as she danced around James.

'Shut up, Madge!' Bruno boomed. Madge simmered down but remained unconvinced of James's credentials. Creeping over to Bruno with her tail between her legs, she shot malevolent glances at the newcomer and growled low in her throat.

Meanwhile, Lizzie had crossed her hands over her chest guiltily. She was doing some quick thinking.

'James!' she cried again, this time trying to sound shrill not just with surprise, but also with delight. 'How nice that you're early! You're just in time to help Bruno here put in the tap.'

James looked at her in wonder. 'Sorry, what?' he asked. She didn't like his expression at all. You wouldn't expect a person to be delighted to be called on, unexpectedly, to help install a tap, but Lizzie had a shrewd suspicion his dark glower went deeper than that.

Gosh. Could he be jealous? Or was he just plain disgusted?

'Yes! Isn't it great? Bruno's putting in a tap. There wasn't one – can you believe it? I mean, who'd have a big garden like this without an outside tap? You can't absolutely rely on the English weather to be pissing down rain every day, after all. He asked me to help, but handyman stuff really isn't my thing, as you know. So what luck that you got here early! A whole hour and a half early! Traffic was good, was it? Non-existent, probably. You must have absolutely *whizzed* over here. How long did it take you, forty-five minutes? That must be some sort of record.'

Lizzie became aware that both men were looking at her a bit oddly. Oh dear. She was babbling. But what else could you do when your husband came upon you in an outgrown bikini, helping a half-naked man with some plumbing?

Then Bruno stepped forward and stuck out a big damp hand. 'Bruno Ardis,' he said in hearty tones. 'Landscape gardener.'

Automatically, James shook the proffered hand. 'James Buckley,' he replied. 'Architect.'

Lizzie beamed maniacally at both of them. 'Gosh, you two are sort of in complementary professions, when you think about it. Can't have a garden without a house, and vice versa. Well, technically you can have a house without a garden, lots of people do, but not the sort of people James works with. They always have gardens. I bet you'd like to chat. Pity Bruno has to go home now. Another time maybe. Gosh, look at the time! You'd better pack up quickly. Remember what you said about ... about not wanting to be late for your, erm, your wife's steak and kidney pie.'

'Look, Lizzie, I'll be out of here in ten minutes or so, but I just have to get this thing finished now or I won't be able to turn the water back on.'

Twisting a little so her back was to James, Lizzie shot Bruno a beetle-browed grimace. 'Hurry up,' she mouthed, jerking her head in James's direction. Then, spotting Bruno's shirt in a sodden heap, she scooped it up and bundled it into his arms. 'Nice and dry now,' she sang out in her mothering voice. 'You can put it back on.' Ignoring Bruno's incredulous look, she turned to James, forcing her face back into a smile. Really, her jaw was beginning to ache with the strain of all this grinning. 'So, where are the twins, then? Did they go straight inside?'

'They're in the car,' said James, his face set in grim lines. 'Asleep.'

'Well, come on, let's get them into the house.'

'No rush,' said James. 'They're out cold. Why don't you go and put some clothes on first?'

Lizzie felt the blush rise from the tops of her feet, all the way up her lumpy legs, across her burgeoning chest, over her neck, and into her hairline. 'Right,' she whispered, and hurried inside.

It wasn't so much what James had said but the way he'd said it. No, it was the way he'd *looked* at her as he'd said it, not with the look of a man who wants his wife to cover her body because he can't bear to share her glorious nakedness with the rest of the world. No. Rather, with the look of a man who is pained by the sight of his wife making a spectacle of herself by sporting flesh that is no longer sportable.

By the time Lizzie had ripped off the despised bikini and thrown it into the rubbish bin, she was in dire need of a brown paper bag to breathe into; failing that, she was just about ready to put a plastic bag over her head instead. But as she pulled on her leggings, she told herself, out loud, to get a grip. Why should she be hyperventilating with humiliation just because James had given her a withering look? What did she care if he didn't like the redistribution of flesh about her person? She'd borne him two children, and if he didn't like the effect this had had on her body, then he could jolly well haul himself out onto the club and pub scene and find himself a younger model. Which he was probably doing already, come to think of it. Bruno, who wasn't even a father, could at least appreciate the body of a mature woman. Or so she gathered.

Lizzie yanked an oversized T-shirt down over her head. Then, with a flushed face, accelerated heart beat, and distinctly combative air, she walked back outside.

Bruno was gone. Probably a good thing, on the whole. James was leaning on his car, keeping a watch on the twins.

'Right,' Lizzie called, walking towards him. 'I'm covered from head to toe. Are you happy now?'

James stood up, pushing the floppy fringe out of his eyes. 'Delighted,' he said dryly. 'By the way, your man said he turned the mains back on.'

'He's not *my* man. He's a friend of my neighbour's.'

'Oh?' James raised his eyebrows. 'I thought he was a gardener.'

Lizzie felt a flash of irritation. 'He's a landscape gardener *and* a friend of my neighbour's. The two aren't mutually exclusive, you know. And while we're on the subject of Bruno: I was in a bikini because he arrived unexpectedly while I was sunbathing, and *he* didn't have his shirt on because—'

James held up a hand. 'Lizzie, please, you don't need to explain. Let's just unload the twins and call it a day, if you don't mind.'

Lizzie stamped her foot. 'I wasn't bloody *explaining*. I was telling you the facts. But apparently you don't want to know. Apparently what I do means absolutely nothing to you. Fine. I'll bear that in mind from now on.'

'Shush,' said James. 'You'll wake them up.'

Lizzie glanced through the window at the sleeping twins in their car seats. 'What did you do to them, anyway? Normally they spring back to life the minute I turn the engine off.'

James shrugged. 'None of us got a lot of sleep last night,' he said shortly.

'Is that why you brought them back early?' Lizzie wondered.

'Not really.' James looked surreptitiously at his watch. 'I brought them back because the whole thing was a bloody nightmare. They were howling for you by mid-morning, and Mum was ready to bite a chunk out of somebody.'

'Ah,' said Lizzie in a neutral tone of voice, trying to disguise the little stab of joy she felt to know they'd missed her. She'd half-feared they'd be spoiled rotten by everybody at the manor and never want to come back to Sevenoaks again. 'I hope this isn't going to be a problem,' she said thoughtfully, after a moment. 'The children need to see you on a regular basis, you know.'

'I know,' said James. 'But don't worry, they won't be spending any more time at the manor. I've found a little house in Chipping Norton.'

What? What was that? Found a house?

But James didn't give her time to ask any questions. Looking at his watch again, he groaned, 'It's later than I thought. Better get a bloody move on.'

'Oh, right.' Ironically, now that he was leaving, Lizzie felt all her rage and indignation draining away. In its place, pure panic rushed in. She took a deep breath and burst out, 'How about a coffee for the road?' Oh dear. She'd meant to sound so casual.

He gave her a surprised look, then dropped his eyes. 'I'll get a drink when I fill up with petrol. I really have to get back now. Catch up on some work.'

Lizzie shrugged. 'OK, maybe next time.' She unbuckled Alex and eased him out of his car seat. It was heavenly to feel the warm heft of the little boy in her arms again. She looked at his sleeping face; the rosy cheeks and ridiculously long eyelashes. Gently, she placed a kiss on the spot between his eyes.

'You've missed them.' James stood cradling Ellie in his arms, watching Lizzie.

'What can I say? I'm a real sucker for punishment. Come on.'

James followed her into the house and up the stairs to the twins' room.

'Blow-up mattresses?' He stood in the doorway, frowning at the floor-level beds and wicker baskets stuffed with clothes.

'Well, it seems ridiculous to duplicate all the furniture,' Lizzie whispered defensively as she put Alex into bed, gently easing off his shoes and socks. The twins could sleep in their clothes, just this once. 'They have perfectly good beds in Gloucestershire.' She watched as he knelt down and laid Ellie on her mattress, tucking a blanket over her small body. He ran one hand tenderly along the child's cheek, then turned to whisper, 'If we're going to rent the place as a holiday house again, all the furniture will have to stay.'

'But . . . but those are *children's* beds. They're shaped like sleighs!' Lizzie's voice rose, and Alex stirred and moaned. She clapped her hand to her mouth in alarm. James stood up carefully and crept out of the room, Lizzie following on tip-toe.

Out of earshot in the passageway, James told her, 'We're going to target *families* this time. Rich American families with little kids. So we don't need to change the nursery. I don't have time to be doing that sort of thing right now. If you really wanted to, we *could* get the beds moved here then buy more for Mill House, but it would be silly, don't you think? Why not just buy some decent beds here?'

'Well, I will, then. I'll buy myself one, too.'

'Don't tell me you're also sleeping on the floor? Wouldn't it have been easier to get a furnished place?'

Lizzie took a huffy breath. 'Yes, I could have got a furnished place,' she said between clenched teeth. 'There were all kinds of little hovels with tatty sofas and smelly mattresses. But I liked *this* place.'

He glanced down the crooked passageway. 'Fair enough. Since I'm here, do you mind if I take a quick look around?'

See what I'm paying for, she could imagine him adding in his head. 'Be my guest,' she said.

Quick was the operative word. He sped through the house, giving each room a cursory but professional once-over. Lizzie puffed along behind, trying to see things through his eyes, wondering what he would make of it. Thank goodness she'd cleaned up and added a few softening touches.

When they entered the bathroom, Lizzie recoiled. She'd temporarily forgotten about the state of the wall. James went over to the pock-marked plaster and ran his finger over one of the holes. 'You need to talk to the landlord about this bathroom. It's a shocker. This wall is in terrible shape.'

Lizzie began to take a keen interest in the state of her cuticles. 'It's not *that* bad,' she said. 'A bit of filler and some paint would soon put it right. I could probably do it myself.'

James shook his head. 'I wouldn't mess with it. Landlords can be funny about that sort of thing. Besides, it's not your responsibility.' He looked at his watch again. 'Oh God, I really have to go now. Look, I won't take the twins next weekend. I'll be in Scotland. Let's talk when we get back.'

And then he was gone.

'I've just come in from the butcher's and they've got this really good sale on mutton.' Lizzie's mother's voice rang cheerily down the phone-line the next morning. 'A forty per cent discount if you buy half a carcass. Would you want to split one with me, I wondered?'

Lizzie was trying to get the children ready for nursery school.

Ellie didn't want to get out of her pyjamas. Alex, on the other hand, had changed all by himself and was very proud of his feat. Lizzie didn't suppose it really mattered if he went to 'school' in inside-out shorts and a purple T-shirt belonging to his sister. Perhaps Ellie could even go in her pyjamas.

'Lizzie? Are you listening?'

'Oh, right. Something about mutton?'

'Yes, half a carcass. Shall we split it?'

'Mum, the children won't eat mutton. And I don't think I can eat a quarter of a sheep all by myself.'

'Well, not all at once, of course! You'd freeze it, silly.'

'Mum, my freezer's about the size of the glove compartment in my car. No, smaller. Why don't you just freeze the whole thing yourself?'

'I suppose I'll have to. If only Janie hadn't gone off like that to Australia.'

'Yes. Well. Was there anything else, Mum? I'm in a bit of a hurry. Early mornings are sort of a bad time for me.'

'Obviously, and I wouldn't call you in the mornings, only I can't seem to get you at all at night.' Lizzie gave a guilty cringe. She was still unplugging her phone in the evenings, not sure that her composure would hold through a friendly conversation at that time of day. 'Have you got another minute? The thing is, I thought I'd better let you know ...'

'Mum?'

'Still here. Just taking a sip of tea. Thought I'd let you know I ... erm ... I bumped into that woman, Sofia or whatever her name is. James's secretary.'

'Sofia? Oh. Sonja. And she's a PA not a secretary.' Lizzie waved Ellie's panties at her as she zipped through the kitchen on her tricycle.

'A what?'

'Personal assistant.'

'PA, secretary, same thing. Anyway, I bumped into her over the weekend in Cheltenham. Shopping.'

'Oh. Well. Good for you.'

'The thing is, Lizzie, I just thought I'd give you a heads-up.'

'Heads-up?' Lizzie's head did indeed jerk up.

'A bit of a warning, I mean. That Sonja, she's changed.'

'Changed how?'

'Well, didn't she used to have brownish hair and wear brownish clothes and peer at one through thickish glasses? And wasn't she a bit skinny and round-shouldered? The type to hang back and not make her presence felt?'

Lizzie thought about Sonja. It was difficult to think for long about Sonja because there was so little to think *of*. Sonja was like a piece of office furniture. Necessary, useful, rather cheaply put together, extremely neutral in appearance. She'd begun work at James's office in Chipping Norton just before the twins were born, and had never given anybody a moment's trouble ever since. Lizzie had been very glad indeed when her predecessor, a sharp little thing in black polyester and dyed blonde hair, had taken herself off to Newcastle to be with her boyfriend. Sonja was not the sort of PA to give the boss's wife any cause for concern.

'Yes, brownish just about describes her,' Lizzie said after a moment.

'Well, not any more.'

Lizzie felt a flicker of unease. 'Really?'

'Really,' Lizzie's mother said grimly. 'She's gone sort of ... golden. Gold highlights in her hair. Frosting, I think they call it. And lots of gold jewellery, although it's improbably just costume stuff. And glittery eyeshadow. Not gaudy or anything. Very subtle. I swear she even had some sort of glitter on her arms.'

'Good grief.' Lizzie tried to picture a golden Sonja, but simply couldn't.

'The glasses are gone, too. Did you know, she has very green eyes?'

'No. I didn't. I would have thought her eyes were—'

'Brownish? Exactly. But they're green. And her clothes are all different, too. Expensive-looking. Nicely cut. She doesn't look skinny and round-shouldered any more. What's more, she seems to have a bosom.'

'Are you sure this person *was* Sonja?' Lizzie asked. 'I mean, you've only met her once or twice. How on earth did you recognize her if she's changed so much?'

'I didn't,' Lizzie's mother admitted. 'She recognized *me*. Came right up to me, cool as a cucumber, and introduced herself. She's probably having to introduce herself to her own *family* these days. Anyway, she asked how you were doing, and said wasn't it a shame you and James had split up.'

'Bit of a cheek.'

'That's what I thought. She never used to be that way, did she? Quite shy and retiring, I thought when I saw her at the Christmas party.'

Lizzie winced as she always did when people mentioned the Christmas party. She had drunk too much and made a bit of a fool of herself on that occasion. She brought her mind back to Sonja. 'That's how she's always been – a total nonentity, really.'

'Well, she's definitely an entity now. And you know what it all means?'

Lizzie said nothing. Her heart was hammering unpleasantly. She knew what her mother was getting at.

'It means she's after James. Got to be. She's single, she's thirty if she's a day, her biological clock is probably ticking so hard it keeps her awake at night. And there's James, suddenly single, too. James is really quite attractive, you know. And she works with him *every day*.'

Lizzie's palms were sweating. She couldn't think of a thing to say.

'Liz? Darling? I didn't mean to upset you. I just thought someone ought to tell you. Don't ... don't throw it all away, Lizzie-bean. I mean, James always doted on you. Are you *sure* you can't work things out?'

Lizzie sat down on the kitchen floor and squeezed the bridge of her nose with her left hand.

She was remembering James's flat voice: '*I want to ask you a favour ... Don't keep phoning all the time.*'

She was remembering his face when he came upon Bruno

grappling with the tap, the scathing look he'd given her when he asked her to go and put some clothes on.

She was remembering the words 'divorce lawyer'.

She shook her head savagely. It was all a farce, this split of theirs, and she wouldn't let her mother scare her.

'Calm down, Mum. I haven't given up on him yet. But can I ask one thing? Please don't start inventing trouble for me. I've got enough on my plate as it is. For all I care, Sonja bloody Jenkins could dye her hair purple and start wearing a thong to work. It's none of my business.'

'You know best, my dear.' Her mother sounded huffy, as well she might. 'Just don't leave things too long, will you? Men have their needs, after all.'

Chapter Eight

On the first of June. Lizzie stood outside Chipstead village hall at noon in dark glasses, waiting for the door to open so she could grab the twins and bolt. She was glad now that the other women more or less ignored her. She didn't want to meet anybody's eye. Her own eyes were too red and swollen.

That morning, James had phoned for a 'talk'.

She'd been chewing a pencil and trying to think of a rhyme for 'silk worms' when the ring half-scared her to death.

She'd known exactly who it was, even without caller ID, and felt an immediate, intoxicating surge of hope. It was ages since he'd phoned her. Maybe he'd had time to think and was finally calling to make peace. But her excitement was almost immediately doused by his tone of voice, which was businesslike.

He wasn't phoning to try to work things out; what a groundless hope, in hindsight.

He was phoning to tell her that she needed to find herself a lawyer. His own lawyer advised that the best course of action, if they wanted a quick resolution, was for Lizzie herself to initiate the divorce petition.

'The ... what?' Lizzie croaked.

'Divorce petition. The bit of paper that gets the ball rolling.'

'Oh. And *I've* got to send it to *you*, you say?'

'That's right, and you'll need a lawyer to draft it. We have to establish irretrievable breakdown of the marriage.' His voice held no inflection. 'Since there wasn't any adultery, one of us has to charge the other with either desertion or unreasonable behaviour. We don't want this thing to drag on and on.'

Lizzie was clutching her chest in pain. Could she be having a heart attack? She cleared her throat. 'James? Do we need to be in such a hurry? Can't we just ... wait and see? I've been sort of hoping we could, you know, patch things up. That e-mail—'

'Lizzie, do you want to know the truth?' James interrupted, his voice louder than usual. 'I'm not interested in patching things up. I want this divorce at least as much as you do. The way things were between us – do you think it was a one-way street? Let's have the guts to be honest. Staying in a marriage for the sake of the children just doesn't bloody work. Take it from me, no kid wants to spend his childhood watching his parents ignore each other. Look, let's just end it in a civilized way, and move on.'

'For the sake of the ...? I didn't realize ... I thought ... All right, then. Crikey. OK. So. Can't we ... can't we just say we had – what do you call it? – irreconcilable differences, and leave it at that?' She was surprised at how normal her voice sounded. She was surprised she could speak at all.

'Apparently not. It's adultery, desertion or unreasonable behaviour. Or else we have to live separately for two years by mutual consent.'

'Oh.'

'So if we want this done quickly, we have to come up with a plan.'

'I see. Well, desertion seems the obvious thing, doesn't it?' She couldn't keep the edge out of her voice.

'You'd have thought so.' His voice was dry. 'But since I've been paying the rent on your Sevenoaks house, apparently we can't use that. So we're down to unreasonable behaviour.'

'Right. But surely you're the one who should be doing the petition thingy then. I mean, it all started with me being unreasonably exhausted in bed, didn't it?'

He didn't contradict her. 'I can't put that on a legal document, Lizzie. No, it's much better if you just come up with something about me. Apparently, it doesn't have to be that bad. I mean, you don't have to say I was beating you senseless or getting blind drunk every night. My chap says the courts aren't very demanding. Just a couple of paragraphs will do.'

Lizzie's fingers were turning white around the receiver. 'All right,' she said. 'I'll ... I'll have a quick look in the Yellow Pages then, and find a lawyer.'

'Don't procrastinate on this one, Lizzie. There's some sort of time limit on the unreasonable behaviour charge. We can't leave it too long, or we'll end up having to wait for years. Just remember, whatever you put in the petition, I won't be defending.'

'OK. I'll ... I'll come up with something.'

'Good. There must be a million things you could say. I'm sure I was a bugger to live with.'

'Yeah, well ...' She cleared her throat. 'James? This isn't some sort of ... joke, is it?'

There was a silence. 'No,' James said at last. 'Of course it isn't.'

The ice-packs Lizzie had used on her eyes hadn't been very effective, so she kept her sunglasses on and her eyes strictly down, making a detailed study of everybody's footwear. She hadn't realized how popular those espadrilles with wedge heels were becoming.

At last, the door of the village hall opened. Lizzie shuffled into the room at the back of the crowd.

'Mrs Buckley?'

Lizzie saw a pair of brown suede slip-ons stop in front of her. She looked up cautiously. Mrs Kirker, the nursery school director, was standing before her, eyebrows raised, mouth pursed. She didn't look quite as motherly and benevolent as usual.

'Mrs Buckley, I'd like to have a word, if I may. About some, ah, issues that have cropped up.'

'Issues?'

'I've asked Mrs Shay to settle Alex and Ellie at a table and keep them occupied just for a moment.'

'Oh. Right. Fine.'

'So, if you wouldn't mind?'

Lizzie followed Mrs Kirker towards a tiny table and chairs,

her back burning as she imagined the other mothers watching and speculating.

Mrs Kirker lowered herself onto one of the child-size chairs and indicated that Lizzie should do the same. Lizzie sat down gingerly. She was beyond caring about personal comfort, given that she was sleeping on a deflating blow-up mattress every night, but she didn't like the mental image of herself with her knees so close to her chin.

As she arranged her legs, she was struck by a sudden unpleasant thought: since there wasn't going to be a reconciliation with James after all, she really was going to have to buy some beds.

She wondered briefly what sort of bed James would buy when he moved into the house in Chipping Norton. She hoped he'd have the decency not to opt for a king-size mattress. She hoped the house was a narrow one with a steep stairway that simply wouldn't *let in* a king-size mattress.

'Mrs Buckley?'

'Hmmm?' Lizzie jumped guiltily to find the canny brown eyes of the nursery school director fixed on her in intense speculation.

'So do you have any suggestions?'

Belatedly, Lizzie realized that she'd missed something vital. Possibly, she'd missed an entire conversation. She swallowed nervously. 'Aaaah ... could you run that by me again? Sorry. Bit preoccupied.'

Mrs Kirker's eyes narrowed. Lizzie had no doubt at all that she was taking the measure of her, from her unkempt head of hair to her shabby moccasins. She was probably cataloguing all the signs of imminent breakdown – ragged fingernails, torn jeans, unstyled hair, sunglasses indoors, shiny forehead, small fat roll just visible above waistband – and making a mental note to phone Social Services.

'I was talking about Alex's behaviour. Not to say that Ellie doesn't have issues all of her own. But Alex is the one displaying the most overt aggression.'

'Aggression?' Startled, Lizzie glanced across the room to the low table where the twins were busily creating play-dough shapes. Mrs

Shay, doubled up in her own tiny chair beside them, gave her a wave and a thumbs up signal. Lizzie smiled back weakly.

'Dis is dog pooh,' Alex happened to say in a carrying tone just at that moment.

'Yes, it's the biting mainly,' Mrs Kirker explained in that stagily hushed voice she'd been using all along. 'Unfortunately, while we can make sure there are no sticks or pretend guns in the classroom, we can't take away a child's teeth.'

Lizzie's eyes widened as an image of a toothless Alex sprang to mind. 'Of course you can't,' she said with a small laugh. But Mrs Kirker didn't look particularly amused.

Lizzie was aware that Alex occasionally sank his choppers into another child, but didn't all children bite now and then?

'Many children display some sort of biting behaviour between the ages of about nine months and two,' Mrs Kirker declared, as if she had vast personal experience of this fascinating phenomenon. Which, very possibly, she did. 'It's nothing to get excited about. Generally, biters are just experimenting. They're not purposely trying to hurt other children.'

Lizzie nodded vigorously. 'That's what I've read,' she said. 'He'll grow out of it any minute now.'

Mrs Kirker frowned. 'We-ell. In Alex's case I think we're running into quite different territory.'

Lizzie's head froze mid-nod. 'Different territory?'

'That's right. After all, he's well over three, now. I think he's perfectly aware, at this stage, that when he bites another child he's inflicting pain. Let's face it, Mrs Buckley, he's using his teeth as a *weapon*.'

Lizzie burst into a guffaw, then covered her mouth hastily. 'A weapon? Are you saying Alex is *armed and dangerous*?'

Mrs Kirker eyed her coldly. 'You may choose to make a joke of it, Mrs Buckley, but here at Chipstead we've noticed some rather disturbing tendencies, not only in Alex but also in Ellie.'

'What? Don't tell me Ellie's savaging people, too?' Ellie had never bitten anyone in her life, Lizzie could safely say, but what if she was pulling pony-tails or giving children Chinese burns?

'No, Eleanor is not an aggressive child, as I'm sure you know. But she is capable of passive aggression. Pretending not to hear when a teacher talks to her; using most of a toilet-roll when she goes to the loo and then not flushing; refusing to follow simple class rules like putting away the toys once she's finished with them. That sort of thing.'

Wearing pyjamas to school, Lizzie could have added. Squishing Rich Tea biscuits into the floor with her trainers. Mimicking whatever anyone said to her in a sing-song voice.

Personally, Lizzie wouldn't have classified this sort of silliness as 'passive aggression'. Ellie was just going through a bit of a maddening stage, that was all. She was a lovely child at heart. So was Alex, for that matter.

Lizzie began to feel jittery and flushed. She was overcome with an urge to shove Mrs Kirker off the tiny chair ... Oh God! That was where the children got it from: their mother!

She took a deep breath.

She burned to give Mrs Kirker a tongue-lashing about her inability to deal with minor discipline issues. But Mrs Kirker was a nursery school director. Clearly, she out-ranked Lizzie.

'Sorry they're causing trouble,' she mumbled. 'Ellie's just showing off, you know. I'll talk to them both.'

Mrs Kirker put out a hand and patted Lizzie kindly on the shoulder. 'I didn't tell you all this to upset you, Mrs Buckley. But I was just wondering – is everything all right at home? You see, children often start playing up when they're stressed about things beyond their control: a death in the family, a big move, any sort of upheaval.'

Lizzie was too tired to break down in tears. She just nodded and began to bite her cuticles.

'So ... there is something?' Mrs Kirker asked gently.

Lizzie took a finger out of her mouth to mutter, 'Their daddy's gone.'

'I beg your pardon?'

'Their father. My husband. He's not with us any more.'

'Oh my! I had no idea. Oh, you poor thing. If you can bear to talk about it ... when did he pass away?'

Lizzie broke into a high laugh, quickly suppressed when she saw the look on Mrs Kirker's face. 'No, I don't mean that,' she explained hurriedly. 'I don't mean he's dead. He's just not with us any more. He's with his parents in Gloucestershire. We're here.'

Mrs Kirker frowned. 'Ah. I see. A separation. You had some serious issues in your marriage, I take it?'

'Yes, well. You know. This and that.'

Mrs Kirker glanced quickly over at the children, who were now dumping puzzles out on the floor. She lowered her voice. 'This is trespassing a little, so don't feel you have to answer. But was there any violence in the marriage? Was he hitting you at all?'

'Good God! No!' Lizzie stood up, her sense of outrage finally overcoming her inborn deference for figures of authority.

Mrs Kirker jumped up, too. 'Oh, my dear. I'm sorry. I can see I've offended you. I do get carried away sometimes. Please forgive the intrusion. But honestly, you'd be surprised – *astonished* – how often I come across domestic abuse in families that you'd think were *quite* above all that. I was just checking, that's all.'

Lizzie's chin wobbled. 'My husband is a lovely man,' she said. 'He doesn't *hit* people. We're not a family of . . . of *thugs*.'

'Of course not,' cried Mrs Kirker.

But Lizzie was already limping off as fast as she could. (Unfortunately, her left foot had gone to sleep during her session in the miniature chair.) Mrs Kirker scurried after her, tutting her distress.

'Come on, you lot, let's tidy up Mrs Kirker's room,' Lizzie ordered her children.

Something steely in her voice must have penetrated their three-year-old brains because, to their eternal credit, Ellie and Alex both leapt to attention and began shoving puzzles back into boxes. Lizzie tried to maintain a dignified posture while scraping blobs of play-dough off the floor.

'Oh, please don't worry about clearing up,' Mrs Shay begged.

'Really. Leave it to us,' Mrs Kirker chimed in. 'You have enough on your hands.'

But Lizzie wasn't content until every last puzzle piece was in its box and every last toy and book was on a shelf. Then she hissed at the twins to say thank you and goodbye. She might look like a battered wife, but she'd show the old cows that she expected impeccable manners from her children. She was sure the two women couldn't wait for her to be gone so they could put the kettle on, wheel out the real chairs, and start discussing her wretched case. To think she'd ever liked Mrs Kirker!

She drove home in a silence so ear-splitting that even Alex noticed. As they bounced up the lane, she sped straight past the cottage and on to the barn.

Ingrid Hatter came to the door with a surprised look. 'Lizzie? How lovely to see you.'

'Ingrid, I'm terribly sorry, but can you take the children for about half an hour?'

'Of course I can. Is it an emergency?' Ingrid's eyes lit up with curiosity.

'Yes. I need to go running.'

Lizze loped down the muddy lane in her shiny new trainers until she reckoned she was out of earshot of the barn. Then she began to sprint. As she picked up speed, she did what she'd been longing to do since the phone call with James that morning. She let rip with a blood-curdling, spine-chilling, ear-piercing scream.

It was a short-lived scream because she didn't have enough breath to make it last. But she kept on running as fast as her quivering legs would carry her over the rough terrain of the lane.

Strangely exhilarating to hear the wind in her ears, to see the mud flying away beneath her feet, to feel her heart working so hard. She was so powerful, so fleet of foot, so ... crikey, she was airborne.

Lizzie picked herself up out of a puddle and checked for injuries. Nothing major, but her shoes might never be white again.

She started to run again, darting right at the corn field along the footpath used by hikers and dog-walkers. Naturally, she couldn't sustain the sprint for very long. Soon she was hobbling along at a pace barely faster than a walk, with a flame of pain flickering up each shin, but still she was running. Every time she came to a downhill slope she broke into a faster lollop, determined to flee all the frustrations and mortifications of the day.

After about fifteen minutes of noble endeavour, Lizzie's hard-driven body began to assert itself. *Stop*, it said loudly. *Stop this minute. Stop or I'm going to seize up right here, right now, in the middle of the footpath.*

She stopped and sat down on a large, rough rock. Her mud-splattered legs were shaking and her heart was thumping so hard someone might as well have been playing bongo drums inside her chest. There was sweat on her face, sweat trickling down between her breasts, sweat making her hands too slippery to clasp together.

Gosh. It felt pretty good.

Her exhilaration didn't last long, though. As she cooled down, the sweat began to make her shiver, and after a while she noticed that tears were dripping from her chin.

She must have sat on that rock for at least twenty minutes, breathing in, breathing out, letting the tears slide down her face, gazing vacantly across the green and friendly landscape. *I want this divorce at least as much as you do.* The words had shaped themselves into a slightly sinister chant by now, and eventually they drove her to her feet.

She tried to run again, but she was soon reduced to a hobble. Every now and then she attempted a slow jog, but her body was having none of it. It had suffered more than enough insult and injury for one day, and it was as much as she could do to force her jellified legs to take all the necessary steps to get her to Ingrid's barn.

When Ingrid opened the door and took in her red, tear-streaked face and swollen eyes, for once she asked not a single question.

That evening, while the children ate their spaghetti and cheese in front of a *Kipper* video, Lizzie plugged in the phone and made a call.

When Tessa answered with a cheery 'hello', Lizzie's throat suddenly constricted and she couldn't speak. After a moment or two of strangled noises, Tessa said, 'Listen, mate, if this is a crank call, you can just—'

'Tessa,' Lizzie managed at last. 'It's me. Don't hang up.'

'Lizzie? Oh God, what's the matter?'

'It's ... it's James.' She broke into hoarse sobs.

'James? What? An accident?'

'Oh. No. Nothing, nothing like that. It's just ... he phoned me today. Tessa, he's not bluffing. He's not teaching me a lesson. He's dead serious. He thinks we're finished and done for. He's asked me to get a lawyer. He wants to get shot of me as qui-quickly as possible.'

For a moment Tessa herself was speechless, but then she rallied. 'Lizzie? Look, just calm down for a second. Take a few deep breaths. In through the nose, out through the mouth. That's right. Now, this sounds bad, but you don't want to over-react. Remember, a man's pride is his vulnerable underbelly – and you pretty much *walloped* him there with that e-mail of yours. It's going to take him a while to recover. He wants to strike back at you, of course he does. But don't give up on him just yet. It's not over till it's over. What have I been saying to you all along? You've got to pull yourself together and make a concerted effort to win him back.'

Lizzie wiped at her eyes with the back of her hand. 'But, Tessa, he says he wants out. He says he's not interested in patching things up. And d'you know what? I get the distinct feeling that he just doesn't give a flying f-feather any more.'

'Listen, Lizzie, I don't believe it. Not for a moment. Maybe he thinks that right now, but he's dead wrong. You used to be the happiest couple I'd ever seen. Love like that doesn't just go up in a puff of smoke. And he's not involved with anyone else, and nor are you, so ... Lizzie, I don't like to kick a person when they're down, but I do have a theory. You see, the way you are right now? Well, you're not really the same girl he married. You used to be so *interested* in everything. You used to care about your clothes and your make-up and your hair. You used to watch the news and read the papers and have opinions. You used to laugh a lot. But now? Well, your main topic of conversation is the kids and, to be honest, that's, well ...'

'Boring?'

'No. Just, maybe, not as fascinating as you think. Oh God, I'm sorry. Don't cry! Look, I really think you should go and see a therapist. My friend Petronella has one. She says she's great. What harm could it do?'

'Not a chance, Tessa. I may be a bit of a wreck, but I can sort myself out. Really, I can.'

'Lizzie, don't be obstinate. You're depressed and you need to do something about it. Seeing a therapist doesn't mean you're mental. It just means you're ready to move on. Ready to be proactive about your, you know, issues. Oh Lizzie, I just want to ... to grab you by the scruff and shake some life back into you.'

'Well,' said Lizzie lifting her chin, 'I *am* doing something about it, if you want to know. I went running this afternoon. Didn't you say exercise is good for depression?'

'You went running?' Tessa shrieked. 'Good grief! That's ... that's *wonderful*. How did you feel afterwards?'

'Like hell. What do you expect? I'm sore all over. But do you know what? I'm going to stick with it. Does your offer still stand to, you know, train with me? Could you bear it? Because I think I can get the teenager down at the barn to babysit.'

'Does my offer still stand? Lizzie, it does a lot more than stand. In fact, I can guarantee that I'll be up at your cottage every day, *forcing* you into your trainers. This is progress, Lizzie! Progress!'

Lizzie gave a quivering sigh and took a final bite of the carrot cake she was eating for supper. 'I don't know, Tessa. Don't get your hopes up. It's just running, for heaven's sake.'

From: janehawthorn@yahoo.com
Sent: 2 June
To: lizbuckley@hotmail.com

You get yourself a GOOD lawyer. Take him for every penny, the bastard.

Janie

Chapter Nine

'Hi, Lizzie, how's life?'

Lizzie glanced up from the magazine she'd brought as protection against looking lonely and pathetic as she waited for the children to be let out of school.

One of the nursery school mothers was smiling at her cheerily. Several others were looking benevolently on.

She cleared her throat. 'Life?' she squeaked. 'It's all right, I suppose. How's yours?'

Something odd had happened since yesterday's tête-à-tête with Mrs Kirker about the children. The mums were talking to her. She'd noticed it at drop-off, too. They were also staring at her quite a lot.

She didn't know why her stock had suddenly risen at Chipstead nursery, but it had.

Another funny thing was that Mrs Kirker didn't seem to bear a grudge against her. In fact, she was friendlier than ever; had even made a point of crossing the floor that morning to ask how Lizzie was getting on. In the face of such behaviour, Lizzie was going to find it difficult to go on bearing her own grudge, which she'd meant to drag around like rolling luggage for the rest of her children's career at Chipstead.

Last night, after her conversation with Tessa, Lizzie had extracted a promise from Alex that he'd never bite another child at school again. She'd been restrained enough to bring up the subject only when everybody was bathed, fed and ready for bed. Then, quite calmly and rationally, she'd settled herself on the bedroom floor and remarked, 'Alex, Mrs Kirker says you've been biting children at school again.'

Alex picked up a toy car and spun its wheels against the palm of his left hand. 'Vroom, vroom,' he said.

'Alex. Look at me.'

Reluctantly, he flicked his eyes at her for a second, then turned his attention back to the car. It was a very noisy car, apparently.

'Alex, please look at me when I'm talking to you. And stop that noise. This is serious.'

The blond head continued to bend over the toy car.

'Look at me,' she said through gritted teeth.

'Brum,' he said.

An unreasonable fury took hold of Lizzie. She leaned forward, snatched the car out of his hand, and threw it as hard as she could against the wall. It hit the plaster with a clatter and fell to the carpet, spinning its wheels stupidly in the air. Lizzie noted that part of the bodywork was smashed.

Great, Lizzie, she said to herself. What a fine job you're doing, showing your son that violence is not the answer.

At least she had his attention now. He was staring at her with wide eyes, his determined little chin trembling ever so slightly.

'You are not to bite your friends, do you understand? Biting is naughty and it hurts. Do you want to hurt other children?'

Alex started to nod his head and then quickly turned it into a shake. He was watching her as you might watch a volatile dog capable of occasional savagery. His expression infuriated her.

'If you bite one more child, I will take away your fire engine. Got it?'

'Naughty Mummy,' he suddenly wailed, pointing an accusing finger. 'I woll tell *Daddy* on you! Daddy *gived* it to me. Daddy won't *let* you take it away!'

'Daddy will take it away himself if he hears that you're biting your friends,' Lizzie snapped back. 'You *know* biting is bad. Why on earth do you keep doing it? Would you like it if I bit you? Would you? Would you?' She bared her teeth at him and made violent gnashing noises.

He shrank away and gazed at her nervously. His face seemed to go small and triangular.

But still she couldn't stop herself. She grabbed him by his narrow, pyjama-clad shoulders, feeling her fingers sink into his soft flesh. 'Don't you *ever* bite anyone again. Do you think I like being the mummy of the nasty little boy who bites people at school? You just clean up your act or you'll be lucky if I don't smash every one of your toys into little bits. Do you hear?'

Ellie, sitting on her bed 'reading' a book to Panda, gave a sudden hysterical giggle. Lizzie turned on her like a wounded she-elephant. 'That goes for you, too, Eleanor Buckley. You behave yourself at school or I'll take Panda off you and give him to the starving children in Ethiopia. Understand?'

Ellie nodded.

Alex's eyes glittered with tears. He wore an expression of deep concentration; possibly he was trying to suck the tears back inside through sheer will power. Lizzie knew how that felt. Then, in a whisper, he said, 'No more bitin'. Pwomise.'

She'd had to rush out of the room then so that she wouldn't break down in front of the two of them.

Thank goodness none of the mums who were now being so friendly knew anything about this shameful incident.

Maybe they weren't such a bad crowd after all, even if their kindness was all *Schadenfreude*.

A week after James's phone call, Lizzie still hadn't looked up a lawyer in the Yellow Pages. Instead, she found herself sitting in a shabby waiting room in a Victorian house in Sundridge, watching a youngish receptionist read a Mills and Boon and pick her teeth.

Lizzie glanced at her watch, then dug a tissue out of her bag and dried her sweating palms.

Just at that moment, a buzzer sounded on the receptionist's desk. She glanced up from her book. 'Ms Buckley? You may go in now. Through that door, and turn left.'

The therapist didn't look as scary as Lizzie had expected. Just a bit *older* than she'd expected. Not that she'd been expecting someone in their twenties, of course, but this woman had probably been around at the onset of the Second World War. She was definitely of the same generation as James's mother, though poles apart in appearance. Unrepentantly old-school, with iron-grey sheep's curls and woolly jumper, and blessed with an unusually big bottom, she didn't look as if she'd ever heard of micro-dermabrasion, let alone Botox. The word 'contemporary' didn't spring to mind when you looked into the reflective surfaces of her spectacles.

How on earth was Lizzie going to talk about sex in front of her? If only she hadn't let Tessa push her into doing this. But the image of herself as a dreary whinge-pot had struck home. Besides, she was tired of unplugging the phone at night for fear of breaking down in messy tears if she spoke to anybody even halfway sympathetic once she'd had a gin and tonic.

And maybe Tessa was right. Maybe she'd have half a chance of winning James back if she could just find her old self again.

The woman stood up as Lizzie came in, and held out her hand. 'You must be Lizzie,' she said. 'Call me Ivana. Take a seat wherever you like, my dear.' She indicated three possibilities: a wooden kitchen chair, a fold-up office chair, and a bean-bag.

'No couch?' asked Lizzie with an attempt at a laugh.

The woman raised her eyebrows politely. 'As you see,' she said. 'No couch. But you may lie on the floor, if you like. I have a cushion.'

'Oh no, the bean bag will be lovely.' Lizzie sat down on it accordingly. Immediately, Ivana picked up a clipboard and wrote something. Was she noting that Lizzie had chosen the bean-bag? And what did that mean? That Lizzie was childish? Had low self-esteem? Showed poor taste in décor? Put creature comforts above formality?

God, Lizzie could see this whole therapy thing was going to be a minefield.

'So,' said Ivana, settling her large behind into her own seat, a snugly upholstered armchair. 'What brings you to my office, Lizzie?'

Lizzie glanced up into the woman's kindly but dispassionate face and burst into tears.

She cried for a good thirteen minutes of her half-hour appointment. Very extravagant.

She almost wished she'd gone to someone through the National Health so she could have afforded to cry for the full half-hour. But she didn't want it on her medical record that she was having a nervy-breaker. Besides, Tessa had warned that she wouldn't get an appointment with any sort of mental health professional at all unless she told her GP she was thinking of topping herself. Even then, they might only give her drugs. On the other hand, if she played up her nuttiness just a shade too *much* in an attempt to secure a referral, she'd run the risk of being carried off in a straitjacket.

No, going private had been her only option, and this woman came highly recommended by this seriously disturbed friend of Tessa's.

Lizzie scrabbled in her bag for a clean tissue, and blew her nose. 'My friend thinks I'm depressed,' she muttered.

'Ah,' said Ivana.

'My husband left me,' said Lizzie.

'Ah,' said Ivana.

'He wants a divorce.'

'Ah,' said Ivana.

'And I want to know *why*,' said Lizzie.

'But of course,' said Ivana.

Then they sat in silence, Lizzie occasionally blowing her nose.

Bloody hell, thought Lizzie. What's she up to now? Going through her diary? When is she going to start the flaming *therapy*?

'We had a lovely marriage,' Lizzie blurted out, hoping to bring the woman's attention back to her case. 'Nothing wrong with it at all. Except one teeny problem, but I'm sure ... I'm pretty sure he didn't know about it.'

Ivana glanced up. 'Yes?' she asked absently.

'Yes. It was ... you know, the bedroom stuff.' Lizzie was fiery red now, but it was OK because the woman wasn't looking at her. 'I'd sort of ... gone off the bedroom stuff. After my babies were born, you know.'

'Babies?'

'Twins. A girl and a boy. Not identical. Obviously. Anyway, having them was a horrible shock. I mean, it was lovely, of course, but it was also, you know, a bit *gruesome*, to be honest. Nobody tells you how bad it's going to be, that you're never going to get any sleep, like someone being tortured in a medieval dungeon or something. And then there's the blood and the spit-up and the pooh. Nobody warns you about *that* side of things.'

Good grief. Lizzie couldn't believe she'd said the word 'pooh' in a doctor's consulting room. Maybe it wasn't going to be so hard to say 'sex', after all.

'Ah,' said Ivana, and flipped a page in her diary, or whatever it was. She hadn't turned a hair.

Lizzie began to feel a little bolder. 'So, anyway, I started sort of dreading the ... you know, the ... you know, going to bed with my husband.'

'What is his name?' Ivana asked mildly.

'Huh? Oh. James.'

'Ah.'

'Anyway. So I started losing interest in ... in, you know. But James had no idea, of course. I mean, he says now that it wasn't a one-way street, but ... I don't even know what that means. He certainly always seemed, you know, very keen.'

'I see.' Ivana took up her pen. 'How often were you having the sex, would you say?'

Lizzie's face broke into fresh flames. 'Erm, how *often*? Let me see, oh, probably twice or three times a week.'

'I see. So, let's think. You would have the sex on a Friday night, probably. That is the usual pattern. And then maybe again on Saturday? And then again mid-week?'

Lizzie shifted uncomfortably in the bean bag. 'Yes. Erm, most Friday nights. Except when he was away on business. Or if he fell asleep while I was in the bathroom.'

Ivana raised her eyebrows.

'See, Alex was a bit of a night-owl. My little boy. I'd be up rocking him to sleep until past eleven most nights.'

'How old are your children?'

'Three.'

'And you rock Alex to sleep?'

Lizzie paused a moment. 'Actually, not any more,' she said

135

slowly. 'Not since I moved out.'

Ivana noted something down. 'Ah,' she said.

'And then I'd go and have a shower. Before bed.'

'I see. A quick shower to get ready for the night of love.'

Lizzie cringed. People were obviously a lot more forward about this sort of thing in Croatia, or wherever Ivana hailed from. 'Yes. Except maybe not such a very *quick* shower. I love showering, you see. Well, *used* to love it. The only bit of peace and quiet I'd get in the whole day. So I didn't take quick showers, exactly. Actually, they could be rather long.'

'Ah.'

'So my husband would sometimes be asleep when I'd go to bed.'

'Sometimes?'

'Well, often, then.' Lizzie could see what the woman was driving at. OK, so maybe there hadn't been sex three times a week, or even twice a week. But it had still been pretty frequent. At *least* three or four times a month. And she'd always made him think she was enjoying herself.

So she was still no closer to understanding how a single rogue e-mail message could have ended her marriage. It wasn't even as if they'd had some big falling-out before she'd sent it off.

Ivana looked at her watch. 'Time is over,' she said. 'You need another appointment. Talk to Katriona at the front desk.'

'I'm not going back,' Lizzie told Tessa as they did some stretching exercises before their now daily run. 'The woman is useless. She sits looking through her diary while you talk.'

'Bloody cheek!' said Tessa. 'I wonder why Petronella thought she was good.'

'Dunno. Maybe she's more interested in whatever brand of loony your friend is. I'm certainly no expert in psychotherapy, but I expected some sort of ... *input* from her. She didn't give me any advice at all! I'm worse off than I was before I went.'

'Worse off? How come?'

Lizzie shrugged. 'I don't know. I'm just dwelling on things again.

Thinking too much. Probably breaking down even *more* often than before. D'you know what? I think I'll go and give the old bat a piece of my mind.'

She was back in the bean-bag a week later. 'Ivana,' she said, clearing her throat. 'Ivana. I have something to say to you.'

'Yes?'

'I'm not coming back after today.'

'Ah.'

'I only came back at all because I thought someone should mention to you . . . the thing is, you might want to do some extra courses in psychotherapy. I've done a bit of Internet research, and I believe things may have changed since you got your degree. I think today's mentally disturbed client wants a little more, what do you call it, intervention? A little more to and fro, at any rate. A bit more bang for their buck.'

'Ah,' said Ivana. 'Now, where were we.' She looked at her notes, not at all perturbed, while Lizzie churned with the double stress of having spoken her mind, and not seeming to have offended the injured party.

'Yes, frequency of relations,' Ivana said calmly. She closed her notebook, tipped her spectacles up off her nose, and looked straight at Lizzie, who was startled to see that her eyes were periwinkle blue.

'I want to tell you a story,' the therapist announced. 'A young couple is getting married. She is in the beautiful white gown, he is handsome in his tuxedo. When she arrives at the church, he is there outside. So she whispers to the bridesmaid: "Tell the organist to keep on playing." Then she pulls him into the little cloakroom. The organist keeps playing for maybe six minutes, then the husband comes out fiddling with his flies, and he is smiling from the cheek to the cheek. He walks up to the front of the church and goes in the pew next to the best man. "Where were you?" the best man asks. "I thought maybe you bolted." "I was in the cloakroom with the bride," says the bridegroom, and he is grinning. "I've just had the *best*—"

'OK, I think I've heard this story,' Lizzie interrupted. 'And the bride comes out smiling, too, because she's never going to have to give him another one of those again.'

Ivana looked at Lizzie with tranquil interest. 'So you have heard that joke before?' she asked.

The woman was a nutter. She should be in therapy herself. 'Yes, I've heard it, and maybe two or three more in the same vein.'

Ivana leaned back and folded her hands across her stomach. 'Why do people tell jokes like that, I wonder?'

Lizzie shrugged. 'I don't know. To make people laugh, I suppose.'

'But why is such a joke funny?'

Lizzie was at a loss. Was she supposed to explain the mechanics of punch-lines now? Was this some sort of test of mental fitness? If she couldn't explain how jokes worked, did that confirm she was losing her mind?

Just then, the door cracked open and the receptionist poked her head into the room. She was dressed, oddly enough, in jeans and scuffed cowboy boots.

'You buzzed?' she asked.

'Ah, yes, Katriona. I have just told Lizzie here joke number forty-two.'

Lizzie curled her toes, but Katriona nodded her head in a businesslike way. Did she really have a mental catalogue of at least forty-two jokes?

'Can you explain why that joke is funny?'

Katriona smiled pleasantly. 'Well, it's not that funny when *you* tell it, Ivana. You don't have the timing quite right. But basically, it's funny because it illustrates a stereotype that we all have about marriage and sex.'

'Which is?'

'Which is that women use sex to catch a man, then lose interest in it once they're married.'

Ivana nodded her head sagely, like a professor of literature when a student has explicated a theme in one of the classics. 'People do not have the trust in stereotypes,' she pronounced.

'But they're usually based on a partial truth,' Katriona recited back.

'Lizzie here believes she has the very unique problem with her husband,' Ivana told Katriona.

For God's sake, weren't there rules about patient confidentiality?

'Katriona, tell her of the other night, when you went out for dinner with the ladies of your baby's playgroup. You phoned to your husband before you left the restaurant, yes? Will you explain Lizzie why?'

Katriona grinned. 'I rang him to warn him that I had a really, really bad headache. You see, he thinks that if I only get a bit of booze in me I'll be up for anything. I didn't want him lying in wait with the massage oils and mood music.'

'Thank you, Katriona.'

The receptionist gave Lizzie a bright smile and withdrew from the room.

'So,' said Ivana, 'this unique problem is not so unique, we see. Katriona has a baby. Katriona's body says no more babies now. It is very simple. Let us move on to other areas. You said last time you had a lovely marriage. What does this mean?'

'Well, it's obvious, isn't it? We were compatible. We loved each other.'

'Did you ever have the fights?'

Lizzie thought. 'Not really. I mean, we'd squabble a bit sometimes, but no big fireworks.'

'If there was the one thing you could have changed about this marriage, what would it be?'

'I wouldn't live in Mill House,' Lizzie said quickly.

'Mill House?'

'His house. It's on his parents' estate. It's beautiful, really, but not my sort of thing. Too many antiques. And his mother was always breathing down my neck, looking after the garden, making sure I didn't break things. I never felt it was truly my own.'

'Ah,' said Ivana with a sigh. 'Tell me of the mother.'

'She doesn't like me.' Lizzie had a sudden quick vision of Lady

Evelyn's thin, supercilious face, and the way her nostrils had pinched in when she'd first laid eyes on Lizzie. Of course, Lizzie must have made a very poor first impression with her motley crew of inappropriately-dressed friends, turning up at the manor doorstep, but still. The woman could at least have cracked a smile for the sake of politeness. 'She thinks I'm a bit common and sort of . . . vulgar.'

'Vulgar?' The way Ivana pronounced the word, Lizzie wasn't sure she knew what it meant.

'Yes, you know, in bad taste. I mean, I always seem to be in the wrong clothes, and, to be honest, I think she thinks I'm too, sort of, busty.'

'Busty?'

Lizzie gesticulated at her chest. 'You see, it really doesn't matter what I wear. As soon as I put anything on, unless it's up to my chin, it looks a bit indecent. I mean, you should have seen her face at the last Christmas party up at the manor. I was wearing this lovely green velvet dress. Thought I'd better make a bit of an effort, you see, as I'd been slouching around in sweatshirts for ages. So anyway, I'd put on a bit of weight, and maybe I didn't quite realize when I tried the dress on, but it was more or less skin-tight, and, well, probably a bit much. The thing was, nothing else I tried on was any good either, so I really didn't have much choice. I had to wear it or go in a sack. Of course, I never meant to go swimming in it.'

'Swimming?'

Lizzie nodded. She could hardly bear to think of the Christmas party now. It had started out well enough, with James wiggling his eyebrows appreciatively at her dress and pretending to whistle. 'Do you really think I should wear it?' she'd asked nervously. 'It's a bit low, isn't it?'

'Lizzie, you look gorgeous,' he'd replied. 'I haven't seen you look this good in ages.'

Bit of a double edge to that compliment, but she hadn't blamed him. After all, when she'd looked at herself in the mirror of the changing room, she'd been taken aback to see how unkempt and just plain *wide* she appeared in her leggings and woolly jumper.

Most of the dresses she'd tried on for the Christmas party had been absolutely nightmarish, of course, making her look like a ship in full sail, or a haggis squeezed into a sausage skin. But the green dress was cut just right. In it, she'd felt rather sophisticated and statuesque.

James's father had liked the dress, too. He'd lifted his monocle to get a better look, then done a sort of bow and kissed her hand in a rather theatrical way. But Lady Evelyn had sucked in her cheeks and averted her gaze from Lizzie's cleavage.

Later, surrounded by a good helping of the men at the party, Lizzie had felt invigorated and invincible. Her father-in-law's famous punch probably had something to do with her euphoria. She'd glanced at James every now and then to see if he was taking note of her triumph. It wasn't often that she could rouse herself, these days, to be the life and soul of the party, and she wanted him to notice that she was a big hit. But he never seemed to be looking at her; he always appeared to be bending forward to hear something some willowy brunette in pearl-coloured satin was whispering to him.

Lizzie had given up feeling jealous about the way women reacted to James. She knew perfectly well that he didn't encourage them. Still, it had looked just a little bit like encouragement, the way he'd touched the willowy woman's shoulder and then let his hand graze her side.

'Show us a bit of the synchronized swimming, then,' one of the chaps in Lizzie's group of admirers suddenly suggested. For some reason, she'd been regaling them with a story from the glory years of her synchronized swimming career at school.

'What, *now?*'

'Why not?' somebody else cried, a raffishly handsome character with blond hair and bloodshot eyes whose name, for the life of her, she couldn't remember. 'I mean, we're in a room with a pool.'

'Come on, Lizzie! Show us some of your moves!'

Lizzie had no idea what was in that punch, but it was obviously lethal. The next thing she knew, she found herself toeing off her shoes and doing a swan dive into the water. In her green velvet dress.

As she surfaced, she realized that the entire party had gathered at the pool's edge. People were clapping and egging her on.

Feeling strangely detached from the situation, she'd floated about in a back layout for a while, staring up at the cherubs. 'Come on, show us a trick or two,' somebody called hoarsely. Lizzie remembered glancing at the spectators, and catching sight of James in his dinner jacket. The willowy woman was still by his side, laughing now and clinging to his elbow for support. In one swift movement, Lizzie pointed a ballet leg at the ceiling, and then disappeared underwater in a back somersault followed by a continuous descending spin or two. People were still clapping and cheering, but when Lizzie emerged and glanced at James, he was watching with a stony face.

When she swam up to the steps, her dress suddenly heavy and cold on her skin, it was the blond chap with the bloodshot eyes who pulled her out of the water and gave her a bear hug. James merely gave her a towel.

'You'll have to borrow something of Mum's,' he'd said in an even voice. 'Though I'm not sure anything will fit.'

They'd left the party shortly afterwards, Lizzie with her hair still wet, bundled up in a monogrammed terry-cloth dressing gown and one of Roger's overcoats, her green dress in a Waitrose shopping bag. Evelyn had produced the clothes with a look on her face that suggested she would probably toss the dressing gown into the fire with a pair of tongs when it was returned to her.

The walk from the manor to Mill House had never seemed longer. Lizzie kept peeping at James, trying to think of something to say to break the strained silence, but he never looked back at her, not once. By the time they got home, her teeth were chattering and her lips were blue. She took a long, hot shower to drive the chill out of her body, and when she came out, James was sound asleep – or pretending to be so.

Lizzie glanced at Ivana now, but couldn't read the expression behind her flashing spectacles. 'I . . . I put on a bit of a synchronised swimming show at the party,' she confessed.

'Ah?' said Ivana.

'Yes, you see, everyone was egging me on and I'd had a tiny bit too much to drink. And you know what, I don't believe James liked it very much.' Lizzie closed her eyes. She could see James's face, definitely annoyed and possibly embarrassed, as he draped the towel over her shoulders.

'I think I made a bit of a fool of myself,' she said quietly. She remembered trying to push the towel back at James, and turning merrily to the fun-loving, red-eyed blond chap, who showed signs of wanting to boost her up on his shoulder and do a victory lap around the pool.

James had thrown the towel over her shoulders again and almost frog-marched her into the changing room, like some recalcitrant child.

Ivana looked at the watch she kept pinned to her blouse. 'Our time is up,' she announced. 'I am sorry you will not be coming back. I feel we are making the progress.'

'I have to go again,' Lizzie told Tessa as they shuffled along the perimeter of the maize field near Back Lane Cottage. 'I don't think she wants me back, but I'm going anyway.'

'Look, can you move just a little faster?' Tessa asked. 'We're not actually running right now. Barely even jogging. That's better. Keep it up now. About Ivana; I know I sent you to her in the first place, but I thought you said she was useless.'

'Oh, she is,' puffed Lizzie. 'But there's something about that room of hers. Just sitting there in that stupid bean-bag sort of makes me remember things. Hang on, stop a moment. Let me catch my breath.'

With an exasperated sigh, Tessa stopped. 'What kind of things?'

'Oh, just things I did that James could've sort of – taken the wrong way,' Lizzie panted. 'Like, there was this chap at somebody's fortieth birthday party who got a bit touchy-feely while we were dancing. I mean, I didn't encourage him at all but I was too polite just to walk away. I think maybe James saw that. And there was this other guy who was learning to do head massages, and I ... well, I let him try his technique on me in somebody's summer house. James got a bit worked up because he couldn't find me, and then, when he did find me, he didn't seem to be that supportive of me letting his friend practise on me.'

'I've never had a head massage,' said Tessa, jogging on the spot. 'Was it any good?'

Lizzie shook her head. 'Actually, it gave me a bit of a headache. But anyway. It seems I also put on a ... well, a synchronized swimming show at Lady Evelyn's Christmas party.'

'Synchronized swimming at the *Christmas* party? Why didn't you tell me?' Tessa was wide-eyed.

Lizzie wiped the sweat off her forehead and began to shuffle on. 'I don't know. I think I was too embarrassed to talk about it, afterwards. Plus I was a bit plastered at the time. I don't really remember all the details. Obviously, I thought it was a runaway success when I was doing it, and all the blokes seemed to think so, too. But James clearly reckoned it was a bit off. That much I do remember.'

'And so?'

'So maybe James sort of started to see me through his mum's eyes. Maybe my whole strategy back-fired.'

Tessa stopped in her tracks. 'What strategy?'

Lizzie stopped, too, already struggling for breath again. 'My strategy to ... well, to keep him interested.'

Tessa looked puzzled. 'Why did you need a strategy? Did he show signs of straying or something? You never said so.'

'Actually, he didn't really. It's just that he always sort of gathers a flock of women around him. You know how it is. They naturally gravitate towards him. I just ... always felt I needed to sort of demonstrate to him that men also found *me* fascinating. You know, in case he should suddenly wake up one day and realize he'd somehow slipped the shoe on the ugly sister.'

Tessa gaped at her, then shook her head. 'So the touchy-feely dancing, the head massage, the swimming were all to demonstrate your fascinating side?'

Lizzie looked sheepish. 'Things got a bit out of hand now and then.'

Tessa continued to stare at her in wonder. 'Lizzie,' she said, 'don't you see what you did? You flirted with his mates. Let them cosy up to you. Gave them synchronized swimming shows. Kept giving *him* the cold shoulder in bed. Then sent him that bloody e-mail. There's no mystery about why he left you! How could you expect him to *stay*?'

Lizzie began to jog again. 'I wasn't cosying up to anybody. I was just trying to be charming, that's all. I was just trying to have one-tenth of the effect on men that he always has on women. So that we'd be *equal*. So that he'd look over at me at some party and see me in the thick of things and think to himself what a bloody good choice he'd made.'

Tessa sped ahead of Lizzie and began to run backwards so that she could make her point better. 'Lizzie, you idiot, he always knew he'd made a good choice! He loved you. But you know what, I've known you virtually all your life. You're not the sort of girl who goes off for creepy head massages. You don't jump into pools in your party clothes. Lizzie! Watch it!'

But it was too late, Lizzie had put her foot down right in the middle of a large pile of horse manure that turned out to be rather fresh and slippery. With a strangled cry, she went down elbows first in the rough grass. Aghast, Tessa knelt down beside her. 'Oh, God! Oh, Lizzie, I'm sorry. I was distracting you. Here, take my hand and stand up. Carefully, now.'

Slowly and painfully, Lizzie got back up on her feet. 'Oh, bugger,' she said as she tested her weight on her left ankle. 'Oh, bugger and blast. It's not broken. It's not even sprained.'

'Excellent!' cried Tessa. 'Come on, now, don't worry about the muck, we'll hose you down afterwards. Let's just keep going!'

'You still love this James?' asked Ivana.

Lizzie nodded dumbly. She'd just finished recounting the head-massage incident in the summer house. At the time, she hadn't thought she was breaking any unwritten rules – well, not really. After all, hadn't this same chap, Luke, a local organic herbalist and a bit of a free spirit, been giving head massages to all sorts of people in

Laingtree, including Roger Buckley? And hadn't Roger even offered to put head massages on his list of spa services at the conference centre if Luke was any good at it?

Of course, she wouldn't have liked it if James had ever gone off to a summer house with a pretty girl for, say, a haircut or something. But still. The whole incident had been perfectly above board.

If only she and Luke hadn't jumped so guiltily when the door of the summer house suddenly opened and they saw James standing there, looking tight-lipped.

Ivana took off her spectacles and rubbed them with a tissue. 'Lizzie,' she said, 'I am willing to make the bet that your husband thinks you love him no more. Now,' she looked at her pinned-on watch, 'before you leave, I will summarize what I believe you have shown me in these visits.' She began counting items off on her gnarled fingers. 'Yes, you have been depressed. Yes, you have suffered from the lack of sexual appetite; this is very normal for new mothers; not unusual at all. Yes, you still love your husband.' Her hands sank down onto the arms of her chair, and she began to shake her head. 'But you did *not* have a lovely marriage. You did not fully believe in your husband's love. You did not show *your* love. It is probable he thinks that you are turned away from him.' Turned away? Oh, turned *off*. 'That is why he left you. My advice is simple. Tell this James of your feelings.'

Lizzie heaved herself to her feet, shaking her head sadly. 'Look, I've already *told* him I still love him. I've already *told* him I don't want the divorce. But d'you know what? I think *he's* just gone clean off *me*. I think he's finally come round to Lady Evelyn's point of view; she always had me pegged as cheap-and-nasty.'

Ivana shrugged. 'That may be,' she said peaceably. 'We all see a different truth.'

Lizzie slung her bag over her shoulder. 'My friend, Tessa, thinks I could win him back,' she said a little defiantly. 'She thinks if I was thinner and better dressed and a bit more lively, he'd be all over me again.'

Ivana looked up at her. 'For men, so much of love is in the pack-agings,' she mused.

Lizzie waited for more pearls, but Ivana had returned to her diary. Lizzie sketched a little wave and walked out.

'And this time I'm definitely not coming back,' she told Katriona as she counted out the cash.

Katriona smiled and gave her a receipt.

'Maybe you should just trot off to the doctor and get some drugs, after all,' Tessa said doubtfully as they jogged at a snail's pace over the meadow at Knole Park.

'No,' Lizzie panted back. 'I don't need them now. I'm getting better. I think the running helps. Look, can you slow down a moment? Anyway, I can't have Prozac on my record. What if I have to fight for custody of the kids?'

Tessa gave Lizzie a startled look. 'Don't talk that way, Lizzie. You're going to get him back.'

Lizzie shrugged and fell back to a walk, forcing Tessa to walk, too. 'Ah, ouch, when will I stop getting stitches? Look, if Ivana did one thing, she showed me that our marriage was knee-deep in trouble before I ever wrote that e-mail. I mean, half the time I was in some sort of zonked-out, sleep-deprived zone, all covered in baby sick, and then, when I'd shake myself out of it for some dinner party or other, I'd end up doing all these stupid, show-offy things. His mum was probably whispering in his ear, telling him that bad breeding will out, that sort of thing. The whole thing was unravelling for years. I don't know how we stayed together as long as we did.'

Tessa frowned. 'Come on, it wasn't like that,' she said. 'You guys were happy. You were in love. I saw you. You couldn't have faked it.'

Lizzie swiped at her eyes with the back of her hand. 'We *were* in love, weren't we? Oh God, I miss him so much. I just wish we could go back and start all over again.'

Tessa reached over and grabbed Lizzie's sweaty hand. 'You *can* start over again,' she insisted. 'I'm convinced you can. Come on, ignore the stitch, let's *run*!'

Chapter Ten

'I knew you'd go out on a date with me eventually.'

It was Saturday morning. Bruno lay on his back on the picnic blanket, gazing up at the uneasy sky, where bright patches of blue were pitted against scudding grey clouds.

In the thick of her therapy sessions with Ivana, Lizzie had allowed herself to be persuaded to go on this jaunt with him. Exactly why, she wasn't quite sure, except that the weekends were long and lonely, and Bruno had a way of cheering her up.

'You can't call this a date.' Lizzie was arranging crisps, pieces of apple and peanut butter sandwiches on paper plates. Occasionally, she swatted at a fly or bee with a napkin.

'Picnics are notoriously romantic,' Bruno insisted. He closed his eyes and made kissy noises with his lips. As lips went, they were OK, Lizzie reflected. Rather full, for a man, but by no means repulsively so. They'd probably feel silky but firm to the touch, definitely not wet. Lizzie felt that men's lips, unlike dogs' noses, had no business being wet. Any suggestion of spittle, dribble or drool was a definite turn-off in her book.

Lizzie stopped herself short, surprised by the trend of her thoughts. Was this the attitude of a woman whose sensual side had withered up and died?

Her fit of self-analysis was abruptly curtailed. '*Aaaargh*!' She yelled.

'What the hell?' Bruno leapt to his feet and crouched in some sort of martial arts stance.

'Relax, Bruno, no one's attacking us. Your stupid dog just dropped this bloody great stick on Ellie's plate, that's all.' She held up the offending item, silvery with saliva. Madge yipped with excitement and began leaping around the blanket, sending apples and sandwiches flying.

'Here.' Bruno grabbed the stick and threw it as far into the woods as he could. With a wild lunge, Madge disappeared into the undergrowth after it.

'I have to say, if you're trying to get back into the dating game by taking women out on picnics, that dog is a liability.'

Bruno propped his head up on his hands. 'And I have to say, if you're trying the same thing, those twins are a double liability.'

'OK, just because I was kind enough to let you come on a picnic that we were going on *anyway*, don't let your imagination run away with you.'

The pupils of Bruno's gypsy brown eyes suddenly dilated, and Lizzie's stomach did an odd little flip. 'And where do you think my runaway imagination is taking me?' he asked in a suddenly husky voice.

'Straight to the gutter, I would guess,' she managed to quip back. Good grief, was she flirting?

Hastily, she stood up and bellowed, 'Ellie! Alex! Lunchtime!'

Alex appeared from behind a tree. He stood still a moment, then scraped the ground with one foot before letting out a roar and charging towards the picnic blanket. With a flying leap, he launched himself at lounging Bruno, landing with a thud on his stomach. Bruno doubled up in exaggerated pain, grabbed the wriggling child, and held him at arm's length in the air above him. Alex began raining punches down on Bruno, most of which swished harmlessly through the air. Every now and then, Bruno lowered the little boy slightly so that his small fists could make contact with their target.

'Uh! Oh! Ouch! You got me!' Bruno groaned.

Ellie crept onto Lizzie's lap. 'Daddy likes wrestlin', too,' she remarked.

The sun clouded over and the brilliance was gone from the day in an instant, as if someone had turned off a switch.

Lizzie wrapped her arms around the little girl and pressed her cheek into the petal-soft skin of her neck, closing her eyes. For the millionth time, she wondered how deep the sadness went in this inscrutable daughter of hers. Ellie began to squirm. 'Ooosh, ticklish.' Within seconds, she slipped out of Lizzie's arms like a wet bar of soap, and went to join forces with Alex against Bruno.

The rain began to plop down. Suddenly, the picnic turned into a mad scramble to pack everything so they could escape to the relative shelter of the woods. There, huddled under the canvas picnic blanket, they waited for the weather to pass. The twins ate their sandwiches in the dripping shelter with great relish. Lizzie tore up a French loaf and handed hunks to Bruno, who was hacking at a round of Brie with a penknife. It was the nicest lunch Lizzie had had in days.

The phone was ringing as Lizzie fell through the door after her evening jog, panting and clutching her left side.

Barely able to talk, she picked it up and breathed heavily into the receiver. Tessa, sweaty but not nearly as out of breath, grabbed her car keys, jangled them, and indicated with a jerk of her head that she was leaving. Shaking her head, Lizzie detained her with a frantic hand on the elbow.

After a few 'yeses' and 'of courses', Lizzie hung up the phone and turned to Tessa.

'James wants me to get my stuff out of the house over the weekend,' she told her in a tone of wonder.

'This weekend? Talk about short notice. The flaming gall of the man!' Tessa's eyes snapped with anger on Lizzie's behalf.

'It's OK, Tessa. We discussed this. We agreed it was best to open the place to the holiday market as soon as possible. I'm sure he needs the money, what with ... everything. I bet he wasn't expecting to get bookings quite so soon, though. I certainly wasn't. But it'll be OK. I'll phone Maria in a moment and ask if I can stay with them. I just wish ... I just wish James hadn't asked Sonja to sort it out. That was her on the phone. There's something so ... humiliating about dealing with his PA.' Lizzie blinked quickly.

'It is a bloody cheek,' agreed Tessa. 'But never mind. Chin up. Look on this as an opportunity. You'll be back at Mill House, you're bound to see him there, and it's guaranteed to jog a few fond memories. Come on, remember what we said, it's not over till it's over.'

Lizzie's eyes widened. 'What, you expect me to sort of throw myself at him over the packing cases?'

'I'm not saying throw yourself at him,' said Tessa. 'Just, you know, wear something decent, for one thing. Get your hair done. Put on some perfume. And maybe, I don't know, show him a few photos from an old album or something. To stir the heart strings.'

Lizzie was shaking her head doubtfully when her little monsters came thundering down the stairs and rushed at her, flinging their arms around her legs. Caught off guard, Lizzie toppled. They all went down in a wriggling heap, the twins screaming with laughter. From the floor, Lizzie saw the frayed flares of Sarah Hatter's jeans rounding the corner. She managed to struggle into a sitting position.

'So?' she asked the teenager as jauntily as she could. 'How were they?'

Sarah blushed. (She was always blushing.) 'They were fine,' she said with a little shrug. 'We had fun.'

Tessa was waving her car keys again. 'Look, Liz, I really have to go or Greg will be after me with the carving knife. It's my turn to cook tonight.'

Lizzie waved Tessa out of the room, then turned to Sarah. 'Let's see, how much do I owe you?'

While Lizzie dug around in her bag, Sarah stood awkwardly in the hall, trying not to look too eager to get her hands on the money. As Lizzie poured pound coins into her palm, the girl suddenly took a sharp breath and said, 'I read some stuff of yours, Mrs Buckley. I didn't mean to. There was a a pile of papers on the kitchen table, and the children wanted to draw, so I took a quick look, thinking if it was shopping lists or something like that, they could just draw on the back.'

The blush on Sarah's face was painful to see, especially as Lizzie's own face seemed determined to match it blaze for blaze. She knew exactly what Sarah was talking about. Quickly, she bent down and busied herself with straightening Alex's clothes. Astonished at suddenly having his T-shirt tucked into his shorts, Alex began to stomp around in a circle, flailing at his mother's busy hands.

'Oh. You ... you read my verses?' Why on earth had she left the embarrassing things lying around in plain view?

'Yeah, I'm really sorry. I didn't mean to stick my big nose in or anything.'

Lizzie stopped fiddling with Alex's clothes and let him go. She watched him scamper off, with a regretful pang that she couldn't do likewise.

'Mrs Buckley, they're so good!'

'What?'

'The poems. Honestly. They're great. I think they're really funny.'

Lizzie looked at the bright red, slightly pimpled Sarah in wonder. The wonder was chiefly at the fact that such an unprepossessing person could suddenly afford her such keen joy.

'You liked them?'

'Yeah, yeah. They're really cool. But ... how come they all stop in the middle? Why don't they have proper endings?'

'You really mean it, about liking them? You're not just saying that?'

Sarah began to bite her fingernails. 'Some of them made me laugh until I nearly wet myself,' she said with another shrug. 'But I got sort of frustrated because you never find out what happens in the end. Is there any chance you could quickly finish the one about the boy who lost his hamster during assembly? You got up to the place where the hamster is sitting on the headmaster's shoe, grooming its whiskers, and the whole school can see it except the headmaster.'

'Quickly *finish* it?' Lizzie repeated faintly. 'But I don't really know how it ends.'

By now, they had walked out of the front door and were standing in the lovely late-afternoon light, near the gate. The children had followed them outside and were using Alex's toy fire engine to put out an imaginary blaze among the violas.

'Oh.' Sarah sounded disappointed. 'I thought people who wrote stories and things always had everything planned out before they even started.'

'Well, maybe some people do. But I don't.'

'So you're not going to finish any of them?'

'Well, as a matter of fact, I'm planning to work on them to-night.'

'That's great then. Maybe you'll have the hamster one finished by tomorrow? Well, I'd better get back, Mrs Buckley. Homework to do. Thanks for the dosh.'

That night, Lizzie sat down with the hamster poem, determined to prod it towards some sort of ending.

Alas, it was heavygoing. Her head felt muzzy and her body ached from the run. Only the thought of Sarah turning up expectantly the next day kept her plodding on.

Around ten o clock she gave a frustrated sigh and decided to pack it in for the night. Standing up from the table and stretching, she told herself she'd make a cup of tea and have a little snack before turning in. Mabye the words would flow better in the morning. But as she paced the cold kitchen floor, waiting for the kettle to boil, words and lines began to form effortlessly in her head. She grabbed paper and a pen and started jotting things down, completely forgetting about the tea and chocolate biscuits.

Just before midnight, it was done. She'd written the ending and returned to the beginning to re-write large chunks so that everything would tie in properly. Flushed with the unusual feeling of finishing, Lizzie couldn't help congratulating herself on a job well done. She only hoped Sarah would agree. It would be such a pity to disappoint someone who'd nearly wet her pants laughing at the first version.

From: lizbuckley@hotmail.com
Sent: 20 June
To: janehawthorn@yahoo.com

Dear Janie

Why no word? I'm guessing if there was major news, like premature labour, we'd know.

I'm OK. Been jogging every day this week. It still hurts like hell.

Up at dawn tomorrow to go and pack up the stuff at Mill House. Still can't believe it's really come to this.

Bye now, must sleep. Seem to have kicked the insomnia habit. Knock-on effect of the running. Beginning to feel more human, less zombie.

In haste,

Lizzie

Chapter Eleven

According to the digital clock on the microwave oven at Mill House, it was 11:17 a.m.

Lizzie picked up her mug of tepid tea and went back to the living room, where she'd made considerable progress in stripping away all traces of her personal occupation of the house. One box was already taped shut, full of books, CDs, candles and framed photographs. A second box was beginning to fill up with knick-knacks: a jar of perfect shells collected over a lifetime of beach visits; a couple of handmade plates bearing the imprint of two tiny, pudgy hands.

From above came occasional shrieks of laughter or bellows of rage as the twins re-discovered their bedroom and fought over the treasures still housed there. That room, Lizzie reckoned, was going to take the longest.

Things like china, glassware, cutlery, towels, linen, vases, casserole dishes, silver teapots, even board games were all to be left *in situ*. The idea was to give visiting families a sense of being in a home away from home. But all 'clutter' had to go. To that end, a skip had been rented and stood waiting at the end of the driveway. Anything Lizzie didn't pack or throw away this weekend would be subject to another sort by James (or possibly Sonja) on Monday.

James, apparently, had taken everything he wanted already. Lizzie noticed that he'd removed a quirky wrought-iron wine-rack, shaped like a waiter holding a tray, which she'd once given him as a birthday present. She'd bought it as a joke, really, a good-humoured dig at his irreproachable taste. He must have thought it would offend the house guests.

'Hello.'

He'd come in soundlessly. And why should he knock, walking into his own home?

Lizzie looked up from wrapping a misshapen blue and pink bowl, and caught her breath.

His dark hair was damp, presumably from a shower, and he was wearing a plain white T-shirt that draped softly over the hard planes of his chest, planes that for long years she'd been quite entitled to touch, if the fancy took her. On his feet were the carefree surfer-style sandals she remembered him buying in Greece, ages ago, on their last child-free holiday together.

He'd worn those same sandals the day he'd bought them, putting them on as they sat on a stone wall in the sunshine, sharing an ice cream that melted faster than they could lick it. Suddenly she remembered the exotic little jolt of pleasure as their warm tongues met amid the icy swirls of sweet vanilla.

'You're late.' She spoke quickly, her heart beating hard enough to cause a tiny flap-flap in her T-shirt. When she'd got out of bed at six that morning, she'd meant to follow Tessa's advice and make a bit of an effort with her clothes. But, looking at her reflection in the propped-up bathroom mirror, she'd instantly thought better of wearing the summer dress she'd put out the night before. After all, James had last seen that little number at the church fête, and who wears a party dress to pack up a house, especially one with such a deep decolletage? Much more dignified to wear jeans and a T-shirt. As for her hair, she had at least washed it, and that would have to do.

James gave a rueful shrug. 'Sorry. Got off to a slow start this morning.'

Lizzie bent her head over the ugly little bowl. 'Oh, I didn't mean to criticize. I'm a bit relieved, really. You've always been late – you're on Buckley time, after all. That weekend when you were so punctual, even *early*, was a bit freaky, to be honest.'

'Buckley time' was fifteen minutes slower than Greenwich Mean Time on a good day, twenty minutes slower on a bad day.

'You could put that in the divorce petition,' James said. 'That I was always late for everything.'

Lizzie looked up and met his eyes, then looked away quickly. There was no warmth in his gaze, no laughter. He wasn't kidding.

'Hey, what's that monstrosity?' he asked, looking at the bowl she held. 'Looks familiar. Something of Ellie's?'

Not trusting herself to speak, Lizzie nodded stiffly. Ellie had made the bowl at nursery school for Mothers' Day the year before. Alex had made a pencil holder, a tin covered in green felt. Sniffing it before she packed it, Lizzie could still smell diced tomatoes.

'Right. Well, you'd better get on with things.' James frowned at his watch. 'I'll get the kids. Sounds like they're upstairs? I hope they're going to settle OK in the new house.'

Lizzie said nothing, just carried on packing. So much for stirring up fond memories.

Ten minutes later, Lizzie was waving the children off with an air of hearty good cheer, as if she were sending them on a lovely holiday with her full blessing.

She hoped some small and harmless incident — a trail of broken eggs, a smashed antique vase — would happen at the beginning of the weekend to put James on his mettle.

James was a devoted father, but he was a man. A man was always reading the newspaper when a child dragged a chair across the kitchen, climbed up on the kitchen cabinets, and started dumping flour, rice and spaghetti all over the floor. A man was always watching rugby when a child got hold of a stapler and decided to see whether it was possible to clip together a flap of tummy skin.

Men, it seemed to Lizzie, reserved their powers of peripheral vision solely for playing sports or driving fast cars. This was all well and good, but if James let anything happen to either of the children, she was going to have to kill him.

Two hours later, Lizzie made her way into the master bedroom. It was hard to look at the four-poster bed without remembering the first time she'd seen it, years ago, before she and James were even engaged. They'd been living in each other's pockets for a couple of months when James suddenly invited her to Sunday lunch at the manor, to reacquaint her with his family.

'I don't know if you remember my mother?' he'd asked when he suggested the outing.

'Oh yes. I remember her.'

'Well, you'd better see her in the full light of day, when you're stone-cold sober. Just so's you know what you're getting into.'

They'd both laughed as if he were joking. But Lizzie could still remember the piercing thrill she'd felt at the assumption that she was 'getting into' something. Until that moment, the only assumption she'd made was that she'd better enjoy every moment she spent with James, because his interest couldn't outlast the summer any more than daffodils could outlast the spring.

She couldn't have cared less, at that point, if his mother had been a gargoyle.

In fact, Lady Evelyn Buckley was no gargoyle. In her youth, she'd been beautiful, her long neck, thick eyelashes and haughty mouth giving her the elegance of a scornful giraffe. All the men of her circle had clamoured for her, or so Lizzie gathered as she paged through old photograph albums and scrapbooks in the library at the manor. Fading pictures of tennis tournaments, charity balls, hunt meetings and 'coming out' parties showed Lady Evelyn with a succession of young men, all good-looking, all apparently gratified to be squiring the slim blonde beauty with the pinched-in nostrils and sceptical brow.

Roger Buckley, elegant in sepia tones, didn't appear any more frequently in the photo archive of Lady Evelyn's glorious social career than his rivals. But somehow or other, he'd won through. Perhaps his grace and ease had allowed him to pip everybody to the post. Perhaps his possession of Laingtree Manor had given him the extra cachet he needed to win the hand of the ice princess.

The lunch at the manor that day, all those years ago, had been an excruciating affair, with James trying to protect Lizzie from his mother's version of the Spanish Inquisition, and Lizzie trying to figure out which was the fish knife, which the butter knife, and which the knife most suitable to be aimed at her hostess's jugular.

Apparently, Lizzie's violent fantasies went undetected beneath her demeanour of docility and politeness. As she left the dining room for a quick trip to the loo to apply powder to a face she was sure must be gleaming with the effort of remaining civil, she heard Lady Evelyn say in her carrying voice, 'She doesn't seem *too* bad, does she, Roger? Not abrasive, at any rate, like that brassy Californian. Of course, I can't understand a word she says – she will mumble. And she's very middle-class. What did you say her father does? Some sort of agricultural salesman?'

'Oh, shut up, Mum,' Lizzie heard James say without rancour. But her heart swelled with pride. He'd stood up for her!

After lunch, Lizzie and James escaped into the private grounds, rowdy with relief. As they sat chortling in the wild meadow near the orchard, James took a key from his pocket. 'Come on,' he said, pulling her to her feet. 'I've got something to show you.'

He took her to the cottage she'd already noticed, set in a picture-book garden next to a fast-running stream where an eighteenth-century watermill still turned. As he unlocked the door, he said with simple pride, 'Welcome to my house.'

She was deeply impressed, of course. First, there was the bare fact that he had a house at all. Second, there was the perfection of the house itself.

Mill House looked rather small from the outside, but some cunning architect (she didn't know then that it was James) had knocked down interior walls and added on rooms, so that once inside you had an airy impression of space and a sense of almost limitless possibilities, a bit like the feeling of being in a rambling country hotel and glimpsing archways and doors leading into uncharted territory.

And the furniture! Actually, the furniture scared her. This was furniture with frets and cartouches and finials, pediments and curlicues and floriated scrolls. Lizzie felt very middle-class indeed, gazing at the lovely faded silks and damasks, the velvets and brocatelles, the gleaming tortoiseshell and metal inlays, and thinking of her Mum's blue 1970s sofa and wobbly bamboo drinks cabinet.

James led her from room to room, showing her his favourite pieces and telling her things she couldn't take in about chairs that had to be addressed by name (Louis XIV, Princess Charlotte) and ugly knick-knacks with impeccable pedigrees.

How could he be the owner of such magnificence? It was almost a turn-off. She'd always thought of him as a slightly scruffy frequenter of obscure London pubs. One of the lads. Now he was turning out to be a country property owner and connoisseur of roll-top desks, the sort of person who might easily take over a slot from one of the Sotheby's types on *Antiques Roadshow*. Not really *her* type at all.

'This is the room I really want you to see,' he said, throwing open the door into the master bedroom.

Lizzie had never seen such a bed, not in real life.

It was a massive, tea-brown, Jacobean four-poster draped in dull gold fabric adorned with scarlet lions. The drapes pooled extravagantly on the floor at each corner and were tied back against the posts with heavy, tasselled ropes.

'Oh. My. God,' she said.

He gave a sheepish laugh. 'It's a reproduction, of course. The real ones are too narrow for a kingsize mattress. Would you care to . . . ?' He quirked his eyebrows at the bed.

'To . . . what?'

'You know . . . try the bed?'

In the golden gloom, behind the heavy drapes, Lizzie and James made love with such passion that James managed to rip one of the sheets with his toe.

Of course, Lizzie hadn't known then that the bed, with its carved roses and exquisite linen, was for hire. The house happened to be free of paying guests that weekend. James explained the holiday rental thing to her afterwards as he bundled the linen into the washing machine and scrambled around in closets trying to find a replacement for the ripped sheet.

As they sat waiting for the tumble-dryer to finish, James told Lizzie all about the house, how his father had allowed him to draw up plans to expand and re-design it while he was still an under-graduate; how James had used a small inheritance from his paternal grandmother to fund some of the construction; how his parents had paid a top interior decorator to handle the refurbishment, incorporating many pieces that were already in the family's possession;

and how they'd eventually transformed Mill House into a highly lucrative holiday cottage.

When James graduated from university, his parents' gift to him had been the opportunity to buy the house. His mother had wanted to give it to him outright, but his father insisted that James should come up with some money. 'He was trying to give me an education as much as a house,' James explained. The asking price had been ridiculously low, but it was still substantial. James had been stretched to organize a loan at all, young and inexperienced as he was.

'Dad deliberately gave me no help at all with that end of things,' he remarked cheerfully. 'He was even obstructive, telling his own bank manager not to deal with me. He wouldn't stand guarantor, and he set a time limit on how long I had to raise the money. A month.'

'But you did it,' Lizzie said with pride, looking around the luxurious kitchen, its lustrous panelling concealing the humdrum gleam of household appliances.

Many women might have sat at that enviable scrubbed oak kitchen table in a frenzy of covetousness. Not Lizzie. Even though he'd introduced her to his parents, Lizzie knew in her heart that she had slightly less than a snowball's chance in Saudi Arabia of ever hanging onto James Buckley for the long haul. She was just glad to be there, in that moment, still flushed from their romp on the four-poster, cradling a cup of James's trademark strong, sweet bricklayer's tea.

'Yeah, I did it,' said James. An odd look flitted over his face. Indigestion, Lizzie wondered, or an unpleasant memory?

Later, as they made the bed, flicking the freshly laundered sheets up into the air between them, Lizzie suddenly asked, 'Who's the brassy Californian?'

She hadn't meant to ask at all. Had planned *not* to ask. But the question simply popped out of her mouth of its own volition.

James stopped shaking out the sheet for a moment. 'The brassy...?' His brow crinkled.

'Your mum reckons I'm *slightly* better than some brassy Californian you used to bring round,' Lizzie said patiently.

'Oh . . . I went out with an American girl for a while. Mum never took to her.'

'Goodness, you astonish me. And your mother so easy to please. So, where did you meet her?'

'London. She was from Santa Barbara, doing some kind of study year abroad.'

'Oh? So she was only here a year?'

'Well, as a matter of fact, she stayed on a bit longer.'

'How much longer?'

'A year or so.'

'Was she pretty?'

'Boot-faced and bandy-legged. Now, is the interrogation over?' He grabbed a feather pillow and gave her a playful clubbing.

Naturally, she seized her own pillow and began clubbing him back. Feathers flew, and, in the excitement of the tussle, a corner of James's pillow, which, for some reason, had a coin sewn into it, caught Lizzie hard in the eye, instantly giving her a shiner. This was rather difficult to explain away when they dutifully trooped back to the manor for a cup of tea before James's dad drove them both to the railway station.

How fondly Lizzie always remembered that eye injury. James had been absolutely stricken. He'd held ice to her face with such tenderness – a big man hunched down over a kitchen chair, face stiff with remorse – that Lizzie had known there and then she'd never be able to stop loving him.

The eye had remained swollen for a couple of days. She'd booked off sick, not too devastated to be missing another day in front of the computer screen with G. H. Brightman and Associates, the public relations company she worked for.

Of course, she'd told G. H. Brightman she had pink eye. Better a childhood disease than a black eye from the boyfriend, no matter how playfully inflicted.

In those days, James was the mere employee of a busy firm of architects based in Ealing Broadway. He took a long lunch that Monday, turning up at the flat with, among other things, an eye patch, a box of maximum strength pain-killers, a bunch of the kind of pale ivory lilies that sprinkle brown pollen stains everywhere, a bottle of wine, a loaf of French bread, and several different cheeses.

She and Tessa lived off cheese for days afterwards, Lizzie remembered.

But the memories were slowing her down. How long had she been sitting on the bed with the drapes drawn, cradling a pillow?

And how long had the doorbell been ringing?

The visitor was her father-in-law. He sauntered into the house, swinging his ridiculous monocle and looking about him with that faintly amused air she'd always found a bit daunting.

'Making progress?' he asked, running his eyes over the jumble of boxes.

Lizzie shrugged. 'Sort of,' she mumbled.

'Evelyn's after some tupperware container she once lent you. Leftovers from a meal up at the manor, apparently.' He raised his eyebrows ruefully, and, for the millionth time, Lizzie thought how much he looked like James. An older, more worldly, vastly disillusioned James.

'Oh. Tupperware? I don't remember. Let's have a look.' No need to ask why Lady Evelyn hadn't come herself. From the moment James had turned up at the manor with his suitcase, Evelyn had excommunicated Lizzie from the church of Buckley.

Lizzie went into the kitchen and pulled out a drawer. Although she'd already cleared away most of the plastic, several containers and a jumble of lids still remained.

'It could be any of these,' Lizzie said. They both contemplated the drawer in silence. Roger Buckley even raised his monocle to get a better look, then let it fall and gave a fastidious shudder.

'Oh, just give me one or two of the better-looking ones,' he said. 'God knows, whatever I take back is bound to be the wrong thing.'

Lizzie found a plastic bag and dumped a handful of containers and lids into it. 'Here, give her a wide selection. Rich Americans don't want to be storing leftovers, I'm sure.'

He gave a brief chuckle. 'I'm going to miss you, Lizzie,' he said regretfully. 'Miss you like the devil. Do you really have to go? Was my boy such a dead loss?'

Lizzie wished fervently that he'd shut up. She could feel her eyes going hot and prickly. If the tears couldn't be suppressed, she'd have to bolt to the loo with a fake sneezing fit or something. 'He wasn't a dead loss at all,' she said. 'He was ... well, he was great, if you want to know.'

'Really?' Roger was carefully looking for lint on the lapels of his tweed jacket; a very absorbing task, apparently. 'He swears he wasn't messing about with other women, by the way. I asked him point-blank.'

'What?' The question came out as a squeak.

He put down the bag of tupperware, pulled out a kitchen chair and sat down with a weary sigh. 'Yes, I asked him. Wanted to get to the bottom of it all. The whole thing makes no sense to me, and I can't abide mysteries. Why would he leave you? Why would you want him to? You two have always been so ... so *happy*. So I thought to myself, if that boy of mine has gone and flushed away his marriage for the sake of a quick ... Well, you get my drift. I was going to give him what for.'

Lizzie gazed at her father-in-law in amazement. 'What were you planning to do? Cane him?'

He gave a lopsided grin. 'You flatter me, Lizzie. He's a decade or two too old for a caning, but I'd have sorted him out.' He looked down at his well-manicured hands and slowly clenched them into fists. 'Rest assured, I'd have sorted him out. He'd have come back to you on hands and knees.'

Lizzie just shook her head, completely at a loss for words.

Roger leant forward and patted Lizzie's lifeless hand where it lay on the kitchen table. 'So anyway, I wanted to let you know he hasn't been cheating on you,' he said. 'In case you had your suspicions. In case that was the problem.'

'It wasn't the problem.'

'So I gather. Well, is the shoe on the other foot, then? Have you been messing about with some chap? Evelyn seems to think so.'

Lizzie snorted. She could just imagine Lady Evelyn's comments on the subject. 'Of course, I haven't been messing about! Bloody hell! I'm a married women with a pair of children to keep track of. I don't have time to go to the *toilet* by myself, let alone go sneaking off for any extramarital quickies.'

Roger laughed gently. 'Don't get all worked up, my girl. That's exactly what I told Evelyn. Plus I happen to think you're rather fond of our boy. So, if that's not it, what the devil is it?'

Lizzie rubbed her face and tucked some stray hair behind her ear. 'I ... I really can't tell you, Roger. It's complicated. And it's ... well, it's between the two of us.'

'It's between more than the two of you. What about Ellie and Alex?'

'They're fine, thank you very much.'

Roger stood up slowly and shrugged his elegant shoulders. 'All right,' he said. 'All right. But just you be sure you know what you're doing, Lizzie. Just don't let the game get away from you. The stakes are pretty bloody high.' Then he turned, picked up his tupperware and let himself out of the house.

Lizzie's friend, Maria Dennison, and her fiancé, Laurence Hendershott, lived in a small house in Laingtree village. Maria and Laurence had caused a mild scandal in the village five years ago, when he'd moved in with her, selling his flat in Cheltenham and parking his tiny car in her driveway, alongside the well-known black convertible she'd been driving around the countryside for years.

It wasn't so much that Maria and Laurence hadn't bothered to get married. It was more that nobody had expected Maria to pull a boyfriend out of the hat in the first place. People had expected Maria to soldier on alone in her small house, perhaps accompanied by a ginger cat or sensible dog, growing ever so slightly more eccentric as the years went by.

Maria, the only vet in a five-mile radius, worked out of a tiny animal hospital next door to the doctor's surgery, just across from her house. Lizzie had liked her from the moment they'd been introduced at the annual church fête, the summer she and James got married. Maria had looked so straightforward and no-nonsense in her jeans and T-shirt, with her honest brown hair caught back in a school-girlish pony-tail. But Lizzie only got to know her well after Laurence moved in with her, because Laurence and James, who met playing cricket for the local team that summer, took to each other immediately.

Laurence was a big quiet man with a full beard and warm eyes – the sort of chap you'd want to be stranded on a desert island with, not because he was sexy, but because he looked as if he'd know how to make a cabin out of palm trees, or quickly knock together a seaworthy raft out of dried rushes, or catch a tuna with his bare hands. Disappointingly, he worked as an actuary, a job that sounded so stupefyingly dull that Lizzie always forebore to ask him anything about it.

The Buckleys had spent many evenings with Maria and Laurence, preferring to lounge around in their untidy kitchen eating Laurence's goulash than to attend the smart dinner parties of the young married set in Laingtree and surrounding villages.

Lizzie had last seen Maria on the miserably cold day she'd left Laingtree for Sevenoaks. That day, while Lizzie raced about shoving things into suitcases and boxes, Maria had distracted the children with games and new toys. She'd even provided ham and cheese sandwiches (for Alex and Ellie), not to mention tissues, aspirins and Rescue Remedy (for Lizzie). Just the sight of Maria sitting calmly on an old blanket in the garden, doing her level best to keep the twins away from their frantic mother, had brought tears of gratitude to Lizzie's eyes.

Now, as Lizzie drew up alongside Maria's house, she felt a sort of shyness come over her. It was so long since they'd seen each other face to face, and Lizzie had left in such high drama. She felt slightly silly to be back again, so tamely, and with nothing resolved.

But as she opened the car door, Maria was already walking down the garden path to meet her.

'Lizzie! Christ, it's good to see you. It's been like a morgue around here without you lot. Come on, let's get you inside with your feet up and a drink in your hands. Sorry I didn't pop round to the cottage today. I was working flat out. Saturday's my busy day, of course. Most people can only get their creatures in to see me after work or over the weekend.'

Maria normally didn't chatter so much, bless her, but she was obviously trying to give Lizzie time to deal with her watery eyes.

In the kitchen, Laurence hailed her with a silently raised glass of Guinness, then set about pouring a stiff gin and tonic. As usual, dinner – poached Atlantic salmon with a white wine sauce – was better than most meals you'd get in a restaurant. But for the first time ever in that kitchen, Lizzie found the dinner conversation stilted. Laurence was trying very hard not to mention James, and Maria kept telling long stories about various beasts she'd treated in the last month or so, which made Lizzie uneasy because Maria didn't generally talk much about her work.

When the plates had been cleared, Laurence stood up, flexed his grizzly bear shoulders, and said, 'I'll take a stroll down to the pub, then. See you later.' Lizzie could have hugged him for his heavy-handed tact.

The minute he was out of the door, Maria stopped fussing with the dishwasher and came back to the table, glass of white wine in hand.

'So how are you *really*, Liz?' she asked. 'You don't look too bad. Bit of colour in your cheeks, at least.'

Lizzie shrugged. 'I'm OK,' she said. 'Keeping my head above water. Has ... has Laurence seen much of James?'

'Oh, he sees him once in a while. James pulled out of the cricket for the season, did you know? But Laurence calls him up now and then, asks him round to the pub.'

'Has he been round here? To dinner, or anything?'

Maria nodded, her pony-tail bobbing. 'Once or twice.'

Lizzie could feel a pulse beginning to beat in her throat. 'Has he ever, erm, has he ever brought anyone with him?'

Maria looked at her with calm compassion. 'No,' she said. 'He always comes alone.'

The relief made Lizzie grin like a lunatic. 'That's great. That's fantastic. Look, would you do me a favour? Keep on asking him over, and if he ever shows up with someone – you know, a woman – let me know. OK?'

Maria swirled the wine in her glass, then took a slow sip. 'You're asking me to spy on him?'

'Well, not exactly *spy*. Just keep me posted. If he starts seeing someone, I think I'm entitled to know.'

'Wouldn't he tell you?'

Lizzie shrugged. 'I don't know. His PA, Sonja, I don't think you've ever met her, seems to be cosying up to him. I swear I've had more conversations with Sonja recently about the children and Mill House than I've had with James.'

'He's never said anything about her to me. I'll ask Laurence if he ever mentions the name.'

'So, you're going to spy for me?'

Maria sipped her wine again, then gave a big, slow smile. 'I'll do it if you'll do something for me.'

'What?'

'Start looking after yourself again. Do something with that hair. Put on a bit of make-up. Sit up and take a bit of notice.'

Later on, Lizzie took a long, thoughtful soak in the tub. Maria had given her carte blanche to use whatever bathroom supplies took her fancy. Bemused by the range – who'd have thought Maria would be a connoisseur of bath products? – Lizzie found herself trying out a sea salt and ginger exfoliating cream. As she rinsed off, she had a sudden image of herself as an elderly lizard shedding an even more elderly skin. Finding a slightly rusted plastic razor in her own toiletry bag, she set to work on her legs and armpits, half-fearful that she'd clog the plug with the thickets of excess hair that were coming off. How odd. She couldn't have looked at her own armpits for weeks, possibly months.

As she snuggled down in the narrow bed in Maria's spare room, Lizzie was astonished at how smooth the sheets felt against her bare legs. She was put in mind of the first time she'd ever shaved her legs, when she was about thirteen, and her worn old cotton sheets had suddenly felt like satin.

Drifting off to sleep under Maria's down duvet, Lizzie was visited by a minor revelation. It was suddenly crystal clear to her that the mums of Chipstead nursery hadn't shunned her in the beginning because they'd spotted at a glance that she suffered from terminal personality defects. No. They'd shunned her because she looked like a bag lady. But then they'd found out about her broken marriage, and everything had changed. Because a woman whose husband has walked out on her has a right to hairy legs and greasy hair and unlaundered clothes.

The relief of finally solving this riddle was balm to Lizzie's troubled soul. With a little smile playing about her lips, she fell into a deep and healing sleep.

The work at Mill House went quickly the next day, with Maria there to help. By two in the afternoon, Lizzie had thrown away or bagged up for charity almost as much as she'd packed. As she and Maria stood gazing at the rubbish piled up in the skip, Lizzie felt an unexpected sense of relief and even virtue, as if she'd purged herself of past folly and was not only cleansed but also, in some weird sense, free to start all over again.

Throwing a last bag of odds and ends onto the pile, Lizzie rubbed her hands together in satisfaction. 'Done,' she said. 'Let's go back and celebrate.'

As they pulled away, Lizzie looked out of her rearview mirror at Mill House. 'It was always too postcard-pretty for me, anyway,' she said.

Maria, wedged among the black bags of clothes and toys bound for Oxfam, wisely said nothing at all.

Out in Maria's small, untidy back garden, as they sat sipping Earl Grey and eating HobNobs straight from the bag, Maria suddenly asked, 'You're still coming to the wedding, right?'

Lizzie almost choked on a wodge of biscuit. 'Christ! The wedding!'

Maria pulled a face. 'Come on, Lizzie, don't tell me you've forgotten about it?'

Lizzie took a quick slug of tea. 'Forgotten? Good grief, of course not. It's just ... I hadn't really thought about it much lately.'

'Well, that's not surprising, really. Anyway, Laurence says James is still prepared to be best man.'

Lizzie's eyes began to bulge. She knew what was coming next.

'Are you still OK with matron of honour?'

Maria and Laurence were getting married at the end of August. She'd known this for almost a year now. The date had always seemed so hazily distant that she'd shelved it away in her mind as something to be thought about much, much later. But she did, of course, remember, quite clearly now that Maria mentioned it, that she'd promised to play the bride's side-kick. Maria had asked her in September last year, in this very garden, over cocktails and a lovely dip made with cream cheese, pesto and sun-dried tomatoes. Lizzie even remembered how apologetic Maria had been about not including the twins in the wedding as flower girl and page boy. 'Only we've decided to make it an evening thing, no kids allowed,' she'd explained, slightly red in the face.

Back then, Lizzie had no inkling that, by the following summer, it would be awkward for her to play matron of honour to Laurence's choice of best man.

Lizzie took a deep breath. 'Bloody hell, Maria. You're not going to hold me to it?'

Maria gave her most winning smile. 'No, sweetheart, of course not. Not if you don't want me to.'

'But?'

'But I'd still love you to do it, obviously. I mean, if you're coming to the wedding anyway, why not be matron of honour?'

'Shit, Maria. Tongues will be flapping.'

'Tongues are always flapping. It's the nature of tongues. All kinds of people know you're supposed to be matron of honour. They'll think you chickened out if you don't do it.'

'Yeah, well, I *feel* like chickening out.'

'OK, it's your decision. But I'll give you till the end of the week. If I don't hear from you by then, I'll ask someone else.'

'Who?' Lizzie was curious. It seemed to her that Maria didn't have any confidantes in Laingtree, besides herself.

'What, you think I don't have any mates?' Maria asked with

mock indignation. 'Don't worry, I can rustle up a substitute, even at short notice. But if you are going to do it, you'll need to have dress fittings and so on.'

Lizzie studied her friend a moment. It was so odd to hear sensible, denim-clad Maria say 'dress fittings'.

'What made you decide to get married?' she asked suddenly. 'You and Laurence. Why do you feel you need that piece of paper? It's not public pressure, surely? I mean, apart from a few old bats, nobody thinks twice about you living together, do they?'

Maria put her tea cup down carefully. 'It's not the piece of paper,' she said. Pulling her pony-tail over her shoulder, she began to stroke it gently. 'We're getting married because we want to. Well, I suppose there're two things we want. We want the big party, the celebration of us being a couple. And then we want the total commitment of marriage.'

Lizzie frowned, still puzzled. 'But you *are* totally committed. Have been for years. Everybody knows it. And, well, I just thought you were so unconventional. I didn't think you'd go in for the wedding dress and the wedding cake and all that stuff. It just doesn't seem like *you*. Oh, and by the way, who says marriage is about total commitment? Look at me and James.'

Maria shook her head. 'You and James. Somebody needs to bash your heads together, that's all I can say. But anyway, think about the matron of honour thing. I'd really like to have you. No pressure, of course.'

Lizzie gave a crooked grin. 'No pressure at all. Look, I don't need a week to think about it. I'll do it, of course I will.'

Chapter Twelve

Standing with Tessa amidst a crowd of restless runners, some jogging on the spot, others stretching and lungeing, Lizzie forgot all about Sarah and the children on a picnic blanket under an oak tree somewhere, eating Smarties. Her heart was galloping and her hands were slick with sweat as she wrung them together anxiously.

She couldn't believe it. She, Lizzie Buckley, was in a race. A race!

She felt as jittery as a thoroughbred at Ascot for the first time. Perhaps she'd astonish everybody and take off like a greyhound, leaving far more seasoned runners coughing in her dust. The way she felt at this moment, anything was possible!

'Lizzie!'

'What?'

'Lizzie, get moving? We're off! They've started us!'

'Oh God, I didn't hear the whistle.'

'Just get moving! Come on!'

Lizzie felt as if the crowd were sweeping her along, without any effort from her own legs. The throng of runners was moving as one, a human wave, carrying Lizzie in its midst like a piece of flotsam. It was marvellous! She'd be able to run like this for hours, let alone the thirty or so minutes required to finish the five kilometres.

The runners streamed effortlessly down the valley towards Knole House, picking up speed on the descent.

'Don't go too fast,' Tessa shouted over to her. 'You'll burn out.'

'No bloody fear,' Lizzie yelled back. 'I could keep this up all day.' And she ran like the wind, strong and free.

Then, all of a sudden, they were faced with a sheer cliff of a climb. No longer did Lizzie feel that the runners all around her were sweeping her easily along in a human tide. Instead, she began to feel like a big boulder in a riverbed with a flood swirling by on either side.

'You're doing really well,' Tessa called back over her shoulder. 'Just keep breathing in through your nose, out through your mouth.'

'Shut up,' Lizzie panted back.

But soon enough Tessa had to slow to a virtual walk to allow Lizzie to catch up. When they were within earshot of each other, Lizzie begged, 'Don't wait for me, Tess. Please. Go on.'

'You sure?'

'I'm sure. Run! I want to do it in my own time.'

'OK.'

Lizzie watched in admiration as her friend accelerated away out of sight. Poor Tessa had no hope of making a decent time, now.

The runners had thinned out at the back. Lizzie was keeping pace with an elite group now: a seriously old chap whose shorts seemed to be tucked under his armpits; a pudgy girl of about ten; and a heavyset woman of indeterminate age who wore bandages around one ankle and both knees.

But the spectators cheered them on as if they were in *Chariots of Fire*. That was the lovely thing. Every time they rounded a corner and puffed into sight of the people dotted around on picnic blankets under trees, they were met with a burst of applause and many hoarse cries of encouragement: 'You can do it! Don't give up! Keep going! Nearly there now!'

Even the deer seemed to gaze after them with newfound respect as they hobbled by.

Lizzie didn't come absolutely last. The octogenarian slowed to a walk in the last hundred metres, and she pipped him to the post.

She was feeling quite proud of herself, standing about in her sweaty running gear with the other competitors after the race, sipping a sports drink and discussing the course, until Ellie piped up, 'Mummy, did you win?' And she was forced to admit that no, she hadn't won, and no, she hadn't come second or third, or even tenth or twentieth.

'Din't you come *anywhere?*' Alex asked in amazement.

'Of course she came somewhere,' Tessa said with a little snort. 'She came second last.'

Even at three, the twins knew what second last meant.

They gazed at her in silence.

Then Ellie said, 'Is that the very bestest you can do, Mummy?'

Lizzie made a vow then and there. She didn't know if she'd ever run five kilometres in less than forty-five minutes, but she was going to try. She was pretty sure that vying for last place with an old-age pensioner and a schoolgirl was by no means her personal best.

'This is Petronella,' Tessa said one evening, casually flapping a hand at the petite woman in a purple tracksuit who stood at Lizzie's gate, holding onto the fence for balance as she bent one leg up behind her and tugged on it in a businesslike way. 'She's thinking about the London Marathon, too.'

Lizzie made an effort to wipe the slight frown from her brow. 'Hi there,' she called brightly. Petronella? What kind of a poncey name was *that*, for heaven's sake?

The woman waved back but didn't pause in her stretches. Sketching a few quick lunges herself, Lizzie snatched more covert glances at the stranger. She was little and delicate, and very thin. Her dark hair was worn in a boyish, cropped cut that made her green eyes look huge. Tendrils of hair curled around pixie-like ears. Lizzie wondered if such a fragile-looking person could actually run.

Lizzie herself *could* now actually run.

Ever since the 5K fun run at Knole Park, running had taken on a whole new meaning.

She was used to making vows and then turning a blind eye on herself as she broke them. She was an avid New Year's Resolutionist, and her favourite resolution had always been to Lose Weight. She'd been resolving to do so since the age of, oh, twelve or thirteen, with indifferent results. She'd had lean years, certainly, but the fat years seemed to outweigh them, especially latterly.

The vow to become a decent runner was a first. And, for one reason or another, it seemed to be sticking.

No longer did she stretch her imagination for Tessa-proof excuses to skip her runs; no longer did she hope to turn an ankle or develop a mild case of asthma that would make running impossible. On the contrary, she was finally getting used to the dry taste of exhaustion. She knew how to push beyond it now. She'd also come to tolerate, even to relish, the mid-run sensation that someone was sandpapering the inside of her lungs while she waded through hot molten fudge.

Lizzie was astounded by her own progress, as the weeks passed by. It was such a pleasure to pound along beside Tessa, matching pace for pace yet still able to hold a conversation without puffing as if she only had half a lung. As her body rose to the unexpected challenge, Lizzie found herself *liking* it in a way she'd never dreamed possible. Most of her life, frankly, she'd felt her body was a bit of a liability.

Of course, she'd gained a new respect for her body when it went into overdrive and produced twins, but she hadn't felt immediately connected to the work at hand. In fact, her body had seemed perfectly able to manufacture fingernails, earlobes and eyelashes without the slightest need for any input from the conscious Lizzie Buckley. And, distressingly, all this activity had seemed to call for even deeper layers of body fat.

Now, the boot was on the other foot. The conscious Lizzie Buckley was pushing her body to its limits, and, bless it, her body was working away to make the necessary changes to accommodate these new expectations. Her lung capacity had increased, her resting pulse rate had decreased, her breasts had resigned themselves to being bound flat every day, and, the cherry on top, she was now sporting more muscle than body fat.

She couldn't understand why the world wasn't on fire with the joys and rewards of running. The first weeks of training had been unspeakable, of course. In those early days, she'd roll out of bed and groan, wondering why she didn't remember being run over by a bus or falling out of a moving train. But once she'd outrun those first aches and pains, her whole life seemed to swing suddenly upwards into a clear new place where the view was better, the air sweeter and the colours inexplicably brighter.

'You have more energy,' Tessa told her matter-of-factly when she tried to explain the upward-swing phenomenon. 'Of course you're going to feel better.'

Lizzie had never realized that energy was such a component of mood. Perhaps energy was really what happiness was made of; perhaps if you felt strong and full of vigour, even a day in the garden pulling up weeds was a good, sweet day. Maybe the experience of falling in love shot you chock-full of energy, and that's what made you want to sing and dance and stay up all night doing the business.

Maybe, oh Christ, maybe everything was simpler than she thought. Maybe her marriage had really fallen apart because her energy had simply ebbed away, as if she'd been on a slow bleed ever since the twins were born.

Nowadays, Lizzie was taking all the herbal remedies, vitamins and iron pills Tessa had given her when she first came to Sevenoaks. She tended her body like a slightly temperamental furnace that needed constant stoking with choice kindling. She wanted it to burn at optimum speed, not too fast, not too slowly, because she wanted to run, run, run.

She'd even changed her approach to food. 'God, you're becoming a complete pain in the backside,' Tessa snorted as they toured Waitrose, Lizzie painstakingly reading every food label and rejecting anything that was too high in salt, sugar, preservatives, fat, red food colouring, or any ominous-sounding chemical. She was vetoing all kinds of blameless foods until Tessa told her that ascorbic acid was really vitamin C and selenium was actually good for you.

Nowadays, when the children had gone to bed, she either worked on her nonsense verses or immersed herself in the running literature Tessa had brought over to Back Lane Cottage weeks ago. With the zeal of the newly converted, she was taking all the advice about nutrition very much to heart. It was so much easier to be virtuous about food now that she was working towards a goal, now that a tiny voice in her head said that maybe, just maybe she'd be able to manage at least a *half*-marathon next summer without being borne away through the crowds on a stretcher.

She hadn't yet told Tessa about her modest hopes. Tessa's own running ambitions were burning very bright. Even though the real marathon training wouldn't begin for months, she was pushing herself hard, often running before work in order to stuff more miles into the week. 'I'd better not bloody fall pregnant now,' she said one evening as they slogged through a light drizzle, mud splattering their calves. 'I'm going to run this bloody marathon in under three hours if it kills me.'

Lizzie played the game. 'Yeah, heaven *forbid* you should fall pregnant now. It'd be *years* before you'd be fit to try again, and by then you might be too exhausted to give it your best shot. Best you start taking some precautions, you and Greg.'

Tessa grinned. 'Steady, Lizzie,' she said. 'Fate's not an idiot, you know. Fate knows the difference between being tempted and being *taunted*.'

Lizzie didn't have the nerve to tempt Fate on her own behalf, let alone taunt it. She feared that the minute she opened her mouth to announce she was thinking of having a bash at a half-marathon, Fate would give a giant guffaw and immediately strike her down with a sprained ankle or shin splints. So she kept quiet and bided her time.

As for Tessa's thin and snooty friend Petronella, she'd heard the name before, but couldn't quite remember in what context. Lizzie had certainly never seen her behind the counter at Boots.

But as the three of them took off down the lane, feet pounding rhymically on the hard-packed dirt, Tessa said conversationally, 'You'll never guess where Petronella and I met, Lizzie.'

'Where?'

Petronella shook her cropped head. 'In a doctor's waiting room, actually,' she said in a bored voice that discouraged further discussion.

But Tessa wasn't easily discouraged. 'Yeah, back when Pet was trying to figure out what was up with her ovaries. You've certainly moved on since then, huh?'

Petronella shot Tessa a dark look. 'Don't know if I'd call it moving on.' Without looking at Lizzie, she said, 'I'm divorced now, so I'm out of the whole infertility-doctor scene, thank *God.*'

Lizzie was silenced by the bitterness in her voice.

Tessa suddenly picked up the pace until the other two were stretching to keep up. Without the slightest sign of exertion, she then remarked, 'You two have so much in common, you know – the running, the marriage issues, and you both go to Ivana. That's why I thought you should meet.'

'Gosh, thanks, you're so thoughtful,' Lizzie hissed. So *this* was Tessa's loopy friend!

Petronella simply glared ahead, her face apparently clenched in pain. Would that be a stitch, Lizzie wondered, or just general misery at the turn the conversation was taking?

'So, have you heard anything from your divorce lawyer recently?' Tessa asked Lizzie, perhaps in a bid to make Petronella feel better, on the commonly-held assumption that misery loves company.

'Yes, we've had a couple of conversations. I'm still working on the petition.' Lizzie was taking for ever to eke out a few paragraphs that would convince the court that James was guilty of unreasonable behaviour: '*He had a nasty habit of brushing his teeth in the shower. He always threw his clothes on the floor instead of into the hamper. He didn't believe I could read a map. He didn't like me to phone him at work. He said he thought I'd never make a true golfer. His mother looked down her nose at me.*'

Tessa shook her head. 'I still can't believe this whole thing.' She turned to Petronella, who'd started to exhale in a loud steady hiss through her mouth as she scissored her slender arms back and forth. 'This woman is married to one of the nicest men on the face of the earth. And one of the sexiest. She has one stupid misunderstanding with him, and now it's all up in flames.'

Petronella looked Lizzie up and down. 'The trouble with having a sexy man is you can't afford to let yourself go,' she remarked with a sniff. 'I bet you were thirty pounds lighter when you got married.'

Lizzie was speechless. Talk about random acts of bitchiness.

Petronella went on, 'My ex is drop-dead gorgeous. Never

thought *anything* could come between us. But this whole baby thing – it just blew us out of the water, in the end.'

'They say it's hard to get pregnant if you're too *thin*,' Lizzie muttered.

Petronella shrugged. 'It wasn't my weight,' she said. 'It was ... oh God, I don't feel like explaining. Tessa, you tell her.'

Tessa shook her head gravely. 'Every now and then, apparently, a woman's, erm, cervical mucus takes against a certain type of semen. Sort of goes into attack mode when that kind of sperm shoots into the tubes and makes a dash for the egg. How did the doctor put it again? Oh yes. He said Pet's fluids were *hostile* to her husband's best efforts. The mucus was simply murdering the poor bloody sperm on contact.'

Lizzie looked at Tessa, aghast. OK, so Petronella *was* a bit hostile, but you didn't joke about this sort of thing. 'Come off it, Tessa,' she protested.

'She's not kidding,' Petronella said. 'Bloody twisted, isn't it? What hope did we have with that kind of stuff going on?'

'Couldn't they sort of *disarm* your, erm, mucus?' Lizzie asked.

'Yeah, they suggested *in vitro*, but by that time *we* were too hostile to go through with it.' Petronella managed a small, painful laugh at her own joke.

Ah, sense of humour. *That* must be what Tessa saw in her.

The running was doing Lizzie so much good that she felt the need to show her new self off to the maddening, sheep-like Ivana. Striding into the little office one morning, she deliberately shunned the bean-bag and claimed the kitchen chair instead.

'Hello again, Lizzie,' said Ivana. 'Long time no see. You have more issues? Same issues?'

Lizzie sucked in her stomach and squared her shoulders. 'Actually,' she said, 'I just dropped in to give you a tip or two.'

Ivana flashed her spectacles and took up her diary. 'Ah?'

'You want to tell the unfortunates who come in here that most of their "issues" would go away if they'd just get up off the sofa and go running.'

'Ah?'

'Yes. Look at me! Can't you see the difference? I'm a new person! I'm fit and I'm lean and I'm much, much happier.'

Ivana lowered her glasses and peered at Lizzie with the disconcerting periwinkle blue eyes. 'You have lost the weight?' she asked doubtfully.

Lizzie bridled. 'Of course I've lost weight! Can't you tell? But that's not the only thing. I'm full of endorphins now. Just bursting with them. You know all about endorphins, right? The hormones your body sprays around when you start exercising too much? To deaden the pain of all the exercising? Anyway, they make you feel a lot happier, I can tell you. As a therapist you should be *prescribing* that people go running.'

'I see.' Ivana found a pen and noted something down. From her vantage point on the kitchen chair, Lizzie found she could now see the pages of the familiar diary. She narrowed her eyes and tried to read the spidery letters.

'So altogether I'm in a much more positive frame of mind,' Lizzie insisted. Really, Ivana could at least acknowledge her client's progress in some obvious way – pat her on the back or give her a high five. Maybe just look up and crack a decent smile for once in her life. But Ivana just kept writing. Lizzie peered at the book. She made out a loopy E and maybe an X.

'Yes?' Ivana murmured in a preoccupied sort of way.

'Yes. And I've been thinking.' Lizzie cleared her throat. 'Tessa's right. I'm pretty sure I gave up on James too easily. I mean, maybe I turned out to be a bit of a dud for him, but ... but I *know* he loves the children, and he *used* to love me. So, I'm thinking maybe I could persuade him to give things another shot if I could just convince him that I really haven't been myself since the twins were born. That e-mail I sent him about needing a break from being married—'

Ivana paused in her notes. 'E-mail? You sent him e-mail?'

Lizzie heaved a deep sigh. 'Yes. I didn't tell you because, well, I thought it would complicate your take on the marriage. But the thing is, this whole crisis blew up in the first place because I sent him an e-mail that was supposed to go to my sister, Janie. *Accidentally* sent it, of course. I was having a bit of a rant – you know, wishing I could switch lives with a single woman, going on about how I'd rather have a cup of tea in front of the telly than go to bed with him. Just ... just the usual stuff.'

Ivana removed her glasses and gave Lizzie her undivided attention.

'Please to continue,' she said.

'Well, he didn't like it, obviously. Couldn't understand that it was all just hot air. Talked about not wanting us to end up like his parents. They have separate rooms at the manor, you see. Anyway, it was all nonsense, but I couldn't make him *see*—'

'Ah.' The glasses were back on. 'You were angry when you wrote this – this ranting?'

'Angry? Well, I suppose. I must've been.'

'Why angry?'

'Oh, I don't know. Things were just getting too much for me. For one thing, he was always travelling so he could never help with anything at home. He was the breadwinner, his sleep was sacred, so he never got up to deal with the fall-out at two o'clock in the bloody morning. So I felt a bit like a single mum anyway, without any of the perks. And, well, I've already told you about his mother poking her nose into things all the time.'

'A-ha!' cried Ivana. 'Lots of anger, lots of blame. You need to introspect this rages. This anger is good, it helps you understand.'

Lizzie took a shaky breath.

'This is usual in the marriage,' Ivana was explaining. She seemed rather excited. 'This is the old, old struggle of man and woman. But I'm thinking you never spoke of these things with James.'

'No, of course I didn't. I didn't want to be a nag.'

'But this anger becomes like exploding device if you are bottling it up. You need to open the bottle.'

'Yes, but can we get back to the depression? I'd like to concentrate on the depression more. You see, I've been thinking that if you could, maybe, give me a bit of paper, a letter or something, saying I was definitely depressed at the time? Then I could show it to him, and he'd finally *understand* about that stupid bloody e-mail, that it wasn't the gospel truth or even close, and maybe he'd give me another chance.'

Ivana put down her diary. She took off her glasses. She stood up and held out her arms. Lizzie, taken by surprise, stood up too and took a couple of stumbling steps towards the woman. The next thing she knew, her nose was smooshed up against a woolly shoulder, and Ivana was patting her gently on the back. Not the sort of back-pat she'd been hoping for when she bounced into the office, but still.

'My poor girl,' Ivana was murmuring. 'I will give you a piece of paper, yes, but this will not solve. Only talk will solve. You need to *talk* to this husband. You need to speak of the rage inside. The rage is normal, many women have the rage, many times it is part of the loving. Maybe this husband loves you still, maybe no. For sure, he thinks you love him no more. You need to tell him what is for real in your heart.'

Lizzie was sniffling and nodding, torn between acute discomfort, because she could smell the garlicky, lavendery smell of this old woman who was more or less a stranger, and deep gratitude, because her shoulder was so broad and accommodating.

The patting stopped and Lizzie straightened. Just for a moment, before she pulled out of Ivana's grasp, her eyes fell on the open diary. She was able to make out the words 'exercise addiction' and an emphatic question mark.

That night, as Lizzie crept into the children's room to tuck them in one last time, she couldn't help but stand and gaze, struck by an unusual sense of how lucky she was to have these two small, impossibly demanding, impossibly lovable persons to care for.

After all, Ivana might think that she, Lizzie, was a desperate case, lurching from protracted post-partum depression straight into outright exercise addiction, but to her children, she knew, she was all-powerful, all-knowing and without flaw (well, if you discounted her inability to win fun runs).

Asleep, the twins looked blameless and helpless all at the same time. She couldn't hold any grudge about pen marks on the new sofa or beheaded peonies in the garden when she watched them sleep. Instead, she started to feel very sentimental and grateful to Panda the panda for standing guard over them so faithfully all through the night.

One morning, Lizzie woke up and realized that she felt pretty good. This was strange and inexplicable, but it was true.

She still missed James the way you'd miss a limb, and she couldn't imagine that ache ever going away. But other things had healed, and she was growing a little stronger every day, in spite of everything.

Besides, she now had a plan.

The plan was very simple. On the day of Maria's wedding, Lizzie, looking thin and gorgeous, would dazzle James with her transformation. When the band struck up, she'd brazenly ask him to slow-dance. She'd be bold out on the floor, running her fingers over his back, pressing herself against him the way she used to in the old days. Later, when the moment seemed right, she'd push an envelope across the table to him. Inside would be the letter from Ivana, the letter certifying, in Eastern European syntax, that Elizabeth Buckley had been clinically depressed when she'd written the e-mail in which she stated that she preferred a cup of tea to a night of passion with her husband. Perhaps, if she had the courage, she'd also tuck inside a letter of her own, a letter listing all the lovely things she'd like to do to him if he would only give her another chance.

She didn't think she'd mention the rage inside. At least, not at first.

Lizzie stretched slowly in bed – a real wooden bed with a headboard – then stood up, went over to the window and tied a knot in the sheet she still used as a curtain. Sunlight lay in bars across the dewy lawn and burnished the brash new bramble branches that were fingering their way through the fence again. Lizzie flexed her hands. Her plan wasn't all that far-fetched, because she really *had* changed.

Daily life had begun to make her happy again, not sad and resentful. For example, just looking out of the window today, she felt a quite uncomplicated joy because it was so plainly a day for gardening.

Strange that she should feel so much satisfaction at the simple prospect of walking out of her own door and hacking away at rogue flora.

Lizzie went over to her dressing table, a warped wicker one bought from the secondhand shop that delivered, and studied her pale face in the mirror. She picked up a brush and began to run it through her hair. Then she put her fingers to her cheekbones.

Yes, she was a lot happier in so many ways these days, but something had been bothering her for ages.

Nobody, not one single solitary soul, had properly commented on her weight loss. Oh, now and then somebody would say something like, 'Lost a pound or two, have you, Lizzie?' But nobody seemed to realize the full extent of it. Nobody seemed to notice that she'd lost *at least* the equivalent in body mass of Bruno's collie, Madge.

It was all a bit discouraging, really. There she was, running her heart out every day, supposedly in the interests of health and well-being, but really with a view to getting rid of the stubbornest case of malingering baby bulge any woman had ever had to deal with, and all to no avail. Not even Tessa had patted her on the back. Not even inquisitive Ingrid had said more than a throwaway word or two. Bruno, who dropped by on a regular basis to help with the garden, hadn't made any sort of crack about it at all.

As for the women at Chipstead nursery, who more or less wel-comed Lizzie to their bosom these days, not a single one of them had reeled back in amazement at her accomplishment. Nobody had demanded to know what diet she was on. Nobody had asked how on earth she'd managed it. Mrs Kirker had once said Lizzie was looking 'very well', and somebody else had wondered whether she'd coloured her hair or whitened her teeth. 'You look different, somehow,' the woman had said. 'I just can't put my finger on it.'

What was the use of slimming down, Lizzie wondered, if nobody could see the difference?

Still pondering the issue half an hour later, as she doled out cereal to the children, Lizzie began to wonder if she'd really lost any weight at all. Maybe her scales were lying? Maybe they were defective? Probably. They'd been the cheapest ones she could find. Perhaps she'd only lost her marbles.

Leaving the children to slop milk and sprinkle sugar at will, Lizzie sprinted upstairs. (Amazing. She could now sprint upstairs without raising her heartrate or suffering shortness of breath.) Snapping the light on in her room, she began stripping off her clothes – her favourite frayed old jeans and big sweatshirt. In her underwear, she stood on her bed and peered at herself in the the warped wicker mirror.

No matter which way she looked, she did in fact seem thinner. Also more muscular. There could be no doubt about it. The scales weren't defective. She *had* lost weight.

But why didn't anybody *say* anything? They couldn't all be in a conspiracy to demoralize her, surely?

Slowly, Lizzie climbed back into her clothes. Then she stood up on the bed to take a last look.

'Oh God!' She clapped her hand to her mouth in horror. Because suddenly she was fat again. 'Bloody hell! It's the *clothes!*'

She was still wearing the clothes she'd thrown into her suitcase when she'd first left Mill House. These clothes had one thing in common. They were chosen to disguise her figure.

And they were doing exactly that.

They were disguising her new, trimmer, leaner, virtually flab-free body so well that nobody could even tell there'd been a change. Even her running clothes were bulky. Her 'new' tracksuit, bought at the peak of her weight gain, had enough spare fabric about it to conceal a small watermelon in its folds. She never ran in lycra shorts; she didn't even possess a pair.

The size of her bust was no help. Since she was still wearing tent-like clothes, of which her current sweatshirt was a prime example, people were free to imagine that her stomach was somewhere out there in line with her breasts.

Well, by God, things were going to change. As soon as possible, she was taking herself to Bluewater for a skinny-me shopping spree.

At ten thirty the next morning Lizzie was standing in front of a proper full-length mirror. She was in a place she'd avoided for years – the harshly-lit confines of a boutique fitting room. In a crumpled heap in the corner lay the clothes she'd arrived in: a pair of thick black leggings and a giant T-shirt that hung down to her knees. She'd realized just the other day that people were wearing leggings again. Of course, until they began to pop up on the High Street, she hadn't noticed that she was the only person still slouching around in them. At least their comeback meant she was suddenly, if inadvertently, in fashion. But looking at the things objectively, she could see they were hardly flattering.

In place of her ghastly old clothes, she was wearing a black and white halterneck top (with built-in bra) above a pair of fabulously-cut black bootleg trousers. And she was crying.

She knew this svelte, well-dressed young woman looking back at her. For years she'd been able to see only her feet. But she'd have recognized her anywhere.

'My God, Lizzie Indigo,' she muttered with a catch in her voice. 'Where the hell have you *been* for the last four years?' Then she sniffed and gave herself a pink-eyed smile. 'You know what? You look better than ever. But for God's sake, do something about the *hair*.'

The new Lizzie, the Lizzie who was going to bowl James over at Maria's wedding, was finally beginning to emerge.

She left the boutique at top speed, the gorgeous halterneck top and black trousers nestling in a glossy carrier bag. She wasn't even going to think about how much the outfit had cost. But, out of respect for James's bank account, she vowed to stick to cheap-and-cheerful shops for the rest of the morning.

Three days later, Lizzie had yet to wear any of the lovely new clothes she'd bought that morning in the mall. A strange shyness had come over her, and suddenly she didn't feel up to bursting out dramatically in a new persona. Also, she was distracted by her non-sense verses, because, wonder of wonders, they were complete!

Buoyed up by young Sarah's enthusiasm, she'd managed to force each and every one of them to a conclusion. Then she typed the lot of them up on the outdated old computer she'd brought from Mill House. She didn't have a printer, so she took the disc over to Ingrid's and printed the verses out there. Then she spent days combing through each verse, looking for errors and making eleventh-hour changes. Now, at last, she had a clean copy of a manuscript, and no idea what to do next.

She bought a book about first-time publishing, in which she read that she couldn't expect any respectable publisher to so much as look sideways at her unsolicited work. Far from being thrown onto a slush pile, her verses would be tossed directly into the recycling bin if she presumed to approach anybody without the proper preliminaries. And the proper preliminaries meant finding a literary agent.

The book advised her to network and attempt to meet agents face-to-face. Lizzie didn't want to network and meet anybody face-to-face. While she was no longer the unwashed wreck she'd been a few short months ago, she still felt too raw and vulnerable to launch herself on the world as a one-woman silly-verse marketing machine. She preferred to deal with people on paper, through the Royal Mail, with a nice comfortable distance, both geographically and temporally, between herself and the unknown. So she went to the Sevenoaks library and perused a massive volume containing the names, addresses and submission requirements of all the literary agents and publishers in the United Kingdom.

She was so confused by the number of agents claiming to represent children's books that she ended up selecting a name on the basis that it sounded honest. Jemima Straight, literary agent, promised at least to *consider* unpublished writers, but rather sternly forbade multiple queries. Ms Straight offered to take a commission of 15 per cent and stipulated that queries be submitted with complete manuscript, synopsis, biography, SAE and a vial of the writer's blood, sweat and tears.

Lizzie sat down and wrote a self-effacing little note about her poor, defenceless verses, rattled off a synopsis ('ten barmy tales told mostly in iambic pentameter, always in silly verse, at least one of which caused my neighbour's daughter to wet her pants in mirth'), and chewed her lower lip over her biography.

She wasn't worried so much about the first part. A Bachelor of Arts in History and English Literature didn't look too shabby. And her London career with G.H. Brightman and Associates could be pumped up to sound rather impressive, even though poor old Brightman's main client was a manufacturer of feed for hamsters, gerbils and other domesticated rodents.

Then there was her stint at the Food Research Institute near Laingtree, post-marriage, pre-twins. She'd had a fancy title – in-house public relations manager – but the scope of the job had been modest. On a regular basis she'd churned out press releases about Brussels sprouts and mutton; and once a month she'd produced a staff newsletter. The fact that this newsletter generally ended up being turned into origami and/or shredded to provide bedding for the secretary's son's pet rabbit never failed to produce in Lizzie the uncomfortable sense that the Food Research people perhaps overestimated their need of a public relations manager.

None the less, she was glad now that she'd been given such an impressive title. It was the work of a moment to make her career with the institute sound nothing short of stellar.

But what could she write about the last few years of her life? 'Mother' conveyed nothing of the complexity of the job she'd been doing since she'd given up working. 'Home executive' didn't even begin to describe the diversity of her experience during these past years. If she were to break the job down into titles, the list would be endless: housekeeper, food and beverage manager; general purpose and personal shopper; childhood sleep disorder therapist; nutritionist; potty training expert; household appliance technician; nurse practitioner; chauffeur; toddler dispute resolution consultant; arts and crafts administrator; juvenile music and dance director; juvenile fashion consultant; laundress and seamstress; festive season interior decorator; chief executive in charge of vomit clean-up and vomit zone decontamination; chief cook and bottle-washer.

She wrote it all down, hoping to tickle Jemima Straight's funny-bone. It was a gamble, of course. Ms Straight might not even have a funny-bone.

Then she took her clean and typo-free manuscript and slid it tenderly into a padded brown envelope along with all the other paperwork. After she had dropped the children off at nursery, she drove to the Post Office and handed over her hopes and dreams to a bored-looking clerk.

'Could I insure it?' she asked the woman.

'What is it?'

'It's ... well, it's the manuscript of a children's book.'

'Uh-huh. Printed matter, no commercial value. Insure it up to twelve pounds, if you like.'

Lizzie said she didn't think she'd bother. 'How about if I sent it registered mail?' she wondered humbly.

'You could do that,' the clerk conceded with a shrug.

So Lizzie did, then gave the envelope a furtive good-luck kiss before relinquishing it to careless hands to be weighed, stamped and thrown casually onto a large heap of waiting mail.

To celebrate this step towards becoming a famous children's author, Lizzie decided to have her hair cut and blow-dried. Lord knew, it was high time she sorted out the split ends.

She hadn't meant to do anything more than get a little trim, but the moment she sat down in the pivoting chair, and Luis, the bald stylist, strode up, she was overcome by a strange recklessness.

'What do we want to do today?' Luis asked, pulling strands of hair this way and that in an experimental manner. 'A trim? Or something completely different?'

Lizzie looked Luis boldly in the eye. 'Cut it off,' she said. 'I want it jaw-length. I'm tired of this long-haired look. I want something very, very stylish.'

Luis's eyes began to gleam with excitement. 'Very good,' he said. 'And what about colour? Are we interested in highlights today?'

Highlights? What an excellent idea. 'Absolutely,' said Lizzie. 'Give me something really dramatic.'

Luis was almost quivering with anticipation now. 'How about some face-framing slices in a really pale blonde? You natural tone is warm, of course, but I think we need to go cooler to get the drama you're after.'

Cooler? What on earth did that mean? Never mind, the man looked as if he knew what he was doing. 'Go on, then,' said Lizzie. 'Do whatever you like.'

Chapter Thirteen

'Jesus, Lizzie, what have you done to yourself?'

The twinkle was gone from Bruno's eyes as he gazed at her in frank astonishment.

'Bruno, I wish, wish, *wish* you'd ring and let me know you are coming before just *materializing* in my garden. You're not supposed to be in this neck of the woods today, anyway. Down, Madge, *down*.'

Bruno batted a gnat away from his face. 'Christ, woman, you've been starving yourself. They could use you in anatomy class instead of a real skeleton.'

'Why thank you; you're too kind.'

It was the day after her hair-cut, and Lizzie had put on some of her new clothes, just to get the feel of wearing them around the house before she burst upon the world with her new image. She'd chosen a pair of tailored white capri pants topped with the snug black and white halterneck that fitted like a second skin. Her feet were resplendent in black sandals with three-inch heels.

'And your hair! Your gorgeous bloody hair. Why've you gone and cut it off?'

Lizzie put her hand up to her shiny new, jaw-length bob. 'Now, don't go insulting my hair,' she said fiercely. 'I like it this way, thank you very much.'

Madge began to bark in agitation. She didn't like the raised voices.

'Shut up, dog!' Bruno shouted.

He took a few steps back and folded his arms across his broad chest. Cocking his head to one side, he contemplated her as a hen contemplates a shiny pebble that might or might not be edible.

'I just don't think it suits you,' he said bluntly. 'The skinniness, and all those streaks in your hair. You look like a different type of person.'

'Yeah? Different in what way?'

He shrugged. 'I don't know. Tougher. Meaner. Nastier.'

Lizzie broke into a delighted grin. 'That's *exactly* the effect I was aiming for,' she cried. Turning around slowly, she asked, 'Do I look tough and nasty from the back too?'

'You look a complete and utter bitch from the back,' Bruno told her sorrowfully. 'It's something about the way they've cut the hair shorter at the nape, I think. And the way your shoulder blades stick out like knives. You could step in front of a TV camera this minute and be one of those terrifying bloody anchorwomen. You're even wearing the right kind of make-up.'

'Yes, yes, *yes*,' said Lizzie, punching the air with glee. 'Things are definitely looking up.'

Bruno shook his head. 'Not for me,' he lamented. 'I like a woman with a bit of flesh on her. Toast-rack ribs just don't do it for me. Where's my cuddly Mother Earth girl with the mussed-up long hair and all the curves? For crying out loud, woman, you've starved off your best assets.'

Lizzie looked down at her bosom, respectably restrained in the built-in size C cups of the halterneck top. 'I *wish*,' she said ruefully. She'd dropped a bra size, but she'd never have the little fried-egg breasts she admired in women like Tessa – at least, not without surgery.

'What I want to know is, how did you do this to yourself in just a couple of weeks? I swear, when I saw you last, you looked quite normal. Did you go on a crash diet? Give up eating altogether?'

Lizzie gave what she hoped was a mysterious smile. 'No crash diet,' she said, quite truthfully.

'You've been ill, then? A touch of the old gastric flu? Talking to the white telephone all night? Oh, God, it's not something worse? Some sort of terminal illness?'

'No, no, *no*. Can you stop going on about it now? What are you doing here, anyway?'

Bruno shrugged. 'I had some time on my hands, and I was driving past the lane. I thought if I did a bit of weeding and digging, you might offer me a cup of tea?'

Lizzie gave a grudging smile. 'OK, I'll change into some gardening gear and put the kettle on.'

'Great! By the way, I see the ground elder is trying to make a comeback near the fence.'

When Lizzie walked out into the garden ten minutes later, she was in her usual tracksuit pants and big T-shirt. As she set the tea tray down on the lawn, Bruno straightened up, garden fork in hand, to look at her.

'My God,' he muttered. 'The real Lizzie Buckley returns! Except for the hair, of course. *Now* I see how you did it. You've been wasting away for weeks, haven't you? And none of us the wiser.'

Lizzie knelt down and busied herself with the tea things. 'Not wasting away,' she said. 'Shaping up.'

'Shaping up? Mmm, thanks, that's a damn fine cup of tea. Shaping up for what?'

Lizzie stood up and took a sip from her own steaming cup. 'I don't know,' she murmured. 'Just ... life in general.'

Bruno put down his tea. 'The single life, you mean. Here, let me take your cup.' Before she knew what he was up to, he'd set her cup on the tray and taken her hand. 'Could it be you're *really* shaping up for this sort of thing?'

And he kissed her.

His mouth was hot from the tea, but his lips were cool and smooth. His hands on her back seemed to be feeling out the newly-exposed ridges of her ribs and shoulder blades through her over-sized T-shirt.

Taken completely by surprise, Lizzie struggled at first to be free. But only moments later, she found herself leaning into the warm hard body, giving herself up to the disturbing sensation of his tongue probing her mouth.

Bam! It hit her like a piano falling out of a second-storey window. Arousal. Lust. Passion. Whatever you cared to call it. Shocking in its intensity, yet sweetly familiar, like an old friend she hadn't seen in a long, long time.

All of a sudden she wanted nothing better than to get this big, warm man into her inadequately-sized bed and rip all his clothes off. But why waste time? Why not rip his clothes off right there in the garden?

'Ahem. Ahem-hem-*hem*.'

Blast and damnation.

Lizzie jumped away from Bruno as if she'd been electrocuted. A chorus of barking broke out – Madge shouting the odds at Ingrid Hatter's hyperactive terrier.

Ingrid herself was standing by the fence, hanging onto a taut leash and wearing a huge, lopsided grin. 'Having fun, you two?'

Bruno scowled at her. 'Couldn't you just walk on by?' he growled. 'Snogging is not a spectator sport, you know.'

But Ingrid was hardly listening. 'Lizzie!' she brayed. 'Your hair! It's fabulous. You sneaky thing! You never said you were going to have it done. You look so . . . so *chic*. I love the highlights. I've been thinking of getting some myself, you know. What do you reckon, maybe a coppery blonde?'

Lizzie gave a shaky sigh, part regret, part relief. 'I'd try ash blonde, if I were you. Too much red in the coppery tones. Look, why don't you come on in, Ingrid? Have some tea. Let the dogs have a proper go at each other.'

'Oh no, I must be getting on. Jack needs his exercise.' Jack, the terrier, was bouncing like a basketball, his pointy little head appearing and disappearing over the fence.

'Let him chase sticks with Madge. That'll give him a work-out, I promise you. Come on, I've just made a huge pot of tea.' Lizzie gave Ingrid a beseeching look, rolling her eyes briefly in Bruno's direction.

'Oh. Right. Very well, then, I'll come round.' Walking towards the gate, she began to reel in her dog as if it were a nimble little fish.

'Coward,' Bruno whispered out of the corner of his mouth.

'Wolf in sheep's clothing,' Lizzie hissed back.

Yes, she was a coward. Thank God, thank God! Who knew *what* would have happened if her highly commendable cowardice hadn't reared its gibbering head. And thank God too for the unapologetic curiosity of Ingrid Hatter, and her heroic lack of diplomacy and tact. If Ingrid had acted the way nine people out of ten would act after inadvertently sneaking up on a couple in a clinch – namely, melt away into the middle distance as quietly as possible – Lizzie would by now be … oh, never mind. Much more sensible to be pouring out a third cup of tea in the sunshine.

But that kiss had been a wonderful thing. That kiss had shown her that she was indeed fully recovered from the worst effects of her depression. Finally, after years of blurry apathy, she seemed once again to be a woman in fully working order. When she whisked James out onto the dance-floor at Maria's wedding, she wouldn't even have to pretend to be frisky and frolicsome.

From: lizbuckley@hotmail.com
Sent: 16 July
To: janehawthorn@yahoo.com

Dear Janie

Thinking of you lots lately. Only two months to go and you'll be a mother.

I've been a real wet blanket about marriage and motherhood just lately. Not v. supportive of me, knowing you've decided to chuck the job and take it all on. Just want to say you won't regret it. Staying home with small children is the most back-breaking, thankless, unglamorous job in all the world – how could you not love it?

I know you and Simon will be fine, by the way. Come on, he's loved you since you were thirteen. He'll know what to do when you're round the bend with sleep deprivation. It'll be just like when you were fifteen and wore only black, told everyone to eff off all the time, and had a stud in your tongue. He'll know it's just a phase and that the real Janie will come home in good time.

Wish James had known it was just a phase.

Have you thought of a name yet?

Lots of love

Lizzie

PS The gardener bloke grabbed me and pressed his attentions on me today. Jolly nice attentions they are, too! It's been so long since

Lizzie stopped typing and stared at the screen.

After a long moment, she put her hand back on the mouse and deleted the whole of her postscript. Some things you didn't tell anybody, not even your sister. If she'd realized that ages ago, she could have saved herself a lot of grief.

Lizzie stood at Tessa's door, alternately knocking and ringing the bell. It was a Wednesday evening and they'd arranged to run from Tessa's house in The Dene to the High Street and from there to the school running track near Knole. Depending on how they felt after a couple of laps, they might then run on through the Kissing Gate towards Knole House and do a half-circuit of the park itself.

That was the plan, anyway, if Tessa would answer the door.

Lizzie gave the doorbell another impatient jab and began to stretch. As she leant forward over her left leg, she looked at it in wonder. What had happened to the acres of orange-skin dimples? Likewise, the little pocket of flab that used to hang down under her thigh and wobble if she wriggled her leg? And where had that long, lean calf muscle been hiding all her life?

She'd taken to wearing lycra cycling shorts, à la Tessa, because the sight of her glorious new legs always added a spur to her labours out on the road. If she was flagging even slightly, she only had to look down at all that lovely muscle to be pumped full of energy and conviction all over again.

She'd never forget the first afternoon Tessa had seen her in the cycling shorts.

'Blimey,' Tessa had said. 'Are those prosthetics? What happened to the trusty old Roman columns?'

Then she'd rushed over to give Lizzie a rib-cracking hug. The two of them had run like blazes that day; they'd run as if they had wings on their heels, as if they were on steroids, as if running were as natural a state of being as lying slumped on the sofa, eating Maltesers by the handful and watching re-runs of *Men Behaving Badly*.

Lizzie rang the doorbell again.

It wasn't like Tessa to keep a person waiting. Tessa had a lot of bad habits, one of which was excessive punctuality.

At last Lizzie heard footsteps approaching, but the gait didn't sound like Tessa's. Too slow and hesitant for her; too light for a man, so it couldn't be Greg.

The door opened slowly, but Tessa always flung doors open. Who on earth could it be?

'Tessa? Tessa! Oh, God, what's happened?'

Tessa just shook her head and gestured to Lizzie to come inside.

At a glance, Lizzie could see there'd be no running tonight. Tessa looked a complete wreck. Her eyes were bloodshot and swollen from crying; her face was blotchy and damp; her hair hung lifelessly at her shoulders, as if she'd taken a shower and then forgotten to blow-dry or even brush it.

When they were both sitting down on the black leather sofa, Tessa heaved a wobbly breath and said, 'It's OK, Lizzie, don't look at me like that. I'm fine. I'm absolutely fine. Just being a bit of a prat, is all.'

'You don't look fine.'

'Yeah, well, nobody's died or anything. I've just been having a little sob session because, well, because the bloody curse is back again, if you must know. Two days late, sod it. I was beginning to get my hopes up, that's the worst of it.'

'Oh. Oh, Tessa, I'm sorry. It just doesn't seem fair, does it?'

'Fair? Nothing's bloody fair. Fairness is a man-made construct, and we can't even make it work in our own justice systems. Why would it work in nature? I don't think nature's ever even *heard* of "fair". The only thing nature knows is survival of the fittest. And I have to assume there's something *not* fit about either my eggs or Greg's swimmers, or both.'

'Hey, no aspersions on the little guys! For all we know, they're swimming for England.' The sound of Greg's suave, public school voice gave Lizzie a bit of a start, given the circumstances. She jumped up and flashed him a bright, nervous smile.

His strained face softened slightly and he gave her an answering grin. It was more than eight years since Lizzie had first laid eyes on Greg Martin at Evelyn Buckley's summer pool party, but he hadn't changed much. He was still the wry, rough-hewn chap with impeccable manners who'd tended to Tessa's wounded ego when she'd failed to dazzle James.

Urbane as ever, even with a wife in tears and the prowess of his own sperm up for discussion, Greg walked over and placed a hand on Tessa's shoulder. He kneaded her lightly in the collar-bone area, then ruffled the bedraggled-looking hair.

Only after Tessa had glanced up at him with a watery smile did he turn to give Lizzie an appraising look. He pursed his mouth in a silent whistle. 'Well done, Lizzie,' he said with feeling. 'You look bloody fantastic. Tessa told me you were whipping yourself into shape, but I had no *idea* you could look so ... so ...' He described a narrow shape in the air with both hands, apparently at a loss for words.

'So lean and mean? So tough and bitchy?' Tessa suddenly piped up, forcing her ravaged face into a smile.

'Whoa, Tess!' Greg raised his eyebrows at this unwarranted attack on their guest. 'Steady on, woman. Claws in, claws in.'

'I'm only quoting somebody else,' Tessa defended herself.

'Don't worry, Greg,' Lizzie grinned. 'I take it as a compliment. You don't know how hard I've worked to look tough and mean and bitchy.'

'Well, I'm sorry to say it, old girl, but you look as sweet-tempered as ever to me. Just thinner, that's all. Are you girls still planning to run? No? In that case, who's for a snifter? Might as well have a double, Tess. Medicinal purposes.'

'You two have a drink,' Lizzie said. 'I think I *will* run, after all. Just a quick one.'

That's when she knew she *was* an addict; nobody turns down a double gin and tonic and the chance of a good gossip to go running alone in the drizzle.

Phones are not supposed to ring at two in the morning unless there's some terrible news. Or unless, of course, you have a relative in another time zone who doesn't always think before she dials.

Jolted awake in the deep, black stillness of the night, Lizzie didn't panic at all. She just stumbled to the 'office', hoping the ringing wouldn't wake the children. Bloody Janie. She'd give her an earful.

'Lizzie? Is that you, Lizzie?'

Still half-asleep, Lizzie was nonetheless able to identify the disembodied voice of her brother-in-law.

'Yes, yes, it's me. Do you know it's the middle of the night here, Simon?'

'Lizzie, Jane's in hospital.'

'What?'

'She's got something bad. Pre-eclampsia, it's called. Her blood pressure's one sixty over a hundred and ten.'

Pre-eclampsia? Wasn't that one of the few things that could still cause death in childbirth?

'And Lizzie, they're getting ready to induce labour.'

'Calm down, Simon. That can't be right. The baby's not due for a couple of months.'

'Lizzie, I'm telling you, they're saying it isn't getting enough blood.'

'Oh, God, Simon. Oh, God.'

'Will you tell your mum and dad? I don't feel up to breaking the news.'

'I'll tell them. Look, give me the hospital's phone number. Bloody hell, where's a pen that works? OK, OK, got one. So what's the number there?'

Simon gave her the details and she scrawled them on the back of an envelope with a shaking hand.

'Jane's asking for you to come,' Simon blurted out suddenly. 'Oh, Jesus, Lizzie, you wouldn't recognize her. She's all yellow and swollen. She hasn't been able to put on a pair of shoes for days. And she says her head is killing her and she has a horrible pain in her side. Will you come, Lizzie? For God's sake, say you'll come.'

Lizzie mind was racing, but she didn't even hesitate. 'Of course I'll come. You tell her to bite the bullet. I'll be there as soon as I can.'

'I've got to go now,' Simon said abruptly, and hung up the phone.

There was no question of taking the twins to Australia. Just as soon as James understood what she was talking about when she phoned him at 3 a.m., he said of course he'd have them in Chipping Norton for the week.

'Do you absolutely have to go yourself, since your mum and dad are going?' he asked mildly.

'James, she's asking for me specifically. And she's scared to death.'

'Good God, Lizzie,' James said the next day, as she opened the door. 'You've cut your hair.'

Lizzie patted her bob self-consciously as the twins burst out from behind her and launched themselves at their father. 'Yes, it was time for a change. Look, thanks awfully for coming at such short notice ...' But Lizzie's rehearsed speech dried up as she registered that somebody was standing on the pathway behind James.

'Mrs Buckley, hello. So sorry to hear about your sister.'

There, in the flesh, stood a woman who was still recognizable as Sonja Jenkins – but only just. She had extremely blonde, extremely straight long hair cut in a jagged geometrical style, such as you might see in an avant-garde magazine at the hairdresser's. She wore a needlessly formal black suit, which managed to look slightly indecent because of its tight fit over her strangely upstanding bosom. She looked anything but skinny and round-shouldered. All the bits of her that were on show gleamed with the sort of rich bronze tan you get topless-bathing in a place like Mykonos. Or in six seconds at a Hollywood tanning booth. As reported, her eyes were startlingly green.

Lizzie had a sudden urge to slam the door in their faces.

'Sonja?' she croaked. 'Well ... hello. I didn't realize you were there. James, could I talk to you a moment?'

'Fire away,' he said, hoisting Ellie up onto his back.

'Inside? If you don't mind.'

'Oh, all right. Come on, you lot.' He plucked Alex off his leg and stowed a twin under each arm.

'Without an audience,' she added, looking meaningfully at the children.

He raised his eyebrows but set the children down. 'Ellie, Alex, can you find me a dandelion? Or maybe three or four dandelions?'

'Yes, yes,' they shrieked, not stopping to ask why on earth he'd want three or four dandelions.

'I'll find them first,' Ellie yelled.

'No, I woll, I woll,' Alex roared.

And off they scampered.

'Please keep an eye on them, Sonja,' James called over his shoulder as he followed Lizzie into the house.

Lizzie closed the door and they stood looking at each other in the big empty hallway. Now that they were alone, Lizzie felt suddenly too embarrassed to say what she wanted to say. Her imagination was probably running away with her, anyway.

James nodded at a suitcase propped against the wall. 'That theirs?'

'Yes, and that big bag there.'

He picked up the case and slung the bag over his shoulder. 'What's the latest on Janie?' he asked, before Lizzie could rally her thoughts. To his credit, he'd always liked her sister.

Lizzie bit her lip. 'They're holding things off as long as they can. Trying to keep the blood pressure down. Monitoring the baby.'

He nodded. 'And you? How're you coping? You look tired. And ... thin. When did you get so thin?'

Lizzie shrugged. So much for dazzling him with her new image. 'What's *she* doing here?' she asked in a rush, jerking her head at the door.

'Sonja? I asked her to come. To help on the drive home – sing songs, tell stories, that sort of thing. The Smalls don't travel terribly well, I've found.'

Lizzie took a deep breath. She squeezed her eyes shut, then opened them. 'Listen, James. I just want to say one thing. Well, maybe more than one thing. All this is very hard for me. Going away. Leaving the twins.'

He nodded, watching her intently.

'So I just want to have as little to worry about as possible. If you get my meaning?' She flicked her eyes towards the door again.

'Yes, of course. No, hang on ... What *is* your meaning?'

'Look, I just don't think we should confuse the children at this point. I mean, we *are* still legally married. So I'm asking you – I mean, I know I probably don't need to mention it – but I'm asking you *please* not to have any women stay over while Ellie and Alex are with you.'

She was trying to shake the awful image that had popped into her mind of the children running into Daddy's room in the morning to find the preternaturally bronzed Sonja with her strangely pneumatic bosom and cat-like green eyes lying on the pillow where Mummy should be.

'For God's sake, Lizzie,' James burst out angrily. He spun on his heel and made as if to walk away, but at the last minute, he turned back and said, through gritted teeth, 'I'll put off all the hot dates I was planning until *after* you get back. Was there anything else?'

'Yes, actually. There's this.' She dug in her handbag and produced a piece of paper. 'All the contact details for Sydney. You can probably still reach me at my e-mail address, too.'

He took the paper, folded it, and tucked it into his pocket.

'Um, James? When I said that about women staying over? It's just ... I worry so much about the kids, whether we're screwing them up for life. You know?'

He nodded curtly.

At that moment the door fell open with a crash. Ellie stood on the step, red in the face, hands on hips, tears coursing down her cheeks. 'Daddy, there's ... huh ... no ... huh ... dandelions. Mummy, Mummy, we can't ... huh ... find any dandelions.'

Getting a firm grip on the suitcase, James strode over to his daughter. 'Come on, Ellie-Belly, there has to be a dandelion out there somewhere. Let's go and take another look.'

Walking out after them, Lizzie called, 'Try the field on the other side, there should be plenty over there.'

She felt a small jolt of satisfaction to see Sonja Jenkins, in the middle of the garden, balancing on one high-heeled shoe while she scraped at the sole of the other with a stick. A gleeful Alex raced around her, chanting, 'You stood in *dog* pooh, *you* stood in *dog* pooh.'

Good old Madge, or, possibly, good old Jack.

Lizzie directed Sonja to Bruno's garden tap so that she could clean her shoe properly. After all, the children had to sit in the car with her for two solid hours.

At last, Sonja's shoe was more or less clean, Ellie had her four dandelions, both children had been persuaded to visit the potty one last time, the suitcase and bag had been thrown into the boot, and the moment of parting arrived.

Lizzie squatted down beside the car and held out her arms for the twins. Alex rushed up and roughly head-butted her. She pulled his golden orb towards her and deposited a kiss somewhere in the region of his left eyebrow. He wriggled away, giggling, and climbed up into the car. Ellie lingered, soft and clinging as a cat. Lizzie gave her a hard hug.

'You be good to Daddy, now,' she whispered in the child's ear. 'Help him with things. And look after Alex for me.'

Ellie nodded. 'Don't worry, Mummy. I know yus what to do.'

Lizzie blinked rapidly. 'Course you do. I'll phone from Australia as soon as I can. And I'll see you in a week.'

Ellie put her arms around her mother's neck and squeezed to the point of strangulation. 'Be a good girl, Mummy,' she said.

'Come along, Ellie-Belly, we need to get going,' James called. 'Hop in. No more dawdling.'

As they pulled away, Lizzie was just able to see her apparently nonchalant son's face suddenly crumple, as he craned his head to watch her disappear. His mouth formed a big black 'O', and she knew he was treating the car to a full-volume, grief-stricken bellow, the sort of roar he gave when he couldn't find his fire engine last thing at night.

'Attaboy, Alex,' she muttered to herself, dashing away her own tears. 'You give Sonja Silicone-Boobs the ride of her life back to Gloucestershire. Maybe her green contact lenses will pop out with the strain.'

From: lizbuckley@hotmail.com
Sent: 21 July
To: mdenn@optonline.com

Dear Maria
    Janie and baby are stable.
    They induced the day we arrived, as Janie's liver was starting to pack up. She was all swollen and blotchy and yellow. Horrible. Writhing on the bed with back pain and also, this is the weird thing, almost beserk with hunger. Mum kept saying, 'For God's sake, give the poor girl some food', but they'd only give her ice cubes.
    Labour was quick once they got the petocin going. Worst thing was the magnesium drip, Janie says. Baby girl born just after midnight, 3lb 1oz; in neonatal intensive care. Every rise and fall of her chest seems such an effort. I stand at the window watching her breathe.
    Janie in hospital until further notice.
    Maria, will you do me a favour? James phones to let me talk to the children, and they sound fine, but I worry anyway. Could you give James a ring and check up on them? Maybe even ask them round to tea on Sunday? This is definitely not espionage, just friendly observation.
    Thanks a million,
    Lizzie

From: mdenn@optonline.com
Sent: 22 July
To: lizbuckley@hotmail.com

Hi, Lizzie

So Janie's been discharged! What a relief. So glad to hear the baby's getting stronger and gaining weight.

James gave us the good news. He was over with the kids for tea this afternoon, as per your instructions. We gave them fish fingers, smiley-face potato thingies, and ketchup (a nod in the direction of greens). Then they watched *Kipper* and fell asleep while we had a glass of wine and polished off some curry.

James is looking a bit rough around the edges, but the twins are in good nick. James kept muttering things like, 'I had no idea how little they sleep. I mean, how little they sleep *concurrently.*' Apparently they've been waking up in relays, asking for water, potty trips, night lights and so on.

When I asked James how he was liking the Chipping Norton house, he said he'd liked it fine until the children turned it into a complete tip. Apparently they fed a box of crayons into the radiator after drawing a mural on one of the walls. Melted wax is now bleeding out onto the white carpet.

But don't worry. I gather he's keeping them fed and bathed and highly entertained. Ellie informed me, 'We like to stay wiff Daddy cos he lets us ride round the house on his back. Mummy never wants to play horsey.'

Are you still coming back on Thursday? When you pick up the twins I'm going to nab you for an hour – dressmaker needs to re-do measurements. James says you've lost a significant amount of weight. Maybe you should tell him about the running and the health food fixation so he won't think you've got cancer or worse.

Hope you get to hold your niece before you come home. Thank God the crisis is over.

Bye now, see you soon.
Maria

Chapter Fourteen

As Lizzie stepped out into the arrivals hall at Gatwick, her eye was caught by a frantic flutter of colour to her left. It was Ingrid Hatter in summer florals, waving energetically and mouthing, 'Welcome home!'

The minute Ingrid deposited her on her own doorstep, Lizzie grabbed car keys and handbag, jumped behind the wheel, and headed for Gloucestershire.

From directions supplied by Mapquest, she drove without a single wrong turn straight to James's house in Chipping Norton.

The place was in a quiet side street with absolutely no parking. Defiantly, she pulled over on the double yellow line outside number 39 – a narrow, unremarkable white house flanked by clones of itself.

As she stepped out of the car, Lizzie was smiling from ear to ear, like some sort of nutter. Heaven only knew, she'd be desperate to palm the twins off on any handy babysitter a couple of hours from now, but right now she couldn't wait to see them.

At the top of the four steps that led up to the front door, Lizzie paused. She was poised to ring the doorbell of her husband's new life. She was about to see it: the space he inhabited without her. This was the future James had chosen; the place where Lizzie didn't fit in. Perhaps he'd never meant her to see it at all.

She took a deep breath and rang the bell.

A loud scampering and shrieking broke out. The door flew open and hands grabbed her at knee level, pulling her bodily into the house. She tumbled down and they swarmed onto her, Ellie sobbing, Alex jabbering at top speed.

Then James walked up, and she was staring at the beautiful feet she'd first seen in the strawberry fields of Longborough, but now she had a child's damp cheek pressed to her face.

'Here, let me help you up.' He took her hand and she stood awkwardly, both children pressing themselves close.

James looked terrible. She'd never seen him so unkempt. He obviously hadn't shaved in a while, nor had he bothered with a comb. He was wearing a vest and a pair of tartan pyjama bottoms, and he held a cup of coffee in one hand.

'How's it been?' she asked.

He shook his head wordlessly, then gave a rueful grin. 'They ran rings around me,' he said. 'Thank God you're back.'

She felt a stab of irritation. 'So they can run rings around *me*?'

His eyebrows rose. 'They wouldn't dare.'

'Don't you believe it. Anyway, are they all packed and ready to go?'

'We packed our bags las' night, Mummy,' Alex yelled, doing a little stomping dance around the room.

'I'll get their stuff,' James said. She watched till he was out of sight, then knelt down and gave Ellie, still tearful, several kisses and a quick hug. 'Come on, sweetie, show me Daddy's house, then.'

Ellie gave a brave sniff. 'All right, but there's nuffin in it.'

She was right. There was almost nothing in it but expensive white carpet, blank white walls, a solitary white sofa, and lots of shiny brass fixtures in the loo. Lizzie smiled when she came to the place where the twins had scribbled their toddler graffiti. It brightened up the décor, at least. When she walked into the kitchen, the first thing she saw was the waiter-shaped wine-rack she'd once given James.

She heard his tread on the ceramic tile behind her and turned. He stood there, nursing his coffee, watching her with an unreadable look on his face.

'You always hated that thing,' she said accusingly. 'What's it doing here?'

He shrugged. 'I don't know. Maybe just ... to remind me of our differences.'

Wump. A blow to the stomach.

'It was a *joke*,' she mumbled, blinking quickly. 'The stupid wine-rack was a joke.' But he'd turned away to run water over his coffee mug in the gleaming new kitchen sink, and didn't hear.

Alex provided a welcome distraction by racing up to the wine-rack and challenging it to fight. 'You duh naughty knight and I gonna rescue duh princess,' he told it solemnly. 'I need a helmet!' and he made a dive for the cupboard under the sink, where Lizzie caught a glimpse of a very shiny set of saucepans. James stepped up, closed the cupboard door smartly, and said, 'No time for duels now, my boy. Time to go with Mummy.' He turned to Lizzie. 'You look shattered. Are you OK to drive?'

She gave a surly shrug. 'I'm fine. I'm only going over to Maria's now. She'll give me some coffee to wake me up.' Unlike you, she added silently.

He considered her a moment. 'I wouldn't like to have to deal with this lot after that monster flight, I can tell you. Are you sure you'll be all right? I can always keep them for another day if you need time to recover. It's a lot tougher than I thought, looking after them twenty-four seven. But it's easier for you, of course; you're much better at it than I am.'

She gave a bitter sneer. 'Oh yes, much better. It's *women's work*, after all. Too mindless and menial for the likes of *you*. But me? I thrive on it, of course. It never gets *me* down. Oh, *no!* Never.'

Oh, dear. Maybe Ivana was right. Maybe she needed to unbottle all her anger so it didn't become an exploding device.

Dashing tears from her eyes, she rushed the children out of the house.

She drove to Maria's house in a tearing rage. How dared he assume that raising children was a doddle for *anybody*, just because they were female? What would he think about her genetically-endowed coping skills if he knew she'd smashed Alex's toy car against the wall and bruised his shoulders?

By the time she was sitting in an armchair at Maria's house, sipping coffee, she was no longer angry, just miserable.

'I wish I'd never gone anywhere near the place,' she told Maria. 'It was depressing. All those spanking new fittings, the granite countertops in the kitchen, and not a painting on the wall, not a knick-knack on the mantelpiece. It barely looks inhabited. And this is where the kids are supposed to spend their weekends.'

'He's only just moved in,' Maria said soothingly. 'I'm sure it will be more homely in time.'

The fact that he'd moved into a separate place at all, a place of his own, was the part that grieved her most. She didn't want it to be more homely in time. She wanted it not to exist.

But she shook her head and turned her attention back to her resentment. 'He has the gall to say I'm better at looking after the twins than he is. Making out he's such a hero to have taken them on when he's their *dad*, for God's sake. Looking as if he hasn't slept in days. The bloody *condescension* of the man.'

'I'm sure he's *much* better at looking after them than you are,' Maria replied with a twinkle.

Lizzie took a deep breath and went a bit purple. Then she caught Maria's eye and gave a rueful laugh. 'All right, all right. But why couldn't he just say it was a tough job without trying to make out that it's not a tough job for *me*? Doesn't he bloody understand that we more or less lost our *marriage* because it's such a tough job for me?'

The doorbell rang, jangling Lizzie's nerves.

'That must be the dressmaker.' Maria set down her tea and jumped up eagerly. 'Try not to think about James now, love. Try to think wedding. For me, please?'

Lizzie had visited the dressmaker in Stowe for a first fitting some weeks ago. How Maria had persuaded the woman to make a house-call, Lizzie had no idea, but she was thankful she didn't have to try to control the twins in the tiny front room where the woman plied her trade.

Lizzie plastered a smile on her face in a bid to pass for a happy matron of honour, not a maddened soon-to-be ex-wife. Not that the dressmaker cared. She looked as if she would have preferred it if all her clients were mannequin's dummies. Clamping her teeth on a handful of pins, she began to re-measure all Lizzie's relevant dimensions. She wrote down the new numbers in a dog-eared notebook, alongside the old ones, tut-tutting as she went. At last, she closed up her book and looked Lizzie in the eye.

'My girl,' she said, 'I hope you're not planning to lose any more inches?'

Lizzie blushed, as if caught out in some decidedly underhand caper. 'I'm not *planning* to,' she said.

'You'd better not, then,' the dress-maker snapped. 'This dress is supposed to fit like a glove, not like a tent. I can't have you chopping and changing your measurements all the time. If we have to alter the dress in any way, it's going to cost Maria here an arm and a leg.'

Lizzie hung her head like a naughty schoolgirl. 'Right,' she said. 'I'll ... I'll monitor my weight then.'

'Never mind your weight, it's your measurements that count,' the woman said sternly. 'Don't go building up any more muscle, either. I'm making this dress to fit you as you are *today*. All right?'

'Got it.'

'After all, I have my reputation to think of,' she went on sniffily as she packed up her bag of tricks. 'I don't think I've ever *known* a body change so much in a few weeks. It's just lucky you've gone *down* in size and not up, or we'd find ourselves without enough fabric.'

Oh, it was lovely stuff. Lizzie had never enjoyed a telling-off so much in her life. It quite boosted her flagging spirits. What bliss to be scolded for being too thin! As Maria showed the woman out, Lizzie wondered if she dared lose another inch here or there, just to provoke a real bombardment of verbal abuse at the final fitting. A blistering ticking-off about her skinniness would buoy her up nicely for the ordeal of facing James in a dinner jacket.

Lizzie had the luggage loaded and the children strapped in the car before Maria dropped a bombshell of her own, and it had nothing to do with Lizzie getting too thin for her dress.

'Oh, sweetheart, one last thing,' she said a shade too casually, just as Lizzie was about to reverse out into the lane.

'Uh-huh?' Lizzie felt her ears prick up, as if she were a dog. Something about Maria's tone put her on the alert.

'While James was with us on Sunday he asked a sort of favour.'

'Yeah? Alex, stop kicking like that. You'll damage something.'

'He wondered, um, if he could, ah ...'

Maria never ummed and ah-ed.

'Come on, out with it. What did he wonder?'

'If he could bring a, um, a partner. To the wedding. You know, given that it would be a bit awkward if the two of you were obliged to, ah, partner each other.'

'I ... see.' Lizzie saw nothing at all except a rapidly receding image of herself seductively slow-dancing with James.

'There's the dancing,' said Maria apologetically. 'The two of you will probably have to manage one dance together, I'm afraid, but after that, if you bring partners ...'

'We need never get within spitting distance of each other again. I see his point. Who's he bringing, anyway?'

'I'm sorry, sweetheart. I don't know. I got the feeling that he didn't have anyone special in mind.'

'It's that bloody bitch, Sonja Jenkins, I bet. Did I tell you she's gone and had a boob job?'

Maria twirled her pony-tail thoughtfully. 'Really? That doesn't sound like James's scene.'

'He likes big boobs,' Lizzie hissed, glaring down at her own bosom, which was looking modest and discreet for the first time since she was about thirteen. 'He's a man, for God's sake. Do you think he cares if they're made of jelly?'

Maria leant into the car and said in a low voice, 'Calm down, sweetheart. You've got to drive this lot safely back to Kent. Don't work yourself into a state. James simply asked if he could bring a partner if he felt like it, and Laurence said yes, of course he could. The same goes for you, obviously. It might just make things easier, Lizzie.' Then, in a fierce whisper, she suddenly added, 'Oh, bugger, bugger, bugger, our timing's just so screwed up, isn't it?'

Lizzie had never seen Maria lose her cool before. It was unnerving. 'It's not *your* timing that's wrong, Maria,' she assured her hastily. 'It's ours. Don't worry about me. It's no big deal. I can bring a bloody partner if I have to.'

And she pulled away quickly so they wouldn't have to talk about it any more.

It was as she rounded the bend onto the High Street that Alex piped up, 'Sonja's boobs aren't made of jelly, Mummy.'

Lizzie slammed on her brakes in shock. The car behind her screeched to a halt a couple of inches from her bumper. Horns blared from every direction. Lizzie eased her foot back onto the accelerator, telling herself to take deep breaths.

'Really, darling? What are they made of?' she asked as conversationally as she could, when she was able to speak.

'Skin, just like yours, silly.'

'Oh? And how do you know?'

''Cause I seed her bare naked, you know. At Daddy's house. But don't worry, you gotta bigger bottom than her.'

When the children were in bed, Lizzie staggered downstairs, half-drunk with jet-lag, and picked up the portrait Ingrid had so admired the day they'd shared the bottle of Chardonnay. Lizzie admired it, too; always had. She'd never seen such a speaking picture of family life. The expressions on the children's faces were so typical of each, and so well caught – Alex's face brimming with mischief, Ellie's full of merriment, and James ... well, what could you say about such a battered, handsome, rueful face. He could have been a model for extreme sports practised by laconic athletes in effortlessly elegant clothes.

The bastard.

Lizzie took the picture carefully out of the frame. She went to the kitchen and found a pair of scissors. Very slowly, she cut around the image of herself and the children. She'd have to take up scrap-booking now, so that she could use the butchered portrait on a cheerful page decorated with ribbons and stickers and pressed flowers. Maybe no one would notice the excision of the central image: her husband.

She picked up the offcut from the kitchen floor. The face smiled crookedly up at her. With a sort of low growl, she tore it viciously into shreds and threw it into the rubbish bin.

He'd broken his promise. Lizzie gave a strangled snort, somewhere between a shout and a sob. He'd broken his promise that he wouldn't have a woman in the house while the children were with him. Well, that was it, then. There'd be no reconciliation. He'd gone beyond the pale.

Lizzie yanked open several kitchen cabinets until she found a large jar of peanut butter. She opened the lid, grabbed a spoon, and was about to begin shovelling the stuff into her mouth when a ragged cry from above gave her pause. One of the twins was having a nightmare. She pushed the peanut butter back into the cupboard and hurried off upstairs to soothe and cajole. Being a mother was ironic, that way. So often, some mundane parenting task saved you from yourself.

Lizzie was now looking forward to Maria's wedding about as much as she'd looked forward to having her wisdom teeth removed. Maybe slightly less.

The worst thing was, she'd have to pick up the phone and ask Bruno to squire her to the grisly event. It was either Bruno, or the bloke in the white coat and pony-tail who worked at Boots with Tessa. They were the only two single men she knew. Thankfully, the thing was still some weeks away, so she wouldn't have to pop the awkward question just yet.

And it *was* going to be awkward. The last time she'd seen Bruno, he'd been looking reproachfully at her over a cup of tea while Ingrid wittered on about that weekend's car boot sale. And she'd been trying not to look back, because she'd had no intention of letting him know that only moments before she'd been plotting the quickest way to get him out of his clothes and into her bed.

Altogether, Lizzie was reluctant to think too hard about Bruno, let alone ask him to partner her to a wedding. But Tessa didn't think Lizzie should be putting off the evil hour. 'You want to nail things down ahead of time so you can relax,' she advised one evening in late July as they cooled down after a surprisingly hard forty-minute run along the hilly bridleway off Back Lane. 'It's no good phoning him up the week before, only to find he can't make it. I mean, if James really is having a thing with this Sonja bitch, you have your pride to think of. You can't go to the wedding alone. It's absolutely crucial that you have a partner.'

Tessa was right, of course. The embarrassment of having to ask Bruno out on a date would be nothing compared to the embarrassment of watching in solitary splendour as James snuggled up to Sonja during the slow dances. Even so, she couldn't quite bring herself to dial Bruno's number. After all, he was bound to turn up on her doorstep sooner or later and then she'd be able to ask him face-to-face, without making a big production of the invitation.

But the days went by and Bruno failed to darken her doorstep. Probably, he was appalled that he'd ever kissed her. Perhaps he was too ashamed of his cheek to show his face in her garden again.

Only that didn't sound like Bruno.

Then, on 15 August, with just two weeks to go until the wedding, Lizzie heard the distant snarl of a lawn-mower. After a moment or two, she set down her pencil – a rhyme for 'pomegranate' refusing to materialize, anyway – and wandered over to Ingrid's.

She stood at the gate watching Bruno mow, aware that it wasn't much good shouting to attract his attention. Nor did she feel like running after him over the newly-shaven lawn. But Madge soon spotted her, and came tearing over the gravel driveway to jump up at her.

As Bruno turned the mower at the far end of the lawn, he finally noticed her. He hesitated a moment, then switched the machine off and came striding over.

'Hi, Lizzie. Have you come to see Ingrid? She's not in, you know.' The chill coming off him was reminiscent of the draught she often noticed when she walked past her fridge, which really didn't seal at all well.

Lizzie gave a taut smile. 'Actually, I just popped over to say hi to *you*.' The attempt at carelessness didn't quite come off, largely because of the blush that swept over her entire body. 'Haven't seen you since ... well, in quite a while, anyway.'

He looked hard at her, frowning slightly, and she blushed more, if that was humanly possible. After the *barrage* of flirtation he'd subjected her to since the day they'd met, you'd think she'd be entitled to walk over for a chat without him acting as if she was presuming on a friendship that didn't exist.

'Yes, it's been quite a while,' he admitted. 'As a matter of fact, I've been studiously avoiding you.'

'What?'

'I've been keeping out of your way. I thought you'd be grateful.'

'Grateful? To be snubbed?'

He gave a shrug of his large shoulders, and, for the first time ever, a touch of awkwardness crept into his manner. 'Well, you know. After the public snogging incident. I'm not as thick-skinned as I look. I saw you rolling your eyes at Ingrid.'

'Oh, for God's sake, Bruno.'

'Do you deny you were rolling your eyes?'

'Well ... maybe I was. But to be honest, I was desperate to make her stay so that I wouldn't ... do anything silly.'

'Oh. You were tempted to do something silly, were you? God, the relief. I thought you were just flat-out desperate to be rescued.'

Lizzie was relieved to see the twinkle back in his eyes. Bruno without a twinkle was like a gin and tonic without ice and a slice of lime.

'Anyway, I really came over to ask if you'd go with me to a wedding,' she said in a rush. 'It's friends of ours in the Cotswolds. My husband's going to be best man and I'm matron of honour, so it's a complete bloody balls-up. He's gone and asked if he can bring a partner, so now I've got to produce someone, too. Either that or pretend I'm in casualty with third-degree food poisoning.'

By now, Bruno was grinning broadly. 'How could I refuse such a flattering invitation? When is this shindig?'

'Last Saturday of the month.'

'The thirty-first?'

'That sounds right.'

'Oh, bugger. I'm sorry, Lizzie. I have something else on. If you'd asked me sooner ...'

Lizzie was aghast. How dared he have something else on, after all the Saturdays he'd begged her to go on a date with him and she'd turned him down? It just wasn't fair. She forced her lips into a smile. 'No problem. That's absolutely fine. I'll find somebody else. Maybe I'll take Tessa and pretend I've gone lesbian or something.'

He gave a great big belly laugh. 'Relax, Lizzie, relax. Of course I can do it. I was just winding you up. I mean, you deserve it, after all the rejection I've had to bear.'

She made as if to cuff him over the head, and Madge gave a warning snarl. 'Whoa girl,' Lizzie said. 'I'm not really trying to clobber him, although it would do him the world of good.'

Bruno just laughed again. 'What do I have to wear? Full regalia?'

'Yup. Black tie, cummerbund, the lot. And ...'

'And what?'

'We'll have to sleep over. Bed-and-breakfast, because Maria's house will be full of relatives and whatnot.'

'Ah.'

'Separate rooms, of course.'

'Of course.'

Lizzie's face was as red as a ripe tomato again. God, he'd think she was setting them up for some sort of shag-over. She hastened to change the subject. 'The twins will be with my in-laws. Maria decided against kids at the do, I've no idea why.'

'Gosh, me neither. Why wouldn't she want the little angels there? They could hand around hors d'oeuvres and kiss grandmothers.' They both burst out laughing at the thought of Alex in such a role.

'Yeah, well, apparently there wasn't a chicken nugget or fish finger option on the caterer's menu,' Lizzie joked.

As she jogged effortlessly back to the cottage, she thought with satisfaction that if she had to turn up with a partner, she was glad it was Bruno. At least he was always good for a laugh, and she dearly wanted to look light-hearted and carefree if James was going to be flaunting the detestable Sonja.

'Mummy! Somebody atta door!' Alex bellowed much later that same day, racing past Lizzie at the kitchen table on his black plastic scooter.

The doorbell rang again, but Lizzie didn't move. She sat at the table with a large manila envelope in one hand and a letter in the other. The letter was short, but she was reading it over and over again.

'Mummy, iss Sarah atta door,' Alex called again. 'She says get Mummy to come open.'

'Yoo-hoo! Mrs Buckley? I mean, Lizzie? It's Sarah. Is everything OK?'

Lizzie stood up slowly. 'Yeah, fine. Come on in. I'm more or less ready to go.'

Sarah edged diffidently into the room. 'I can stay about forty-five minutes, I think. Will that do? Oh my godfathers, what's wrong? Has something happened in Australia?'

'No, no, it's nothing at all. Janie's fine, the baby's fine. It's just this stupid letter. From a literary agent. Remember I sent off the manuscript? Well, this is what they saw fit to send back.'

She handed the letter over and Sarah scanned it quickly. Lizzie already knew it by heart.

Dear Ms Indigo

Thank you for letting us read *Hamming it Up*. I'm afraid we do not feel able to represent the manuscript. The juvenile fiction market is tricky, and we do not see a niche for your verses, which are rather long and sophisticated for the early reader, but perhaps too facile for the pre-teen reader. Of course, another agent may feel differently.

Yours truly,

Jemima Straight, Literary Agent

Sarah was flushed with indignation by the time she'd read it through. 'They're just *idiots*,' she burst out. '*I'm* a ... a juvenile reader and I think the verses are great! They're *miles* better than most of the rubbish they're putting on the shelves at the library.'

'Oh, Sarah, thank you,' Lizzie said, looking at the letter forlornly.

'But perhaps you're not the average kid. Perhaps the average kid is way too cool to read my facile stuff.'

'Way too *stupid*, more likely. Anyway, who says I'm not cool?'

Lizzie ruffled Sarah's hair. 'You're the coolest kid I know,' she said honestly. 'But you're not dead average, are you? You read weird stuff – well, weird for your generation, I mean. Richmal Crompton. Dodie Smith. Georgette Heyer. Agatha Christie. Mazo de la Roche. I don't suppose you're any more in touch with the tastes of today's juvenile reader than I am. To think I had the nerve to start writing another volume of the stuff! Anyway, it was worth a try. At least now I'll never need to find a rhyme for pomegranate.'

And with that, she tossed the thick manila envelope, containing the sum of her literary ambitions, into the kitchen rubbish bin, where it came to rest on a small pile of banana peel, junk mail and cooked spaghetti. 'I'm off to run now,' she said with a big, false grin. 'Don't let the little monsters have any more ice-cream. They've already had two helpings.'

Running alone around the maize field, because Tessa wasn't feeling well and had cancelled at the last minute, Lizzie reflected bleakly that she'd been living in a fantasy world for weeks. She'd allowed Tessa to convince her that she could win James back, but it was obvious that he was no longer hers to reclaim. She'd permitted herself to dream that she could make a living as a writer, but it was obvious that she hadn't a hope in hell of even being published.

She'd better start living in the real world. She'd better draft those paragraphs for the divorce petition. And she'd better find herself some work that paid. If only there was something she could do from home. If only she'd suddenly discover that she was a hugely talented painter or sculptor. Yes, she'd be able to do oil paintings of people's pets, or make busts of local children. Except, of course, she'd consistently been given D's for art throughout her otherwise blameless school career.

She couldn't bear the thought of dumping the children in a crèche and going off to work in London. There must be *something* she could do in her little upstairs office. What a pity that her only marketable skill was writing press releases.

Hang on ... Surely she could write press releases from home? Perhaps her old company, G.H. Brightman, could be persuaded to send some work her way. Now, there, finally, was an idea worth pursuing.

When she'd worked for him, Gilroy Herbert Brightman had never asked Lizzie to lunch at his club. This was a lucky escape, she now realized. His club seemed to specialize in the kind of food she'd last encountered in her school dining hall.

The roast beef looked like tree bark, but luckily there was gravy to soften it up. Of course, it was the sort of gravy that had a skin on it, but, if you broke the skin, you could coax a few glutinous splodges of brown stuff out of the gravy boat and onto your plate.

'Married life seems to suit you, Lizzie,' G.H. Brightman ventured, peering doubtfully at her over his reading glasses as she shook salt over her food. 'You're looking very ... I don't remember you being quite so ... Anyway. How is your chap? What's his name? Lawyer, wasn't he?'

Lizzie picked up her knife and fork and began to saw away busily. 'Architect, actually. He's ... um ... he's fine.'

'Kids? Didn't you send us a birth announcement?'

'Twins. Yes. They're doing awfully well.' She took her first bite and settled in for a long chew.

Brightman took a thoughtful slug of red wine. 'Good of you to.... Always wondered how you were doing. Nice to catch up.' He stared at her in frank mystification.

He'd been surprised to hear from her at all, puzzled but polite when she asked if they could go to lunch. He thought she was the happy wife of a well-placed young man and living in bucolic Gloucestershire.

'How's the office?' Lizzie asked after a gulp of her own wine. 'Busy?'

'Oh, doing pretty well. Did you know we're thinking of opening an office in Glasgow? There's a gap in the Scottish market. We got Peabody on board. You know, the recycled pet bedding people.'

'Wow. Good job. I bet everybody's pretty stretched now.'

Brightman shrugged and picked his teeth discreetly. Apparently he was having trouble with the beef, too.

Lizzie took a deep breath and rushed into her prepared speech. 'I was just wondering whether you might possibly have some freelance work to send my way. You see, I'd really like to keep my hand in. The Internet makes it so easy to telecommute these days. I could easily help you out from home.'

Brightman blinked at her. 'Sorry? What?'

It wasn't the answer she'd hoped for.

'I could do the Petlove press releases. Mr O'Brien always said he liked the way I handled them,' she said desperately.

'Freelance? You think you could do the press releases freelance?' He adjusted his glasses so they were on the very end of his nose. Then he made a steeple out of his hands and pressed his lips together. 'It's a thought,' he conceded. 'But it wouldn't work. The whole telecommuting thing ... Sorry, my dear. You know how Mr O'Brien operates. He likes to do things face-to-face. I must say, he always did like *your* face in particular.' He leaned forward and patted her hand. 'Pity you got married – er, from my point of view, that is. You were an asset, a real asset, my dear. If you ever think of going back to work full-time ... But you won't, of course.'

Lizzie flashed him a phoney smile. 'I won't, of course. Look, I'm terribly sorry but I don't think I can manage any more of this beef.'

'Ah well, then you'll have room for the bread-and-butter pudding,' G.H. Brightman said with relish.

'So the fat old bastard wouldn't give you any freelance work?' Tessa asked as they ran that evening.

'No. Apparently it's my face the client values, not my press releases,' Lizzie replied grimly. 'By the way, what's the best place in Sevenoaks for daycare?'

'How would I know?' Tessa snapped. 'I'm childless, haven't you noticed?'

'Of course you'd know. You know everything.'

Tessa couldn't suppress a gratified little smile. She'd always been susceptible to flattery. 'Well, people do say Little Folks is good. Nice bright facilities and an outdoor playground. Who wants to know?'

'Me, of course. If I can't do freelance, I'm going to have to go back to work.'

Tessa turned to stare at her in surprise. 'But Lizzie, you swore you wouldn't go that route. You made the choice to raise your kids *yourself*. You're always going on about it – how rotten it is and how much you love it. I mean, isn't it a bit soon, anyway? You and James aren't even divorced yet. Maybe this thing with Sonja will blow over. It was probably just a one-night-stand. Plus, he's not going to cut you off without a penny, is he?'

Lizzie pushed herself to run faster. 'We haven't talked about money at all yet. You don't get to that part until after the divorce petition's filed. I've been stalling on the petition, but I can't do that for ever. And anyway, how can I go on paying the rent out of his bank account, buying my clothes on his credit card, and getting my hair done with his cash, now I know he's with someone else? It's a matter of pride. Besides, what if he doesn't have enough money? Between us, we're running *three* bloody houses now.'

'But one of them's earning money.'

Lizzie shrugged. 'The fact remains, I've been living in a dream world. I had this idea I could make some money out of my nonsense verses, but it turns out I'd probably have to *pay* to get them published. No, I need to sort myself out, one way or another. I've got to start bringing home the bacon. I'm on my own now.' She stopped talking to catch her breath. For some reason, the pace wasn't quite as comfortable as it should have been; maybe something to do with the fact that she'd wolfed down a large box of Smarties in the car that morning. She hadn't meant to eat the Smarties, but, as she'd opened the glove compartment to see if she'd left her missing sunglasses there, the box had fallen to the floor with a lovely rattle. She must have hidden them there weeks ago. She defied any normal person not to eat a Smartie or two if a large box of them fell unexpectedly into their hands.

Maybe pouring them wholesale down your throat as you drove

along was slightly less than normal. Still, the Smartie-guzzling was a minor aberration, a reaction to the stress that seemed to crackle in the air around her. She'd always been a bit of a panic-eater, and ever since Alex had mentioned seeing Sonja naked at James's house, she'd been panicking like mad.

'Let's not talk about this now,' she told Tessa. 'Let's just do some sprints. I need to work off all that chocolate.'

Tessa stopped in her tracks. 'Chocolate? You've been eating *chocolate?*'

'Smarties,' Lizzie called over her shoulder. 'Children's emergency box. Ate them on my way to the supermarket this morning. Don't worry, they've made me feel so sick, I won't be touching sugar again for weeks. Well, probably for years.'

She felt quite confident as she made this statement. Which just goes to show how wrong a person can be.

Chapter Fifteen

In the next five days Lizzie ate up the entire stock of her larder and fridge, including dry goods. Everything was grist to her mill: raisins, hot chocolate powder, peanut butter, mild cheddar cheese, condensed milk, stale Rich Tea biscuits, bright blue kids' yoghurt, cartons of custard, even an entire jar of her mother's homemade lemon curd. That stray box of emergency Smarties had started something.

And what was the point of being thin, now that her chances of winning James back had been blown out of the water? Why not find comfort where she could? Where was the sense in depriving herself of anything that could make her happy for a few short moments? She knew she was on a juggernaut of self-sabotage, but she lacked the will to jump off.

In ten short days, she was due to appear in front of two hundred or so people, including Sonja Jenkins, in a lilac, shot-silk matron-of-honour dress that was designed to fit like a glove, but what did she care? She might just as well go back to being fat and spineless. What difference was it going to make, after all?

To take her mind off the wedding, she worked on her CV, not the jokey one she'd sent to Jemima Straight Literary Agent in all her innocence, but a deadly serious one that she could send off in response to exacting advertisements in the *Guardian* and the *Independent*. As she sat tapping away on the keyboard, she munched through bowls of Readybrek and Weetabix with thick crusts of sugar.

Wearing the frayed old jeans from her fat days, Lizzie paid a visit to Little Folks. The place was run by a polished young woman who was the very antithesis of plump and homely Mrs Kirker. This woman was chic and sharp and thin. She made Lizzie fill out a slew of forms, all of which had to be submitted to some distant Little Folks head office, where Lizzie's credentials would be scrutinized and either accepted or rejected. Lizzie suspected that 'zero' was not the right amount to have filled in under 'household income'.

'What was it like, then?' Ingrid Hatter asked, as Lizzie sat in the barn's big bright kitchen, morosely staring into her mug of green tea. 'The daycare place?'

'It had a padded cell,' Lizzie said. 'They called it their soft room. All brightly lit and full of colourful foam cubes. But it was a padded cell.'

'You'll have to find somewhere else,' said Ingrid. 'Maybe someone does childcare at home.'

'There's nowhere else,' Lizzie said. 'Nowhere else with room for twins. I've already phoned around.'

'Do you really have to get a job, then?'

Lizzie gave a great, deep sigh. 'How can I not, Ingrid? I'm single. I'm about to be divorced. My husband is sleeping with his PA. I've gone and signed a year-long lease on Back Lane Cottage. Every time I use the credit card or make out a cheque on the joint account, I feel sick to my stomach. There *is* no joint anything any more.'

Sometimes, as Lizzie sat on the kitchen floor beside the fridge late at night, eating ice-cream straight out of the carton, she realized she'd like to poke Maria in the eye for putting her in this position.

Why hadn't she simply told James he couldn't bring a partner?

But that wouldn't have helped, not really. The mere fact that he'd *asked* if he could bring a woman with him would have been enough to destroy all Lizzie's fragile hopes and plans.

If only Maria and Laurence would suddenly have a change of heart and not get married at all. No, she couldn't wish that. If anybody deserved their special day, it was those two. But oh, how Lizzie wished she didn't have to be part of it.

She dreaded seeing James with Sonja on his arm. She dreaded going on show, newly single, before a fascinated crowd of village acquaintances. She dreaded bumping into Lady Evelyn at the manor, when she dropped the twins off.

Then there was the issue of Bruno and the bed-and-breakfast. She'd booked them into separate rooms, but each room contained a double bed. She had a horrible fear he was going to jump to conclusions.

There was only one small grain of hope in this veritable desert of dread, the hope that James, seeing her with Bruno again, might be struck down with jealousy and remorse.

It wasn't a logical or sensible hope. James had given her ample reason by now to assume that he didn't give two hoots what she got up to. After all, he'd given up their marriage without a fight, he'd forged ahead with divorce plans at a speed of knots, and he'd moved so swiftly into some sort of relationship with Sonja Jenkins that she could only conclude he'd been just itching to be on the loose again.

The fact was, she really didn't know if James still retained any residue of affection for her at all. But even if he didn't, he might still be vulnerable in a dog-in-the-manger sort of way. If she could just make him sting, even the tiniest bit, she knew she'd feel better.

The only problem was, by the end of the month she was going to be exploding out of her lilac dress like a pig in a party frock, not at all the sort of figure to inspire jealousy and remorse.

Lizzie had experienced binge-eating before. She'd just never experienced it alongside exercise addiction. By now, running had become her daily fix and she simply couldn't do without it, no matter how much she'd been wolfing down all day.

One evening, when Lizzie, Tessa and Petronella were scheduled to run laps at the high school track, Tessa dropped out at the last moment. Apparently, Greg had decided to come home early from work to take her out to a spontaneous romantic dinner. Lizzie speculated that the change of plan might have something to do with Tessa's ovulatory cycle.

While she wished the two of them nothing but luck, she also wished she didn't have to run laps with the snooty Petronella. In her current state of mind, she didn't feel like facing supercilious looks from Miss Zero Per Cent Body Fat.

Since she'd consumed the better part of a large Cadbury's slab only moments before easing her feet into her trainers, she wasn't surprised to be doubled over with a stitch just twenty minutes into the session.

'You go on,' she panted, dropping back to a walk and waving Petronella away. But Petronella slowed down and turned her high cheek-bones towards Lizzie with sudden keen interest.

'What's the problem? A stitch?'

'Yeah, and it's pretty bloody vicious.'

'You mostly get those from eating or drinking too much right before a run.'

Lizzie glanced up from her half-crouch. 'That's what I hear,' she mumbled. Was Petronella about to yell, 'Busted!' and cart Lizzie away in cuffs because she'd broken one of the golden rules of running?

'So, d'you know what I do?' There was something peculiar about Petronella's voice, something self-conscious and strained.

Lizzie straightened up, wincing. 'You throw a stone and the stitch disappears?'

'No. Before I run, if I've over-eaten, I ... I stick my finger down my throat.'

Lizzie gaped at Petronella, aghast. 'You what?'

'I didn't think you'd be so shocked.' Petronella sounded defensive. 'I mean, you've obviously got your own issues with food and weight, right?'

Lizzie squeezed her eyes shut and shook her head very quickly. 'I'm not *shocked*. Just ... surprised. You're so *thin*. You don't look as if you've ever had any kind of weight problem. I would never have taken you for a ...' She stopped and bit her lip.

'A bulimic,' Petronella finished matter-of-factly. 'Don't worry, I'm not in denial any more. I know what I am. I even know it's a stupid way to be, but God, it gets results.'

'Really?' With a swift movement, Lizzie raised her left hand behind her head and threw an imaginary stone. 'Aaargh, I think that makes things *worse*,' she cried, clutching her side. 'Maybe I'll just keep walking for a while.'

'I'll walk with you,' Petronella offered.

Lizzie shrugged. 'Don't feel you have to, honestly. You're here to get a decent work-out, after all.'

'Don't worry, there's plenty of time for that,' said Petronella. 'D'you know why I'm doing all this stupid running, anyway? To replace the throwing up. It doesn't work nearly as well, I have to tell you. Every now and then, if I really go overboard on the food, I still have to purge afterwards. It's ... it's a sort of compulsion.'

Lizzie was astonished that Petronella, who'd always scared her a bit, had decided to confide in her. She couldn't help feeling rather flattered. Obviously, she had the sort of face that inspired trust in people. She must look like the kind of person who could keep secrets and give good advice.

'I've never told Tessa about the bulimia, by the way,' Petronella warned. 'I mean, she knows I was in therapy about my marriage and my body image and so on, but she doesn't know about the chucking up. She's so ... I don't know ... *in control* of her life. She'd think I was pathetic. But you're different. You're obviously pretty screwed up, yourself. I mean, look at the way your weight yo-yos. For weeks there, you were whittling down your body. Now I see you're beginning to go the other way again. So I knew you'd understand and wouldn't start trotting out a whole lot of bloody advice.'

'Right, no, obviously. Erm, if chucking up works so well, why would you even want to stop?'

'Phwah, don't you know *anything* about eating disorders? Bulimia can kill you in the long run. Heart failure, generally. But more importantly, it rots your teeth and gives you foul breath. Plus, men don't like it, for some reason. They don't think it's normal. They think it means you're sick, or something. They also think it makes you infertile. They want to cart you off to counsellors and hospitals and whatnot.'

'Is that what happened? With your husband?'

Petronella broke into a very slow jog and Lizzie joined her. 'Yeah, that's what happened. He was all for checking me into some kind of treatment centre, and I wouldn't go. The funny thing is, a couple of months after we split up, I took myself off for treatment anyway. So now I'm officially a recovering bulimic, which is great – except I've lost my marriage. Life's a bitch and then you die, right?'

On that happy note, Petronella suddenly accelerated away, leaving Lizzie to plod along behind, nursing her stitch and an uncomfortable sense of *déjà vu*.

Enough was enough.

Something about Petronella's confession had chilled Lizzie to the bone. She'd never really thought of her love affair with food as 'addiction' or likely to flip over into illness. But gazing into Petronella's troubled green eyes, she began to wonder if she herself was poised on the edge of some ruinous slippery slope. Best not to find out, really. She decided to take evasive action while she still could.

That night, Lizzie went through her kitchen cupboards with a fine-toothed comb. Out came all the culprits – the cooking chocolate, the Boudoir biscuits, the honey, the Readybrek, the sugar, the salt and vinegar crisps, the custard powder, the tins of sticky toffee pudding, the raisins, the cashew nuts, the digestive biscuits. Not one of these things had been consciously bought for herself. Everything was 'for the children'. Otherwise, she'd be staring at Belgian chocolate and over-ripe Camembert, avocados and crème brûlée, pistachioes and chocolate mousse.

She piled everything on the cracked formica counter.

'There.' she said out loud. 'That's all of it out in the open.'

Watching the pile of food as if it might slide off the table and bury her, Lizzie opened her handbag and fumbled around until she found a card. 'Ivana Sanader, Emergency Number' was inscribed in the centre in a large, plain font.

She picked up the phone and dialled the number.

'Ivana? It's me, Lizzie. Lizzie Buckley. No, sorry, I don't want to use my credit card. Could you just send me the bill? No, it's not a crisis of the heart. It's . . . it's a crisis of greed. I'm binge-eating. No, not drinking. EATING. Can you talk me down?'

*

Tessa phoned the next morning to invite Lizze and the twins to lunch. 'Just come straight here after you pick them up from nursery,' she said. 'I've taken the day off to catch up on some stuff around the house.'

'Right, sounds good. Should I bring something?'

'How about dessert?'

Lizzie paused for a moment. 'OK, dessert it is. See you later.'

When Lizzie turned up at Tessa's door, clutching a bowl of fruit salad in one hand and hanging onto Alex with the other, Tessa gave the fruit one sniff and said, 'You call this dessert? I was hoping for cheesecake. Or lemon meringue pie. A hot sponge pud would've been good. But *fruit*?'

'Sarcasm does not become you,' Lizzie said, thrusting the bowl at Tessa, who'd never been seen so much as *touching* cheesecake, let alone eating it. A slight scuffle ensued as the children pushed past Lizzie's legs into the house. 'Don't *break* anything!' Lizzie called as they disappeared around a corner.

Thank goodness it was a clear day, so they were able to go outside. Lizzie was on tenterhooks whenever the children were cooped up in Tessa's house. People with no children always had so many fascinating breakables lying around within easy reach of grasping little hands.

With the children happily jumping in and out of the sprinklers, Tessa and Lizzie were able to settle down at the patio table in relative tranquillity. 'What's for lunch?' Lizzie asked as casually as she could.

The truth was, she was starving. After a long dark night of the soul, spent talking to Ivana at hourly intervals, and wrestling with her will power and the entire contents of her larder, she'd made it through to morning without touching so much as the crumb of a single chocolate biscuit. The comfort food was all in a black bin bag now, tightly secured and summarily dumped in the garage. She'd even thrown coffee granules and old cooking oil over everything, to make sure she didn't sabotage herself one night by going and scrounging out of the bag.

From now on the children would be snacking on wholewheat

bread and Marmite, with the occasional apple thrown in for variety. She'd had one miserable banana for breakfast, washed down with a cup of green tea. The whole experience had drained her, both emotionally and financially, and she sincerely hoped she'd never have to repeat it.

Lunch, thank goodness, would be diet-style food. Tessa tended to think an enormous bowl of field greens seasoned with a squeeze of fresh lemon juice, a dash of ground pepper and perhaps a thimbleful of pine nuts, was a fitting lunch for a grown woman – unless, of course, she happened to be running more than five miles later that same day, in which case she was entitled to a side dish of handmade wholewheat pasta stuffed with spinach.

'Pizza,' said Tessa.

'Well, for the children, obviously.' Using a method of thought control Ivana had taught her, Lizzie directed her mind away from images of oodles of melted cheese on golden crust. 'But what about us?'

'Pizza,' Tessa repeated blithely. 'Oh, and some garlic and herb sausages.'

'*Sausages?*' Lizzie couldn't believe her ears.

'Yes, why not? Gosh, was that your stomach growling? I'd better get the starters. Crisps and dips sound OK?'

Crisps? And *dips*? High sodium, high fat foods, here at Tessa's house in The Dene? Lizzie groaned. 'Oh, Tessa, don't *do* this to me. I'm trying to get back on the straight and narrow. You see, I've been on a bit of a bender with the calories lately. To be honest, I had to make some emergency calls to Ivana last night. In the end, I did a deal with Fate about the whole thing. I'm going to lose the roof over my head and the clothes off my children's backs if I don't pull myself together and stop binge-eating. I didn't think I'd be in any danger *here*. What's going on? You're supposed to be the food police.'

Tessa shrugged. 'A girl can let her hair down every now and then, surely? Look, I'll get the nibbles. You don't have to overdo it. Just go slow and you'll be fine.'

She went into the house and came out with a tray of dishes that didn't include a single crudité. With a pleased smile, she set the food down and helped herself to several sesame seed crackers dipped in something that seemed to be made entirely of double-thick cream and crushed garlic. Lizzie sat and looked at a mound of guacamole. Tears blurred her vision.

'I'm not going to eat it,' she said in a choked voice. 'Not any of it. For God's sake, Tessa, get me a plate of raw carrots. I'm not going to this bloody wedding looking like a sow in a silk dress.'

Tessa raised her eyebrows but went away and made up a plate of cucumber slices, tomatoes and broccoli. Lizzie sat and crunched stolidly, trying not to look at the spot of cream on Tessa's chin, trying to ignore the slurping noises Tessa made when she licked avocado off her fingers.

To take her mind off the food, Lizzie asked, 'What was Petronella's husband like? Did you ever have them over to one of your infertility dinner parties?'

Tessa presided over quite an active social circle made up of couples she and Greg had met in their quest for fertility. Lizzie and James had once been present at a gathering. All the talk had been of sperm counts and motility, ovulatory cycles and basal thermometers. Lizzie had felt horribly uncomfortable, being pointed out in hushed tones as a totem of fecundity because of the twins.

Tessa shrugged. 'I never met him, actually. They were already on the verge of divorce when I first came across her at the doctor's office. She was making some last-ditch attempt to sort things out, but it didn't work, obviously. Anyway, she doesn't talk about him much, and I don't like to pry.' Tessa put another heavily-loaded crisp into her mouth and chewed contentedly. Lizzie averted her eyes.

Tessa didn't like to pry? That was rich. Petronella must have warned her off the subject in no uncertain terms.

They ate steadily for a bit, watching the children play. Then Tessa suddenly jumped up. 'Hang on,' she said. 'I've got to bring on the *pièce de résistance.*'

She dashed into the house and came back moments later, walking slowly with both hands behind her back. Lizze leaned forward in her seat, fascinated. Was Tessa going to produce the most fattening dip the world had ever seen?

'Ta-da!' Tessa cried, and pulled out something that looked like a digital thermometer. She set it gently on the table and stood back, grinning from ear to ear.

Lizzie stared at the white stick with dawning comprehension. Right in the middle of the stick was a clear window, and running across the window were two thin pink lines, one slightly lighter than the other.

'Is this what I think it is?' she gasped, terrified of jumping to the wrong conclusion.

Tessa simply nodded. Lizzie noticed that her eyes were sparkling and that she was blinking quite a lot.

Lizzie leapt to her feet, knocking over her chair, and gave Tessa a tight bear-hug. 'Oh, you *wicked* thing. You've put something soaked in your own urine on the table! Why on earth didn't you tell me straight away? When did you find out? Is that why you and Greg went out last night? To celebrate?'

Tessa nodded. 'Best celebration of my life, even without the bubbly,' she said. And then she burst into very un-Tessa-like tears.

Lizzie felt her own lip wobbling and her eyes prickling in sympathy. 'Bloody Fate!' she railed. 'Just when you were getting all set to train properly for the marathon.'

Tessa gave a snort of laughter through her tears. 'Yeah, well, what can you do? Maybe in three or four years' time, huh? But you know what this means, don't you?'

Lizzie raised her eyebrows. 'Well, it seems to mean you've given yourself permission to eat naughty food for the first time since you were twelve.'

'Well, I'm eating for two now, aren't I? But that's beside the point. I'm talking about the *marathon*. The marathon's my lucky talisman. I can't give up on it completely or something horrendous is bound to happen. So I've got to pass the baton on to you.'

Lizzie felt her stomach clench painfully. 'To me? I'm no good with batons. Give it to Greg.'

'Greg's not a runner; he has flat feet.'

'Well, how about Petronella?'

'Honestly, don't you know anything? That won't work. She's

already running the thing for her own reasons. You can't double-dip. Look, I've *got* to have someone out there running for me. For this baby.' And she put her hand protectively to her stomach. 'Fate demands it,' she added for good measure.

'That, and the roof over my head and the clothes off my children's backs,' scoffed Lizzie. But something strange was welling up inside her, something like a full orchestra playing crescendoing music in her chest. She thought of her new niece, Elizabeth, tiny and powerless and covered in hairy down, barely recognizable as a human, yet more precious than all the combined crown jewels of England, Monaco and any other European monarchy you cared to mention. In a few short months, Tessa would be bringing just such a creature into the world, though, with a bit of luck, hers would look more like a baby and less like ET.

'OK,' she said with a small sob. 'I'll do it. I'll do it for your baby. I'll run the bloody thing.'

As she spoke, she felt a pair of cold wet arms curl around her knees, and a plaintive voice whined, 'Mummy, wassa matter? Why's evvybody cryin'? Where's our *lunch*?'

Ellie peered up at her, shivering and soaked, her brow positively bulging with worry.

'We're crying with happiness, sweetie,' Lizzie said, ruffling her daughter's wet hair. 'Auntie Tess,' she glanced at Tessa, who nodded, 'is going to have a baby. And I ... well, I've just decided I'm going to run one of the hardest races in the whole world.'

Ellie's face relaxed. 'That's good, Mummy,' she said. 'I like babies. But you better practise lots for the race so you don't come last dis time.'

Lizzie met Tessa's eye. The side of Tessa's mouth was quivering slightly. Lizzie gave her a quelling look.

'I will, sweetie, I will,' she assured Ellie.

A sudden loud crash put paid to the conversation as Alex plummeted out of a low tree, bringing down the branch he'd been swinging on. Lizzie leapt as if a games mistress had fired a starting gun, and reached his side before Tessa had even moved halfway across the lawn. When she got there, Alex was already standing up and examining his elbows and knees for grazes.

'Alex!' Lizzie cried, her heart in her mouth.

'Don't shout, Mummy,' he said, his face bright red and very earnest. 'I dint *mean* to break the tree. I woll fix it. If you find me some sticky tape, I pwomise I woll fix it.'

From: lizbuckley@hotmail.com
Sent: 26 August
To: janehawthorn@yahoo.com

Dear Janie

Thanks for the photos. I'm impressed. Both you and Elizabeth have made huge strides! Such a relief to see you looking your old self. Yellow never suited you. As for E, not a bouncing baby quite yet, but at least she looks less like a textbook pic of the foetus at seven months! What beautiful eyes, though. Give her a kiss for me, and tell Mum and Dad to come home. You must be driving each other up the wall by now.

Bye and love

Lizzie

PS Have put self on strict diet. Nothing but apples and water until the wedding. If matron of honour dress won't fit on Sat, the dressmaker will have me arrested for reckless endangerment of property or similar. Wish she hadn't taken measurements when I weighed less than eight and a half stone.

'Are you sure you don't want me to drive?' Bruno asked as Lizzie tooted at an ancient Mini that had suddenly pulled into their lane, just as she was speeding up to merge onto the M25.

'Little old men who drive Minis wearing Andy Capp headgear should be forced to re-take their drivers' licences every six months,' Lizzie muttered as they pulled out and surged past the offending vehicle. 'And no, I don't want you to drive. How do I know you don't drive like a maniac? You can't take chances when you have kids in the car.'

So saying, she suddenly pulled into the slow lane to pass a lorry that was thundering along down the middle of the highway.

'Interesting manoeuvre. I usually overtake on the right,' Bruno remarked mildly.

'Oh, shush. If you're going to back-seat drive all the way to Laingtree, I'll have to get out my ear-plugs.'

'Ear-plugs?'

'I keep them for when the children won't stop squabbling. They're also useful if your passenger won't stop second-guessing every single thing you do.'

'OK, I'll shut up. Let's find something soothing on the radio.'

'Soothing? We don't need soothing. We need rousing; we need upbeat; we need funky.'

'Funky?'

'You know, something to get us into party mood. So, what did you do with Madge?'

'Well, I thought of bringing her, but I wasn't sure if the B-and-B would have her. So I asked my neighbour to keep her.'

Things weren't as bad as they could have been, then. They could have had Madge along for the ride, trailing a long tongue out of the window and roaring at passing cars.

'Mum-*my*, are we there yet?'

'No, we are *not* there yet. We've only been in the car ten minutes.'

'Mummy, I'm hungwy.'

'Mummy, Alex is tryin' to spit at me.'

'Telltale, telltale.'

'Oh, for *heaven's* sake. Bruno, would you look in that bag behind your seat? You'll find a couple of tapes from the library.'

'Let's see ... The Wiggles? Raffi? *The Tale of Jemima Puddleduck*?'

'Wiggles! Wiggles,' came the cry from the back.

'Wiggles it is, then,' Bruno said cheerfully. 'So much for funky and rousing.'

'Oh, I don't know,' Lizzie shrugged. 'Have you heard their fruit salad number?'

More than two hours later, after a stop for lunch in Oxford, and just as both twins had finally dropped off to sleep, Lizzie turned off the main road and sped along a series of narrow, hedge-lined lanes snaking through picturesque fields dotted with sheep. After a while they began to drive past rolling parkland. Lizzie slowed down and put on her indicator as they approached a massive stone gate.

'What are you going in here for?' Bruno asked. 'We don't have time to start popping in at National Trust houses, surely?'

'It's not a National Trust house,' Lizzie snapped. 'It's where my in-laws live.'

'Christ Almighty! Why didn't you tell me you'd married minor royalty?'

Lizzie had almost forgotten her own shock and amazement when she'd first laid eyes on the myriad chimney pots and flying buttresses of Laingtree Manor. 'It's not as grand as it looks,' she said, not quite truthfully. 'Anyway, James's folks only live in one wing nowadays. The rest of the place is a sort of hotel. And they're not titled – except for Lady Evelyn. His family only bought the place three or four generations back, with money they made from something not very glamorous – wool trading, I think.'

'Where's your house, then? Somewhere nearby?'

'Mill House? It's down there, see? That cottagey place with all the trees around it.'

'Cripes,' he breathed. 'Now *that*'s what you call a garden! Can we drive over so I can take a closer look?'

'No, we can*not*,' Lizzie said, more sharply than she'd meant to. 'Some fabulously wealthy American businesswoman is there this weekend, apparently. It's hardly good manners to go and gawk.'

'Who takes care of the grounds, then?'

Lizzie pulled a face. 'My mother-in-law does the master-gardener thing, with a couple of local chaps once or twice a week to take care of the grunt work.'

'She knows what she's doing.'

Lizzie nodded. 'Yeah, you have to give the devil her due.'

Minutes later, they stood at the tall Gothic archway of the front door, Lizzie carrying Ellie, still groggy from her doze, and Alex hanging onto Bruno's hand.

As she sounded the enormous knocker, Lizzie found herself praying that her father-in-law would answer the summons. But she was out of luck. The heavy, carved door creaked open to reveal Lady Evelyn Buckley, attired for a casual country weekend in cashmere twinset, hairy burgundy skirt and matching burgundy pumps.

'Poor children, they're worn out!' was the first thing out of her mouth. 'Eleanor's as white as a sheet! I suppose you've been letting them stay up till all hours, Elizabeth. Well, come along, don't hang about, let's get them inside. And who might this be?'

'Erm ...' Lizzie couldn't think of Bruno's name for the life of her. This was the effect her mother-in-law had on her. No wonder the woman thought she was a ('middle-class') imbecile. Oh, not to mention a trollop, turning up with a man she barely knew from Adam.

'Bruno Ardis,' Bruno said firmly, and stuck out his hand. 'I'm Lizzie's partner. For the wedding.'

A fraction of a second passed while Lizzie's mother-in-law viewed Bruno's proffered hand with raised eyebrows and nipped-in nostrils. Then she extended her own for a fleeting shake.

'Ardis? That's unusual. It's not English, is it?'

Bruno shrugged slightly. 'I've always thought it was,' he said without rancour.

'Well, it isn't. It can't be. You'd better look it up on the World Wide Web. I'm sure you'll find your people come from somewhere peculiar, like Italy. And what is it you do, Mr Ardis?'

Lizzie, still clutching Ellie even though the child was struggling to escape, thought her heart might stop entirely. She should have primed Bruno. She should have told him to lie. If he opened his mouth now and said he was a gardener, she would simply sink through the floor with sheer mortification.

'Investment banker,' Bruno said smoothly. 'Retired.'

'Retired? At your age? I suppose you made a fortune gambling away old ladies' nest eggs. Really, it's quite criminal the way flashy young men with absolutely no ability to produce a *single* useful thing are allowed to make indecent amounts of money, just gabbing on the phone all day to their chums. At least James has an honest profession, I always say.'

Alex, hopping from flagstone to flagstone, suddenly piped up. 'Bruno cuts people's grass, Granny.'

Lizzie felt one of her eyelids twitch crazily. A nervous tic. This was new. 'He has his own landscaping business,' she explained hastily. As she spoke, Ellie oozed out of her grip, fell in a heap on the floor, and began to sob quietly.

Meanwhile, Lady Evelyn looked poor Bruno up and down. 'How ... interesting,' she murmured. Then she turned her attention to the whimpering child and her voice softened. 'Come on, Eleanor, stop that silly crying. Let's get you into the kitchen and give you some bread and milk.'

'She's just waking up, that's all,' Lizzie said defensively. 'Give her a moment and she'll be fine.'

'Don't worry, Elizabeth, I'm quite aware of that,' Lady Evelyn replied with a dismissive wave of her hand. 'A little discipline and structure go a long way, though, you'll find. Now, Mr Ardis, if you'll just set their luggage down against the wall over there, I'll get somebody to take it up to their room later.'

Obediently, Bruno put down the overnight bag he was carrying. He looked over at Lizzie with raised eyebrows. 'Shouldn't we get going?' he asked. 'Don't you have to pick up a dress, or something?'

'Oh, God! So I do.' But Lizzie couldn't bring herself to leave. She crouched down on the floor next to Ellie. 'Ellie, my love, do you want to lie down and finish your nap, maybe? How about if Gran lets you watch a video?'

'Good heavens, do you allow them to watch television at one o'clock in the afternoon? Remind me to give you an article I cut out about the detrimental effects of too much television on the unformed brain. Eleanor doesn't want to watch a video, do you, darling? She just needs to get some decent food inside her and then I'll read her a nice book. All this fast food stuff makes children quite irritable, I understand.'

Lizzie was just choking back a howl of rage when a familiar voice rang out, 'Oy, Alex, put that down right now! Ellie-Belly, what are you doing on the floor?'

'*Daddy!*' With a shriek of joy, Ellie jumped up and bounded over to her father. Alex hastily set down the large pewter jug full of dried flowers he'd been fiddling with and slammed himself into his father's knees.

Lizzie felt an absurd rush of relief. Thank God! James was here. Already, Ellie was bouncing back to her normal self.

But relief turned into blazing fury within fractions of a second.

Oh, God! *James* was here.

James, who'd asked Sonja Jenkins to stay over at his new house while the children were in his care, against Lizzie's express wishes. James, who'd let his three-year-old son see his PA's bare breasts.

James, who'd then bolted off to Scotland for two weeks, on the flimsy excuse of finishing the renovation of some barn, so that she, Lizzie, hadn't had the opportunity to confront him in person with his perfidy.

The bastard.

She stood up slowly, keeping her eyelids low so he wouldn't see the rage flashing in her eyes. Now was not the time to cause a scene.

James didn't seem to notice either Lizzie's suppressed fury, or the presence of Bruno. He was too much occupied with the twins, who were swarming all over him. Bruno, leaning against the wall, arms folded, viewed the scene with calm interest.

'Oh, don't let them do that, darling, they'll ruin your clothes,' Lady Evelyn said sharply, as Alex hooked his hands in the waistband of James's trousers, preparatory to rappelling up his frame.

'Relax, Mum, it's just a bit of fun.' James didn't seem in the slightest bit ruffled to be scolded as if he were yet another child. By now, Alex was sitting on his shoulders and chanting that he was king of the castle.

'OK, we'd better get going,' Lizzie said stiffly.

James looked at her at last. 'Hi, Lizzie. You look well. Have you put on some weight? You were so thin last time I saw you.'

Bruno stepped forward. 'Yeah, I kept telling her to be careful in the bath or she might trickle off down the plug-hole,' he remarked, almost as if he and Lizzie were in the habit of taking baths together. Lizzie could have kissed him in gratitude for the sly implication.

James's eyebrows shot up. 'Trickle ...? Oh, yes, right.'

Bruno stuck out his hand again. 'Bruno Ardis,' he said heartily. 'Lizzie's partner. We've met before, in Sevenoaks.'

'That's right,' Lizzie chimed in. Her voice sounded strangely shrill to her own ears. 'Only Bruno didn't have a shirt on, so maybe you don't recognize him fully dressed.' There. Let him not imagine for a moment that he was the only one who could have romps with bare-chested people.

'Of course,' said James as he clasped Bruno's hand. 'Bruno. The garden tap chap. With the wife who makes steak-and-kidney pie. Nice to see you again.' He hoisted Alex down from his shoulders. 'Come along, kids, let's go to the kitchen, then. Granny has a snack for you.' And he sauntered off with a twin hopping and skipping along at each hand.

He really hadn't looked particularly perturbed to see her with Bruno, Lizzie thought sadly. That was probably because he thought Bruno's wife had lent him out for the evening. Never mind, Bruno was bound to look fabulous in a dinner jacket, and James couldn't fail to feel a few twinges at the wedding, surely? Especially if they somehow conveyed to him the fact that there was no steak-and-kidney wife waiting in the wings.

Lady Evelyn shot Lizzie a reproving look. 'Goodbye, then. We'll see you tomorrow morning when you come for the children. *Enjoy* yourselves.'

Back in the car, Lizzie sat with her hands on the steering wheel for a moment or two, taking a few deep breaths.

Bruno got in beside her and fastened his seat-belt. 'Is your mother-in-law always so ... so charming?' he asked with a twinkle.

Lizzie shook her head in wonder. 'Did you see the way she *looked* at us? As if ... as if ...'

'As if we might suddenly strip off our clothes and start going at it right in front of her?'

'Yeah. Something like that.'

'Don't worry about her. Obviously, she's upset that you've hurt her son's feelings.'

'Oh no, she *always* looks at me as if I'm about to do something obscene. As a matter of fact, she's relieved to be shot of me. It would be good riddance, I'm sure, if I didn't happen to be the mother of her grandchildren. To be fair, she dotes on them. She's actually quite good with them, in her way.'

'Ah. I see. You bring out the worst in her, do you? But James doesn't seem a bad bloke.'

'He gives a good impression, doesn't he? Looks like the kind of chap who'd keep his word, do right by his children, that sort of thing. In fact, you'd probably be surprised to hear that he's a lying swine who thinks nothing of letting his three-year-old son see his new girlfriend naked.'

'Crikey. He doesn't seem the type! He was a bit taken aback to see me here, don't you think?'

'I was hoping he'd react a bit more, to be honest. You're going to have to be a lot more flirtatious with me. And we'll have to let him know you're divorced, too. He'll have the bitch, Sonja Jenkins, on his arm at the wedding.'

'Sonja Jenkins?'

'Yes, his personal assistant. She's assisting him in the most personal ways possible just at the moment.' She started up the car. 'I hope the twins are OK.'

'They'll be fine. Tough as old boots, those two. So where next?'

Lizzie heaved a sigh that seemed to come up from the very soles of her feet. 'The dressmaker's in Stowe,' she said. 'I have to do a final fitting, then head over to Maria's house to help her get ready. I'll drop you at the B and B now. The wedding starts at five. I'll show you the church.'

'And what am I supposed to do at the B and B all afternoon?'

Lizzie cast him a frantic look. 'I didn't think of that. Did you bring a book or something? Maybe you could nap.'

'Don't worry,' said Bruno soothingly. 'I can look after myself.'

Chapter Sixteen

The apple and water diet had worked.

It was touch and go, but the dressmaker finally managed to get the zipper up and fasten the hook and eye of the silk dress under Lizzie's left arm. She then stood back with a mouthful of pins, and remarked, through gritted teeth, 'You went ahead and put on some weight, I see.'

Lizzie opened her eyes very wide. Whoops, there went that tic again! 'Really? You think I've put on weight? I suppose it's *possible*. I mean, I was trying very hard not to *lose* any weight, after our conversation last time.'

The dressmaker shook her head crossly. 'You girls. Up and down like see-saws. I don't know. Still, it doesn't look *too* bad – only you'll have to remember to suck in that stomach.' She gave Lizzie's middle a little dig with the flat of her hand. With a hiss of indignation, Lizzie pulled it in as far as it would go. It was quite an effort. Really, she should have brought some support pants. Or a corset.

'Take a little look,' the dressmaker said, and gestured towards a full-length mirror on the other side of the room.

Lizzie looked.

It was a beautiful dress, excellently cut, a long sheath of softly draping lilac that wouldn't have looked amiss on the red carpet at the Oscars. In it, Lizzie looked tall and curvaceous, elegant and composed. If breathing was a bit difficult, that was a small price to pay.

Lizzie turned to the tetchy little dressmaker. 'Thank you,' she said with real warmth. 'Thank you, thank you, *thank you*. I feel ... so much braver, now.'

Astonishingly, the woman allowed herself a small, tight smile through her pins. 'You look like a million pounds, though I say so myself,' she replied. 'I'm certainly not ashamed to have you wearing one of my dresses. But if I were you, I wouldn't eat anything.'

Getting out of the dress was more difficult than getting into it, but between the two of them they managed to ease it over her head. Then the dressmaker wrapped it tenderly in tissue paper and hung it in the car for her. 'Good luck, my dear,' she said, and Lizzie felt as if she'd been blessed at the pulpit.

Maybe the whole event would go swimmingly, after all.

Maria's house was in a state of chaos, heaving with people Lizzie had never met. Maria, wearing a tatty old dressing gown and brightly-coloured spiral curlers, was circulating calmly, offering people coffee and asking them if they'd had enough to eat.

When she spotted Lizzie, who'd walked in without ringing since the front door was standing open, she sailed forward and wrapped her in a hug that smelt crisply of oranges and lemons.

'Hello, sweetheart. How's the dress? Everything OK? Any news from Australia?'

'Everything's fine. Janie and the baby are doing really well, thank God. And the dress fits. But Maria, what are all these people doing here? Shouldn't you be getting ready in peace and tranquillity?'

Maria gave a chuckle. 'Well, it would be nice, wouldn't it? But I couldn't possibly turf this lot out. Some of them have come all the way from the Borders.'

'Well, at least stop waiting on them hand and foot,' Lizzie hissed. 'It's time we started prinking and preening, isn't it?'

But it was at least twenty minutes before they managed to sneak away, because of course Maria had to introduce Lizzie to her father, her aunts, her uncles, her niece and nephews, and several ancient relatives, all of whom wanted to know her maiden name and her mother's maiden name so they could try to work out whether they'd ever known any of her 'people'.

When they finally got away, the hairdresser, brought in from Evesham, followed them upstairs to unroll the curlers and comb out Maria's 'do'. Lizzie, who was burning to tell Maria all about the encounter at the manor, was obliged to sit and chat about the weather and Maria's choice of flowers while the hairdresser worked.

But when the woman was done, Lizzie was absolutely astonished. Plain Maria Dennison, with her schoolgirl pony-tail, was transformed into a glorious Medusa, with glossy corkscrew curls tumbling down her back.

'Good grief,' Lizzie breathed. 'You're ... beautiful.'

Maria tossed her hair and chuckled. 'Don't sound so bloody surprised.'

The hairdresser, whose name was Mandy, then went to work in a businesslike way with a box of make-up. The result was almost unnerving. Lizzie had never known Maria could look so lovely – and so formidable. If Lizzie had first met Maria in this guise, she probably wouldn't have had the guts to say more than, 'How do you do?'

'Stop staring, Lizzie,' Maria said. 'You're making me nervous. Anyway, it's your turn now. Get going, Mandy; we seem to be running late.'

With great efficiency, Mandy washed and conditioned Lizzie's bob. She then went at it with a blow-dryer and several different kinds of brushes. 'There,' she said with satisfaction when it was done. 'What do you think? Lots of texture now, and loads of movement.'

It was fabulous. Mandy was some kind of magician. Lizzie's hair looked more groomed and stylish than she'd ever seen it. Without wasting a moment, the woman turned her attention to Lizzie's face.

'You should be working for a fashion magazine, or one of those makeover shows on TV,' Lizzie blurted out in heartfelt wonder when her make-up was finally done. 'You're absolutely *brilliant*. What on earth are you doing in Evesham? You should open a place in London.'

Mandy smiled graciously as she packed away her make-up and hair brushes. 'Just be careful not to smudge anything when you're getting into your dresses,' she said.

By the time she'd helped Maria into her ivory satin gown, and squeezed into her own lilac one, Lizzie's heart was beating uncomfortably hard.

It was show time.

At ten past five, Lizzie marched slowly down the aisle behind Maria to a swelling rendition of Wagner's 'Bridal Chorus'. She kept her eyes on the row of satin-covered buttons running down Maria's back. It wasn't that she was too nervous to look at the congregation. OK, it *was* that she was too nervous to look at the congregation. Apart from all the curious stares, she was terrified of spotting Sonja Jenkins, and being so put off her stride that she'd trip and fall into Maria's train. That said, the tiny buttons on the back of the dress were a real work of art, well worth staring at.

'Lizzie,' a voice hissed. She risked a quick sideways glance. Bruno, sitting at the edge of a crowded pew on the bride's side of the church, gave her a big grin and a quick wink. Lizzie saw a series of nudges and whispered conversations break out like a mini-whirlwind around him. She gave him a repressive scowl and went back to counting buttons.

At the right-hand front pew, Laurence and – oh my God – James stood half-turned, watching the approach of the bride. Laurence seemed shinier than usual, and was beaming from ear to ear. James wasn't smiling. He looked rather pale and stern. Lizzie had forgotten how raffishly handsome he was in a dinner jacket.

When Maria's father lifted the veil from Maria's face, a faint titter passed through the church at Laurence's reaction. First, his jaw fell open slackly. Then he was heard to mutter urgently, 'Maria? Is that *you*?'

The weight of a couple of hundred stares made Lizzie's back prickle as the wedding party stood at the altar, waiting for the minister to do his business. Had there ever been such a slow and measured delivery of the marriage service, in the history of Christian ceremonies? And had there ever been a noisier congregation? The whispers and shufflings were like the faint roar of a cornfield in a stiff breeze. Lizzie was convinced people were so overcome with the need to gossip about the matron of honour and best man that they couldn't observe the normal proprieties of the occasion.

Lizzie couldn't help wondering for the hundredth time why Maria hadn't opted for a registry office ceremony, or – better still – one of those destination weddings on some remote island on the other side of the world. Yes, a destination wedding would've been perfect. Right now, they could be standing barefoot on a beach, wearing garlands of tropical flowers, jumping playfully out of the way of happy little waves – blissfully free of this great gaggle of villagers and the boring drone of a long-winded Church of England minister who didn't know how to get to the point.

Dammit, if any of her friends ever asked her to be matron of honour again, she'd *demand* a destination wedding. At this very moment, Ellie and Alex could be building sand castles in the background, because that sort of wedding was obviously so informal that children were welcome. In fact, there'd probably be hordes of barefoot local kiddies throwing confetti or blowing bubbles at them. Best of all, that sort of wedding was so casual – and so costly to get to – that nobody would *dream* of bringing a partner.

A sudden tug on her elbow brought Lizzie back to the cool, dimly-lit altar with a jolt.

'Huh?' she said in surprise.

For the second time, the congregation tittered discreetly.

'My *bouquet*,' Maria muttered out of the side of her mouth.

Hastily, Lizzie took the flowers Maria was thrusting at her. She'd entirely forgotten the bouquet-holding aspect of her duties. Come to think of it, she'd been delinquent in the dress-fluffing department, too!

Still, now was probably not the time for fluffing, given that they were saying their 'I do's'. Better leave it till later.

Concentrating hard now, Lizzie watched James produce the rings out of his pocket. With a pang, she noticed that he wore nothing on his own ring finger but a small band of pale, untanned skin. She wasn't wearing her rings either, but that was mainly because they kept slipping off her finger now that she'd lost weight.

'You may kiss the bride,' the minister intoned at last.

With great alacrity, Laurence twisted one hand in Maria's Medusa-like curls and almost bent her over backwards as he pressed his mouth to hers.

People clapped and laughed, then the organ struck up and everyone filed out of the pews and began milling around.

Standing on the church steps beside Maria, Lizzie suddenly remembered her obligations.

'For heaven's sake, what are you doing?' Maria demanded, as Lizzie began tweaking and rearranging her skirt.

'I'm fluffing,' said Lizzie. 'Would you rather I didn't?'

'I'd much rather you didn't. I mean, it's not as if I'm wearing a bustle or anything. Just relax. Enjoy the moment!'

So Lizzie straightened up and tried to relax. With a permanent smile plastered on her face, she kept a sharp look-out for Sonja Jenkins, but there was such a crush of people that she couldn't spot her. She noticed James gazing out across the crowd, and wondered if he were looking for Sonja, too.

When she caught sight of Bruno among a thicket of smart young Laingtree matrons, she suddenly realized they hadn't discussed how he'd get to the reception, which was being held at a country hotel several miles away. 'Excuse me, I have to talk to Bruno for a second,' she hissed in Maria's ear.

It was hard to scuttle through the press of flesh in an unobtrusive way when you were wearing a long, shot-silk gown and holding a bouquet of mixed summer blossoms, mainly lilac roses. People kept trying to waylay her, shouting things like, 'Fabulous dress, Lizzie. How's London treating you, Lizzie? What have you done with the twins today, Lizzie?'

At last, she reached Bruno's side. 'You OK?' she asked casually, bursting into the little circle in all her finery. A couple of the women greeted her with fulsome cries of spurious joy, and she gave a general little wave and smile in return.

'I'm fine, Lizzie, just fine,' Bruno said with an easy smile. 'Shouldn't you be up there on the church steps with the bride, though?'

'Don't worry, I'm heading back right away. I just wanted to ask if you could drive my car over to the reception. I don't think it would be quite the thing for you to arrive with the wedding party.'

'Oh, don't you worry about Bruno,' one of the women called out. 'He can travel with us. Travis will be delighted.'

Lizzie wasn't entirely sure that Travis would be delighted to be chauffeuring a young(ish) man with cherubic curls whom his wife couldn't seem to stop touching. Every time this woman (Lizzie recognized her as a teacher from the local primary school) made any conversational point, no matter how mundane, she seemed to need to underline it by patting Bruno on the shoulder with her long, manicured fingers, or touching his elbow, or nudging him gently in the side.

'No, honestly, he'd better take the car,' Lizzie said. 'We'll need it to get back afterwards. The keys are at the desk at the B and B.'

'Well, he can follow us there, in that case,' said the persistent teacher. 'It's a tricky route.'

'Thanks, I'll do that,' said Bruno.

'See you later, then,' Lizzie muttered, and raced back to her post on the church steps.

As she dashed up the steps, holding her skirt so she wouldn't trip, she became aware that someone was staring at her. Glancing up she caught James's blue eyes boring into her. Their gazes snagged together, like fish hooks caught in mid-cast. Lizzie's stomach did an odd little swoop. Maybe he'd seen her talking to Bruno. Maybe the jealousy and remorse were setting in. He certainly looked like a thundercloud.

The crowds began to disperse now, as people moved on to the reception. Lizzie watched like an anxious mother as Bruno walked away towards the car park, escorted by the school teacher and her long-suffering husband. He turned and gave her a little wave and a thumbs-up just before they rounded a corner and disappeared out of sight.

Soon there was nobody left at the church but the wedding party.

The obligatory photo session passed in a blur for Lizzie. With one part of her brain, she followed the photographer's instructions

– hold up your bouquet, hold it down, put your hand on the bride's shoulder, turn slightly sideways – while the rest of her brain darted about restlessly.

Was Sonja Jenkins lying low, perhaps, too ashamed of herself to show her face? Had she decided not to come at all? What would she be wearing, if she was here? Scarlet, probably. Did James feel any guilt about breaking his promise to Lizzie that he wouldn't confuse the children by having women stay over in his house? Probably not. He wasn't baulking at breaking his promise to love her till the end of time.

'That's it! We're done here, people,' the fat little photographer announced, placing lens caps on lenses and packing away his equipment. Funny how photographers were always so bossy, Lizzie reflected. In their way, they were quite the wedding despots, marching people from pillar to post and making them stand in unnatural positions, clasping each other in unnatural embraces.

'Psst! Lizzie!'

She almost jumped out of her skin. Somehow or other James had snuck up on her.

'Come around the side here, quick,' he said, indicating the wall of the church with a flick of his head.

Lizzie's pulse went haywire. What on earth was going on? Was James seizing the moment to apologize to her about Sonja? Oh, God, was it possible he had something even more momentous to say?

She gave a quick look around, but nobody was watching them. Almost everyone was clustered around Maria and Laurence, as if they'd been transformed by the last hour and a half's work into minor celebrities.

'OK,' she muttered, 'you first. I'll follow in a moment.'

He gave her an odd look, but did as she suggested, striding purposefully round the side of the building. She waited a couple of heartbeats and then sauntered after him, hoping that her back conveyed the casual look of a person intent on viewing the architecture from another angle. Even though her heart was thumping with excitement, she was still level-headed enough not to want to set any more tongues wagging about the state of play between the Buckleys.

'Right, there you are.' James popped out from behind a bush. 'We'd better be quick.'

'Er ... quick?' Lizzie's mind boggled. What on earth did he mean? This didn't sound like the prelude to an important speech.

'Quick, lift your arm.'

'*What?*'

'Lift your arm! Don't you *know* that your zip's split?'

'My zip?' The dignified and reproachful speech Lizzie had been preparing regarding James's behaviour with Sonja went out of her head with a ping. She glanced at her left side. Holy mackerel! She was open from armpit to hip bone, flesh-coloured strapless bra and lilac panties cheerfully on display.

'Oh, shit,' she said quickly, a painful blush rising as she grabbed at the sides of the dress and tried to hold them together. 'Why didn't anyone tell me?'

'It only happened a moment ago. Come on, let's see if I can fix it.'

Humiliated to think of the wild hopes she'd entertained just seconds before, she bowed her head and held up her arm. He half-knelt at her side, trying to slide the little plastic moving part back down from the top of the zip to the bottom. It was hard work, apparently.

'Can you, sort of, suck in your tummy?' he asked.

She pulled it in as hard as she could, and for once didn't feel even slightly ticklish as his fingertips bumped against the bare skin of her side.

He managed to wiggle the fastener back down to the bottom of the zip again, but as he eased it upwards, it was clear that he was going to have some trouble squeezing everything back inside. Oh, God. She might as well just have worn a sign saying, 'Too fat for this gig.'

'It's a bit on the tight side,' he remarked through clamped teeth. 'But, there, I've got it. Let's hope it holds.'

'Thanks,' Lizzie muttered, still red in the face, and on the verge of tears.

'Don't mention it,' James replied. 'Come on, we'd better get back. I could murder a double whisky right now, couldn't you?'

Determined to salvage a little of her dignity, Lizzie called after him, 'By the way, Bruno isn't really married. It's . . . it's a real date. He's not, you know, out on loan or anything.'

James looked back at her over his shoulder. 'Oh. Excellent,' he said. 'I'm glad to hear it.'

Chapter Seventeen

Sonja Jenkins wasn't at the wedding. Lizzie had scanned the room again and again from the bridal table, and the woman simply wasn't there. James must have come alone, after all.

What on earth did that mean?

Maybe she'd made a huge tactical error, making sure James knew Bruno was single.

Still shaken by the shameful ordeal of the split zip, Lizzie hardly dared glance at James, sitting just a few feet away on the other side of Laurence. But the moment he stood up to make his speech, her armpits began to gush with sweat. Oh, no! She'd all but forgotten that it was the best man's duty to propose a toast to the matron of honour.

But James was good at toasts. There wasn't a trace of awkwardness about him when he asked the assembled company to raise their glasses to 'Lizzie, as lovely today as we've ever seen her.' If you weren't in the know, you'd never have guessed he was talking about the wife he'd walked out on.

For some reason, this toast seemed to strike a chord with the wedding guests. There were calls of 'Hear, hear' and 'Bravo, Lizzie', almost as if she'd done something worth applauding. Maybe they were cheering her for losing so much weight. Although she'd put on a tad recently, she'd still shed, overall, the equivalent of a six year-old child, pound for pound. Maybe they violently approved her new hairstyle. Maybe they were simply impressed that she'd had the gall to show her face at all. Whatever the reason, their unexpected kindness made Lizzie's eyes prickle and her heart swell with an odd combination of mortification and gratitude.

As the speeches went on, she wondered how she'd act when the time came for the matron of honour to dance with the best man. Certainly, she didn't have the courage, or even the inclination, to revert to her original plan to beguile and bewitch him on the dance floor. Sonja might not be here at the wedding, but that didn't prove for a moment that James had excised her from his personal life. Any number of things could have prevented her from coming; gastrointestinal flu, for instance.

As it turned out, Lizzie didn't have to dance with James at all. The wedding party numbers were out of kilter because Maria's mother had died of leukaemia years ago. With great forethought, Maria had primed her father to ask Lizzie for the first dance. Lizzie was quite happy to take a spin around the floor with Mr Dennison's enormous walrus moustache hovering above her shoulder while James did his duty by Laurence's mother. As a matter of fact, Lizzie felt strangely fond of the old chap, because his few words about Maria had been absolutely spot-on.

'I never thought I'd see this day,' Mr Dennison had told the upturned faces with disarming honesty. 'She's a grand lass, of course, but not exactly the nesting variety. All I can say is, thank God the Hendershotts taught their son to cook. No, seriously. Here's to my girl, who grew up so strong and tall and good, without a mother to guide her.'

After that first waltz, the dance floor was quickly swamped with slightly tight wedding guests, and the danger of being forced into some sort of exhibition waltz with James passed harmlessly by.

Wandering away from the dance floor, Lizzie decided she'd better find Bruno.

He was sitting at his table, chatting to some weather-beaten farmer chap as if he'd known him all his life, showing no signs at all of wondering where his partner was. But his face lit up in a heartening way when he saw her.

'Ah, Lizzie! There you are. I was about to come up and claim you for a dance.'

'You weren't in too much of a hurry, I see. Never mind. My

feet are killing me in these shoes. Why don't we go and get a drink, instead?'

Obligingly, he stood up and led the way towards the bar. Spotting a handy sofa against the wall, Lizzie sank down thankfully while he ordered the drinks.

When he eased himself down beside her with the two glasses, she pulled a wry face and said, 'You know what? It looks as if I needn't have brought you, after all.'

'Ouch,' he said, taking a sip of his red wine. 'You're so good for my ego. What do you mean?'

'Sonja Jenkins doesn't seem to be here. I think James came alone.'

Bruno set his glass down on a table. 'Um, Lizzie, he didn't come alone.'

Lizzie's heart clenched. 'What ... what do you mean?'

'You know when you went to have your dress fitted? Well, I took a stroll to the pub. Everybody was there.'

'Everybody?'

'The wedding crowd. Laurence, of course. Good bloke, that Laurence. A whole mob of people from Laurence's side. James, too. Bit bloody awkward, that. And ... and James's partner was there.'

'So, who is she?'

Bruno looked a bit shifty now. 'I'm sure you've never met her,' he said. 'She's American.'

'American?'

'Yeah, from some place called Santa something in Florida.'

Lizzie's hand tightened on her wine-glass, and her skin popped up in gooseflesh. '*Show* me,' she said, and downed her wine in one.

Bruno sighed and heaved himself to his feet. 'Come on, then.' As they wove their way among the tables, Lizzie ignored a few yells of her name, her mind focused on one thing only. When they passed an empty table, she picked up a random glass of white wine and took a slug. She had a feeling she was going to need medicinal alcohol.

'There,' Bruno said suddenly, jerking his head towards a table on their left.

Several people were seated at the table, and, as they watched, James strolled up and took a seat next to one of the women. Lizzie had noticed this woman earlier, when she'd been looking for Sonja Jenkins. You couldn't miss her, really.

'Oh, no! Not *her*,' Lizzie whispered.

She had red hair. Real red hair, not the dyed variety. In most people, this was a misfortune. If somebody had come up to Lizzie and said, 'James is going out with a redhead', Lizzie would've been relieved. Even a little incredulous. Huh, she'd have thought, couldn't he do any better than that?

But this woman's hair was her crowning glory. It was thick and sleek, positively rippling with health, good styling, and expensive serums. And it wasn't that carroty red that gets kids bullied at school. It was a strange, wine-dark colour, full of burnished coppery lowlights, like a very old cabernet sauvignon held up to candlelight.

And this woman didn't have the redhead skin tone. Lizzie doubted whether either freckle or blush had ever blemished the luminous perfection of her exquisitely whipped-cream complexion.

She was easily the most beautiful woman Lizzie had ever laid eyes on, outside of a movie screen.

As the woman leaned over James to talk to his neighbour, Lizzie saw that her black dress was backless enough to show more than a hint of bottom cleavage. Bottom cleavage, in this case, didn't look like an embarrassing *faux pas*. It looked like the height of sophistication, the very pinnacle of classy North American chic, designed to make all the women in Gloucestershire feel hopelessly dowdy and provincial.

Settling back into her chair after making some point, the woman swept her eyes lazily around the room. Just for a moment, her confident, unconcerned gaze caught and held Lizzie's. Lizzie froze like a deer in the headlamps. The stranger allowed herself a barely perceptible smile and a swift lift of her perfect brows. Then she deliberately turned towards James and placed her hand on the inside of his thigh, quite high up. With her lips less than quarter of an inch from his ear, she whispered something, and he laughed. As he turned to whisper back, Lizzie could see the light in his eyes. Then the woman lifted her hand to the back of his head and casually pulled him into a kiss.

'Come on, Lizzie, let's get out of here,' Bruno said gruffly. 'You've seen her now. No point loitering.'

Lizzie let him take her by the arm and lead her out of the room. As the swinging doors closed behind them, the insistent beat of the music was abruptly muffled. Bruno kept on walking, towing Lizzie along, until he found a couple of fireside chairs in a little nook of the hotel's reception area.

Lizzie was shivering, although the evening was still quite warm.

'Should I get my jacket for you?' Bruno said.

'No,' Lizzie said quickly. 'Don't. Don't leave me. I'll be fine. I'm not really that cold.'

He took one of her arms and began to rub it briskly. 'Would you like a cup of tea? I'm sure I could order one.'

'No. Nothing. I don't want anything. Why didn't you tell me? Why didn't anybody tell me?'

'Tell you what?'

'Come on, Bruno. You're not a *complete* idiot. Why didn't anyone say James was going to be here with ... with *that*.' Lizzie threw a hand into the air in a despairing gesture. 'And to think I thought he was bringing ordinary little Sonja *Jenkins*.'

'But Lizzie, did you see her teeth?' Bruno asked.

Lizzie frowned, slightly puzzled. 'Well, no,' she admitted, allowing him to go on rubbing her arms.

'Perfect,' he said. 'An absolutely perfect set of teeth. So white, they'd blind you if she ever gave a proper smile.'

Lizzie began to feel vaguely indignant. 'And you're telling me this to *comfort* me?'

'Well, in a way. I mean, they're too perfect, if you get my drift. They give you the feeling they can't be real. It's not just the teeth. It's the whole woman. She's like a Stepford Wife. Or a Barbie doll. I'd find it all a bit creepy, if I were James.'

'Did you ... did you talk to her at all, in the pub?'

Bruno shrugged. 'A bit,' he admitted.

'Well? What did you find out?'

Bruno seemed strangely reluctant to impart any further information. 'Does it really matter?' he asked.

'Of course it matters. Come on, spit it out. What do you know?'

'If you insist, then. She's ... erm ... her name is Erin. Erin Wilde.'

'*And?*'

'What makes you thinks there's any and? OK, OK. *And* she's staying at your house.'

'*Mill House?*' Lizzie was incredulous.

''Fraid so.'

Lizzie shook her head, at a loss for words.

'He works pretty fast, doesn't he?' said Bruno, almost in admiration. 'First the PA, now this tourist. He must have met her in the last couple of days, and already he has her coming to a wedding.'

'No, Bruno,' Lizzie croaked. 'I think he's known her for ages. She's ... I'm pretty sure she's an ex-girlfriend.'

'An ex-girlfriend?'

'You said she was from Florida, but I think you got it wrong. It's California, isn't it?'

Bruno thought a bit and then nodded. 'That's right,' he said. 'Santa ... Barbara, maybe? I'm not that hot on geography.'

Lizzie huddled down in her chair. 'Definitely the ex-girlfriend, then.' She was crying now in the way she'd perfected when she first went to Sevenoaks. Soundlessly, without any movement of her facial muscles at all. Tears simply slipped down her cheeks, as if she had incontinence of the ducts all over again.

'I'll have some tea now,' she said.

As Bruno strode off to find a waiter, Lizzie tried to dry up the tears with a tissue, but it was useless.

She could have forgiven James Sonja Jenkins, maybe. Proximity, opportunity, all those extenuating circumstances; she could have allowed herself to be convinced that he'd unwisely taken comfort because it was more or less shoved in his face.

But he must have gone to some lengths to reclaim Erin, his 'brassy Californian'.

Maybe he'd been having an affair with her all along? Yes, he'd probably been meeting up with Erin for months before he left Lizzie. He went away on enough business trips to facilitate any number of affairs.

Maybe he'd been planning to leave Lizzie for Erin long before he read that dreadful e-mail. Maybe Lizzie's silly blunder had given him the perfect excuse to bail out. Now that Lizzie had seen Erin with her own eyes, nothing seemed more likely.

How could James ever have let Erin go in the first place? If she, Lizzie, had so much as glimpsed a photo of Erin at the outset of things with James, she'd probably have thrown in the towel there and then. Boot-faced and bandy-legged Erin was not. Nobody could have expected Lizzie to hold her own in the shadow of a woman like that.

Bruno arrived with a tray and poured them each a cup. He put three spoons of sugar in Lizzie's. 'For shock,' he said. 'Swallow it down and blow your nose. You can't let them beat you, Lizzie. You've got to get out into the fray again. Maria needs you there, for one thing.'

After two cups of tea and some mundane chatter about Ellie, Alex, Madge, Ingrid Hatter, and the peculiarities of dogwood, Lizzie was able to get her tears under control. It was a bit like staunching a wound. Given enough time, the beginnings of a scab were bound to form, even over a severe injury.

'All right,' she told Bruno. 'I'm ready to go back in.' Nothing tangible had changed, after all. She and James were still on the brink of divorce. The only difference was that now she finally knew it was irrevocable.

'You might want to pop into the loo,' Bruno suggested. 'You've got some black stuff . . .' He gestured at his under-eye area. She gave him a watery smile and went off to re-apply her make-up.

Lizzie was on auto-pilot for the rest of that ghastly evening. Somehow she managed to smile and chat and circulate. People asked her about her new home, and she told them. People asked her if she had a job, and she told them. People even had the flaming cheek to ask if there was any chance of her and James getting back together again, and she told them.

But she wasn't prepared to stand in the line-up of single women waiting to catch the bride's bouquet. She wasn't that much of a sport. Several voices, made loud and tactless by too much wine, urged her to join the spinsters, but she shook her head and stood her ground, forcing a smile when she caught Maria looking at her anxiously.

The American girl, stylish and supercilious, allowed herself to be pushed into the scrum. As the bouquet arced gracefully through the air, she put up one long arm and caught it. Finding it in her hand, she pulled a little moue of surprise, and quickly tossed it to one side, as if she'd rather not be seen dead with such a thing. Maria's awkward niece made a dive for it, and snagged it by the petals. Hugely entertained, the wedding guests laughed and clapped.

At last, the bride and groom took off in Maria's convertible, towing sardine tins and an old boot, with the obligatory white writing all over the sides of the car.

Most of the guests went out into the car park to see them off. Lizzie felt a stab of misery to see James and Erin standing hand in hand. They made such a striking couple among the ill-assorted throng of relatives and friends. Looking at them, both so tall and elegant, so obviously a cut above everybody else, Lizzie had to remind herself that she'd once been the woman at James's side. Watching Erin, she marvelled afresh that she, Lizzie, had ever qualified for the job.

Maria and Laurence were bound for a week-long seaside idyll in a romantic cottage in Pembrokeshire. Lizzie just hoped it wouldn't rain all day every day, and that there was a decent dishwasher. Then again, it was a honeymoon. Maybe they wouldn't care if they couldn't sunbathe. Maybe there'd be no dirty dishes because they'd be eating strawberries and oysters off each other's naked tummies.

As the car sped off, Bruno took Lizzie by the elbow.

'I think we should call it a night,' he said. 'You look completely knackered.'

'Thass nice to know,' Lizzie said. She was having some trouble talking. Her tongue seemed too thick for her mouth. Perhaps those last two or three glasses of wine had been a mistake. 'I'm feeling better already.'

'I don't mean you look awful. I just mean you look tired.'

'Yesh, well. Iss been a tiring old life.'

Turning to walk back into the hotel, she found herself face-to-face with James and Erin. Somehow, she managed to swallow down the choice expletive that sprang to her lips. Unfortunately, Bruno had less self-control.

'Bugger,' he said with feeling, only partly under his breath.

'*Shit*,' James muttered simultaneously.

The only person who didn't look thoroughly jangled was Erin.

'Hi, er, Lizzie,' James managed. 'Having fun? This is a friend of mine, Erin Wilde. Erin, this is ... erm ... this is ...'

'Your wife,' Bruno prompted.

'Exactly. My ... um ... *estranged* wife.'

Erin held out a long-fingered hand, apparently expecting Lizzie to shake it. Lizzie touched the cool fingers for the briefest possible moment. 'Great to meet you,' Erin announced in a loud, authoritative voice, as if she had a concealed megaphone tucked into her cleavage. 'I've heard a lot about you.'

Lizzie always felt stumped when people said that. She knew she was supposed to smile graciously and say something coy, like, 'All good, I hope?' But the only response her brain suggested was, 'Shut your face, you vicious, red-headed husband-snatcher.'

It was probably just as well she couldn't seem to operate her tongue.

'I gotta hand it to you for not tweaking things at Mill House,' the loud drawl continued. 'It takes a real restrained woman not to want to put her stamp on a place. I guess you had the sense to know you couldn't improve on anything. It's so classy, totally killer décor, if classic English country does it for you. Right now I'm more into the whole Bauhaus thing.'

Lizzie gaped at the woman. An acute sense of outrage robbed her of the power of speech yet again. If she weren't careful, Erin

Wilde would go away with the impression that Lizzie Buckley was a mute.

Bruno broke the awkward pause with an entirely new conversational gambit. 'So what brings you to darkest Gloucestershire, Erin?'

Erin gave Bruno a quick once-over. 'We met at the Grey Goose, right?' she asked.

'I'm flattered you remember,' Bruno replied drily.

Lizzie noticed suddenly that Erin was an inch or two taller than Bruno. She guessed that Erin didn't mind towering over men.

Erin smiled a blinding smile that didn't cause a single crow's foot. Lizzie took note of the teeth. A tribute to orthodontistry, she had to agree. 'I'm in London on business,' Erin said, snuggling up against James. 'But Gloucestershire is pure pleasure.'

Pure pleasure? Lizzie glanced at James. Erin's hair was tickling his jaw and his hand rested lightly on her shoulder. He wouldn't meet Lizzie's eye.

'And what's your business, Erin?' Bruno ploughed on.

'I'm in realty.'

'Reality? As in reality television?'

Erin pulled a face that seemed to say, 'God, you people.'

'Real estate,' James explained briskly. 'You must have heard of Wilde and Enfield?'

Wilde and Enfield. Even Lizzie had heard of them. Their purple and yellow 'For Sale' signs were all over the place in Kent. If she'd thought much about them at all, Lizzie would have assumed they were an English company.

'We're one of the bigger realty multinationals,' Erin said importantly, shaking back her wine-coloured hair. 'Britain is our fastest-growing market right now.'

'How ... how nice for you.' Not much of a rejoinder. Lizzie realized, but at least her voice was working again.

'Well, we'd better get going.' Bruno put his hand under Lizzie's elbow. 'We were just about to say our goodbyes.'

Erin opened her eyes very wide. 'Really? Not in party mood tonight?'

Bruno gave his most wicked cherub grin. 'Oh, we're in party mood, all right. More of a private party mood, though. Gloucestershire is pure pleasure for us, too.'

Lizzie suppressed the urge to punch the air and cry, '*Yes*, Bruno!' At least one of them had enough gumption to strike a blow for the deserted wife.

She stole a look at James's face as Bruno propelled her away. She might as well not have bothered. His expression was completely impassive. To look at him, you'd have to assume he really didn't give a flying feather that his wife was apparently off to a night of pure partying pleasure in the chintzy bedrooms of a local bed and breakfast, with a short but well-muscled landscape gardener from Kent.

Just as they were almost out of earshot, Erin Wilde bugled, 'Lizzie, you might want to throw on a jacket or something. Your zipper's splitting.'

Chapter Eighteen

'Thank you, Bruno, thank you.'

'For what?'

'For keeping my end up with Ms Britain-ish-our-fashtest-grow-ing-market.'

'Christ, could you believe the woman?'

Lizzie, fiddling with the knobs under the passenger seat, suddenly crashed backwards into a reclining position. She'd asked Bruno to drive because it was just possible that she was over the legal limit for alcohol in the bloodstream.

'You think she was consheited? Not just, you know, impreshively confident?'

'She was confident the way the Queen speaks the Queen's English. Way, way beyond the call of duty.'

'Men like confident women,' Lizzie said.

Bruno was quiet for a moment. 'Either he likes her or he doesn't,' he said after a while. 'Nothing you can do about it, lass. If he prefers that sort of woman to a woman like you, then it's his loss.'

Lizzie felt a great surge of affection for Bruno. 'You think so, Bruno? You really think so?'

'Phwargh, there's no comparison! A real estate queen over a *poet*? He's clearly lost his marbles, love.'

'I'm not really a poet,' Lizzie said, but she felt a bit better. 'More of a ... a vershi— a vershifier. Can't even get published, you know.'

'You're a poet and you know it. Next time you see Ms Wilde, you let her know you're above all the trappings of commerce. You're made of finer stuff.'

'Oh, God. Do you think I'll *have* to see her again?'

Bruno shrugged. 'Chances are, love, chances are.'

They made the rest of the trip in silence.

As they let themselves into the dark house with the key Bruno had been given earlier when he checked in, Lizzie felt a terrible sense of letdown and sadness. In some weird way, she'd been looking forward to this wedding, even after she'd found out James was bringing a partner. Yes, she'd been looking forward to the chance to show off her hardwon new body to the assembled cast of characters of her old life in Laingtree. Most of all, she'd been looking forward to twirling around, all slim and satin-clad, looking more sophisticated that she'd ever looked in her life, in front of James.

Whoever said looking good is the best revenge hadn't factored in an opponent like Erin Wilde. Sure, Lizzie could look good. But what did mere 'good' matter if the enemy was fabulous?

All Lizzie's ludicrous hopes of bringing James to his knees with jealousy and remorse had been swept away once and for all now. Her husband was being unfaithful, not only with his nasty little PA, but also with a goddess-like redhead from his past, possibly in the Jacobean bed where Lizzie's children had been conceived. A marriage didn't recover from a double whammy like that.

By now, Bruno had brought Lizzie to the doorway of a bedroom. She was aware that, without him there to support her, she might have had slight difficulty walking in a straight line. 'Bag's in the car,' she told him muzzily.

'No, it's not,' he replied, swinging it down from his shoulder. 'I brought it in for you.'

'Well done, jolly good.' Lizzie fell into the room and searched the wall for a switch, blinking a bit when the light actually flicked on. 'Gosh, will you look at that?' she drawled, waving an expansive hand at the pink and green floral fabrics that seemed to cover every surface. 'Bloody killer décor, dontcha think?'

Bruno grinned. 'Bloody killer,' he agreed. 'Well, I'll say good-night then. See you in the morning. Not too early, right?'

Lizzie turned and grabbed Bruno's hand. 'Wait,' she cried. 'Don't go. I . . . I can't get this flaming dress off without help. Besides, you promised.'

'Promised?'

'A night of pure pleashure. Remember?'

'Bloody hell, don't do this to me,' Bruno groaned. But Lizzie had already thrown herself against his compact body in its dazzling white shirt and cummerbund. In the course of the drive home, she'd made up her mind that she'd better sleep with Bruno. It was pointless not to, really. James thought she was going to. Erin thought she was going to. The whole of Laingtree probably thought she was going to. She might just as well go ahead and put everybody out of their misery.

Bruno stood rigid for a moment, apparently resisting. Lizzie hoped he was frozen in the grips of a moral dilemma, and not by acute embarrassment and reluctance. At last, he slipped his hand into the gaping slit of her zip, which was now open again from armpit to hip.

'I've been wanting to do this all night,' he murmured, his finger-tips cool along her side.

Without warning, Lizzie doubled over at the waist, like a rat trap closing. She collapsed onto the carpet and lay in the foetal position, arms clamped to her sides.

'God, Lizzie, what's the matter?' Bruno knelt down beside her, appalled.

'It's . . . it's nothing,' she managed to utter. 'Just . . . just don't *tickle* me. Please.' Then she reached up and pulled him down beside her.

Lizzie was aware of the weight of an arm across her body as she woke up. Relief whooshed through her. She'd been having the most terrible, convoluted dream. How lovely to find herself back in her bed in Mill House, with James beside her snoring softly. What on earth could she have eaten to give herself such a monstrous night-mare? Sonja Jenkins had been in it, with a whole new body; also, some predatory American female who wanted to steal James off her. And she'd been living in some ramshackle old farmhouse in Kent, ripping up nettles as a hobby.

Blue cheese, probably. It had always been a failing of hers.

She turned over languidly in bed, opening her eyes a slit.

Hang on. The sheets were wrong. She'd never owned sheets with a flower motif on them in her life.

Her eyes flew fully open and she found herself staring into the sleeping face of a man with curly dark hair.

Bruno.

Lizzie sat bolt upright in bed, clutching the sprigged sheets to her naked bosom. 'Aaaargh,' she groaned, clapping a hand to her head. Not a nightmare, then. Reality.

Shit, shit, *shit*.

Perhaps she'd been in an accident; her head felt as if someone had driven over it. Yes, that must be it. She and Bruno had been in a car accident and they were in hospital together. In the same bed. Naked.

No, for pity's sake, it couldn't be that.

Then she remembered.

Oh, dear. Oh, dear. Oh, dear.

She'd burnt her bridges. Well and truly burnt them.

Lizzie eased herself cautiously out of bed, keeping a weather eye on the sleeping form of Bruno. She didn't want him to wake up until at least one of them had some clothes on. As she slid off the bed, the sheet seemed to slide with her and Bruno was suddenly exposed in all his glory.

Gosh, rather a nice body.

Lizzie flicked the sheet over him hastily, grabbed the lilac silk dress from the floor where it lay in a heap, wrapped it around her like a sarong, and scuttled off to the bathroom.

Closing the door softly, she stumbled over to the hand-basin and looked at herself in the mirror. Little piggy eyes, lost in the swollen folds of her eyelids, stared back at her in bloodshot horror.

She splashed her face hastily with cold water, then looked again. No discernible improvement. Creeping back into the bedroom, she managed to retrieve her overnight bag. As she was easing herself out of the room again, Bruno suddenly turned over and muttered something that sounded like 'Smelly-bear'. He was losing the sheet again. Lizzie tore her eyes away and locked herself up in the bathroom.

Digging in her toiletry bag, she found some eye drops and aspirin. She downed the pills with three glasses of water from the tooth mug, then turned the shower on full blast and stood under it with her eyes closed, grimly relishing the way the jets of water pummelled her body. By the time she'd slapped some make-up on her face and dressed in jeans and a T-shirt, she was beginning to feel almost human again.

A sudden knock on the door nearly made her jump out of her skin. 'Did you leave any hot water for me?' Bruno called.

She took a deep breath and opened the door. Steam blossomed into the bedroom where Bruno stood, dressed in shorts and a T-shirt, hugging his elbows as if he were cold, and grinning lazily through his stubble.

Lizzie went hot with embarrassment.

'Morning,' she croaked. Clearing her throat, she tried again. 'Did you ... ah ... sleep well?'

'Like a baby,' said Bruno. 'You?'

'Very well, thanks. Only now I have sort of a headache. It's pretty bad, actually.'

Bruno walked over and ruffled her hair. 'Commonly known as a hangover,' he said kindly. 'You had quite a lot of wine last night.'

Lizzie jumped away from his hand like a nervous horse. 'Look, you go ahead and shower. I have to dash. I want to pick up the twins so we can get out of here. It's already nine.'

He gave her a measuring look. 'OK,' he said after a moment. 'I'll see you later.'

Gunning the car along the narrow lanes towards the manor, Lizzie felt sick with nerves. She couldn't get over the fact that she, a married woman, had slept with a man who wasn't her husband. It wasn't that she didn't like Bruno. She liked him a lot. In fact, maybe what she felt was *more* than just liking.

But still. She was *married*. She was a *mother*.

And damn it all, up until now, whatever she'd done to bring about the death of her marriage, at least she'd always been certain that she stood on the moral high ground. More or less. If you discounted that episode when she'd given her mother-in-law's party guests a synchronized swimming demonstration in her cocktail dress. Because, strictly speaking, you couldn't really put a high moral spin on that. And perhaps the incident with the head-massager also fell into ambiguous moral territory. Not to mention one or two other small infringements. Still, she'd never had anything but the best of intentions.

But things were getting a little murky all of a sudden.

To Lizzie's infinite relief, her father-in-law, not Lady Evelyn, answered the door at the manor. 'Lord, you don't look very well, my dear,' he said immediately, peering at her through his monocle. 'Come in and have a cup of tea. The children are outside with a babysitter. Evelyn's of the old school – doesn't believe a man can manage children, so she got somebody in for this morning. She's at some sort of pow-wow with the vicar.'

Poor vicar.

Roger herded her gently into the amber drawing room and onto an armchair.

'There, sit down. I'll just ask for the tea. No, on second thoughts, let's have coffee.' Lady Evelyn employed a succession of *au pairs*, usually Australian, to help in the kitchen, but none of them ever stayed very long. Lizzie had no idea who was currently in charge of the Aga stove and enormous blackened kettle.

Roger was back within minutes. He sat down close by and said, 'Come now, tell me about the wedding.'

But Lizzie said, 'Why would Lady Evelyn go to the trouble of getting a babysitter if she's already got the *au pair*?'

Roger gave a rueful shrug. 'Anja has her work cut out today. Cleaning silver for some shindig this evening.'

'A Sunday dinner party?'

Roger sighed deeply. 'That's right. A little gathering for that American girl who's staying at the cottage. You must have met her?' He looked at Lizzie rather sharply from under craggy eyebrows.

'Erin Wilde. I met her.' Lizzie bit her bottom lip. 'She was ... the one before me, wasn't she?'

Roger didn't pretend to misunderstand. 'Yes, she had her claws in James for a while, years ago. Evelyn can't stand her, of course, but ... well, she's trying to put a good face on things. You know, in the circumstances.'

Lizzie pulled a pretty good face, herself. 'She probably thinks Erin's at least one step up from me.'

'Ptuh,' said Roger. 'She *abhors* Erin's manners, but she half-suspects that back in California the woman actually comes out of a drawer very near the top, if not the top drawer itself. It's a real treat, seeing her trying to "place" Erin. She can't do it in the usual way – family, schools, accent, house. So she's only got money to go on, and Erin was born filthy rich. All terribly confusing for poor Evelyn.'

He was trying to make her see the funny side. It *was* mildly amusing to think of Lady Evelyn's gut-level snobbery being forcibly redirected by her intellect, like a bloodhound being dragged off the wrong trail. But not amusing enough to raise a smile.

'What I don't understand is why Erin is staying in *our* house,' Lizzie muttered. 'There's no shortage of bed-and-breakfasts, surely? Why did James have to book her in *there*?'

'Ah, here's the coffee.' Roger stood up and took the tray from a harrassed-looking young woman with a shiny face. 'Thanks, Anja. How's the silver coming along?'

'Very slow,' the *au pair* said unhappily. 'There is much.' Lizzie thought her accent might be Dutch.

Roger pulled a sympathetic face. 'Rather you than me,' he said. 'Lizzie, this is Anja. Anja, Lizzie. Lizzie has the good fortune to be Alex and Ellie's mother.'

Anja's face lit up for a moment. 'They are so sweet children,' she said.

'Thanks. They have their moments.'

'I go back to polish,' Anja said.

As she walked out, Lizzie turned back to Roger, who was clattering mugs.

'So?' she asked. 'Why is Erin Wilde at Mill House? Why would James choose our own *house* to put her up?'

Roger shrugged. 'Auld lang syne, possibly,' he said. 'Did nobody ever tell you that she helped James raise the money to buy the place from me?'

Lizzie felt as if she'd just accidentally swallowed a bucketful of ice cubes. 'What?'

Her father-in-law heaved a sigh that seemed to come from somewhere very low. 'Yes, in retrospect it was a very poor idea, I'm afraid. You see, I wouldn't let the boy have the house for nothing, as Evelyn would've liked. I wanted him to work for it, so he'd value it more.'

Lizzie nodded. She knew the concept. If she made Alex and Ellie earn gold stars towards a toy they wanted, they seemed to appreciate the piece of plastic junk a lot more than if she simply handed it to them.

'I just didn't know about Erin Wilde at the time. She wasn't part of the equation,' Roger said regretfully. 'I thought he'd have to go hat in hand to the banks, maybe ask one or two of his chums to make an investment. I didn't realize he had this real estate princess in the wings. Her old man made a fortune selling clapboard houses on some beach on the Californian coastline back in the sixties, I gather. To her, the downpayment on Mill House must have been a mere bagatelle, but it put James in her debt.'

'Surely he paid her back?' Lizzie's voice sounded hoarse and scratchy, and she hastily cleared her throat.

'Oh, he paid her back all right, with interest,' Roger said. 'Still, the effect remains. The sense of obligation. Drink some coffee, my dear. Don't let it go cold.'

Lizzie took a large gulp and nearly scalded her throat. She gave a strangled yell and fanned at her open mouth.

'Easy, easy,' said Roger. 'Here, have some milk.'

She chugged the milk straight out of the white porcelain jug. It was blissfully cold and soothing. Somehow, as she set the empty jug back down on the tray, she felt she was losing her tenuous hold on her dignity. She straightened her shoulders and and composed her face.

'So do you think Erin Wilde feels at all ... possessive about Mill House?' she asked as calmly as she could.

'Possessive is a strong word.' Roger sipped his own coffee cautiously. 'But not really strong enough to describe any feeling entertained by Miss Wilde, I shouldn't think. It's obvious she still feels highly territorial about the place. And, I'm sorry to say, quite territorial about James, too.'

She and Roger sat in silence for a while, both deep in unpleasant thoughts, finishing their coffee. At last, Lizzie surprised herself by blurting out, 'Roger, I can't help thinking he must have been seeing her for quite some time. I mean, he wouldn't call and ask her to a wedding out of the blue, would he?'

Roger raised his eyebrows and lifted his monocle to get a better look at her flustered red face. 'My dear,' he said slowly, 'James wasn't unfaithful to you. He told me so, and I believe him. Whatever is happening between him and Erin, it's new.'

Lizzie felt rebuked. She shouldn't have raised the question at all. Naturally, Roger wouldn't admit that James might have lied to him.

Come to think of it, lying wasn't really James's forté.

But if he hadn't been having an affair with Erin all along, then he must have cold-called her. She tried to imagine James picking up the phone, dialling California, putting on a sexy voice, and asking a woman he hadn't seen in years to come and spend a dirty weekend with him.

Putting down her mug, she gave her head a good shake. 'Anyway, the children are in the lower garden?'

Roger stood up and brushed imaginary fluff from the shoulders of his elegantly rumpled linen shirt. 'Let's go and find them, shall we?'

Lizzie's heart lifted. No matter what else went wrong in her life, at least she could count on Ellie and Alex for unconditional love.

'I want chicken nuggets or I won't be your *fwiend* any more,' Alex yelled belligerently as they negotiated the traffic circle and pulled away at speed past the McDonald's in Oxford.

'Let's wait till we get home,' Lizzie said, biting back the more infantile reply – 'Don't be my friend, then, see if I care!' – that sprang to her lips. 'Why don't you close your eyes and have a little nap?'

'Not *sleepy*,' Alex yelled back.

'Are we nearly there?' came Ellie's plaintive cry.

'Not yet.'

'Are we nearly there *now*?'

'No, not yet.'

'Are we nearly there *now*?'

'Ellie! Will. You. Be. Quiet. I'll tell you when we're nearly there.'

Silence. Lizzie glanced over at Bruno. He was either asleep or pretending very well.

She felt a surge of gratitude towards him. He was so kind, so diplomatic. She'd been unbelievably lucky to have him just show up on her doorstep. Most divorced women had to jump right back into their nylon stockings and kitten heels to brave the perils of the man-hunt all over again before they found anyone half as nice as Bruno.

Not that she was 'with' Bruno, of course. She couldn't possibly enter into anything like that until she'd finished things once and for all with James. She wasn't the sort of woman to let men overlap in that way. OK, she seemed to have slept with Bruno, but that was just a blip, and he'd soon find he was very much mistaken if he was expecting more of the same – at least for the moment. She had the children's morals to think about, after all.

When Lizzie drove her cargo of sleepers up the driveway of Back Lane Cottage at last, she was surprised to see two people sitting on her doorstep.

She made out Petronella, in running gear, and Sarah Hatter in a T-shirt and pair of ragged denim shorts.

All at once she remembered that she'd arranged to run five miles with Petronella that night.

'We were about to give up on you,' Petronella called as Lizzie got out of the car, surreptitiously kneading her head, which had begun to pound again.

'Do you think we still have time to go?' Lizzie asked, walking towards her and stretching from the waist to relieve the aches of sitting behind the wheel for two hours.

'Maybe not the full five miles, but ...' Petronella stopped short and stood with her mouth hanging open.

Lizzie looked back to see what she was staring at. Bruno was straightening up beside the car, rubbing his eyes and running his fingers through his tousled hair.

'Who's that?' Petronella demanded more rudely than usual.

'That? Oh. Bruno. The chap I took to the wedding. Remember I said I'd invited my landscape gardener?'

Bruno had now finished yawning and scratching, and was unloading luggage from the boot of the car. In his dozy state, he didn't seem to have noticed that Lizzie had visitors.

'You didn't drop him back at his house, I see. Is he staying over with you?' Petronella wanted to know.

'No, he left his van in my garage,' Lizzie said, wondering why she had to explain herself at all. Petronella seemed to be almost as inquisitive as Ingrid Hatter. 'Don't worry; he's going home straight away. He won't mess up our run or anything.'

Petronella continued to stare at Bruno, who was now stowing things in his van, oblivious to the attention he was arousing. 'Look,' she said all of a sudden, 'let's not do the run today. Quite honestly, I don't really feel like it, and you look like death warmed up.'

'Kind of you to notice,' Lizzie said, relieved to be let off the hook. She smiled at Sarah, blushing in the middle distance. 'Sarah, can you stay a bit anyway? I'd love some help with this lot.' She hated asking the girl to babysit on a certain evening, then just sending her home when plans changed.

Sarah showed her braces. 'Sure,' she said happily.

'Well, I'm off then.' Without further ado, Petronella stalked away towards her bike, propped at a careless angle against the fence. As she drew level with Lizzie's car, Bruno turned from his van and caught sight of her. For a moment he was motionless.

Then Petronella gave him an awkward wave, and he lifted his hand in a brief return salute.

Lizzie felt a stab of ... yes, jealousy. Something about the way these two were behaving made her suspect that she was witnessing an intense case of instant mutual attraction.

Lizzie walked over to Bruno and watched Petronella cycle away.

'Friend of yours?' Bruno asked in an offhand way.

Lizzie shrugged. 'Running partner. Her name's Petronella. I'll give you her number if you like.'

Bruno tore his eyes away from the disappearing bike and fixed them on Lizzie's flushed face and hurt eyes. 'I don't want her bloody number,' he said, taking her chin in his hand and running his thumb gently along her lower lip.

Lizzie bowed her head and laid her cheek against his chest where his heart was pounding in a reassuring rhythm. She felt stupid tears prickle beneath her eyelids. Perhaps she was turning into one of those pathologically jealous women who believe every shop girl and waitress is trying to flirt with their man.

Of course, Bruno wasn't her man.

Bruno lifted her chin and planted a soft kiss on her mouth. Lizzie ripped herself out of his grasp. 'Not in front of Sarah,' she muttered. And then, of course, one of the children began to cry.

Over Alex's sulky golden head, Bruno said, 'Come out to the pub with me? It looks as if you have a babysitter already.'

Lizzie thought for a moment. Her head was seriously hurting now and she felt bruised all over. She knew her eyes were bloodshot and she hadn't had time to blow-dry her hair after her rushed morning shower.

But somehow none of that seemed to matter.

'All right,' she said. 'I'll come, but not to the pub, please. Can we find a restaurant? And you'll have to help me settle the children first.'

'Was it good for you last night?'

Bruno sprang this question on her just as she was sinking her teeth into a crusty bread roll. They were sitting at a secluded table in a tiny French restaurant somewhere in the country near Hever Castle.

Lizzie chewed quickly and swallowed with a gulp. 'Um ... yes. Of course. Very nice, thanks. Was it ... was it OK for you?'

'Fantastic,' Bruno grinned at her. 'I don't think I've ever done that thing where you pretend you're on a merry-go-round horse before.'

Caught taking a sip of water, Lizzie half-choked, snorted a bit of water out of her nose, and had to be patted on the back. When she was able to talk again, she whispered, 'Merry-go-round horse?'

'Is it one of your favourites? Personally, I'm keen to try the French maid game you mentioned.'

'French ... maid?' Lizzie's cheeks were burning. OK, so she knew she'd been a bit tiddly, but saucy little games between the sheets had just never been in her repertoire.

Bruno suddenly took her hand and gave it a sympathetic squeeze. 'It's just no fun teasing you, Lizzie,' he said. 'You're way too gullible. You don't remember a thing about last night, do you?'

Lizzie stared at him, bemused. After a moment she shook her head. 'No,' she confessed. 'Not a thing.'

He kept hold of her hand. 'There weren't any merry-go-round games, Lizzie. As a matter of fact, the field was closed for play.'

She shook her head, not understanding.

'We didn't do anything, Lizzie. Not that we weren't ready to give it a shot. Everybody was more or less primed for action when you suddenly asked me if I could,' he lowered his voice, 'take some precautions. I just nipped off to turn my toiletry bag upside-down, but by the time I got back you'd, er, dropped off.'

'Dropped off?'

'Gone to sleep.'

'Passed out,' said Lizzie with a flash of insight.

Bruno nodded.

They sat and thought a moment, Bruno still holding Lizzie's hand.

'Probably a good thing,' Lizzie said at last.

Bruno's fingers, which had gently been stroking hers, went still. 'Why a good thing?' he asked.

Lizzie looked at him, his bright, dark eyes, his cherubic curls, his generous mouth. 'Always a bad idea to rush into things,' she said with a little shrug. 'If we ... when we *do* get it together we want to know that we really mean it.'

'No drunken one-night-stands?' he asked.

'That's right,' she said.

'I'll drink to that,' he said, raising his half-pint of lager. She raised her water and they clinked.

After she'd taken a sip, she said awkwardly, 'I'm not going to be ... you know, ready for that sort of thing for a while.'

He nodded. 'I know. I'm a patient man.' And he gave her a wolf-ish smile.

Chapter Nineteen

From: janehawthorn@yahoo.com
Sent: 6 September
To: lizbuckley@hotmail.com

I don't know, Lizzie. I'm not convinced. Are you really over James? Are you ready for this thing with the gardener? Just remember, you want a little light relief, not another Big Commitment right now. Give yourself time to bounce back properly. No rebound stuff, OK?

Of course I want Mum and Dad here, by the way. Dad cooks, Mum cleans, and Dad holds Elizabeth when she's asleep. If we put her down on any non-human surface, no matter how deeply she's sleeping, she wakes straight away and screams her lungs out. Dad doesn't mind sitting with her on his lap while he watches stuff about the ozone layer and genetic engineering.

I have to say, I can't believe James has buggered off to France! When exactly did he leave? And he gave you no warning? Lord knows, this isn't the James I remember. Do you think it's the male menopause ? I mean, I know he's not even forty yet but how else do you explain it?

Be careful now.

love

Janie

As Lizzie hit reply, her phone rang. She felt her heart begin to beat a little faster. It could easily be Bruno. She hadn't spoken to him for at least four hours. But the voice on the other end was Maria Dennison's.

'Maria! How lovely! How was the honeymoon?'

Maria gave a low laugh. 'Fabulous,' she said. 'We went surfing.'

'In *Wales*?'

'Oh, yes, it's a big thing there. You wear wetsuits, of course.'

'Good grief!' Lizzie was diverted by the thought of the newlyweds riding big breakers into secret coves side by side, Maria like a mermaid with ringlets flying in all directions, Laurence like Neptune without his trident. 'We must ... I must go some time. But Maria, why did you *really* phone? There's something else, isn't there?'

Maria sighed audibly down the line. 'I'm sorry, Lizzie, but you did ask me to be your eyes and ears, remember? It's about James. You know he's gone to France?'

'Yes, of course.'

'Well, the thing is – he took Sonja with him.'

Lizzie sat down on the floor as if someone had yanked the rug rather suddenly. OK, she'd spent the days since the wedding chanting the mantra, 'I am over James', but this was a nasty surprise. 'Sonja? Sonja Jenkins? You mean Erin, surely?'

'No, *Sonja*. Laurence drove them to the airport just this morning. James was going to get a taxi, but Laurence insisted. Well, he nearly jumped out of his skin when *she* opened the door. He says she was all togged up in her holiday gear, sunglasses and everything even though it was raining, and she was towing this dinky little pink suitcase on wheels.'

'But what happened to Erin Wilde? Was she there, too?'

'A threesome? Come on, Lizzie. This is James we're talking about. He must have dumped her. Or vice versa. Anyway, Laurence was gobsmacked. But sure enough, Sonja hops in the back seat and keeps up a running commentary all the way to the airport – beaches they're going to visit, shopping she's going to do, the tan she's going to get, restaurant recommendations her friends have given her.'

'You're joking. Right?'

'Lizzie, why would I joke about a thing like this?'

'Well, what about James? Was he blathering on about tans and restaurants, too?'

'No. Laurence says James just sat with his mouth shut. Didn't look too good, either, Laurence says. Hadn't shaved, rumpled clothes, that sort of thing. Hangover behaviour.'

'I'm sorry, Maria, I have to go.' Lizzie put down the phone and ran up to her bedroom. She stood there for a moment, looking around wildly, then began to grab things off her dressing table and smash them onto the floor. Her hairbrush, a bottle of perfume, a basket of mismatched socks, a coffee mug with some dregs in it, a notebook containing some unfinished verses. Yes, she was over James (*ker-splash* went the mug against the wall), yes, she was about to embrace a new life (the basket bounced off the plasterwork) but was she unreasonable to expect her husband at least to confine himself to one woman at a time for his extra-marital capers? First Sonja, then Erin, now Sonja again. What was the matter with the man?

Lizzie was about to smash a plate she'd spotted on the window sill when the door burst open and Ellie came in. 'What you doin', Mummy?' she asked, looking at the chaotic room.

Lizzie jumped guiltily and set down the plate. She managed to contort her face into a smile. 'I'm just ... cleaning up, sweetie. Clearing some surfaces.'

Ellie looked at her doubtfully. 'I think you doin' it the wrong way,' she observed. 'You don't jus' frow ebbyting onna floor. You got to find a new place for all dose fings.'

Lizzie breathed deeply and dug her fingernails into the palms of her hands. 'Really, sweetheart? Will you help me do that?'

Ellie's face broke into a smile. 'Of course,' she said kindly. 'Why you cryin', Mummy? You made a big mess, but nobody gonna be cross wid you, cos you the *mummy*, you know.'

Fifteen minutes later, the room was tidier than it had been in weeks, and Lizzie was feeling a lot calmer. After all, she was *over* James. She didn't care if he was in France with Sonja. She had her own new romance to nurture.

The truth was, when she thought of Bruno she couldn't suppress a secret smile. More often than she cared to admit – she wasn't a voyeur, after all — she found herself picturing that moment in the bed and breakfast when the flowery sheet had slipped off his sleeping body. When she married James, she'd certainly never expected to see another naked man in her bed again. But when you got right down to it, there was something exciting about the thought of exploring virgin territory just one more time. Well, *virgin* was perhaps not the *mot juste*. Novel. That was a better word. Novel and, yes, definitely exciting. She hadn't felt so invigorated in years.

By the time the children were in bed that evening, Lizzie felt she'd allow herself the little luxury of ringing Bruno. He'd been calling her on a regular basis ever since the wedding. They'd been out for a drink a couple of times, and she'd even spent an afternoon with the children at his cottage in Dunton Green, but Lizzie had been quite happy to let him make the running. Right now, though, she stood in real need of a dose of his lovely, rich voice gently mocking her down the line.

The only thing was, his phone just kept ringing. There was nobody home. He wasn't even picking up his mobile.

Lizzie still hadn't spoken to Bruno by the time she went in for her appointment with G.H. Brightman two days later.

Feeling more than a little panicky at the cavalier way her many job applications were being rejected, she'd broken down and phoned up Brightman the day before, briefly sketching for him the changed state of her affairs, and the urgent need she now had of going back to work. He'd been kind enough to suggest an interview.

Ingrid Hatter had given her a quick squeeze on the shoulder for good luck when she'd dropped the children off with her that morning, but she'd really been hoping for a good-luck hug from Bruno. Still, he was obviously very busy in people's gardens at this time of the year.

'Good of you to come in,' G.H. Brightman said from the other side of his large, untidy desk. 'I must say, I was a little surprised. That is, marriage is one of those peculiar things. At any rate, it's an ill wind, my dear. Not that any of us here would have wished divorce on anyone. But if it had to happen … In short, it couldn't have happened to a nicer girl.'

Lizzie gazed at her former boss in mild wonder. How he'd made his way in the PR profession, she'd never know. He was possibly the least articulate man she'd ever come across. But beneath his dithery exterior beat a brave heart and a needle-sharp brain. His brain didn't beat, of course, although obviously it had some sort of pulse … At any rate, he was a good man. Not only a good man, but the one man in the city of London who seemed to think Lizzie still had anything to offer the world of public relations.

He eyed her silently for a moment. She met his gaze levelly, trying hard to look eager but not abject, keen but not desperate, poised but not complacent. They both knew he was going to offer to take her back.

'I have something,' he said after a moment. 'Yes, I do have something … It may not be precisely … I do like to deal with people I can trust … I'm not sure exactly how you're placed … In short, we *are* opening that office in Glasgow.'

'Glasgow?' Lizzie was stumped.

'Glasgow. City in Scotland? Not as classy as Edinburgh, some say, but not the industrial wasteland of days of yore. By no means a cultural desert. And of course, home of the new Petlove factory. So, what do you think? Could you possibly …?'

'Could I possibly what?'

Mr Brightman tugged at his left eyebrow. 'After all, the sprogs can't be in school yet. It wouldn't be as much of an upheaval. Unless of course you're wedded to the idea of London …'

'Mr Brightman, are you offering me a job in Glasgow?'

His face lit up with appreciation of her quick understanding. 'Indeed. I am indeed. Not just any job, my dear. I know I'm going out on a limb here … In short, I'm asking you to head up the Glasgow operation.'

'Head … head it up?'

'Yes, absolutely, I understand your feelings entirely. No management experience, I'm well aware of that myself. But it would be a very small operation, you understand. At least, at first. Just you and this young lass we have fresh out of university.'

Lizzie felt her eyes going hot. 'Don't you have *anything* in London?'

Mr Brightman furrowed his brow. 'You've hit the nail on the head, my girl. Nothing in London. Nothing at all. If anything, we're overstaffed. I may have gone a little overboard with the new hires once we got the extra business. But the Glasgow job is a great opportunity—'

'I can't go to *Glasgow*!' she interrupted on a note of anguish. Mr Brightman drew back in alarm. Getting a grip on herself, Lizzie explained with false calm: 'All my friends and family are here. I couldn't go off on my own like that. I'm a single parent; I need all the help I can get. But ... but thanks anyway.'

It hadn't been a good day, obviously. But it was about to get a whole lot better because Lizzie was going to dinner at Bruno's house. He'd sprung the invitation on her that very afternoon and she'd never felt more grateful at the prospect of a night out.

When Sarah walked in at seven that evening, her jaw dropped in amazement. 'Mrs Buckley,' she stammered. 'You look ... great!'

Lizzie did look great, and for once in her life she knew it. Her hair shone with caramel highlights, her skin was brown and glowing from all those hours jogging and gardening, and her stomach was flat as an ironing board again. Plus she was wearing an unbelievably flattering wrap-around dress in the exact shade of blue of her eyes.

Driving to Bruno's house, Lizzie felt pleasantly jittery. She wondered at Bruno's motives in asking her over tonight. He'd sounded slightly strained on the phone. She knew it must be difficult for him to maintain the hands-off policy she'd instigated after the wedding. In fact, she was sometimes aware herself of a slight irritation with him for taking her wishes in that direction so literally and following them so faithfully. She couldn't help thinking that a little French kissing here, a little canoodling there would have done both of them the world of good.

But maybe Bruno had come to the end of his tether at last. Maybe

282

tonight he was going to stage a seduction. Of course, she wouldn't go along with it – not all the way, anyway. She did want to be a single woman before she got entangled again. But it would be nice to feel a bit of skin on skin after so long.

By the time Lizzie had parked her car in the driveway of Bruno's cottage in Dunton Green, she'd allowed herself to get so carried away in speculation about how the evening might turn out that she suddenly felt paralysed by shyness as he opened the door. But then he smiled his cherubic smile, and her shyness evaporated. She stepped forward, arms open for a hug, and couldn't help feeling a little disappointed when he held her for only a moment before patting her on the back and setting her gently away from him.

'Come in, lass,' he said gruffly. 'Sit yourself down. How about a margarita while we wait?'

'Margarita? That sounds good.' She threw herself down onto his squashy old sofa, looking around appreciatively at the homely snugness of the little room. Madge, curled up on an armchair, opened one eye, flapped her tail half-heartedly, and then went back to sleep. The first time she'd been in here, Lizzie had felt like Lucy entering Mr Tumnus's burrow. From the hole-in-the-wall fireplace to the bare black ceiling beams and battered old furniture, Bruno's living room spoke volumes for its owner's unpretentious and quirky charm. It would be a lovely room in winter, Lizzie thought, picturing Alex and Ellie toasting chestnuts in a coal shovel over a cosy blaze while their damp socks dried on the mantelpiece. Why her mind threw up such a Dickensian image, she had no idea.

She sipped her drink and stretched luxuriously, admiring the golden glow of her tanned legs. 'So what are we waiting for?' she called through to Bruno, clattering things in the kitchen. 'Something in the oven?'

There was a silence. Then Bruno walked into the room, holding a small pewter bowl of salsa. 'We're waiting for ... um ...'

He had a really odd look on his face. Lizzie couldn't place the expression. It seemed halfway between dread and excitement, if that were possible.

The doorbell rang, interrupting him. Immediately, Madge leapt up from her deep sleep and skidded across the loose rug into the hallway where she began to scratch at the front door and howl. Really howl, like a wolf at full moon. Before Bruno could make his way across the room, the door flew open and someone walked in. Madge jumped at the newcomer, almost knocking her over, still yowling.

It was a thin, dark woman with short hair tucked behind her ears, wearing a pair of khaki shorts and sandals with rhinestones in them.

Good God. Petronella.

'Down, Madge, down!' Bruno boomed.

'Oh, she's OK, leave her be,' Petronella murmured. She knelt down and spoke softly to the dog, then began to knead her ears. With a moan of pleasure, Madge turned upside down and started bicycling her back legs in the air.

Lizzie stood up, sloshing her drink. She looked from the gate-crasher to Bruno and back again.

'Why's she here?' she asked. Bam-bam went her heart.

Bruno seemed to be blushing. Lizzie had never seen him blush before, hadn't even known he *could* blush. 'She's ... um ... she's ...' Whatever he wanted to say, he couldn't spit it out.

'I'm his ex-wife,' Petronella cut in briskly. She was standing up now with her arms folded across her chest, her face white and tense. Madge still lay upside-down at her feet, her feathery underbelly on display.

'Sorry – what?' Lizzie shook her head. She couldn't have heard correctly.

Bruno stepped towards Lizzie and took her hand. 'Lizzie, the thing is, Nell and I, we ... um, we used to be married.'

Lizzie felt the gooseflesh popping out on her bare arms. 'OK. I mean, really *weird*. But fair enough. And she's here, what, to take Madge for the weekend? She has joint custody? Or what?'

Bruno bit his lip. 'Not joint custody,' he said.

'I haven't seen Madge in two years,' Petronella said. 'Not until a couple of days ago. Bruno and I – we've been avoiding each other like the plague.'

'We were both just ... just *staggered* the other day,' Bruno explained. 'You know, when we came back from the wedding and she was sitting on your doorstep. We've gone to such lengths not to bump into each other. Then suddenly, wham! There she was when I was least expecting it.'

'So, you two have decided to be friends?' Lizzie gulped down some air and looked at them with raised eyebrows.

'Not exactly,' said Bruno.

'Not really,' said Petronella.

'We could never be *friends*,' said Bruno.

Lizzie blinked quickly. 'Well, what then? What is Petronella doing at our romantic dinner, for God's sake? Does she still need evidence for the divorce?'

'The divorce was final more than a year ago,' Petronella said.

'The *divorce* was,' said Bruno. 'But ... not us. Look, sorry to spring this on you, but I wanted to explain properly. Face-to-face.'

Lizzie felt herself go deathly white, then red as a beetroot.

'Sit down,' said Bruno gently. 'Smelly-bear, do we give her sugar water? Brandy? Aspirin?'

Smelly-bear?

'Rescue Remedy,' Petronella said decisively. 'I have some in my pocket. Here, stick out your tongue for a couple of drops, Lizzie.'

Obediently, Lizzie stuck out her tongue. With Bruno patting her on the back and Petronella crouching down at her side like an emergency worker at an accident scene, they told her the tale of their reunion.

Bruno explained that when he'd seen 'Nell' out of the blue last week, he'd been rocked to his very foundations. Not laying eyes on her for two years, he'd convinced himself that she no longer meant anything to him. But the moment he saw her face, all that hard-earned conviction was blown right out of the water.

'It was the same for me,' Petronella said, rubbing Lizzie's hand briskly.

'The timing was wrong, Lizzie,' Bruno explained. 'We would've had a chance, you and I, if I'd met you before I ever came across Nell. Or if Nell had gone off overseas somewhere and I'd never seen her again. But ... but seeing her like that, wobbling off on her bike, right at the beginning of ... of things between you and me ...'

Lizzie took her hand away from Petronella. She felt as if she might be sick. 'I'd like to go home now,' she said.

Bruno continued to pat her on the back. 'Lizzie, I'm so sorry. It's just ... Nell is my *wife*. The divorce didn't cancel things out. We both realize that now. We're ... it's like trying to disown your family or something. We can't do it. We belong together.'

Lizzie stood up, clutching her bare arms. 'I've got to go,' she whispered.

But Bruno took Lizzie by the hand and pulled her into the kitchen, closing the door on Petronella's white face. 'I'm so sorry, Lizzie,' he said again. 'I wasn't stringing you along. Believe me. I was ... I was fighting to be out of this thing with Nell. All this week, that's what I've been doing. Just trying to fight it off. I wanted ... I *so* much wanted to be with you. You're way, way nicer than Nell. If you only knew how she's screwed me around, what a nutter she really is ... But I can't do it. I love her and that's all there is to it. Oh shit, the rice is burning.'

Looking at his stricken face as he snatched the saucepan off the gas ring, Lizzie knew he was telling the truth, but it made no difference. She still just wanted the floor to open up and swallow her in one large gulp. 'I have to go home,' she repeated.

Bruno turned from the stove and folded her in a bear hug. She simply stood there, stiff and still, enduring his touch. He pulled gently away from her when Petronella poked her head through the door. 'Something's burning,' Petronella said, sniffing the air.

Lizzie stared blankly at her. She was a fey-looking creature, really, with the little tendrils sticking out around her pixie ears, and the unnerving green of her eyes. Not the sort of woman Lizzie would ever have thought of as Bruno's type. He'd always claimed to like golden girls with curves, and now it turned out he was sick with love for a raven-haired waif.

'You'll stay for supper at least?' Bruno urged. 'It's duck with a marmalade sauce. My speciality. Ask Nell, it's really pretty good ...'

Lizzie transferred her blank stare back to him. Then she turned, walked out of the kitchen, picked up her handbag, and let herself out of the front door. They followed her out, still apologizing, still pressing her to stay and eat with them. As she drove away, they lingered in the road, waving.

She could only imagine how glad they were to see her go.

Safe in her own driveway at last, Lizzie simply sat in the car, her forehead resting against the steering wheel, feeling that she'd never have the nerve to walk into the bright light of her hallway and pick up the sorry threads of her life again.

She'd made a complete mess of everything, and that was the truth.

Firstly, through what amounted to sheer laxity, she'd estranged her husband. Then she'd gone on to lose her prospective boyfriend, not to some stranger, but to her very own running partner! If that weren't enough, she'd also failed to publish her verses, and then failed to reclaim her old job. On top of all that, she'd rented a house she couldn't afford and committed herself to a marathon she was pretty sure she'd never be able to run.

And now she'd have to endure the mortification of telling her well-wishers and supporters that she no longer had a back-up man waiting to mend her broken heart. Why, oh why, had she ever confided in Janie and Tessa and Ingrid and Maria, let alone her mum and dad? They would all be pitying her, all over again, and she simply couldn't bear the thought.

Sitting in the dark, Lizzie felt an almost overpowering urge to run off into the moonlit fields and never be seen or heard of again.

She couldn't do it, of course. What would happen to the twins?

But how she longed to be able to erase the recent past and start all over again, with a clean slate and a fresh piece of chalk. If only she could just close her eyes a moment, and then open them to find herself in a new world, a new place, a neutral setting where nobody had ever heard of James Buckley, or Bruno Ardis, or Petronella, or even Lizzie herself.

And that was when she thought of G.H. Brightman and his stumbling offer, that morning, of a position in Glasgow.

Glasgow was pretty remote. Glasgow was practically the other end of the world. Glasgow would do just nicely.

Waking up the next day, Lizzie wondered at first why she felt so miserable. Then it all came flooding back to her: the scene of her humiliation in Bruno's house, with Bruno and Petronella looking pityingly on as they broke their crushing news.

She gave a low groan and pulled the covers back over her head. Saturday. She couldn't speak to G.H. Brightman until Monday. Perhaps she simply wouldn't get out of bed today.

But you couldn't go into hibernation when you had three-year-old twins in the house. Minutes later, Alex and Ellie were jumping around her in their pyjamas, chanting, 'Castle, castle, castle!'

Then she remembered. She'd rashly promised to take them to Bodiam that day.

Hours later she was at the edge of the moat, holding Alex by the T-shirt so that he wouldn't throw himself in, when he suddenly turned and, with a gleeful giggle, plucked her brand-new sunglasses from her face. One-handed, she tried to wrestle them back from him, but in the scuffle the glasses flew out of his clutches and went somersaulting into the brown water. Lizzie was leaning dangerously over the moat, trying to fish them out with a stick that wasn't quite long enough, when Ellie piped up, 'Daddy could get them out.'

'Yesh,' Alex chimed in, seeing a chance to divert blame from his small person. 'Where's Daddy? Daddy could get dem.'

Lizzie sat up and put the stick down. She watched her sunglasses float away. 'Daddy's in France,' she said with false calm. 'I keep telling you. He's in France having a nice, long rest.'

'Why dint we go, too?' Ellie whined.

'Yesh, why *dint* we?'

'Because,' Lizzie said.

'Because why?' came the chorus.

Lizzie took a deep breath and steadied herself. Then, in a voice that sounded freakishly calm to her own ears, she said, 'Alex. Ellie. Remember that time Mummy and Daddy talked about getting divorced? And one of you asked what divorce meant?'

'No,' said Alex, but Ellie nodded vigorously. 'Yes, an' you said you'd 'splain anuvver time.'

'Well, I'm going to explain now. Divorce is when a mummy and a daddy stop being married.'

'Woss mawwied?' Alex asked, no longer smiling.

Lizzie thought for a moment. 'Married is ... it's when two grown-ups who love each other decide to live together for ever and ever.'

'Oh,' said Ellie.

'When I gwow up I'm going to mawwy *you*, Mummy,' said Alex. He got up on his haunches and touched her cheek in placatory fashion.

'Me too,' said Ellie.

'You can't marry your mother, my darlings.'

'Then I'll mawwy Ellie,' Alex declared.

'You can't marry your sister.'

'Oh. Then maybe I won't mawwy anybody,' he said gloomily.

She tousled his hair, blinking back inexplicable tears. 'Cross that bridge when you come to it, my boy,' she said.

'OK, Mummy. But I'm not gonna mawwy Mrs Kirker.'

'All *right*. Anyway, when you get married, you promise to stay together for ever and ever. But sometimes it doesn't work out that way. Sometimes the grown-ups find they don't want to live together any more. When that happens, they can get divorced.'

Ellie studied her mother. 'So divorce means not keepin' your promise to live togevver for ever?' she asked.

Lizzie paused, not happy with this wording. But after a moment she nodded her head. 'Yes,' she said sadly. 'That's it in a nut-shell.'

Ellie gave her a stern look. 'How come grown-ups can break promises?' she asked. 'You always tell us not to break promises.'

'Breaking promises isn't right,' said Lizzie. 'It almost always makes people sad. Daddy and I are very sad about breaking our promise, but we've decided to get divorced. We won't be living together ever again, and we won't be going on holiday together, either.'

Ellie began to pat her mother on the back. 'But you'll only get a little bit divorced, right?'

Lizzie shook her head. Why couldn't they understand? 'You can't get a little bit divorced,' she choked out.

'Don't be sad, Mummy,' said Alex. He put his hand into the tiny pocket of his jeans and brought out twenty pence. 'We woll buy you anudder glasses.'

'Silly,' Ellie rebuked her brother. 'She's not cryin' for the *glasses*.'

But Lizzie took the coin and put it in her own pocket. 'Thank you, my love,' she said. 'Every little helps.'

'You *can't* give up the marathon!' Tessa wailed at her on Monday morning, from the phone at work. 'Think of what you're throwing away! The hours of training! All that self-discipline! The miles you've clocked up on your running shoes!'

'I'm sorry, I just won't be able to do it,' Lizzie said.

'But you can't give it up!' Tessa insisted. 'Think of everything you've worked for – your fitness, your weight loss, your ... your sense of pride in what you've accomplished!'

'Tessa?'

'Yes?'

'Will you just shut up and listen a minute? I'm giving up the marathon because I won't be here to run it.'

'What the hell are you talking about now?'

'I'm going to Scotland. Glasgow. I'm going to open the branch office for G.H. Brightman after all. I phoned the office this morning and it's all on.'

That evening, Tessa and Greg arrived at Back Lane Cottage with some cartons of Chinese food and a bottle of wine. 'We need to talk,' Tessa said firmly. 'You can't go to *Glasgow*. Nobody goes to Glasgow. You *must* think again. I mean, what about Bruno?'

Lizzie poked at her beef and broccoli with a fork. 'There's something I haven't told you yet. It's more or less no go with Bruno. He's ... um, he's going back to his ex-wife.' She put down her fork and took a slug of wine.

Tessa stared at Greg, dumbfounded.

Greg cleared his throat. 'Hang on,' he said. 'What do you mean? From what I gathered, this chap was all over you. What ex-wife? What are you talking about?'

Lizzie got up and walked hurriedly to the bathroom. She could hear Tessa chiding Greg: 'You idiot! Did you have to be so tactless and insensitive? Can't you see she's a wreck? Just leave the talking to me, OK?'

Lizzie blew her nose fiercely and sucked the tears back down. She wasn't a wreck, not by any means. She was a woman who'd decided to make a fresh start somewhere new. Straightening her shoulders, she walked back to the table. Greg and Tessa smiled brightly.

'So ... so how did he break the news about the ex-wife?' Obviously, Tessa thought this a delicately-phrased and tactful question.

'He introduced us,' Lizzie said with a bitter twist of the mouth. 'Tessa, his ex-wife is your bloody friend, Petronella.'

'*What?*'

'You heard me.' Lizzie blew her nose hard on a paper napkin adorned with a green and red dragon.

'Well, blow me down,' said Greg.

'But ... but she can't be! I would've known! It's impossible!' Tessa protested.

'Truth is stranger than fiction,' said Greg.

'Shush, Greg, you're not actually helping. Look, she's crying again. Will you *just* be quiet and leave the talking to me? OK, Lizzie, so you've had a little hiccup with ... with getting out there and dating again. Never mind. Early days yet. These things happen. No need to ... you know, do anything rash. No need to rush off to Scotland.'

'Glasgow's a cultural hot-spot these days,' Lizzie told them stubbornly. 'I *want* to go there. Brightman is offering me a good salary. It's cheaper to live there than here. I can't afford to turn it down. As for Bruno and Petronella, I'm happy for them. Really. I hope they can work it out this time.'

Greg and Tessa exchanged glances.

'But Lizzie,' Tessa pleaded, 'you've just settled down here. You've just got this house looking decent. And the garden. All those nettles you destroyed. How can you possibly leave? Uproot the children all over again? I mean, is it really necessary?'

'The twins don't care where they are, as long as I'm there,' Lizzie said fiercely. 'Do you think I'd go to Glasgow just for a jaunt? Of course it's bloody necessary.'

For once in her life, Tessa looked quelled.

'Glasgow has the Burrell Collection,' Greg said thoughtfully after a moment. 'Also that science centre that looks like the Sydney Opera House.'

Tessa was roused from her stumped silence by her husband's flippant attitude. 'Will you shut up, Greg? Lizzie, you haven't thought this through. Ellie and Alex need to see their dad on a regular basis. If you take them way up there, they'll grow up without a male role model.'

Lizzie gave a hollow laugh. 'James? He's the model of a philandering bastard. Did I happen to mention he's swilling wine with Sonja Jenkins in the South of France right now? I'm going to Glasgow, and that's that.' She glared at them both as if she expected another argument, but neither of them said a single thing. 'Brightman's already set me up with a relocation agent and I've found out about day-care places. There's this woman called Fiona who runs a childminding business out of her home. It sounds OK.'

'The twins will grow up saying "och aye",' Greg pointed out.

'Good,' said Lizzie. 'I'm all for the occasional "och aye".'

'You should stay and stand your ground,' Tessa insisted. 'Running away isn't going to solve anything.'

'I'm not running away,' Lizzie said. 'I'm ... I'm embracing new opportunities.'

Tessa's eyes darted about as she considered all the angles. 'Look,' she said suddenly, 'go to Glasgow if you must, but don't give up the marathon. You promised me you'd run it. For the foetus. Remember? So if you really must go to Scotland, couldn't you carry on training up there, and take a few days off work to come down and run it? Please?'

Lizzie shook her head. 'The marathon doesn't matter now. I'll be too busy, too stretched. I won't have the time for it. Besides, I might bump into Petronella on the day.'

Tessa scrunched up her mouth and glanced at Greg. He took her cue. 'Lizzie, we *need* you to run it,' he urged. 'Tessa's very ... superstitious. Don't look at me that way, darling, it's true. She's scared shitless she'll lose the baby if you don't run. So, please?'

Great. Nothing like a dose of emotional blackmail to round out her day. Lizzie glared at Tessa. 'You idiot,' she said. 'You're not losing this baby. OK, I'll run the bloody thing if you're going to make such a big deal out of it.'

Tessa surged at her and tried to hug her, but Lizzie batted away her hands. 'I know it's a lot to ask,' said Tessa, 'but I think it might also do you some good, you know? Help keep you sane with everything you've got on your plate.'

'Help keep me out of size sixteen jeans, you mean.'

'That, too.'

Greg was suddenly struck by a thought. 'Hey, does James know you're leaving? Do you think he'll try to stop you?'

'We haven't actually talked,' Lizzie admitted. 'I'll phone him tonight. He's coming back from France next week. We're due to sign the divorce papers as soon as he gets here.' She took a deep breath. Greg and Tessa watched her anxiously. 'I can't bloody wait!' she declared.

Now that Lizzie had made up her mind to move to Glasgow, she was full of impatience to pack up and go. Brightman had offered to give her a month to wind things up, but she'd told him she could do it in two weeks. The less time spent looking over her shoulder in case Bruno and/or Petronella should suddenly pop up out of the woodwork, the better.

Bruno and Petronella didn't seem to realize that it behoved them never to contact her again. They both kept phoning to ask how she was doing. She kept hanging up on them, of course, but it was very unsettling. She couldn't wait to be out of Back Lane Cottage, without a forwarding address and off to parts unknown.

She was packing up the small items in the living room the next day when Sarah and Ingrid Hatter poked their heads through the front door and called, 'Yoo-hoo!' Lizzie set aside the picture she was about to wrap in newspaper – the one of her and Tessa in Greece – and ran her fingers through her dishevelled hair.

'Come on in,' she called. 'It's about time I had a tea break.'

'What are you doing?' Ingrid asked, as curious as ever.

'I'm … I'm packing up my stuff,' Lizzie said. 'I was going to come over and tell you. I've taken a job in, um, Glasgow.'

Ingrid threw herself down on the Ikea sofa. 'You *what?*' she demanded. 'Is this because of that basket, Bruno?'

Basket? Oh, right. One of Ingrid's euphemisms. News certainly travelled fast; Lizzie hadn't actually laid eyes on the Hatters since her disastrous dinner date at Bruno's house.

'Sarah said you came home on Friday night looking as if you'd been crying your eyes out,' Ingrid went on. 'I took the liberty of calling him up, and the cheeky bugger told me he's back with his wife. The absolute nerve of the man. After kissing you like that in the garden! He won't be mowing my lawn any more, I can tell you that for free.'

Lizzie made an explosive noise, a mixture between a sob and a laugh. 'Oh, Ingrid. Don't sack him on my account.' She didn't feel up to admitting to the two of them that the ex-wife was Petronella, her own ex-running partner. 'Look, the truth is, I'm going to Glasgow because I can't really afford to live here. My former boss has offered me quite a decent salary to start up an office there. It's a big opportunity. I can't turn it down.'

Sarah was toeing a rug and looking miserable. Lizzie felt a strange urge to go over and hug her, but she'd never hugged the child before and it would probably be embarrassing for both of them.

'What does James say?' Ingrid barked.

Ah, James.

That was the tricky bit.

She'd phoned him in France last night and he'd had quite a bit to say, none of it very supportive. He'd started out politely enough, asking her to reconsider the whole situation, pointing out all the disadvantages of going so far away from her friends and family, and of putting the children through the trauma of adjusting to yet another new nursery.

'I know all that,' she'd told him. 'I've weighed up all the pros and cons. But I can't really see what else I'm supposed to do. I can't get a decent job around here, not one that would justify me putting the children into day-care. I won't be able to stay in this house in the long run, anyway. It's too expensive.'

'Rubbish,' he'd said. 'I'm quite prepared to keep paying the rent. If that's the issue, just stop worrying about it and stay right where you are.'

That was when she began to bristle. 'I'll do as I see fit,' she'd told him. 'I'm not answerable to you any more.'

There was a silence. And then he said, 'But you're answerable to Alex and Ellie.'

Lizzie was furious. 'So are you!' she spat. 'You should've thought of that when you walked out on us. I'm going to Glasgow because I've sent my CV out to thirteen PR firms, and not one of them wants me! You try taking a four-year break from work and then shoe-horning yourself back in! They don't hold your bloody place for you. And anyway, what are you worried about? If you can keep flitting up to Scotland to re-design old barns, you can make the time to get up there to see your own children.'

'So? What does he say?' Ingrid was nothing if not persistent.

'He's fine with it,' Lizzie lied. 'Can I . . . can I make you some tea?'

'Oh, no, don't worry. We only came over to give you some post,' Ingrid said. 'Don't know how it ends up coming through our door. But still. Where's that letter, Sarah. Go on. Give it to her.'

'I'm sorry,' Sarah muttered, proffering an envelope. 'We've already opened it. But it came to our address.'

'Oh, don't worry,' Lizzie said soothingly. 'I'm sure it's just a bit of junk mail.' And she threw it into a huge wooden bowl, already brimming with neglected paperwork, that took up most of the space on top of the old bookshelf she used as a sideboard.

'No!' Sarah yelped with surprising force. 'Don't do that. You might lose it. Would you please just look at it?'

Puzzled, Lizzie took back the envelope that Sarah was holding out again. Hang on. It didn't really look like junk mail. Nice, thick, cream-coloured envelope. Single sheet of good-quality paper inside, the kind with a water mark.

She took out the letter and opened it, feeling strangely breathless. It was from somebody called Warren Battledon Inc.

Dear Ms Buckley

Thank you for submitting *Hamming it Up* for our consideration. I am happy to say that we'd like to talk to you about representing the book, which strikes us as fresh, funny and commercial.

Lizzie couldn't read any more. The words seemed to have gone into squiggles all over the page. She looked up at the bright, exultant faces of Ingrid and Sarah Hatter.

'How?' she croaked. 'How did this happen? I threw it away.'

Sarah ducked her head guiltily. 'I know. I was there. Remember?'

Lizzie stared at her. 'You,' she said. 'You did it?'

'Mum did all the work,' Sarah admitted. 'I just couldn't let you chuck the book out. So I dug it out of the bin and took it home, not really knowing what to do with it. Then Mum had this idea of sending it off to all the agents for children's books in the entire country.'

Ingrid nodded her head vigorously. 'That's right,' she said. 'Couldn't believe you'd given up after one half-hearted attempt. So I thought I'd give it a go myself. Turned it into a bit of a campaign. It was easy enough. Just a case of writing a form letter on Word and then plugging in the different names and addresses. Did you know you left your disc with everything on it in the A-drive of our computer?'

Lizzie shook her head, bemused.

'Hang on a moment,' said Ingrid, and disappeared from the

room, to reappear within seconds bearing a bottle of champagne and three plastic glasses. She pointed it at a wall and popped it with surprising expertise. Before Lizzie knew it, she was swilling a cold mouthful of bubbly.

She swallowed and took another gulp, and then another. Before too long, a feeling of, yes, *euphoria* began to sweep through her, replacing the numbness of shock.

She, Elizabeth Buckley, née Indigo, might not have a husband or a boyfriend or even the prospect of a boyfriend. But she had something much, much better! She had an agent. A literary agent!

Blinking back tears, she turned to Ingrid. 'I can't believe you did this,' she said. 'You and Sarah. It's wonderful. The best surprise anyone's ever given me.'

Ingrid gave her a big horsey grin. 'It's all down to Sarah, to be honest,' she said. 'That girl really believes in your stuff.'

Lizzie looked fondly at Sarah, who'd finished the thimbleful of champagne she'd been given and was glowing like a beacon. Then she glanced back at Ingrid – nosy, interfering, thick-skinned Ingrid. 'You two,' she said with a break in her voice. 'You've been the best neighbours I could possibly have wished for. I'm ... I'm really going to miss you.'

'But you'll send us a signed copy of the book?' said Sarah. 'It's going to be so cool, knowing somebody famous.'

Speechless, Lizzie went over and gave the big, blushing girl a hug. It wasn't an awkward thing to do, after all. 'You'll come to Glasgow,' she said firmly. 'It's a fantastic place to visit. The cultural hub of the United Kingdom. You'll love it. Promise you'll come?'

By midnight, Lizzie's happiness in her good news had all drained away, as if there'd only been a thimbleful of it, after all. Sleep refused to come. She kept re-reading the letter from Warren Battledon Inc., hoping to recapture the keen jolt of excitement she'd felt the first twenty times. But she might just as well have been reading her gas and electricity bill, for all the kick she got out of the thing now.

On the following Wednesday, the sky was a rare, unbroken blue. Instead of taking advantage of the weather, Lizzie was in the bathroom, dressed in an old T-shirt and the reviled grey jogging bottoms (which she loved to wear now because they were so gloriously baggy she had to fold them over at the waistband to keep them up), a tin of filler in one hand and a cheese knife in the other. She was hoping to fix the drill holes in the wall so that the landlord wouldn't notice them when he inspected the house on Friday.

The packing wasn't finished yet, but she was sure she could manage it before the truck came for the boxes and furniture on Saturday morning. It was astonishing how much stuff they'd accumulated during their summer in the cottage. Of course, James would think none of the furniture was worth packing up and shifting; most of it had been bought from the local second-hand store, after all. But Brightman was paying for the truck and besides, she'd become strangely attached to her eclectic collection.

She and the children would spend their last night at the barn before leaving for Glasgow on Sunday.

All week she'd been tying up loose ends. At the top of the list on today's agenda was the most important loose end of them all: the final signing of the divorce papers.

In a flash of inspiration, Lizzie had packed lunch boxes with cheese sandwiches, hard-boiled eggs and bright green yoghurt, and sent the twins for a long walk and picnic with Sarah.

James, back from France the day before, had promised to be on her doorstep at ten o'clock sharp that morning, but the appointed hour came and went and the doorbell failed to ring. Lizzie, glancing at her watch every thirty seconds or so, was finding it hard to concentrate on the wall-patching job. She felt as if her ears were standing out on stalks, straining for the first sounds of an arrival. At thirty-eight minutes past ten, Lizzie threw down the cheese knife and stormed out of the bathroom.

Without pausing to change clothes or wash the poly-filler off her hands, Lizzie shoved her feet into trainers and wrote a hurried message on a yellow post-it, which she slapped on the front door.

'Gone running,' the note read pithily.

There, that would teach James Buckley to behave as if her time were worthless.

She set off at a sprint along the path that led down past the barn, returning Ingrid's 'yoo-hoo' from her front garden with a terse wave.

As she sped down the hill, the wind lifting the hair from her hot head, her angry heart suddenly had reason to thump at speed. Fight or flight – and she was flying. By degrees, she began to feel better. So what if James was late? Lateness was the least of his sins, and anyway, she was about to be shot of him for ever.

As a matter of fact, she was *glad* he was late. He'd given her the impetus to get out of that bathroom. Here she was out in the fresh air, running through sun-dappled shadows, able to glimpse the blue sky through the tree tops whenever she dared take her eyes off the rocky track. She relished the feeling of power that surged through her body as she fell into a steady rhythm, breathing in through her nose and out through her mouth. She could run like this all day, if she had to. She was ready for anything. Ready for a marathon. Ready to be divorced. Ready to be free.

'Liz-zee!'

Her foot slipped on a rock and she hurtled into the nettles on the verge, struggling to keep her balance. Through her sweat pants, she felt a red-hot prickle from the stinging weeds. Righting herself with difficulty, she looked over her shoulder. It couldn't be? Following her? How had he known where to go? Why hadn't he sat down on the bloody steps and waited for her to get back, like any normal person would? And in his jeans, too. Nobody went running in jeans!

'Lizzie! Hold on a moment, let me catch up.' James ran down the hill with impressive speed and agility, given he was wearing moccasins.

She stood and watched until he was a few paces away, then started running again herself.

'How did you find me?' she asked over her shoulder, between gritted teeth.

'Your neighbour spotted me on your doorstep. She pointed me in the right direction. But I don't get it, Lizzie. Did you forget about our meeting?'

Lizzie's legs picked up speed. She let them go for it. 'Forget?' she spat. 'How could I bloody *forget*? If you went into my dining room right now, you'd see two glasses of water on the table and a list of questions from my lawyer about ancillary bloody relief.'

James didn't seem to be having any difficulty keeping up with her. 'Why the hell go running, then?'

Lizzie stole a look at him. He looked distinctly hacked off.

She took a deep breath. 'Because I'm not operating on Buckley *time* any more,' she hissed. 'I'm back in the world of Greenwich Mean Time, where ten o'clock is still ten o'clock, not ten forty-five. I got tired of waiting around for you!'

James stopped running abruptly and pulled Lizzie to a standstill. 'My flight was delayed. I didn't get in till this morning; I drove straight here from Heathrow. I tried to ring but you haven't been picking up the phone.'

She shrugged his hand off her shoulder. She'd heard the phone ringing a few times last night and this morning, but she wasn't taking any calls at the moment. Bruno and Petronella might still be trying to get in touch, and even if they weren't, too many people seemed to think they needed to reason her out of going to Glasgow.

'Well, it's not as if you've never been late before,' she said irrationally. She gave her head an angry little shake and started running again. Fast. He fell into stride beside her.

'Lizzie?'

'Yes?'

'Shouldn't we be heading back? We've got a lot to cover.'

'Well, OK, if you're getting tired. Let's go back.'

'I didn't say I was getting tired.'

She glanced at him. He certainly didn't look tired, no panting or wheezing, but his neck and arms were beginning to glisten. He must be sweating horribly inside those hot jeans. Possibly chafing too, in the crotch area. All those tough denim seams. Jolly good. Bloody excellent.

'We might as well finish the loop, now we're this far,' she said. 'Pointless turning back. Am I going too fast for you?'

'Too fast?' he asked with something like a snort. 'This is a stroll in the park.'

'OK,' she breathed, 'we'll step it up.'

If they'd been belting along before, now they began to run as if pursued by cohorts of demons, helter-skelter down the rocky path, arms pumping, feet flying, the scenery shooting by in a blur of green. It was stupid. It was dangerous. It was only a matter of time until one of them sprained an ankle.

Lizzie hadn't felt so good in days.

At the bottom of the hill, she raced him along the lane, through a tunnel-like pathway, and then up the long, punishing hill beside the maizefield, towards home. Never before, in all her weeks of training, had she pushed her body so hard. Yet, unbelievably, every time she thought she'd reached the limit of her stamina, she found further reserves of energy and endurance.

She kept stealing sideways glances at James, looking for signs of weakness. She'd never been running with him before, though she'd spent many a drizzly Saturday morning watching him play various ball games with effortless grace. His profile now was stern and determined, yet he seemed to move quite easily. He was a natural athlete, the lucky bugger. She was pretty sure he hadn't been running in years. How he was managing to keep up with her, she had no idea, especially in those heavy jeans and leather-soled shoes. By now, his T-shirt was plastered to his chest, dark with sweat. As they ran, he suddenly pulled it up over his head and, without slackening his pace for a moment, stuffed it through a belt loop.

She looked at him once, naked from the waist up, and then studiously kept her eyes straight ahead.

Treacherous bastard. He was clearly trying to intimidate her with his washboard stomach and rippling muscles. How would he feel if she suddenly stripped off her big T-shirt and began running in her sports bra?

No sooner had the thought occurred to her than she acted on it. After all, her sports bra was black and sturdy, not some flimsy, see-through wisp of lingerie. Lots of women worked out in tops just like it. Why should James daunt her with his flawless French tan? She wouldn't allow it. She'd fight back.

As she tucked the T-shirt into her jogging bottoms, James stumbled and nearly took a nose-dive. He recovered himself quickly. Risking a few glances at his face, she saw that he was looking straight ahead in frowning concentration.

'Not much further,' Lizzie panted as they left the maizefield behind them. 'Just round the bend.'

It was then he began to sprint in earnest, drawing away from her over the grassy meadow with the inexorable acceleration of a sports car leaving a farm tractor in the dust.

Lizzie was at the far end of her tether. She could barely draw breath. She had nothing left; she'd used up every ounce of energy, every reserve of speed, every particle of power in her body. Her chest was on fire; her shins were shrieking; her pulse was so loud you could have used it as the back beat for a rock anthem. James's blue jeans were simply speeding away from her, uncatchable, un-reachable, untouchable, soon to be out of sight.

But she wasn't going to let the bastard beat her.

'Run, Lizzie, *run*,' she growled at herself.

And she ran.

As she did so, she imagined a rope between herself and her hus-band's fleeing back, a rope she was hauling in as fast as she possibly could, hand over hand. She was dragging him back to her, reeling him in with the force of her will.

She gained on him steadily until at last they were level again, running shoulder to shoulder. She heard a loud, wordless yell, like some sort of strangled war-cry, and realized suddenly, with shock, that the noise was coming from her own throat.

James must have heard it, too. He faltered and glanced sideways at her, and, as his head turned, Lizzie saw the dog.

Ingrid Hatter's Jack Russell was trundling along without a care in the world, legs moving so fast it was like a dog on wheels, nose to the ground, apparently oblivious that a 6ft human steamroller was pounding towards it.

'Watch out!' Lizzie managed to yell, gesticulating wildly.

James turned and saw the tiny animal in his path just as he was about to step on its back. The dog suddenly noticed him at the same moment, and skittered quickly to one side. James tried some fancy footwork of his own, but he was moving too fast, and, in an instant, he was down, knees and elbows breaking his fall in the damp grass.

Lizzie stopped, turned and walked back to him.

'You ... OK?' she panted.

He lay on his back, chest heaving, looking up at her with a dazzled expression. 'Fine,' he panted back. 'Fine.'

She extended a hand. 'Here, grab on.' He gazed at the hand a moment, then took it and pulled himself up. His palm was hot and slippery. She pulled her hand away quickly.

For a moment he simply stood, breathing hard, his hands resting on his knees. 'My God, Lizzie,' he wheezed at last, shooting a stunned look at her. 'How did you learn to run like that? I mean, you can really *run*.'

Lizzie's face tried to flush but she was already nearly purple with exertion. 'Anybody can run,' she said. 'You just put one foot in front of the other. No big deal.'

'Well, hello!'

Lizzie jumped like a startled hare. She knew that voice. It was Ingrid Hatter, of course, in brown corduroys and a floppy sun hat, striding down the path with a look of avid curiosity on her face.

'So you two found each other. Jolly good. I was just taking Jack for a walk. Nice sort of day for a walk. Normally I don't take him out till late afternoon but I suddenly found myself with time on my hands. As you do. So I just thought I'd take him for his walk.'

Right. A little walk, motivated by nothing in particular, certainly not by a desire to track down Lizzie Buckley and her soon to be ex-husband, in case they were engaged in any sort of interesting activity along the footpaths or in the ditches. Really, Ingrid Hatter was the limit.

'Well, have a good one,' James said smoothly, as if not at all discomfited to be discovered breathless and sweaty in nothing but a pair of grass-stained jeans, by a woman who was almost a complete stranger to him.

'Jack's lucky to be alive,' Lizzie puffed. 'James nearly trampled him. He fell trying to avoid him.'

Ingrid raised her eyebrows. 'Really? But Jack's so *nimble*. How d'you think he got his name? He never gets trampled. You should see him among the horses at point-to-points. Still, you weren't to know.'

'We weren't to know,' Lizzie repeated numbly. Suddenly catching sight of the pinnacles of her own black sports bra, she fought the urge to cover her chest with her arms. Such a gesture would be downright incriminating, drawing needless attention to her shirtless state. If she just played it cool, Ingrid would think nothing of it. After all, plenty of women worked out in teeny little sports tops.

'Gosh, Lizzie, you're brave, running in a bra. Did you put on any sunscreen?'

'It's a top, not a bra,' Lizzie gabbled. 'Lots of women work out in them. Look, James and I have to dash. We don't have much time now. Sarah could be back any minute and we still have to – you know, do the paperwork.'

Ingrid nodded briskly. 'Tell you what,' she said, 'I bet I know where Sarah took the twins for the picnic. I'll walk Jack in that direction, and if I bump into them on their way back, I'll take them along to the barn. Give you a bit more time.'

'But . . . but they're supposed to be going back to Gloucestershire with James,' Lizzie said. She'd agreed, rather reluctantly, to let them spend a couple of days in the Chipping Norton house before their big move.

'Well, he can pick them up from my place on his way out,' Ingrid offered.

'Good idea,' said James, forestalling any objections from Lizzie. 'Thanks very much.'

'Toodle-oo,' Ingrid trilled, and continued on her way, tiny Jack trundling along in front of her.

James watched her go. 'For God's sake,' he breathed, shaking his head in wonder. 'Is that woman *everywhere*?'

Lizzie nodded. ''Fraid so,' she said. 'But I'm sort of fond of her. Come on, let's go inside and get this over with.'

As they approached the house, James dug a key out of his pocket and walked across to his car. He took a manila envelope from the passenger seat and began to tuck it under his arm, then apparently thought better of it, and instead held it gingerly away from his sweaty body.

'OK, I'm ready,' he said.

As they entered the cool house, Lizzie shrugged her T-shirt back on. Glancing sideways, she noticed that James was doing the same thing. Nothing like a cold, sweat-soaked T-shirt to bring you back to reality. She gave a little shiver. In the hallway, she hesitated. Should she offer to let him shower? Ask him to wait while she took a shower herself? No, all that would take too long and be somehow too – intimate.

Instead, she darted into the bathroom and got them each a towel. 'Here, mop up with this,' she said, throwing him one. Then she ushered him briskly into the dining room where, as advertised, two glasses of water and a list of awkward questions from her lawyer stood waiting.

James finished rubbing down, then folded the towel and placed it on the dining room chair before sitting. Carefully, he laid his envelope in front of him.

Lizzie sat opposite him, lifted her glass of water and drained it in one long pull. Setting the glass back down, she looked up and met his eyes. The expression in those eyes was impossible to read. Lizzie looked away quickly.

'Have a good holiday?' she asked, not even trying to keep the bitterness out of her voice.

'What?'

'Holiday. In France.'

'Oh. It wasn't a holiday.'

'No?'

'Lizzie, I was drafting plans to turn a *fromagerie* into four apartments.'

'Oh. Gosh. Did *Sonja* enjoy it?'

His eyebrows rose. 'Who told——? Yes, she had a wonderful time, actually. She loves France. When I first hired her I had no idea she was such a romantic at heart. But all the wining and dining brought out a completely different side of her. Less inhibited, if you know what I mean.'

Ask a stupid question. Lizzie scowled heavily at the table.

James cleared his throat. 'Look, before we go on, I just thought I'd let you know I've seen this.' He extracted a piece of paper from the envelope; obviously some new exhibit to do with the divorce. Sliding it across the table, he said, 'It came yesterday.'

Puzzled, Lizzie took the piece of paper and scanned it.

From: lizbuckley@hotmail.com
Sent: 13 September
To: janehawthorn@yahoo.com

Dear Janie

Wonderful news. I've found an agent to take my book of silly verse. Actually, I didn't find the agent. My neighbour in the barn did. She sent the verses out to sixty (yes, sixty!) names she found in some book about getting published, and one of them wants to take me on!

If there's any money in this, I may be able to work from home eventually – you know, as a real writer. God, I hope there's some money in it. If only this had come sooner, perhaps I wouldn't be going to Glasgow.

At first, I felt so happy. But now the novelty's worn off, I realize the awful truth. Nothing is going to be that big a deal in my life any more. You see, I think I'm officially heart-broken. It's bloody grim, knowing the man you love is with another woman. Almost unbearable, really. So here I am.

Can't sleep. Can't even eat. Can't stop thinking. It's just so stupid. How can I still be hooked on him after what he's done? I wish I could press some sort of remote control button and turn the love off. Ping. But damn it all, I can't.

Anyway, got to stop this and go to bed. So much to do tomorrow for the move. Make that today. Aaargh!

Kisses to baby Elizabeth.

Lizzie

She could feel her cheeks burning and her chest thumping un-comfortably, almost as if she were running at full throttle again. Suddenly there didn't seem to be enough air in the room. This was probably how she was going to feel about two hours into the London Marathon.

'I'm sorry about what happened,' James said, rearranging his papers. 'With Bruno.'

But Lizzie was hardly listening. 'How did you get this?' she demanded. 'I sent it to Janie. Not you. I *know* I didn't screw up again. I've taken you out of my electronic address book.'

James frowned. 'Janie forwarded it to me. She thought I should see it. Sent me a covering note saying she's worried about you ... Everybody's worried about you. Lizzie, don't you see? Nobody wants you bolting off to Glasgow because of this break-up with Bruno. I'm serious, Lizzie. I have a very bad feeling about you going up there on your own, in this sort of state.'

'I'm not in a state!' Lizzie cried. 'Who told you about Bruno, anyway?'

James shrugged. 'Laurence, as a matter of fact. And Janie, in her note.' He reached out awkwardly to pat her hand, but she shrugged him off.

'Look, I may be a bit battered and bruised, but I'm not unhinged,' she said. 'I've explained to you about Glasgow. I'm not just going because of ... because of Bruno. My reasons are actually very ... what's the word, *sound*. And sensible. And don't try to pretend you're worried about me! We both know you're only concerned about how often you'll be able to see the children. Well, I've told you before, you're just going to have to suffer the inconvenience. That, or move to Scotland. Now, let's just sign the papers, shall we?' Lizzie swiped at her mouth with the back of her hand, half-afraid that she might be frothing.

James stared at her for a long moment, then pushed the pen and paper in front of her. There was a line for her signature. Very care-fully, she signed her name. A tear plopped down and made a bump on the paper, but somehow missed the ink. Then James took the document and signed it himself.

'Done,' he said solemnly.

'Done,' she nodded. She'd managed to get get her breathing and pulse rate back under control. 'I'll hand-deliver it to the lawyer before I leave. And would you take those ancillary relief questions away with you? I'd rather deal with all that by e-mail. I need a shower now, and I need to be alone.'

'OK, but we do need to talk about visitation,' he said. 'If you're really going to go through with the Glasgow scheme—'

Lizzie jumped up. 'I'm not ready to discuss that now,' she said between clenched teeth. 'Isn't a divorce enough for one day? We'll talk about it on the phone, when I'm settled and ready to deal with it. Look, the children's bags are over there. Ingrid will be expecting you to pick them up any minute now.'

'I'll bring them back here to say goodbye,' James offered.

Not sticking around to watch him leave, Lizzie bolted upstairs, slammed her bedroom door, and threw herself onto the bed. After a while, a good long while, it seemed to her, she heard little voices. The children came thundering upstairs to give her a hug and a kiss goodbye. 'See you on Friday,' she whispered into their hair, trying not to cling to them in a strange and frenzied way.

Long after they'd run back downstairs again, and she'd heard the car door slam and then the sound of the engine pulling away, Lizzie simply sat on the bed, motionless, her arms wrapped around her knees.

He was gone.

She realized she'd been holding her breath. Shakily, she let it out.

Yes, he was gone. It was over. She was divorced.

She got up and went downstairs to the kitchen. Before she knew what she was doing, she was standing in front of the counter with a can of sweetened condensed milk in one hand and a can-opener in the other.

But as she pressed the metal tooth into the lid and watched the creamy milk bubble up through the hole, she had a revelation.

She didn't want to drink a can of sweetened condensed milk. What's more, she didn't want to eat a gallon of ice-cream or wolf down half a kilogram of milk chocolate or even open a packet of

HobNobs. No. She was finished with all that. She wanted to take a shower and blow-dry her hair. Then she wanted to get on with her life.

She heard a knock and then the sound of voices in the hall. 'Come in,' she called to Ingrid and Sarah, tossing the full can into the bin as she spoke. It fell to the bottom of the empty rubbish bag with a satisfying thump.

'Everything all right?' Ingrid Hatter caught her eye meaningfully.

Lizzie gave a fierce, dry-eyed smile. 'Everything's fine,' she said. And her smile widened until it took over her whole face, because suddenly, in a weird sort of way, everything did seem fine. For the very first time, she knew she could actually do this. She could go to Glasgow. She could start again. She could live without James, without Bruno, without anyone at all. She had her health, her self-respect, her new job, her running shoes, her agent and, most of all, her twins. With a rush of euphoria, she saw herself blasting up the motorway, her people-carrier packed to the rafters, the children singing at the top of their lungs to something rousing by Raffi or The Wiggles, the big blue sky above them, the whole of England and Scotland before them.

'Everything's fine, fine, fine!' she repeated, pulling out a kitchen drawer and dumping the contents out on the counter with a clatter. 'Now, why on earth do I have these funny little corn forks when I always cut the corn off the cob with a knife? Where did they even come from? Do you want them for your next car boot sale, Ingrid?'

She caught Ingrid and Sarah giving each other baffled looks, and burst out laughing. 'It's OK,' she said. 'I'm not going loopy on you! It's just . . . it feels so good to be free!'

And if she said it often enough, soon it would be true.

'Do you want these?' Tessa asked, holding up one of the wicker baskets Lizzie had used to store the children's clothes.

'Yeah, shove them in a box, they're useful for toys and things,' Lizzie said. 'Hey, out of there, Alex, you're in the way!'

It was Saturday morning, and Alex was bouncing a half-deflated beach ball in the crooked passageway, getting under the feet of two sweating men who were trying to manoeuvre the box-spring bit of Lizzie's bed through the narrow space.

The twins had been delivered home safely the afternoon before by a deeply tanned and smug-looking Sonja Jenkins. She didn't look in the least like a romantic at heart. She looked like a beastly little schemer. James, apparently, was 'in a meeting'. Lizzie had yanked the overnight bags out of Sonja's hands, and sent her on her way without offering so much as a cup of tea or the use of her bathroom.

Alex kicked the ball into the children's bedroom, where his mother and Auntie Tess were hard at work sorting and packing. 'Don't frow dat away,' he cried, diving into a black bin bag to retrieve the shell of a large garden snail. Lizzie rolled her eyes at Tessa.

'When will Sarah be here?' Tessa asked in an undertone.

'Any minute,' said Lizzie. 'I told her ten o'clock.'

As if on cue, one of the movers stuck his head into the room. 'Someone to see you, love.'

'Speak of the devil. Just tell her to come up, would you?'

'No prob.' He withdrew his head and they heard him thump back down the stairs.

Lizzie was taping a box closed seconds later when Ellie ran into the room, eyes bright with excitement. 'Mummy, Mummy,' she cried. 'Guess who's here!'

Lizzie froze above the box, feeling as if her heart had suddenly stopped.

'It's Granny! It's Granny!'

'*What?*' Lizzie jumped to her feet, automatically smoothing her hair down with her hands. Granny? Her mother had flown back from Australia to help her with the move? Her face split into an enormous smile.

But in the doorway, dressed in glacier green, stood Lady Evelyn Buckley.

'GRANNY,' yelled Alex, launching himself at her knees. James's mother rocked slightly as the boy collided with her legs, but she stood her ground, absently stroking his head with one heavily-ringed hand.

'Shit,' breathed Tessa from her corner among the toy cars and picture books.

Lizzie's smile withered and died.

'Lady Evelyn,' she said, reaching for Ellie's hand, her mind racing. 'What are you doing here?'

Lady Evelyn nodded at Tessa, who gave her a weak wave. Then she turned to Lizzie and inclined her head regally. 'Elizabeth, I'd like to talk to you, if I may.'

Lizzie gripped Ellie's hand so tightly that the little girl yelped. Her eyes narrowed. 'Talk away,' she said.

'No,' said Lady Evelyn. 'I mean, I'd like to speak privately.'

Tessa had staggered to her feet. 'I'll watch the twins,' she told Lizzie. 'Go on down to the living room. You'll be pretty private there.'

Lizzie met Tessa's eye indignantly, but Tessa gave a tiny jerk of her head in the direction of the door. Lizzie hesitated for a second, then curiosity got the better of her. 'OK,' she said, 'but I'm very busy. I can't be long.'

Lady Evelyn followed her down the stairs and into the living room, now entirely bare of furniture. The two of them stood on the sun-dappled floorboards, facing each other in the empty silence for a moment. If there'd been the right sort of music playing, and if they'd been wearing cowboy hats, and if Lady Evelyn hadn't been a po-faced noblewoman, they might have been squaring up for a gunfight.

'What are you doing here?' Lizzie demanded again. She'd never spoken so rudely to Lady Evelyn in her life, but all the hairs on her back seemed to be standing up on end, and her whole body was on red alert. What if the old battle-axe had come to kidnap the twins?

Lady Evelyn was looking around the room with a calm, assessing eye. 'So this is the place you've been living in,' she marvelled.

'It's a lovely, light room,' Lizzie said defensively.

Lady Evelyn shook her head. 'Do you know, I don't think I'll ever understand your generation. In my day, you didn't just get married to please yourself. You thought of your family, your name, your place in the world. And once you were married, you stayed that way. You made it work. You didn't expect, oh, a dozen roses every day, violins playing in the background . . . all sorts of romantic nonsense. You just got on with things.'

Lizzie felt her blood pressure beginning to rise. 'You mean, like you and Roger?' she shot back. 'Well, anybody can see there's no romantic nonsense between the two of you.'

Lady Evelyn skewered her with a gaze. 'There may be no romantic nonsense,' she replied, 'but we have a good, solid life together. We understand each other well. We respect each other. But as for you, Elizabeth. I don't understand you at all. You exchanged Mill House for *this*? And for what? Some notion that your marriage wasn't exciting enough any more? Some idea that you weren't quite ready for the tedium of monogamy? I still can't *believe* you just threw it all away. And so lightly. After all, even *you* must've realized you were marrying up when you married James!'

Lizzie felt as if she might choke with pure, white-hot rage. 'Marrying *up*?' she managed to snort out at last. 'You have the absolute brass neck to talk about marrying up? Do you know what you are? You're just plain *rude*. You come barging in here, uninvited, full of airs and graces just because you happen to have inherited some . . . some dusty, useless, ill-gotten old title . . . Yes, thinking you have the right to lecture me because you're so damn superior, born to the bloody purple and all that rot! But when you get right down to it, you're probably the most boorish, ill-bred person I know! I mean, you don't have the manners of a *three*-year-old.' Lizzie stopped and clapped her hand over her mouth.

Lady Evelyn was breathing very unevenly. An ugly red flush had crept across her chest and up her neck. She took a backward step, and staggered slightly. All told, she looked as if she might be about to have some sort of fit.

'Sorry,' Lizzie gasped, rushing over to take Lady Evelyn's elbow. 'I didn't mean it. Oh, God, there's no chair . . . Look, I'm . . . I'm not myself at the moment. Forget I said that . . .'

Lady Evelyn took a deep breath. 'No,' she said. 'You're right.'

Lizzie teetered and had to cling to the older woman's elbow just to remain upright. 'What?'

'You're right,' Lady Evelyn repeated. 'I've been ... unpardonably rude. I've really botched things this time. You see, I didn't come here to pick a fight. I came to reason with you, no, to plead with you. To beg you not to go to Glasgow.'

Lizzie was speechless.

Lady Evelyn gently shook her elbow free. 'Look, Lizzie, it's an open secret that you were never my ideal daughter-in-law,' she said. 'We both know that I was rather ... disappointed when James chose you as his wife. But, and I don't think you've ever understood this, it was nothing *personal*. I am, after all, the daughter of a duke, and a Plantagenet on the distaff side. I was brought up to believe that sort of heritage carries with it a certain amount of responsibility. One has a duty to the bloodline. Is it surprising I'd have preferred someone with a more distinguished pedigree than your own? No, wait, let me finish. The thing is, I never disliked you *per se*. Oh, I admit, I've sometimes found you a little flighty, a little over-the-top. But I always knew that, against all the odds, you were *good* for James. He's had quite a lot of girlfriends, you see, some of them even rather suitable. But bloodlines be damned, I never saw him look at a girl the way he used to look at you.'

Lizzie stared at the woman in astonishment. If Ingrid Hatter's dog, Jack, had suddenly got up on his hind legs and started quoting Shakespeare, she couldn't have been more surprised.

Then a truly unthinkable thing happened. Lady Evelyn took Lizzie's hand, and her eyes – those piercing blue eyes that could quell with a single look – filled with tears.

'Lizzie, I'm really worried about him,' she said. 'He's so extremely unhappy just now.'

In that instant, Lizzie saw, not that spiny old thorn in her side, Lady Evelyn, but a fellow woman, a fellow mother, somebody who loved her son as fiercely as Lizzie loved Alex.

Lizzie opened her mouth, then closed it again. She felt an odd urge to pat Lady Evelyn's back, or press her hand, but she sensed the woman wouldn't tolerate such over-familiarity in spite of suddenly having revealed a human side. 'Could I offer you some tea?' she blurted. 'I haven't packed the electric kettle yet.'

Chapter Twenty

Lizzie stood on the front steps of Back Lane Cottage, looking at the garden for the last time. The lawn was tidy, if a little tall since Bruno had stopped coming by; the rabbit holes were gone; the borders were riotous with late-blooming perennials that she herself had released from a stranglehold of weeds; the roses were enjoying a last flush along the south-facing wall. Nettles and brambles and cow parsley still pressed right up to the fence, but within this green sanctuary, she'd managed to keep the wild things at bay. She wondered how long it would take nature to reclaim the place, if the cottage lay vacant for weeks, or if the next tenant was no gardener.

'Mummy!'

She dashed tears from her eyes and turned away.

The car was loaded, the children were buckled in, and Ingrid Hatter had shoved a picnic hamper full of peanut butter sandwiches into a narrow space between the suitcases and the roof.

'That's it, then,' Lizzie told Ingrid and Sarah. 'All set. Thanks for everything. I'll phone you when we get there.'

'Here, give us a hug,' said Sarah.

Blinking back tears, Lizzie hugged the teenage girl and then her mother. 'I'm going to miss you two,' she muttered in a choked voice.

'Best get off now,' Ingrid replied, pushing her gently towards the driver's seat. 'God knows, it's a long drive. Have you got your passports?'

'Mum,' rebuked Sarah. 'It's Scotland, not Timbuctoo.'

The two Hatters stood in the lane, waving like mad, as Lizzie's vehicle disappeared.

Lizzie had barely made it to the first traffic light in Sevenoaks when Ellie began asking, 'How many minutes till Glasglow, Mummy?'

Lizzie took a deep breath. 'Darling,' she said, 'I've just decided. We're not going to Glasgow. Not today. We're going to Gloucestershire instead.'

It was just after noon when Lizzie unlatched the garden gate at Mill House and walked along the path between beds of asters to the front door. The house seemed diminished to her somehow, as if it had shrunk about an inch all round. As she lifted the heavy black fleur-de-lis door knocker, she had a moment of pure panic. She froze with the knocker in her hand, heart pounding. It wasn't too late to walk away.

Then she squared her shoulders and took a steadying breath. How would she explain herself to Roger and Lady Evelyn, at this very moment presiding over a kitchen lunch for three-year-olds without the *au pair*'s help, if she didn't even sound the knocker? Squeezing her eyes shut, she let it fall.

'Lizzie? What are you doing here?'

Lizzie opened one eye. James was standing on the doorstep in a crumpled T-shirt and a pair of old jogging bottoms that appeared to have been pulled out of a laundry basket unwashed. His hair was lank and dull, his face pale, his eyes sunken, and his stubble approaching the mini-beard stage.

Lady Evelyn was right. He looked like hell.

'I thought you were driving to Glasgow today,' he muttered.

'I was,' she said. 'But then I remembered I wanted to ask you something. I thought you'd be in Chipping Norton.'

'I'm just checking the bath tubs and the sheets here. Mrs Grimes is getting very slack.'

'So your dad said. Look, can I come in?'

He stepped backwards from the door and she walked into the house she knew so well. In the familiar, mahogany-panelled drawing room, she perched on the edge of the rosewood-framed settee and he plunked himself down in the Louis XIV walnut *fauteuil*.

'James, is it Erin Wilde?' she burst out, before she lost her nerve.

He frowned. 'I'm sorry? What?'

'Erin Wilde. Is it her? Did she sort of . . . break up with you? Is she the reason you're unhappy?'

'Who says I'm unhappy?'

'Your mum.'

'*Mum?*' He shook his head in bewilderment. 'Look, Lizzie, Erin was here on business, that's all. She just – went home. No drama.'

Lizzie raised her eyebrows. 'Really? She had business here in Laingtree?'

James shook his head. 'No, no, just in London, of course.'

'So, so you invited her here?'

'No, actually. She invited herself. She's always been very keen on Mill House. The moment it came back on the holiday rental market, she knew. She must have had her spies out. Anyway, she booked herself in straight away.'

'And . . . and you stumbled on her in the gardens and spontaneously asked her to come to the wedding?'

He gave her an odd look. 'No, of course not. Before she came, she rang me up from California to see if I wanted to have lunch when she was in the area.'

'*She* rang *you* up? And *then* you invited her to the wedding?'

James nodded. 'Yeah.'

'Why?'

He shrugged. 'Why not? She was going to be here that weekend. She's an old friend.'

'So, all that lovey-dovey stuff – her hand on your leg, the two of you snuggling up, the kissing – it was all just friendly?'

James stood up and began to pace the room. 'OK, I'll admit, maybe Erin had the wrong end of the stick. Maybe she thought it was going to lead to something more. Maybe I even thought it would be fun to have a little interlude, revisit the past. The trouble is, after about the first ten minutes, she gets on my bloody nerves! But as far as I can see, that's none of your business. Did I ever ask you for the ins and outs of your . . . whatever . . . with Bruno?' He was staring at her so intensely now that the world was reduced to the blazing blue of his eyes.

Courage. She needed courage.

'No, you didn't,' she said. 'And thank you very much for that. But please. Bear with me. Can you tell me what happened with Sonja?'

'Excuse me?'

'Well, you took her to France.'

He raised his eyebrows at her. 'It would've been churlish not to.' He went back to the *fauteuil* and sat down again.

'*Churlish*?'

'Lizzie, when someone works for you for a number of years, you begin to think of them as a human being, not just an employee. For better or worse, you begin to get involved in people's personal lives.'

Christ. *Churlish* not to sleep with his assistant? Were his manners really so impeccable that he couldn't brush her off when she was so obviously panting for it?

'I mean, I don't know what there is to quibble about, anyway,' he went on. 'OK, so it cost some money that I didn't really need to spend, but what the hell? It's rare you can make someone that happy with so little effort. And I don't much need an assistant when I'm on site, so what did it matter if she only worked half a day and spent most of her time in Nîmes?'

Lizzie felt as if she'd lost the plot entirely now. 'Nîmes?' she echoed.

'Yes, that's where Pierre lives.'

'Who the blazes is Pierre?'

He looked at her in astonishment. 'What, you don't know about Pierre? Oh, God, of course you don't. Pierre de la Roche. Her Frenchman. The one she met on her break back in the spring. She's been working on him steadily ever since – steamy phone calls, weekend trips, lingerie in the post, that sort of thing. You must have noticed she's smartened herself up a bit, surely? New hair-do and whatnot?'

Lizzie gazed at him, speechless.

'I thought the whole thing would peter out, of course, but she's even taking French lessons by correspondence now.' James, sitting with his arms folded across his chest, shook his head regretfully. 'It's only a matter of time before she hands in her notice, I reckon.'

Lizzie's face lit up with an enormous smile. 'That's ... that's fantastic. Wonderful! Good for Sonja!'

He raised his eyebrows. 'Gosh, you're really rooting for her. I never even thought you liked her very much ...' A funny expression came over his face. 'Hang on,' he said. 'You didn't think ...? I mean, you couldn't have thought ...? Well, of course, you didn't know about Pierre ... But, I mean, we're talking *Sonja* here ...' She watched the penny drop.

'Never mind what I thought,' she said hastily. All of a sudden it seemed as clear as the nose on her face that James Buckley would never have been interested in the likes of Sonja Jenkins. Even if the woman *had* been naked in his house. 'Look, James, I ... I have to own up. I haven't been completely straight with you.'

'What do you mean?'

'That e-mail. No, not *that* e-mail! The last one. The one Janie forwarded to you? Well, the thing is, I know I let you think it was about Bruno, but, actually, as a matter of fact, it wasn't. Bruno was never the one. I thought he was, oh, just for a few days, but he never made me want to ... to throw things at the wall, and tear up photos, and so on. The note – it was about you.'

James sat very still in his chair. 'I don't follow you,' he said at last.

Lizzie could feel her hands trembling. What if Lady Evelyn had got it all wrong after all?

But she wasn't going to chicken out now. She'd come to say her piece, and she'd say it if it killed her.

'Remember what the note said? That I couldn't eat, couldn't sleep, couldn't think; that I reckoned my heart was broken? Well, it's all true, and it's ... it's not because of Bruno. It's because of ... it's because of you. You, you and only you. In spite of everything.'

He didn't move. No reaction at all. Oh, God. What an embarrassing miscalculation. But Lady Evelyn had been so sure.

'Look, never mind,' she said, and began to gather herself up for a quick exit. But before she could shrug her jacket back on, he leapt off his chair, sending it flying, and grabbed her by the shoulders. 'Don't mess with me, Lizzie,' he said between his teeth.

She'd never seen him treat furniture with such disrespect.

'I'm not messing with you,' she whispered, the tears slipping freely down her cheeks. 'I mean it. Every word.'

And that was when she knew Lady Evelyn had been right. James Buckley *was* pining, not for the fantastically gorgeous, highly success-ful, exotic Erin Wilde, but for ordinary, common-or-garden Lizzie, for his wife.

Oh, dear. His *ex*-wife. But still!

With a groan, he pulled her to his chest and squeezed her so tightly she thought some of her smaller ribs would surely crack. Then he put her away from him and looked deep into her eyes. 'You don't think we've broken it beyond repair?' he asked at last.

She glanced at the chair, which did in fact seem to have a crooked leg. 'There's always glue,' she offered.

'Not the chair, idiot. Us!'

'I know! I know what you mean.' She was smiling through her tears now. 'Like I said, there's always glue.'

He began to smile, too. 'God, I've missed you.'

'Why did you ever go away?' she asked, a catch in her voice. 'Why were you so keen to get divorced? I mean, I know I was an idiot, and that e-mail was ... was unspeakable ... but I *said* sorry! I told you I loved you! So why, why, *why*?'

'Oh, Lizzie. I thought it was over.' He kissed the top of her head and then held her so close she couldn't look in his eyes. 'I thought you'd given up on me. I didn't really need that e-mail to tell me something was horribly wrong. For months I'd had this ... sort of ... sick feeling that everything was falling apart. You only ever seemed happy when you were with other people, flirting with the chaps, that sort of thing. Around me, you could barely raise a smile. You could tell me you loved me till you were blue in the face, but I didn't believe it. I thought the best thing I could do was just ... let you go. You know, the grand gesture. Set you free.'

Lizzie shook her head in disbelief. 'Too bloody noble. The age of chivalry is dead, didn't you know? I was depressed, James. Depressed with a big D. Officially depressed, in fact. Not just the baby blues. The baby purples and blacks and greys. Thundercloud stuff. I felt so miserable, it was scary. So then, when we'd go out, I'd try to make up for it. I'd over-compensate. Go a bit overboard, if you know what I mean. But I was never really *flirting*. Just ... just trying to keep my end up.'

'What do you mean?'

Lizzie felt herself redden. 'Look, James, you must've noticed that women are pretty much all over you most of the time? Well, I just ... I suppose I wanted to show you that men were all over me, too. So you wouldn't, you know, suddenly wake up one day and realize you'd made a shoddy choice.'

He looked at her in wonder. '*What?*'

'Look, half the time I don't know my left side from my right side, let alone my bloody distaff side!' she burst out. 'I think ... I think I was scared, the whole time we were married, that you'd suddenly see through me. I mean, I'm usually a little on the plump side, and ... and so many girls are prettier. And I don't know how to play bridge. Or golf. I can't ride a horse. My parents never use fish forks. Your mum had to point out the proper way to sup soup. I ... I'll *never* be able to tell the difference between genuine Boulle marquetry and a machine-made reproduction.'

James's eyes were suddenly brimming with laughter. He shook his head. 'I see what you mean; you're hopeless. What was I thinking, getting involved with you in the first place? But, you know what? In the circumstances I might just make an exception and overlook all that. Lizzie, you moron, I *love* you. I've always loved you. I don't know how to stop.'

'You do? You really do? This isn't a case of grin and bear it for the children's sake?'

James gave an abrupt crack of laughter. 'Let me tell you something, Lizzie. I never really understood about you being wiped out and exhausted all the time. I thought you were faking it, to be honest. To cover up for the fact that you'd gone off me. Well, now I understand. God, do I understand! Even just one full-time weekend with Ellie and Alex is enough to do me in. And after that week when you were in Australia, it's more like grin and bear the children for *your* sake.'

Then Lizzie broke into a broad grin of her own. She thought suddenly of Bruno and Petronella; of how Bruno had said that divorce couldn't cancel out the fact that they belonged together. She wished them luck, so much luck.

'If that's really, truly the case,' she told James, 'and you're not just trying to stop me from whisking them off to Glasgow, then shut up and kiss me.'

She'd been going to show him the letter from Ivana Sanader, stating that Elizabeth Buckley had been under the influence of 'the depression' when she'd written that she preferred 'partaking of tea and biscuits' to 'having the relations' with her husband. But all at once it seemed that there were more direct routes to the heart of the matter.

James was more than happy to shut up, it seemed. After a minute or two, he asked urgently, 'Lizzie, where *are* the children?'

'They're at the manor. Why?'

'Not lurking in the garden or anything?'

'No.'

'Thank goodness.' He waggled his eyebrows. 'Any chance we could, ah, nip upstairs and, you know, revisit the old bed?'

When she didn't immediately reply, he added quickly, 'Of course, if you don't feel like it, that's OK. No desperate rush. No rush at all. I can be as platonic as the next chap, if that's what you want.'

Lizzie gave a snort of laughter. 'We'd better hurry up; your parents will be wondering why I'm taking so long.' She grabbed his hand and together they ran up the stairs straight into the master bedroom. With a flying leap, they landed on the Jacobean bed.

'Hang on, hang on, hang on,' Lizzie said, even as James began to get to grips with her clothes. 'Before we do this, before we do anything, I've just got to say a couple more things.'

James groaned, every fibre of him apparently yearning to get on with the task at hand. 'Go ahead, then. But quick, quick.'

'First off, why was Sonja Jenkins ever naked in your house?'

'What?'

'Alex saw her starkers.'

'Christ! I'll have to have a word with her about that. She was there to babysit one day when I went to Wales. Why on earth would she strip off?'

Lizzie thought, trying to remember what Alex had actually said to her. 'Maybe just to have a shower?'

He pursed his lips. 'I bet you're right. I came back after eleven that night, it's a long bloody drive. She must have made herself right at home. But never mind Sonja. How do you get this cami thing off?'

'No, wait! There's more. This is really important. You see, I'm different, now. I'm not the same Lizzie I was in the spring.'

'I know, I know,' James said hoarsely. 'You can run like the clappers. And you're as skinny as a whip. And you've got your ... your energy back.' He leaned down to trail his lips over her somewhat smaller but still generous bosom.

'Aargh, stop that and listen. Now you know how tiring the twins are, I'm going to expect a lot more help around the house.'

'We'll get an *au pair*, then.'

'No, we bloody won't. You'll just learn to pick up after yourself.'

He pulled a wry face. 'I know what you mean, actually. All these months on my own, I've sort of noticed that I have a few bad habits. But I think I've housebroken myself now. Honestly.'

She allowed him to kiss her ear, then pushed him away. 'Hang on. I really want you to hear this bit. I'm running the London marathon.'

This really did stop him in his tracks. 'A *marathon*? Are you mad?'

'Yes, absolutely barking.'

'Oh, Lizzie. A marathon! The kids will be so proud.'

Lizzie pulled a face. 'Don't count on it. They'll be very disappointed if I don't win. Wait, wait! That's not all.'

'Your poems? Good grief! I didn't even say congratulations.

We'll have to do something really, really good to celebrate. Like . . . maybe this?' And he bent to kiss her belly-button. It was all she could do to hold still and go on with her speech.

But there was one more thing, and it was the most important of all.

'The last thing, James.'

He groaned again. 'What is it?'

She lifted herself onto her elbow and pushed him slightly away, so that she could look into his eyes. He had to know that she was serious. 'I'm not going to live here at Mill House,' she said quietly. 'Never, ever again. It's a lovely place but it doesn't *fit*. You see, I've worked it all out. All along, I more or less thought I was the ugly sister. But you just gave me the wrong shoe, that's all.'

James looked mystified. 'The wrong shoe? You mean, those patent leather pumps my mum said I should get for your birthday?'

Lizzie gave him a dazzling smile. 'That's right,' she said. 'Those shoes and everything else. None of it fits. So will you come with me to Glasgow and start over?'

'Lizzie, I'll go anywhere in the world with you. We'll sell Mill House, whatever you want.'

'Are you serious? Anywhere in the world? In that case, could we . . . could we maybe try to buy Back Lane Cottage? I'm not really as keen on Glasgow as I've been making out, you see.'

He pulled her down with loving roughness and kissed her again. 'Anywhere,' he whispered at last. 'Wherever you are, that's my home.' And then, just as things began to get interesting, he suddenly sat bolt upright, his head on one side, listening. 'Ah, for crying in a bucket, is that the patter of little feet?'

And it was.